SANIN

# SANIN

## A NOVEL

BY

### MIKHAIL ARTSYBASHEV

Translated from the Russian by
MICHAEL R. KATZ

Introduction by OTTO BOELE

Afterword by NICHOLAS LUKER

## Cornell University Press

ITHACA AND LONDON

First published 2001 by Cornell University Press
First printing, Cornell Paperbacks, 2001

Printed in the United States of America

Library of Congress Cataloging-in-Publication Data

Artsybashev, M. (Mikhail), 1878–1927.
  [Sanin. English]
  Sanin : a novel / by Mikhail Artsybashev ; translated from the
Russian by Michael R. Katz ; introduction by Otto Boele ; afterword by
Nicholas Luker.
    p. cm.
  Includes bibliographical references.
  ISBN 0-8014-3571-4 (alk. paper) -- ISBN 0-8014-8559-2 (pbk. : alk.
paper)
  I. Katz, Michael R. II. Title.
PG3453.A8 S33 2001
891.73'3--dc21

                                            00-011387

Cornell University Press strives to use environmentally responsible suppliers and materials to the fullest extent possible in the publishing of its books. Such materials include vegetable-based, low-VOC inks and acid-free papers that are recycled, totally chlorine-free, or partly composed of nonwood fibers. Books that bear the logo of the FSC (Forest Stewardship Council) use paper taken from forests that have been inspected and certified as meeting the highest standards for environmental and social responsibility. For further information, visit our website at www.cornellpress.cornell.edu.

Cloth printing       10 9 8 7 6 5 4 3 2 1
Paperback printing  10 9 8 7 6 5 4 3 2 1

# Contents

# Acknowledgments

I am most grateful to my two colleagues and collaborators Otto Boele, University of Groningen (The Netherlands), and Nicholas Luker, University of Nottingham (United Kingdom), for their constant support, earnest encouragement, and valuable contributions to this project. I am also grateful to both of them, as well as to Alya Baker (Middlebury College), for their careful reading of my manuscript and their numerous corrections and suggestions. Any remaining inaccuracies and infelicities are, of course, my own. I am grateful to my former research assistants at Middlebury College, Tom Reavley and Katya Neely, for their work on the manuscript and the annotations.

MICHAEL R. KATZ

*Middlebury, Vermont*

# *Translator's Note*

Artsybashev's novel *Sanin* was first published in the journal *Sovremenny-mir* (Contemporary World) in 1907 (January–May, September).

An English translation by Percy Pinkerton, published in 1914 and reprinted numerous times, is inaccurate, incomplete, and expurgated.

The Russian text was subsequently reprinted in an edition of Artsybashev's works, *Sobranie sochinenii v trekh tomakh* (Collected Works in Three Volumes), published in Moscow by Terra in 1994. It is this text that I have chosen to translate.

The system of transliteration is that used in the *Oxford Slavonic Papers* with the following exceptions: hard and soft signs have been omitted and conventional spellings of names have been retained.

M. R. K.

# SANIN

# Introduction

## OTTO BOELE

### I

In the spring of 1908, Leo Tolstoy received a letter from Otiliya Tsimmerman, headmistress of a private school for boys in the provincial city of Perm. In it she relayed a dreadful discovery: her beloved pupils were not the unspoiled creatures she had assumed; they were reading racy novels, frequenting taverns, going on binges, and, worse still, engaging in sex.

The discovery was all the more painful as the headmistress had done her utmost to offer them various forms of uplifting entertainment. She had organized a balalaika class, as well as a workshop where her pupils could master the skills of carpentry. She had even ordered copies of Tolstoy's pamphlets on the nature of sexuality in the hope of satisfying the boys' curiosity about such matters. Alas, they persisted in their dissolute behavior. What was she to do? She addressed her question to Tolstoy himself:

> If I had any talent, I would write. I would write something that would allow them to come to their senses, to return to humanity, to family life. But what do they read nowadays? They engross themselves in *Sanin;* they say the hero's better than anyone else because instead of concealing his depravity, he openly and boldly expresses what others only think, yet dare not say.[1]

Elsewhere in Perm, things were even worse. Eight girls, active members of a secret society of debauchers, had delivered babies. One of them had committed suicide. Although her own pupils were not involved in this organiza-

Research for this introduction was made possible by a fellowship from the Royal Netherlands Academy of Arts and Sciences.

[1] O. V. Tsimmerman to Tolstoy, 15 April 1908, Department of Manuscripts, State Museum of Tolstoy, Moscow, f. 1, l. 4.

tion, the headmistress feared that eventually her boys might be tempted to join it. She wondered if Tolstoy would be willing to write something edifying for these young people to help them mend their wicked ways.

As far as we know, Tolstoy never answered Tsimmerman's desperate plea. He also ignored another request—that he destroy her letter immediately after reading it. As a result, we possess a confidential document that offers a personal perspective on one of the most sensitive issues in late imperial Russia: the "dissipation" of educated youth and their supposed admiration for the eponymous hero of Mikhail Artsybashev's "pornographic" bestseller *Sanin*. Indeed, what is striking about this letter is less the headmistress's dismay at the sexual laxity of her pupils than her assumption that their sexual activities have a direct connection with a literary hero who "does not conceal his depravity." While twenty-first-century readers may regard the boys' behavior as typical of adolescents exploring their awakening sexuality, the headmistress discerned a new, immoral ideology and a corresponding behavioral code: to surrender to one's base instincts, just like Vladimir Sanin.

It is impossible to judge the reliability of the account of eight young mothers and their involvement in a secret sex club. It may have been only a sensational rumor disseminated by tabloids and local gossips. Yet precisely because it was so unclear and because Tsimmerman was so genuinely concerned, her letter presents a vivid picture of what was arguably the greatest scandal in the history of Russian literature before the Revolution of 1917. Not only was *Sanin* temporarily banned by the authorities shortly after its serialized publication in 1907, its author also was nearly anathematized. Many observers viewed Artsybashev's hero as Tsimmerman did, as the embodiment of the cynical "live for the moment" mentality that had supposedly seized the Russian intelligentsia after the failed revolution of 1905. As one critic put it: "You may not agree with Sanin, but it is impossible to ignore him: he embodies a mood apparent in life, and characteristic of many."[2] Such was *Sanin*'s paradigmatic significance that the term *saninism* was quickly adopted as a convenient label for the "moral corruption" rampant among the revolutionary-minded intelligentsia. Judging by Tsimmerman's letter, at a certain point saninism even extended to the ranks of provincial high school students.

Why did this novel inspire such outrage? Why was *Sanin* considered pornographic and at the same time such a powerful statement about the radical intelligentsia? The frequency with which critics proclaimed the central character a "hero of our time," a term that immediately conjures up the image of Mikhail Lermontov's cynical hero Pechorin, suggests that a study of the political background cannot provide an exhaustive answer to these questions. Therefore, it is crucial to look more closely at the sociocultural context of fin-de-siècle Russia, as well as at the literary tradition in which the

---

[2] Ye. A. Koltonovskaya, "Nasledniki Sanina," reprinted in *Kriticheskie etyudy* 70 (St. Petersburg, 1912), 70.

novel was produced and received. Who was interested in *Sanin* and how was the work actually read? Viewing it only as a measure of the moral corruption that allegedly characterized the tsarist empire in its last days, modern scholars have long ignored this work, yet for that very reason it can be a most rewarding discovery. *Sanin* can serve as a concrete starting point for understanding one of Russia's most dynamic yet confusing historical periods.

## II

The idea that the period of "political reaction"—the years that immediately followed the upheaval of 1905—witnessed a dramatic deterioration in morality was always popular in Soviet historiography. Positing the corruption of the tsarist regime as a principal cause implied that the October Revolution of 1917 had been both purgative and inevitable. Yet in the last decades of the twentieth century, both historians and literary scholars began to question the assumptions on which the notion of a cultural and moral crisis early in the century was founded. Research into popular culture of the time has shown that what many worried intellectuals condemned as the "vulgarization" of Russian society was in fact the immediate result of a modernization process that had already begun at the end of the nineteenth century. Technological innovations had led to new forms of entertainment, notably the cinema; activities such as sport, previously confined to the aristocratic milieu, had now acquired a mass character. These developments also affected the literary field. Improved printing techniques and increasing literacy entailed a rapid expansion of the commercial publishing industry as it hastened to cater to the growing numbers of semieducated readers. As more people learned to read, the demand for cheap popular fiction increased. In effect, "serious" literature, understood by the intelligentsia as art that was politically and socially aware, accounted for only a small proportion of Russia's entire literary production. Though it is certainly true that erotic literature and pulp fiction became very popular during the last decade of the tsarist regime, it would be naive to attribute that popularity merely to the intelligentsia's disenchantment with the revolt of 1905 and to ignore the social context or the reforms of that time. The abolition of prepublication censorship in 1905 gave Russia a virtually free press and was far more important to the "vulgarization" of Russian culture than the disappointment of the revolutionary movement.

To understand why *Sanin* could develop into one of Russia's greatest literary scandals, it is important to bear in mind that, despite the political and social changes the society was undergoing, the old dogmas of radical criticism, *realnaya kritika* ("real criticism"), still enjoyed considerable authority. Today, with the benefit of hindsight, it may seem obvious that these doctrines had already been marginalized by the advent of modernism and the emergence of commercial publishing—a development that found its most telling expression in the decline of the "thick journals" in Russia. Yet many representatives of the intelligentsia persisted in viewing literature as a barometer of the nation's political mood. Moreover, some commercially successful authors whose work we would now characterize as middle-brow—and we could include Artsybashev among them—were sympathetic to the traditional call for socially conscious art. Consequently, the legacy of such radical critics as Nikolai Dobrolyubov and Dmitry Pisarev not only continued to manifest itself in the reception of "serious" literature but also exerted a certain influence on the authors of boulevard fiction.

Paradoxically, while literary authorship was in practice becoming an increasingly ordinary profession, the traditional image of the writer as teacher and purveyor of truth proved surprisingly enduring. The cult of Tolstoy as the nation's conscience and the living memory of the "civic" poet Semyon Nadson, who remained one of Russia's favorite authors until the 1917 Revolution, graphically illustrate the durability of this image. Artsybashev fitted into this tradition very well. His work appeared in *Mir bozhii* (God's World), *Zhurnal dlya vsekh* (Journal for All), and *Sovremennyi mir* (Contemporary World), all respectable journals with a marked preference for solid, realist fiction. They offered an obvious platform for a writer such as Artsybashev, who would always remain conscious of his social obligations and showed little affinity for modernist experiments. In an interview in 1913 he made his views on literature clear: "Common sense, consistency, argumentation, a clear and concrete idea of one's subject that constitutes the plot of the work, a thoughtful evaluation of the phenomena introduced in the novel, clarity and concreteness—these are the things I demand of a literary work."[3]

This call for "concreteness" and "common sense" not only demonstrates Artsybashev's stylistic roots in the tradition of realism but also illustrates his typically nineteenth-century concern with the enlightenment of his readers. By raising important and topical issues, an author was meant to heighten the social awareness of his audience and thus contribute to the creation of a better society. The instructive undertone in *Sanin* (which may irritate some modern readers) is not merely an idiosyncrasy of Artsybashev's style or an indication of his lack of talent; it reflects a didactic zeal not uncommon to Russian realism and it shows the influence of Tolstoy, an author whom Artsybashev greatly admired.

Simply to relegate Artsybashev to the realm of the boulevard, as some modern scholars have done, is not as straightforward a proposition as it

---

[3] *Birzhevye vedomosti*, 5 June 1908, p. 6.

[4] "A proposition as it seems" (referring to "some modern scholars"): Neya Zorkaya, *Na rubezhe stoletii: U istokov massovogo iskusstva v Rossii, 1900-1910 godov* (Moscow, 1976), 160–64.

seems.[4] *Sanin* may indeed appear hackneyed from the elevated standpoint of the literary historian who knows how Russian literature developed subsequently; and the novel's life-affirming, hedonistic message may strike us as a peculiar hybrid of vulgar positivism and Nietzschean philosophy. Yet to most early twentieth-century readers, even to knowledgeable and sophisticated reviewers, the supposedly facile quality of Artsybashev's prose may not have been so obvious. The poet and critic Valery Bryusov, for example, wrote a favorable review of Artsybashev's first collection of stories, *Rasskazy* (1905–6); Aleksandr Blok, a leading Symbolist poet, was fascinated by *Sanin* and regarded it as Artsybashev's most remarkable work. Admittedly, one could argue that what we now perceive as Artsybashev's epigonism is betrayed by the fidelity with which he lived up to all aspects of the image of a "genuine" author; he even suffered from tuberculosis. By the standards of turn-of-the-century Russia, however, he was a "serious" writer and he was treated accordingly. His didactic manner, the prestigious journals in which he published, and his public statements on such issues as suicide and poverty were all in keeping with the classical image of the writer as a moral authority. Although he was occasionally attacked for his stereotypes and formulaic language, the vast majority of his contemporaries regarded his work as genuine literature.

It may come as no surprise, then, that *Sanin* is actually a very traditional Russian novel. It is a classic *roman à thèse* with a superior, idealized hero and an omniscient, even meddlesome narrator. The message of the novel is expressed by its epigraph, taken from Ecclesiastes 7:29: "This alone have I found: that God, when he made man, made him straightforward, but men invent endless subtleties of their own." In *Sanin* these "subtleties" are indeed numerous: socialism, asceticism, Christianity, and Tolstoyism, but also vanity, pride, and chastity. The upright man, on the other hand, remains true to himself and "simply" embraces happiness. In the hero's own words: "I know one thing—I live life and I don't want it to be miserable. For that, first and foremost, it's necessary to satisfy one's natural desire. Desire is everything: if desire dies in a person, life dies; and if he kills desire, he kills himself."

Of course, these words apply above all to the sexual ethics that the novel purports to defend, and therefore they betray how deeply Artsybashev is indebted to the ideas of Nietzsche (a debt the Russian author never actually acknowledged). It would be wrong, however, to assume that the novel's sexual preoccupation entirely exhausts its message. In Artsybashev's view, modern society is not simply imperfect or oppressive; it is a distortion of a more natural way of life that needs to be and *can* be restored through the removal of everything artificial.

In its plot development and polemical intent, *Sanin* is clearly patterned on the "tendentious" novel that examined the ideological clash in Russia between the idealists of the 1840s and the nihilists of the 1860s. In the typical tendentious novel, a member of the radical intelligentsia enters an "alien" community such as a family, an estate managed by "liberals," or, in the case of Sanin, a hometown that the hero has not visited for many years. The hero's appearance has a profound impact on the lives of the community's members. Some are shocked by his unconventional behavior; others are fascinated by his ideas. In some cases, the protagonist has a love affair with a high-minded young woman who is chafing to escape her oppressive environment. At the end of the story, the hero disappears again, his eventual fate depending on the author's political stance. In the antinihilistic novel, in which radicals are attacked, he usually dies (Turgenev's *Fathers and Sons* [1862], Dostoevsky's *Devils* [1871–72]) or suffers defeat in some other form. In more sympathetic works, however, the so-called stories about New People, the hero convincingly debunks the outdated ideas of the older generation or successfully puts his own ideas into practice (Chernyshevsky's *What Is to Be Done?* [1863], Vasily Sleptsov's *Hard Times* [1865]).

Artsybashev's bestseller recalls the leftist subgenre of the tendentious novel, the stories about New People. Sanin's hedonistic philosophy is presented as a refreshingly new, viable ideology; in comparison the value systems of other characters appear both dated and untenable. He easily does away with Tolstoy's doctrine of nonresistance to evil by knocking down the conceited officer Zarudin in self-defense. He eloquently expounds his views on unlimited sexual freedom, which he then puts into practice by virtually raping the schoolteacher Zinaida Karsavina. On both occasions, Sanin merely acts as a catalyst, accelerating a process that has already begun. Zarudin himself has provoked the confrontation with Sanin, and thus becomes the victim of his own ego. Even the "rape" scene is intended to suggest that Karsavina enjoys the experience and is initiated into a new, more "natural" way of life. Functionally speaking, Sanin is only an instrument designed to demonstrate the superiority of a higher truth. His unpretentious enjoyment of life is clearly presented as an example to all.

Given this explicitly tendentious orchestration of events, it is not difficult to see why so many contemporaries were dismayed by the novel. The conspicuous idealization of a "rapist" who pursues only the satisfaction of his "natural desires" was bad enough; some readers even produced alternative endings to the work in which the hero was punished for his crimes. One resourceful author, hoping to cash in on Artsybashev's success, wrote a sequel titled *The Return of Sanin* (1913), which shows the hero being sent into exile to Siberia, where he is spiritually reborn.[5]

Turning Sanin into a repentant villain like Raskolnikov, the hero of Dostoevsky's *Crime and Punishment* (1866), may have been acceptable to a nonintellectual Russian audience; to the sophisticated reader, however, the work's most unnerving aspect was its striking timeliness. Many critics

---

[5] Count Amori [I. P. Rapgof], *Vozvrashchenie Sanina* (Riga, 1931).

agreed that Sanin was not merely a one-of-a-kind womanizer conceived by a perverted author but a historical figure (albeit in typified form) embodying the mentality of the postrevolutionary intelligentsia. A most crucial point about Sanin was his past. A former Tolstoyan as well as a sometime revolutionary, he now seemed to care only for women and vodka. Observers maintained that this shift from a worldview based on communal solidarity and shared ideals to a more rugged individualism reflected a major change in Russian society. Sanin was to be understood as the contemporary intellectual who had abandoned his political ideals after the revolt of 1905 and "turned inward," dedicating himself to the pursuit of his personal happiness. According to Yelena Koltonovskaya, a moderate critic writing for the socialist journal *Obrazovanie* (Education), Artsybashev

> was not only the *first* to show us contemporary individualism as representative of a new morality, but he also portrayed it better than anyone else did. Sanin is amazingly logical, consistent, and therefore artistically convincing. All his actions follow from his views, which are united and in perfect agreement with each other. That's why he could be alive, possible in life, deriving from life.[6]

Artsybashev protested against the eagerness of such critics to reduce *Sanin* to a political statement on postrevolutionary Russia, claiming that he had written the book as early as 1903. Yet this rebuttal only seemed to confirm the conclusions of his reviewers. The well-known critic Pyotr Pilsky was quick to point out that even if the novel had been written before the events of 1905, it was not published until 1907. That, Pilsky insisted, could not be a mere coincidence.[7] The Populist Yakov Danilin reminded his readers of Artsybashev's initial intention to make Yury Svarozhich—his fictional student who had been expelled from Moscow University on suspicion of political activity—the main character of the novel (Artsybashev did make a statement to that effect in an interview published shortly after he completed the novel). According to Danilin, the decision to redirect the work's focus from the actual revolutionary Svarozhich to the former revolutionary Sanin, and to portray the latter as vastly superior to all other characters, could have been reached only in light of the events of 1905.[8]

Further contributing to the general mood of indignation were several conspicuous similarities between Sanin and that other charismatic rebel of Russian literature, Bazarov, the protagonist of Turgenev's novel *Fathers and Sons*. They shared an impressive physique and a casual but self-assured demeanor. Both had a way with ordinary people, although they belonged to the intelligentsia. Finally, there was a certain rigor about them that made them both frightening and sympathetic at the same time.

[6] Ye. A. Koltonovskaya, "Nasledniki Sanina," reprinted in *Kriticheskie etyudy*, 70.

[7] P. M. Pilsky, "Reaktsiya zamuzhem," *Problema pola, polovye avtory i polovoi geroi* (St. Petersburg, 1909), 112.

[8] Ya. Danilin, *Sanin v svete russkoi kritike* (Moscow, 1908), 6.

At first glance, it would seem that the similarity ends here, especially if we recall that Turgenev intended *Fathers and Sons* as an attack against the nihilists, whereas *Sanin* continued the more sympathetic tradition of the stories about New People. We should not forget, however, that because of Pisarev's favorable reinterpretation of Bazarov as a new historical type that was about to emerge in Russia, Turgenev's hero had also been transformed into a champion and prototype of the radical intelligentsia. Characteristically, Pisarev had no qualms about grouping Bazarov with Rakhmetov, the ascetic New Man in Chernyshevsky's novel *What Is to Be Done?* This rosy view of Bazarov as a New Man, commonly accepted among Populist and Marxist critics in the 1900s, made it possible to read *Sanin* through the prism of *Fathers and Sons*.

Therefore, it is not at all difficult to understand why any analogy drawn between Sanin and Bazarov was so annoying to the left. The idealization of a hero who was invested with Bazarov's features but mocked the values of the radical intelligentsia seemed to suggest that history was repeating itself. It hinted at a new conflict between fathers and sons, the difference being that yesterday's sons had become today's fathers. Many readers were appalled by the closing scene of Artsybashev's *Sanin,* its hero striding purposefully toward the rising sun. Was Artsybashev suggesting that Sanin heralded the coming of some new New Man?

Precisely because the image of Bazarov as an undaunted revolutionary represented the most sacred ideals of the radicals, comparisons between him and Sanin touched on the most revered traditions of the intelligentsia. Did Sanin betray the legacy of Bazarov? Or was he the ultimate advocate of a materialist worldview that lacked any moral foundations? The former view was expressed by the Marxist critic Vatslav Vorovsky, who argued that Sanin marked a break with the first generation of the *raznochinnaya intelligentsiya,* the nonaristocratic intellectuals who had entered the universities from the 1850s. In the 1860s, this intelligentsia had been the avant-garde of the revolution, a role exemplified by the historic figure of Bazarov. Gradually, however, it had become estranged from its own humble roots, the Russian people, and as a result had lost its revolutionary potential. Acknowledging that Sanin was also a nihilist of sorts, Vorovsky maintained that in the context of 1905 his nihilism merely testified to his reactionary nature.[9]

Another Marxist critic, G. Novopolin, the author of an ambitious study titled *The Pornographic Element in Russian Literature,* also acknowledged that Sanin and Bazarov had a great deal in common. He even went so far as to point out the philosophical similarities in their respective worldviews. Sanin's shocking remark "My life consists of pleasant and unpleasant sensations" was certainly reminiscent of Bazarov's pronouncement: "There are no principles, only sensations." But, the critic insisted, Sanin was no

---

[9] V. V. Vorovsky, "Bazarov i Sanin. Dva nigilizma," *Estetika, literatura, iskusstvo* (Moscow, 1971), 229–55.

Bazarov. He was nothing more than a vulgarized look-alike whose cynicism stood in sharp contrast to Bazarov's zest for real work. True, Bazarov also had an appetite for the fairer sex, but, as Novopolin conjectured, he could love only an intelligent woman, not any woman, as Sanin apparently could.[10]

Across the political divide, Semyon Frank reached an entirely different conclusion. In an essay titled "The Ethics of Nihilism" he argued that saninism was firmly rooted in the legacy of the 1860s. The egoistic hedonism of the present generation did not break with the spirit of Bazarov. On the contrary, it was its logical extension. In Frank's view, the present crisis exposed the ideological bankruptcy of the radical intelligentsia, which was now confronted with the ultimate consequences of a worldview bereft of moral principles.

These mutually exclusive views of Sanin and Bazarov reveal a most peculiar aspect of Artsybashev's novel: despite the popularity it enjoyed and the influence it supposedly exerted on its readers, no political faction was actually willing to claim Sanin as its figurehead. Marxists stressed his reactionary mentality and estrangement from the masses. Conservatives saw him as an outgrowth of the liberation movement. Populists were convinced that Sanin appealed only to the rich and powerful, the elite in St. Petersburg; the common people, they held, rejected the work's depraved message. Always the champion of the political or social "other," Vladimir Sanin does not seem to have attracted any real followers.

## III

How successful, then, really was *Sanin*? In one of the first Western scholarly discussions of the novel, the influential critic D. S. Mirsky contended that it had been the "bible of an entire generation"—an untenable assertion, it would seem, if the response to it was so negative. The indignation it aroused could just as easily be construed as testifying to the moral health of Russian society. Moreover, Mirsky's sweeping statement derives from a rather simplistic view on how a work of fiction can influence its audience. We may know how a reader responds to a text, but it is difficult to tell how it affects his or her behavior.

Nevertheless, the question of *Sanin*'s influence on the behavior of its readers is not entirely trivial. As far as we know, there are no detailed accounts of contemporary efforts to implement the novel's ideas in real life (such as we do have in the case of Chernyshevsky's *What Is to Be Done?*). Yet, as we have seen, the novel is a classic *roman à thèse,* and could therefore arouse

---

[10] G. S. Novopolin, *Pornograficheskii element v russkoi literature* (St. Petersburg, 1909), 244.

the suspicion that some readers interpreted it as a "manual for living." Touring the provinces as a lecturer in the spring of 1908, Pyotr Pilsky observed that this was precisely how audiences approached the novel. They were not in the least interested in literary analysis; they merely wanted to be told how to live, and they believed that *Sanin* could provide the answer. The critic Yelena Koltonovskaya also assumed that this was what readers expected of the novel: not just sex but a doctrine, an ideological program. And, as we saw earlier, this was exactly what worried the headmistress Tsimmerman.

Freed from the fetters of censorship, the boulevard press carried this view to an extreme, assuming a direct relationship between *Sanin* and the sexual practices of its audience. In April 1908 it published a series of titillating reports on the activities of the so-called Free Love Leagues, secret organizations in which educated young people allegedly indulged in sexual orgies. Characteristically, these gatherings were presumed to start with an elaborate prelude that featured hard drinking and a reading of *Sanin* (though the novel does not even hint at the possibility of group sex). Only after these rituals had been observed would the orgy begin.

Some newspapers even began to discover real Sanins in everyday life. People not only identified with Artsybashev's hero, journalists maintained, they also prided themselves on being saninists (*sanintsy*). In March 1908 the *Moscow Voice* reported that a crowd of over three hundred people had broken up a literary evening dedicated to *Sanin* by loudly declaring: "We are saninists! We no longer recognize old-fashioned conventions!"[11] In its report on the same event, the widely read newspaper *Russian Word* asserted that the crowd had consisted not of three hundred but of three thousand hooligans, "all of them students, the majority female!"[12]

The Russian tabloids may have promoted such rumors in efforts to increase their circulation, but the brouhaha does raise the issue of "ordinary" readers and their response to Artsybashev's novel. One way of explaining the paradox of an absolute bestseller that aroused the indignation of its critics is to call it a succès de scandale. It is conceivable that *Sanin* attracted such a wide readership simply because it enjoyed the reputation of a sexy and fashionable novel, not because its views were widely shared. A measure of the commercial perspectives the publicity opened for scribblers hoping to jump on the bandwagon is the six more or less serious adaptations of *Sanin* for the stage. Three were rejected by the censor as early as March 1908; that is, fewer than six months after the last installment of the novel had been published.[13]

One could also speculate, however, that the outrage shared by critics represented only a part, though a significant one, of the reactions provoked by

[11] *Golos Moskvy* 73 (4 March 1908): 3.
[12] *Russkoe slovo* 53 (4 March 1908): 4.
[13] All these plays were rejected by the censor. Manuscripts are preserved in the Department of Manuscripts of the Theater Library in St. Petersburg.

the novel. Pilsky, for example, a resident of Petersburg, was surprised by the solemnity with which provincial readers imbibed the latest literature, especially those works celebrating sexual freedom. And although the Populist Danilin had observed the opposite reaction to *Sanin* in the provinces, the possibility of a significant gap between the professional critic and the "average, gray reader," as Danilin described him, should not be dismissed out of hand.

A survey of the student press and the "Letters to the Editor" sections of various provincial newspapers seems to confirm Danilin's observation that *Sanin* could not boast a considerable number of disciples. The hero's program of sensual pleasure was seen as too vague and one-sided, or simply as incompatible with "real" political and social issues in Russia. In general, the debate among educated youth, from which Sanin's followers were supposedly recruited, showed a tendency, similar to that in the "mature" press, to present Sanin as a hero of the "enemy." Even as students acknowledged that their ranks had been polluted by his ideas, they called upon their comrades to purify themselves and adhere to the straight and narrow. One student, alarmed by rumors of Free Love Leagues, even appealed to his colleagues to sign a petition condemning the "appalling activities of the debauchers."[14]

Are there any counterexamples that support Pilsky's observations? Sometimes one finds an enthusiastic reaction jotted down in the margins of an old edition of *Sanin:* "What a wonderful book! After reading it one wants to live even more!"[15] But it is impossible to tell whether this view is representative of the thousands of anonymous readers who did not record their impressions. Even if it were, it would not necessarily imply that late imperial Russia witnessed a massive imitation of *Sanin,* as some critics maintained. One student, questioned in a poll of readers in 1912, admitted that he had been a follower of the hero for a short time, but he said he had never seriously considered putting his ideas into practice.[16] By all appearances, the enthusiasm inspired by Artsybashev's novel, even if it was authentic, did not last very long.

Nevertheless, without a whole army of active followers *Sanin* was influential in a different sense. By sustaining the illusion of truthfulness and objectivity typical of realist literature, it was seen as a chronicle of contemporary life rather than as a work of fiction. Supposedly it did not merely depict reality; rather it showed life as it really was. Moreover, owing to the absence of a free press, radical critics attached special significance to literature as a vehicle for expressing "true" opinions on Russian society. To them literature was more lifelike and, in a sense, more real than reality itself.

The relaxation of censorship in October 1905 had an enormous effect on

[14] *Minskii kuer* 66 (12 April 1908): 3–4.

[15] Found in a copy of *Sovremennyi mir*, Gorky State Library, Perm.

[16] Ye. P. Radin, *Dushevnoe nastroenie sovremennoi uchashcheisya molodezhi, po dannym Peterburgskoi obshchestvennoi ankety 1912 goda* (St. Petersburg, 1913), 59.

the literary field, as we have seen; yet it did not immediately extinguish the deeply ingrained practice of viewing contemporary life through the lens of literature. Realist fiction continued to serve as an interpretive tool with which one could grasp the main tendencies and conflicts of social reality. *Sanin* was read in exactly this way. It supplied its audience with a prism through which it perceived political reaction and, in retrospect, the revolt of 1905; hence the discovery of saninists in everyday life. What may have been an ordinary drinking bout or student spree suddenly acquired the aura of a conspiracy, a movement of desperate ex-revolutionaries determined to destroy the moral foundations of society.

The boulevard press, which reached its full prosperity during these years, played a vital role in these "discoveries." Investigating rumors and tapping "anonymous but competent sources," journalists meticulously registered the effects of saninism on a day-to-day basis. This is not to say, of course, that everybody believed every rumor. Yet continuous reporting on the debauchery of educated youth indirectly reinforced the status of Artysbashev's novel as a truthful depiction of modern society. Even more skeptical commentators conceded that, while rumors of Free Love Leagues might be a hoax, there could be no smoke without fire. In their opinion, too, Russia was undergoing unprecedented moral deterioration, its most telling indication being the popular success of *Sanin*.

Saninism was less a historical phenomenon than a myth that emerged from the interaction of two separate discourses. On the one hand, "serious" literature and respectable criticism pretended to offer an objective, lifelike picture of social reality; on the other, the tabloid press also claimed to provide nothing but the facts in its relentless search for the ugly truth of post-revolutionary Russia. The significance of Artsybashev's novel, then, lies in its function as a framework for structuring and understanding the confusing reality of a rapidly changing society. Whether it was held responsible for the corruption of educated youth or perceived as an objective document, as a mimicry of reality, *Sanin* seemed to hold the key to understanding what was really happening in Russia. That perception makes it required reading for any student of Russian history or literature today.

# Principal Characters

Sánin, Vladímir Petróvich    *the hero*
Sánina, Lídiya Petróvna (Lída, Lídochka)    *his sister*
Sánina, Márya Ivánovna    *their mother*
Nóvikov, Aleksándr (Sásha)    *family friend; young doctor*
Zarúdin, Capt. Víktor Sergéevich    *cavalry officer*
Tanárov, Lt. Andréi Pávlovich    *cavalry officer*
Svarózhich, Yúry Nikoláevich (Yúra)    *student*
Svarózhich, Lyudmíla Nikoláevna (Lyálya, Lyálechka)    *his sister*
Svarózhich, Nikolái Yegórovich    *their father*
Ryazántsev, Anatóly Pávlovich (Tólya)    *Lyudmila's fiancé; a doctor*
Karsávina, Zinaída Pávlovna (Zína, Zínochka)    *teacher*
Dúbova, Ólga (Ólya)    *teacher*
Ivanóv    *teacher*
Semyónov    *student*
Shafróv    *student*

# Sanin

This alone I have found: that God, when he made man, made him straightforward, but men invent endless subtleties of their own.

Ecclesiastes 7:29

 I

During that most important stage in life when, under the influence of one's first encounters with people and nature, a man's character is formed, Vladimir Sanin had lived apart from his family. No one had looked after him, no hand had borne down on him, and this man's soul had developed independently and distinctively, like a tree growing in a field.

He hadn't been home in many years, and when he returned, his mother and Lida, his sister, could scarcely recognize him: his features, voice, and manner had changed very little, but there was something new about him, something unfamiliar that had matured within him and now lit his face with a new expression.

He arrived toward evening and entered the room as calmly as if he'd left it only a few minutes before. In his tall, fair-haired, broad-shouldered figure and in his serene, almost mocking expression, noticeable only in the corners of his mouth, no fatigue was evident, no agitation; the boisterous delight with which his mother and sister greeted him somehow subsided of its own accord.

While he was eating and drinking tea, his sister sat opposite and didn't take her eyes off him. She was in love with her brother, as only excessively romantic young women can be in love with their absent brothers. Lida had always imagined him to be an extraordinary person, but extraordinary in a way that she herself had invented with the help of books. She longed to behold a tragic struggle and suffering in his life, and the loneliness of a great though unappreciated soul.

"Why are you staring at me like that?" Sanin asked her with a smile.

This thoughtful smile, accompanied by a serene, distant gaze, was his usual expression.

And, strange to say, though this smile was pleasant and attractive in itself, Lida took an immediate dislike to it. It appeared self-satisfied and provided no indication of his suffering or the struggle he was supposed to be experiencing. She fell silent, became pensive, and, averting her gaze, began leafing mechanically through the pages of a book.

When dinner ended, his mother stroked Sanin's head with tender affection and then said:

"Well, tell us what your life was like there, what you did."

"What I did?" Sanin repeated with a smile. "Well . . . I drank, ate, slept, sometimes worked, and sometimes did nothing at all."

At first it seemed as if he didn't feel like talking about himself, but when his mother continued to probe, he began speaking quite willingly. But for some reason it appeared that he was totally indifferent to the way his listeners heeded his account. His manner was gentle and attentive, but there was nothing personal in his attitude, nothing to distinguish the intimacy of his family from the rest of the world; it seemed as if this gentleness and attentiveness simply radiated from him like light from a candle, on everyone equally.

They went out to the garden terrace and sat down on the steps. Lida settled herself to one side and below and listened in silence to what her brother was saying. An imperceptible chill had already penetrated her heart. With her astute feminine instinct she began to sense that her brother was not as she'd imagined him; she began to feel timid and embarrassed in his presence, as if he were a stranger.

It was already evening and soft shadows were falling all around. Sanin lit a cigarette and the delicate smell of tobacco mingled with the fragrant aroma of the summer garden.

Sanin related how life had tossed him from one place to another, how often he'd had to go hungry or roam around, how he'd taken part in the dangerous political struggle and had abandoned it when he'd had enough.

Lida sat motionless and listened attentively, looking lovely and a little strange, as all beautiful young women do in the spring twilight.

The more he said, the clearer it became that the life she'd imagined in such glowing terms was in fact common and ordinary. There was something unusual about it, but Lida couldn't identify exactly what it was. Meanwhile, it emerged as very simple, boring, and, it seemed to her, even banal. Sanin lived wherever he happened to be, did whatever happened to come his way, worked a bit, loafed without a goal, apparently liked to drink, and knew a lot of women. No gloomy, sinister fate plagued his life, as Lida's dreamy feminine soul had desired. He had no guiding idea; he didn't hate anyone and wasn't suffering for anyone.

For some reason Lida considered some of the words he uttered simply unattractive. For example, Sanin mentioned in passing that at one time he was so down and out that he'd had to mend his own trousers.

"You mean you really know how to sew?" Lida blurted out involuntarily, with offended bewilderment; it seemed so unbecoming and unmanly.

"I didn't before, but I learned when I had to," Sanin replied with a smile, having guessed what Lida was thinking.

The young woman gave a slight shrug of her shoulders and fell silent, staring fixedly into the garden. She felt as if she'd awakened one morning after dreaming of the sun, only to find the sky gray and cold.

His mother also felt some distress. She was deeply disturbed that her son had not assumed the place of honor in society that she felt he was entitled to. She began by saying that he really couldn't go on living as he had been doing, and that now he had to find himself a suitable position. At first she spoke cautiously, worried that she might offend him, but when she noticed that he wasn't paying her any attention, she got irritated and began to insist stubbornly, with an old woman's tiresome bad temper, that he was doing it intentionally to annoy her. Sanin was not surprised, didn't get angry, and even seemed not to hear what she was saying. He looked at her with affectionate but indifferent eyes and remained silent. Only when she posed the question "How do you plan to live?" he replied with a smile:

"Somehow or other!"

From his firm, serene voice and his bright, steady gaze one could feel that these words that meant nothing to her contained absolute, precise, and profound meaning for him.

Marya Ivanovna sighed, kept silent for a while, then replied sadly: "Well, it's your own business. You're not a little boy anymore. . . . You two ought to take a stroll in the garden; it's so nice out there now."

"Let's go, Lida, that's a good idea. Show me the garden," he said to his sister. "I've already forgotten what it's like."

Lida was aroused from her reverie; she sighed too, and then stood up.

They walked side by side along the path into the damp, already dark, green depths of the garden.

The Sanins' house stood on the main street of town, but the town was small and the garden looked directly onto the river, beyond which the fields began. It was an old manor house, with pensive, peeling columns, a big terrace, and a large garden, dark and overgrown, like a dark green cloud hovering over the earth. It was eerie in the garden at night: it seemed that there, both in the grove and in the dusty attic of the old house, some ancient, surviving, despondent spirit was wandering aimlessly.

There were spacious, darkened rooms and a parlor on the upper floor of the house; there was only one cleared path through the entire garden, strewn with dry branches and crushed frogs; what modest, quiet life still remained had all been relegated to one little corner. There, right next to the house, scattered yellow sand glistened, leafy flower beds were covered in multicolored blossoms, and a green wooden table stood where, in fine summer weather, tea and dinner were served; this little corner of the garden was alive with simple, peaceful life, at odds with the gloomy beauty of the large, deserted place, left to its natural destruction and inevitable disappearance.

When the house was hidden by vegetation and Lida and Sanin were surrounded only by silent old trees, pensive like live beings, Sanin suddenly put his arm around Lida's waist and said in a strange tone of voice that was both tender and sinister:

"You've turned out to be quite a beauty! The first man you fall in love with will be a lucky fellow."

A hot surge passed from his muscular arm, strong as iron, through Lida's soft and supple body. She became embarrassed, shuddered, and drew back slightly, as if sensing the approach of a hidden beast.

They had reached the riverbank where it smelled of damp and water, and where sharp reeds swayed pensively; the far bank appeared before them with distant glimmers of the first stars.

Sanin moved away from Lida; for some reason he reached for the large dry branch of a tree, broke it off, and tossed it into the river. The water was disturbed and smooth ripples spread away in all directions; and, as if greeting Sanin as one of their own, the reeds along the banks hastened to bow their heads.

## II

It was about six o'clock. The sun was shining brightly, but soft green shadows were once again approaching from the garden. Light, quiet, and warmth filled the air. Marya Ivanovna was making jam: under the green linden tree there was a strong, mouth-watering smell of boiling sugar and raspberries.

Sanin had been working on the flower beds since early morning, trying to revive plants suffering from the heat and dust.

"You'd be better off pulling up the tall weeds first," Marya Ivanovna advised, glancing at him through the shimmering light-blue smoke over the brazier. "Tell Grunka; she'll do it for you."

Sanin raised his sweaty, cheerful face.

"What for?" he asked, pushing away the hair clinging to his forehead. "Let them grow. I like everything green."

"What a character you are!" his mother replied with an amiable shrug, but for some reason she was very pleased by what he said.

"You're the real characters!" Sanin answered with complete conviction, then went into the house to wash his hands, returned, and sat down at the table, quietly making himself comfortable in a wicker armchair.

He was feeling good, relaxed, and radiant. The verdure, the sunshine, and the blue sky cast such brilliant light that his soul opened to receive it with a feeling of complete happiness. Big towns with their noisy hustle and bustle had become loathsome to him. Now he was surrounded by sunlight and freedom; the future didn't concern him because he was ready to accept whatever life had to offer.

Sanin shut his eyes and stretched, flexing his healthy, strong muscles with great pleasure.

There was a faint, cool breeze; the entire garden seemed to be sighing gently and deeply. Sparrows were chirping somewhere, both near and far, hastily and furtively communicating about their small, terribly important, but totally incomprehensible little lives. Meanwhile Mill, the mottled fox terrier, sticking out his pink tongue and cocking one ear, listened to them indulgently from the fresh, deep grass where he lay. The leaves rustled softly overhead and their round shadows slid silently across the smooth gravel path.

Marya Ivanovna was sorely irritated by her son's serenity. She loved him just as she loved all her children, but for that very reason her heart was seething and she wanted to provoke him, wound his pride, offend him—if only to force him to acknowledge the value of her words and her view of life. Every moment of her long existence, like an ant burying itself in the sand, she'd been busy creating the frail and brittle structure of her own domestic well-being. This extensive, prosaic, and monotonous structure, similar both to a barracks and a hospital, consisted of the smallest bricks, which to her, the untalented architect, seemed to be the embellishment of life; but in fact they constrained, irritated, or frightened her, and always caused her anguish. Nevertheless, she thought it was impossible to live in any other way.

"Well, then . . . are you going to go on like this?" she asked, compressing her lips, pretending to be interested in the pot of boiling jam.

"What do you mean like this?" Sanin asked and then sneezed.

It seemed to Marya Ivanovna that he'd even sneezed on purpose, to irritate her, and although that idea was obviously foolish, she became annoyed and sullen.

"It's so nice here," Sanin said dreamily.

"Not bad," Marya Ivanovna answered with restraint, feeling she should be angry, but she was very pleased that her son praised the house and garden in whose company she'd been living as if they were her own kith and kin.

Sanin looked at her and said pensively: "And if you stopped pestering me with all this silly nonsense, it would be even nicer."

The mild tone in which these words were said contradicted their offensive meaning, and Marya Ivanovna didn't know whether to be angry or amused.

"When I look at you," she said with irritation, "I remember that you were a bit abnormal even as a child, and now . . ."

"And now?" Sanin asked cheerfully, as if expecting to hear something pleasant and interesting.

"And now you really are something!" Marya Ivanovna replied sharply, and shook her spoon.

"Well, so much the better!" Sanin said with a laugh; then, after a pause, he added: "Here comes Novikov."

A tall, fair-haired, handsome man was emerging from the house. His red silk shirt, fitting tightly over his slightly plump but strapping, handsome body, flashed its fiery red brilliantly in the patches of sunlight, and his light blue eyes looked affectionate and indolent.

"You two are always quarreling!" he called from a distance in his indolent and affectionate voice. "What about, for heaven's sake?"

"Well, Mama thinks a Grecian nose would suit me better, while I thank God for the one I have."

Sanin looked down at his own nose, started laughing, and shook Novikov's broad, chubby hand.

"Well, what next!" Marya Ivanovna replied with vexation.

Novikov gave a loud, jovial laugh, and its gently sonorous echo rang out agreeably in the green grove, as if some kind, gentle spirit out there had shared his merriment.

"Well, I know what it is . . . it's all those worries about your future!"

"Now even you're joining in!" Sanin said with comic bewilderment.

"Well, it's just what you deserve!"

"Hey!" cried Sanin. "If it's two against one, I might have to run away."

"It seems that I'll soon be the one running away from you!" Marya Ivanovna said with unexpected and, for her more than anyone else, unpleasant malice; she grabbed hold of the pot of jam and headed for the house without glancing back at anyone. The mottled Mill jumped up from the grass, cocked his ears, and watched inquisitively as she left. Then he scratched his nose with a front paw, glanced warily at the house once again, and ran off deep into the garden, preoccupied with his own business.

"Do you have a cigarette?" asked Sanin, very pleased that his mother had gone.

Novikov got out his cigarette case, lazily bending his large, imposing frame.

"It's not fair to tease her," he said with a mild reproach. "She's just an old lady."

"How am I teasing her?"

"Just now. . . ."

"What do you mean? She's the one who keeps after me. My friend, I have never asked anyone for anything; if only they'd leave me in peace . . ."

They were silent.

"Well, how are things, doctor?" Sanin asked, watching attentively as the fantastically intricate patterns of tobacco smoke rose gently in the clear air above his head.

Novikov, thinking about something else, didn't reply immediately.

"Poor . . . ly."

"How so?"

"You know, the usual. . . . Bored. I've had it up to here with this hick town; there's nothing to do here."

"Nothing to do? Why, you yourself complained you didn't have time to breathe."

"That's not what I'm talking about. One can't see patients all the time. There's another life to lead."

"And just who prevents you from leading that other life?"

"Well, that's a complicated question!"

"What's so complicated? What more do you want: you're a young man, handsome, in good health."

"It turns out that's not much!" Novikov replied with good-natured irony.

"How can I put it?" Sanin said with a smile. "I think it's rather a lot."

"But not enough for me!" Novikov laughed. From his laugh it was clear that he was pleased by Sanin's opinion of his looks, strength, and health, and that he felt slightly embarrassed, like a young lady during the inspection of the bride.

"There's only one thing you need," Sanin said pensively.

"What's that?"

"A genuine outlook on life. . . . You're oppressed by the monotony of your own existence; but if someone told you to give it all up and set off into the wide world, you'd be afraid."

"How? As a tramp? Please. . . ."

"Why not as a tramp? You know, I look at you and think: Here's a man who, if given a chance to provide the Russian empire with some sort of constitution, would be willing to spend the rest of his days in Schlüsselburg fortress, to be deprived of all his rights, freedom, everything. . . .[1] And all for the sake of a constitution! But when it's a question of overthrowing his own tedious life and going off in search of new interests and meaning elsewhere, then the question arises immediately: How will I live? I'm a strong, healthy

---

[1] The issue of providing Russians with some sort of legal constitution was a recurrent theme during the eighteenth and nineteenth centuries. Schlüsselburg fortress dominated the entrance to Lake Ladoga from the Neva River, north of St. Petersburg; from the eighteenth century it was used as a prison for high-ranking persons and political prisoners.

man, but won't I perish if I'm deprived of my salary, of cream for my morning tea, of my silk shirts and collars? It's very strange, really it is!"

"There's nothing strange about it. In the first case, it's a matter of ideas, whereas here . . ."

"What is it?"

"Well . . . how can I express it?" Novikov snapped his fingers.

"See how you beat about the bush!" Sanin interrupted him. "Right away you come up with all sorts of qualifications! You don't expect me to believe you're more consumed by your longing for a constitution than by finding meaning and interest in your own life."

"Well, that's another question. Perhaps I am."

Sanin waved his arm in vexation.

"Stop it, please! If someone were to cut off your finger, you'd feel more pain than if they cut off the finger of any other inhabitant of Russia. That's a fact."

"Or it's cynicism!" Novikov tried to reply sarcastically, but it came out comically.

"So be it. But it's true. And now, when there's not only no constitution but not even a hint of one, not just in Russia but in many other countries of the world as well, you're depressed because your own life brings you no comfort, not because of some constitution! And if you say otherwise, you're lying. You know what I have to say," Sanin interrupted himself with a merry twinkle in his bright eyes. "You're depressed now not because your life in general isn't satisfying but because Lida hasn't fallen in love with you yet! Isn't that so?"

"Well, now you're talking nonsense!" Novikov exclaimed, his face turning the color of his red shirt; tears of the most naive and genuine embarrassment welled up in his kind, calm eyes.

"What kind of nonsense is it if you don't see anything else in the whole world except Lida! Why, one wish is written all over you, from your head to your toes—to have her. And you say it's nonsense!"

Novikov winced in a strange way and began pacing hurriedly up and down the path. If it weren't Lida's own brother who was saying this, he might have been ashamed, but it was so strange for him to hear these words about her from Sanin that he didn't even quite understand him.

"You know," he muttered, "you're either posing or . . ."

"Or what?" Sanin asked, smiling.

Novikov shrugged in silence and looked aside. His second conclusion led him to see Sanin as a bad, immoral man, as Novikov understood it. But he couldn't tell Sanin that because he'd always felt genuine affection for him, even as far back as their time together in the gymnasium.[2] It would then appear that he, Novikov, liked a worthless fellow, and that, of course, couldn't

[2] A secondary school that prepared students to enter a university.

possibly be true. As a result, Novikov suddenly felt confused and uncomfortable. The mention of Lida was painful and embarrassing, but inasmuch as he worshiped Lida and cherished his deep and abiding affection for her, he couldn't get angry at Sanin for bringing up her name: it was tormenting but at the same time intensely pleasurable. It was as if someone's burning hand had taken hold of his heart and given it a gentle squeeze.

Sanin remained silent and kept smiling; his smile was courteous and affectionate.

"Well, think of something. I can wait," he said. "I'm in no hurry."

Novikov kept walking up and down the path; he was clearly suffering. Mill came running up, looked around anxiously, and began to rub against Sanin's legs. He was obviously happy about something or other and wanted everyone to know about it.

"What a good dog you are!" Sanin said, stroking him.

Novikov was having difficulty restraining himself from resuming the discussion, but he was afraid that Sanin might once again touch on the one subject that interested him more than anything else in the world. However, everything that occurred to him seemed empty, boring, and dull compared to Lida.

"And . . . where is Lidiya Petrovna?" he asked absent-mindedly, precisely the question he wanted to ask, but couldn't actually bring himself to do so.

"Lida? Where else could she be? Strolling the boulevard with some officers. Nowadays all our young women stroll the boulevard."

With a desolate stab of dark jealousy Novikov replied: "Lidiya Petrovna? How can she, such a clever, mature young woman, spend time with those empty-headed gentlemen?"

"Hey, my friend!" Sanin said with a smile. "Lida's young, beautiful, robust, just like you . . . even more so, because she has what you lack: a thirst for life! She wants to know everything, experience everything. . . . Why, here she comes herself. Just look at her and you'll see! What a beauty she is!"

Lida was shorter and much better looking than her brother. One was struck by her subtle, enchanting combination of graceful delicacy and agile strength, by the passionate, majestic expression of her enigmatic eyes, and by her soft, sonorous voice, of which she was so proud and with which she played. She came down the steps slowly, her whole body in a state of mild excitement, like a beautiful young filly; she held up her long gray dress with dexterity and certainty. Brandishing their spurs and clinking them very loudly, two handsome young officers followed in their shining boots and tight-fitting riding breeches.

"Who's the beauty? Me?" Lida asked, filling the whole garden with her loveliness, her feminine freshness, and her sonorous voice. She stretched out her hand to Novikov and cast a sidelong glance at her brother; she still couldn't get used to him or decide whether he was joking or being serious.

Novikov shook her hand firmly and blushed so deeply that tears welled up in his eyes. But Lida didn't notice: she'd long since gotten used to the timid, reverent gaze he directed at her and was no longer troubled by it.

"Good evening, Vladimir Petrovich," said the officer, the older, fairer, and handsomer one, rattling his spurs cheerfully and musically, standing up straight like an excited, spirited stallion.

Sanin already knew that his name was Zarudin, that he was a cavalry captain, and that he persistently and stubbornly sought Lida's affection. The other officer was Lieutenant Tanarov, who considered Zarudin a model officer and tried to imitate him in all respects. But he was reserved, not very accomplished, and not as good-looking as Zarudin.

Tanarov clinked his spurs in the same way, but said nothing.

"Yes, you!" Sanin said to his sister, in too serious a tone.

"Of course, of course . . . a beauty, and, you should add, an indescribable one!" laughed Lida, throwing herself into a chair after glancing at her brother. Raising her hands to her head and in doing so emphasizing her shapely bosom, she began unfastening her hat, let a long hatpin fall onto the sand, and got her veil tangled in her hair and pins. "Andrei Pavlovich, help me!" she said in a plaintive and flirtatious way, turning to the more reserved officer.

"Yes, quite a beauty!" Sanin repeated pensively, without taking his eyes off her.

Once more Lida cast a sidelong, apprehensive glance at him.

"All of us here are beautiful!" she said.

"What do you mean?" Zarudin laughed, showing his shining white teeth. "We're merely the paltry backdrop against which your beauty is all the more dazzlingly and splendidly displayed!"

"You're so eloquent!" Sanin said in surprise, a note of sarcasm almost imperceptible in his voice.

"Lidiya Petrovna would make anyone eloquent!" replied the more reserved Tanarov, trying to help remove her hat and tugging at her hair, which both angered her and made her laugh.

"And you're also very eloquent!" Sanin drawled in surprise.

"Leave them alone," Novikov whispered insincerely, though with pleasure.

Lida screwed up her eyes and looked directly at her brother; in her darkened pupils Sanin could clearly read: Don't think I don't know who these people are! But this is what I want! It amuses me! I'm no more foolish than you are; I know exactly what I'm doing!

Sanin smiled at her.

Her hat was off at last and Tanarov solemnly carried it over to the table.

"Oh, now look what you've done, Andrei Pavlovich!" Lida exclaimed, instantly altering her demeanor, becoming both plaintive and flirtatious once more. "You've spoiled my hairdo. Now I have to go back inside."

"I shall never forgive myself!" Tanarov muttered in embarrassment.

Lida stood up, gathered up her skirt, and, excitedly sensing all the men's glances directed at her, laughed unaccountably, turned away, and dashed onto the porch.

After she'd gone, all the men felt freer; they relaxed immediately and sat down, losing all that nervous tension men usually feel in the presence of an attractive young woman. Zarudin took out a cigarette and, after lighting it with pleasure, began talking. It was evident that he was talking only out of his habit of facilitating conversation, and that he was thinking about something altogether different.

"Today I've been trying to persuade Lidiya Petrovna to give up everything else and to study singing seriously. With a voice like hers, a career is a sure thing!"

"A fine choice of career indeed!" Novikov replied gloomily, looking aside.

"What's wrong with it?" Zarudin asked in genuine surprise, and even took the cigarette from his mouth.

"Well, what's an actress really? Nothing but a whore!" Novikov answered with sudden irritation.

He was tormented and exasperated by jealousy: he suffered at the thought that the woman whose body he loved would be on display for other men to see, perhaps wearing provocative costumes, revealing her body, and making it all the more sinful and alluring.

"That's going too far," Zarudin said, lifting his eyebrows.

Novikov looked at him with hatred: in his view Zarudin was precisely one of those men who craved the woman he loved; besides, he was terribly irritated that Zarudin was so handsome.

"No, it's not going too far. To appear on stage half-naked! To pose and play voluptuous scenes before the gaze of men who'll leave her tomorrow just as they leave a prostitute after paying their money. Yes, indeed, that's splendid!"

"My friend," replied Sanin, "there's nothing a woman enjoys more than having her body admired."

Novikov shrugged in irritation.

"What a vulgar thing to say!"

"The devil knows whether it's vulgar or not, but it's true. Lida would be effective on the stage; I'd like to see her there."

Even though these words stirred some avid, instinctive curiosity in them all, they also felt uncomfortable. Zarudin, who considered himself cleverer and more resourceful than the rest, considered it his duty to rescue everyone from this awkward situation.

"Well then, what do you think a woman should do? Get married? Pursue her studies and let her talents be wasted? Why, that would constitute a crime against nature, which has endowed her with its finest gifts!"

"Oh," Sanin replied with undisguised sarcasm. "Well, I'll be! How is it that this crime never occurred to me?"

Novikov laughed maliciously, but out of propriety he replied to Zarudin:

"Why do you call it a crime? A good mother or a good doctor is a thousand times more useful than a good actress!"

"Well!" Tanarov retorted indignantly.

"Don't you find it tiresome to keep repeating such things?" asked Sanin.

Zarudin choked on his reply, and it suddenly seemed to everyone that it really was tiresome and useless to talk about all this. Nevertheless, everyone felt offended. It became quiet and very tedious.

Lida and Marya Ivanovna appeared on the balcony. Lida overheard her brother's last phrase, but didn't grasp what he was talking about.

"You seem to have talked yourself to the point of boredom rather quickly!" she observed cheerfully. "Let's go down to the river. It's so lovely there now."

And, walking past the men, she gave a little stretch; for a moment her eyes became dark and mysterious, promising something, communicating something.

"Take a stroll until suppertime," Marya Ivanovna said.

"With pleasure," Zarudin agreed, clicking his spurs and offering Lida his arm.

"I hope you'll allow me to accompany you?" Novikov asked, trying to speak with venom, as a result of which his face assumed a pathetic expression.

"Who's stopping you?" Lida asked, laughing over her shoulder.

"Go on, friend, go," Sanin advised. "I'd go along, too, if she were not, unfortunately, so absolutely convinced that I'm her brother!"

Lida flinched peculiarly and pricked up her ears. Then she cast a swift glance at her brother and gave a short, nervous laugh.

Marya Ivanovna was shocked.

"Why do you say such foolish things?" she asked rudely after Lida had left. "You're always trying to be so original!"

"I intend no such thing," Sanin replied.

Marya Ivanovna looked at him with incomprehension. She didn't understand her son at all, couldn't tell when he was joking or being serious, what he thought and felt when everyone else thought and felt the same as she herself did, or almost the same. According to her own understanding, a person should always feel, say, and do exactly what all other people with the same level of education, economic means, and social status say and do. For her it was natural that people were not simply individuals with all their own traits endowed by nature, but rather were all cast in a well-known common mold. Life around her confirmed this belief: everyone's educational efforts were directed toward this goal, and that was what distinguished the intelligent people from the unintelligent. The latter could preserve their individuality and be despised for it, while the former were divided into groups only according to their education. Their convictions always corresponded not to their personal characteristics but to their position: every student was a revolutionary, every civil servant a bourgeois, every artist a freethinker; every officer had an exaggerated opinion of his outward nobility; and when a student suddenly turned out to be a conservative or an officer an anarchist, then this seemed very strange indeed, sometimes even unpleasant. According to his birth and education, Sanin should have been entirely different from what he was; just like Lida, Novikov, and everyone who came in contact with him, Marya Ivanovna looked at him with an unpleasant feeling of disappointed expectation. With a mother's intuition, she took note of the impression her son made on everyone around him, and that caused her pain.

Sanin saw this. He'd have liked very much to comfort his mother, but he didn't know how. At first it even occurred to him to pretend and express the most reassuring thoughts to her, but he couldn't think of anything; he laughed, stood up, and went into the house. He lay down on his bed and began thinking about how people wanted to transform the whole world into a kind of monastic barracks, with one set of rules for everyone based on the annihilation of all personality and the subordination of its power to some mysterious group of elders. He began to reflect on the role and fate of Christianity, but that proved so boring that he dozed off and slept until late evening.

Marya Ivanovna watched him leave, then sighed deeply and also began thinking. She reflected on the fact that Zarudin was courting Lida, and she hoped it would turn out to be in earnest.

Lidochka's already twenty! she thought. Zarudin seems to be a nice man. They say he'll be assigned a squadron this year. . . . If only he could stay out of debt! But why did I have that awful dream? I know it's nonsense, yet I can't get it out of my head!

For some reason the dream that Marya Ivanovna had had the first night Zarudin had been to their house was really tormenting her. She dreamed that Lida was wearing a white dress, walking through a meadow covered with grass and flowers.

Marya Ivanovna sat down in an armchair, resting her head on her hand in the way old women do, and for a long time gazed at the slowly darkening sky. Trivial but distressing, tiresome thoughts crept into her mind; she felt gloomy and afraid of something.

 III

The strollers returned when it was already quite dark. Their distinct, animated voices resounded from the depths of the garden, gently muffled in the darkness.

Lida, spirited and flushed, ran up to Marya Ivanovna. She bore the scent of the cool, fresh river combined with that of a beautiful young woman excited by the society of aroused young men whom she liked.

"Supper, mama, supper!" she demanded affectionately, harassing her smiling mother. "Meanwhile Viktor Sergeevich will sing for us."

Marya Ivanovna went to arrange supper and, as she left, reflected on the fact that the fate of such an interesting, attractive, healthy, and forthright young woman as Lida couldn't be anything but happy.

Zarudin and Tanarov went in to the piano in the drawing room; Lida sat down in a rocking chair on the balcony and stretched out gracefully and passionately.

Novikov silently paced the creaking floorboards of the balcony, casting sidelong glances at her face, her full bosom, and her shapely feet in black stockings and yellow shoes visible beneath her dress; but, overcome with the powerful and enchanting sensation of her first passion, she noticed neither his glances nor the man himself. Her eyes were closed tight and she was smiling enigmatically to herself.

The usual struggle raged in Novikov's soul: he loved Lida, but couldn't understand her feelings. Sometimes it seemed as if she loved him, sometimes not. And when he thought she did, it seemed altogether possible, easy, and splendid that her young, nubile, virgin body would one day belong entirely and voluptuously to him. But when he thought that she didn't love him, the same idea seemed vile and shameless; then he accused himself of sensuality and considered himself depraved, good for nothing, and unworthy of Lida.

Novikov paced the floor and tried to guess his fortune: "If I step on the last board with my right foot, then she loves me and I must declare myself; but if it's with my left foot, then . . ."

He didn't want to think about what would happen then.

He stepped on the last board with his left foot, broke out in a cold sweat, and immediately said to himself: Ugh! What nonsense! Just like an old woman! Well. . . . One, two, three . . . On "three" I'll go right up and tell her. How will I? It doesn't matter. Well then, one . . . two . . . three. . . . No, on the third time. One, two, three. . . . One, two . . .

His head was on fire, his mouth was dry, and his heart was pounding so violently that his knees were knocking.

"Stop walking around like that!" Lida said with annoyance, opening her eyes. "I can't hear a thing!"

Only now did Novikov realize that Zarudin was singing.

The young officer was crooning an old romance:

> "I loved you; that love, perhaps,
> Has not entirely died in my breast. . . ."[3]

He didn't sing badly, but, like all people who lack formal training, he used

---

[3] An inexact rendering of one of Aleksandr Pushkin's most famous love lyrics, "Ya vas lyubil" ("I loved you," 1829).

exaggerated dynamics instead of subtle expression. Novikov found his singing extremely unpleasant.

"What's that, his own composition?" he asked with unusual malice and irritation.

"No. Don't interrupt! Sit quietly!" Lida ordered capriciously. "If you don't like music, you can stare at the moon."

In fact, a completely round and still reddish moon slowly and mysteriously appeared over some black treetops in the garden. Its soft elusive light slid across the steps, Lida's dress, and her face with its thoughtful smile. The shadows in the garden had grown darker and become as black and deep as in the forest.

Novikov sighed. "I'd rather look at you," he said awkwardly, and thought: What nonsense I can utter!

Lida gave a laugh. "Ugh! What a clumsy compliment!"

"I don't know how to pay compliments," Novikov replied gloomily.

"Will you sit still . . . and listen!" Lida said, shrugging in annoyance.

> "But let my love not disturb you any more,
> I don't wish to trouble you in any way!"

The sounds of the piano spread like resonant crystal splashes in the damp green garden. The moonlight became brighter, the shadows even deeper and darker. Down below Sanin walked softly across the grass, then sat down under a linden tree; he was about to light a cigarette, but changed his mind and sat there motionless, as if enchanted by the stillness of the evening, which was unbroken but somehow amplified by the sounds of the piano and the young singer's passionate voice.

"Lidiya Petrovna!" Novikov blurted out suddenly, as if it had immediately become clear that this moment could not be lost.

"What?" Lida asked mechanically, gazing at the garden, the moon, and the dark branches outlined against its bright round disk.

"I've waited so long . . . I want to talk—" Novikov continued, his voice breaking off.

Sanin turned his head and listened.

"What about?" Lida asked again, absent-mindedly.

Zarudin finished one romance, was silent for a while, and then began another. He thought he had an unusually fine voice and he loved to sing.

Novikov felt that he was blushing and blanching; he didn't feel at all well and thought he might faint.

"I . . . don't you see . . . Lidiya Petrovna, would you care to be my . . . wife?" His tongue was twisted and he felt that this was not at all what one was supposed to say and do at such moments. Even before he finished speaking, it somehow became perfectly clear that the answer would be no and that something shameful, stupid, and unbearably ridiculous was suddenly about to happen.

Lida inquired mechanically: "Whose wife?" and suddenly blushed, stood up, was about to say something, but didn't, and turned away in embarrassment. The moon was staring right at her.

"I love you. . . ." Novikov continued to mumble, feeling that the moon had stopped shining, that the air in the garden was stifling, and that everything was hurtling into some dreadful, hopeless abyss. "I . . . I don't know how to say it, but that's not important and . . . I love you very much."

Why did I add "very much," as if I were talking about ice cream? he thought all of a sudden and fell silent.

Lida tugged nervously at a leaf that somehow happened to be in her hands. She was disconcerted because it was so totally unexpected, unnecessary, and it created an unfortunate, irreparable awkwardness between her and Novikov, with whom she'd long felt comfortable, almost as if they were related, and whom she genuinely liked.

"I don't know, really. . . . I haven't thought about it at all."

Novikov felt his heart sink with a dull ache; he turned pale, rose, and picked up his cap.

"Good-bye!" he said, without hearing his own voice. His lips curled strangely into a ridiculous and inappropriate quivering smile.

"Where are you going? Good-bye!" Lida replied distractedly, extending her hand and trying to smile casually.

Novikov quickly shook her hand and, without putting his cap on, strode briskly along the dew-covered path into the garden. Slipping into the first shady spot, he stopped suddenly and grasped his head in his hands.

Oh, my God! Why am I so unlucky? Shall I shoot myself? This is all nonsense, but to shoot myself . . . This thought came rushing like a whirlwind into his incoherent mind, and he felt that he was the most unhappy, disgraced, and ridiculous man in all the world.

Sanin wanted to call out to him, but changed his mind and then grinned. He found it amusing that Novikov was tearing his hair out and almost weeping because a woman whose face, shoulders, breasts, and legs attracted him didn't want to give herself to him.

Sanin also found it reassuring that his lovely sister wasn't in love with Novikov.

Lida stood motionless on the same spot for a few moments; with keen interest Sanin observed her white silhouette in the pale moonlight.

Zarudin emerged from the illuminated yellow doors of the house onto the balcony and Sanin could clearly hear the meticulous jangling of his spurs. In the drawing room Tanarov was softly and sadly playing an old waltz, its heavy somber tones all-pervading.

Zarudin went up to Lida quietly and, with a gentle, agile movement, put his arm around her waist; Sanin could see clearly how their two silhouettes blended easily into one, swaying strangely in the moonlight.

"Why have you become so pensive?" Zarudin whispered softly, touching her sweet little ear with his lips, his eyes shining.

Lida's head was swimming sweetly and terrifyingly. As always when she was embracing Zarudin, she was overcome with a strange feeling: she knew that he was infinitely below her in intelligence and culture, and that she could never be subordinate to him, but at the same time she found it pleasant and terrifying to permit this physical contact with a big, strong man, as if she were glancing into a mysterious, bottomless pit with the bold thought: What if I throw myself in? I could if I wanted to!

"They'll see us," she whispered, barely audibly, without drawing nearer or pulling away, thus exciting and arousing him even more by her compliant passivity.

"One word," Zarudin continued, pressing closer to her, his ardent passion overflowing. "Will you come?"

Lida trembled. It wasn't the first time he'd asked her this question and every time something in her began to languish and tremble, making her feel frail and weak-willed.

"For what?" she asked indistinctly, glancing at the moon with her wide-open, moist eyes.

Zarudin was unable and unwilling to reply truthfully, although, like all men who so easily become intimate with women, he was convinced in the depths of his soul that Lida herself desired it, and that she knew, but that she was afraid.

"For what? So I can look at you, exchange a few words. This is torture . . . you're tormenting me. . . . Lidiya . . . will you come?" he repeated, passionately drawing her prominent, firm, warm hips toward his own trembling legs.

From the contact of their legs, burning like glowing iron, the warm, fragrant, enveloping mist became even thicker, just like a dream. All of Lida's supple, delicate, graceful body froze, swayed, and drew closer to him. She was tormented by pleasure and fear. Everything around her was being transformed strangely and incomprehensibly: the moon was no longer the moon and seemed to be very, very close, visible through the trellis of the terrace, as if hanging just above the brightly lit lawn; the garden, no longer the one she knew but another, warm and mysterious, suddenly closed in on her. Her head began to swim slowly and heavily. Swaying with strange languor, she freed herself from his arms and immediately whispered with difficulty through her parched, swollen lips:

"I will. . . ."

Reeling, she made her way into the house, feeling as if something terrible, inevitable, yet alluring was drawing her toward an abyss.

That's nonsense . . . it's not that at all . . . I'm only joking. I'm merely curious; it'll be amusing, she tried to convince herself, standing in her room in front of a dark mirror, seeing only her black silhouette reflected on the illuminated door leading into the dining room. She slowly raised her hands to her head, locked her fingers, and stretched voluptuously, observing the movement of her slim, supple waist and her broad prominent hips.

Left alone, Zarudin shuddered on his handsome, well-proportioned legs, stretched, screwed up his eyes, and, baring his teeth in a grin beneath his fair mustache, shrugged. He was usually a fortunate fellow and felt that the future contained even better fortune and greater enjoyment. He fervently pictured Lida at the moment of her surrender as so extraordinarily voluptuous that he himself suffered physical pain from the passion.

At first, when he had begun to court her, and even later, when she had allowed him to embrace and kiss her, Zarudin was still afraid of her. There was something unfamiliar and incomprehensible in her darkened eyes, as if, while allowing him to caress her, she secretly despised him. She seemed so clever, so unlike all those other girls and women he caressed and with whom he was haughtily aware of his own superiority; he was so proud that, while embracing her, he would freeze, as if expecting a slap in the face, and was somehow afraid to think about possessing her entirely. Sometimes it seemed that she was playing with him and that his position was simply foolish and ridiculous. But after her promise today, uttered in a strangely faltering and submissive voice, one that Zarudin recognized from his experience with other women, all of a sudden he unexpectedly felt his own strength and the imminent proximity of his goal, and he understood that it could turn out in no other way than the one he desired. And this sweet, languorous feeling of voluptuous anticipation was combined with a slight and unconscious trace of spite, that this proud, clever, pure, cultured young woman would lie beneath him, just like all the others, and that he would do with her exactly as he wished, just as he had done with all the others. His bitter, cruel mind began vaguely to conceive of imaginatively humiliating, lascivious scenes in which Lida's naked body, disheveled hair, and astute eyes were woven into some wild bacchanalia of voluptuous cruelty. He suddenly had a clear picture of her lying on the floor; he heard the swish of a whip, saw the pink stripe on her tender, naked, submissive body, and shuddering, he staggered at the rush of blood to his head. Golden sparks flashed in his eyes.

It was physically unbearable for him to contemplate all this. With trembling fingers Zarudin lit a cigarette, swayed once again on his strong legs, and went inside.

Sanin, who couldn't hear but saw and understood everything, followed him in, feeling something akin to jealousy.

Animals like that are always lucky! he thought. How the hell is this possible? Lida and he!

They had supper. Marya Ivanovna was in a bad mood. Tanarov was silent as usual, and mused about how splendid it would be if he were like Zarudin, and if a girl like Lida were in love with him. It seemed to him that he would love her in a different way than Zarudin, who was incapable of appreciating such good fortune. Lida was pale, reserved, and didn't look at anyone. Zarudin was cheerful and cautious, like a wild beast on the prowl, while Sanin, as always, yawned, ate, drank a great deal of vodka, and seemed extremely eager to go to bed. But that didn't prevent him from declaring after supper that he wasn't sleepy and that he planned to walk Zarudin home.

It was already late and the moon had risen high in the sky. Sanin and Zarudin made their way to the officer's quarters almost in silence. Along the way Sanin kept glancing at the officer and debated whether or not to smack him in the face.

"Hmm, yes," he began when they'd reached the house. "There are so many different kinds of scoundrels in the world!"

"Namely?" Zarudin asked in surprise, raising his eyebrows.

"Generally speaking, that is. And scoundrels make the most interesting people."

"You don't say!" Zarudin laughed.

"Of course. There's nothing more boring in this world than an honest man. What's an honest man? The program of honesty and virtue has long been known to everyone and there can't be anything new in it. As a result of that archaic rubbish a person loses all diversity; life is lived within a single frame of virtue, narrow and tedious. Don't steal, don't lie, don't cheat, and don't commit adultery. . . . And the main thing is that all this is innate to people: everyone lies, and everyone cheats, and everyone commits as many 'adulteries' as possible."

"Surely not everyone!" Zarudin remarked condescendingly.

"Yes, everyone. One need only examine, more or less carefully, the life of each person to discover his sins. Treachery, for example. At the very moment we render unto Caesar that which is Caesar's, lie down to sleep, or sit down to eat, we commit treachery."

"What are you saying?" Zarudin cried involuntarily, almost in outrage.

"Of course. We pay our taxes and do our military service, but that only means we deliver thousands of people to that same war and injustice that fill us with indignation. We lie down to sleep, yet don't run to rescue those who are perishing at that very moment for our sake, for our ideas. We eat the extra morsel of food, condemning to hunger those whose well-being we should be concerned with all our lives if we are virtuous. And so on. That's understandable! But a scoundrel's different, a genuine, blatant scoundrel! First of all, this man's perfectly sincere and natural."

"Natural?"

"Absolutely. He does what's completely normal for a man to do. He sees something nice that doesn't belong to him, and he takes it: he sees a beautiful woman who won't give herself to him, and he takes her by force or deceit. And that's perfectly natural because this need for and understanding of gratification is one of the few traits that distinguish a natural man from animals. The more animal an animal is, the less it understands gratification and the less able it is to secure it. It merely satisfies its needs. We all agree that man isn't created to suffer and that suffering isn't the goal of human aspirations."

"That goes without saying," Zarudin agreed.

"In other words, gratification is the goal of life. Paradise is a synonym for absolute gratification and everyone more or less dreams of paradise on earth. It's said that originally there was paradise on earth. That legend is by no means nonsense, but a symbol and a dream.

"Yes," Sanin continued after a pause, "by nature man's not adapted to abstinence, and the most sincere people are those who don't hide their physical desires . . . that is, those who, in society, are called scoundrels. Why, take you, for instance."

Zarudin was startled and taken aback.

"You, of course," Sanin continued, pretending not to notice anything. "You're the best person on earth. At least, in your own eyes. Well now, confess, have you ever met anyone better?"

"Many," Zarudin replied indecisively; he no longer had a clue what Sanin was talking about and didn't know whether to be offended or not.

"Name them," Sanin proposed.

Zarudin shrugged in perplexity.

"Well, then," Sanin exclaimed cheerfully. "You're the very best person, and I, of course, am the very best, and yet wouldn't you and I like to steal, lie, and commit 'adultery'. . . especially 'adultery'?"

Zarudin shrugged again. "Very o-rig-i-nal," he muttered.

"You think so?" Sanin asked with a slight tone of offense. "I had no idea. . . . Yes, scoundrels are the most sincere people and the most interesting, because it's impossible even to imagine the boundaries and limits of human vileness. I'll shake hands with a scoundrel with particular pleasure."

Sanin shook Zarudin's hand with unusual candor, looking him straight in the eye, then suddenly knitted his brows and muttered in a completely different tone of voice: "Good-bye. Good night!" and then left.

Zarudin stood motionless for several moments on the same spot, watching Sanin leave. He didn't know how to take Sanin's words and felt confused and uneasy. But then he remembered Lida; he smiled and recalled that Sanin was her brother, that what he'd said was essentially correct, and that he felt some brotherly attachment and friendship for him.

An entertaining fellow, damn it all! he thought complacently, as if, to some extent, Sanin already belonged to him, too. Then he opened the gate and returned to his quarters across the moonlit courtyard.

Sanin went home, got undressed, lay down, and started to read *Thus Spake Zarathrustra*,[4] which he had found in Lida's room, but he felt an-

---

[4] Friedrich Nietzsche's greatest work (1883–84, 1891), a poem condemning traditional morality, especially Christian ethics, and proclaiming the gospel of the Übermensch (superman).

noyed and bored from the first few pages. The pompous images didn't stir his soul. He spat, tossed the book aside, and fell fast asleep.

 IV

Nikolai Yegorovich Svarozhich, a retired lieutenant and landowner who lived in the same town, was being visited by his son, a student at the technical institute.

His son, Yury Svarozhich, had been expelled from Moscow and was under police surveillance as a suspected member of a revolutionary organization. He'd previously informed his family by mail that he'd been arrested, served a six-month prison term, and been expelled from the capital; therefore his arrival came as no surprise to them. Although Nikolai Yegorovich held different convictions, he saw his son's acts as childish foolishness and was sorely grieved by the whole episode; he loved his son, welcomed him affectionately, and tried to avoid conversation on all sensitive subjects.

Yury had traveled for two days in a third-class railway car where the foul air, stench, and wailing babies made it impossible for him to sleep. He was exhausted, and after greeting his father and his sister Lyudmila (who was known as Lyalya, a name she herself had chosen in childhood), he lay down to sleep on the bed in Lyalya's room.

He awoke toward evening, when the sun was setting, its slanting rays outlining the silhouette of the window in red stripes against the wall. Forks and glasses could be heard clinking in the next room, as well as Lyalya's cheerful laughter and a gentleman's unfamiliar but pleasant voice.

At first it seemed to Yury that he was still traveling in a railway car, hearing the noise of the buffers, the rattling of windowpanes, and the voices of strangers in the next compartment. But he soon recalled where he was, and quickly sat up in bed.

"Yes," he said slowly, making a face and running his hand through his unruly, thick black hair. "Here I am!"

And the thought occurred to him that he shouldn't have come home. He'd been granted the right to choose his own place of residence. Yury couldn't explain to himself precisely why he'd chosen to come back here. He thought and he still wanted to think that he'd said the first thing that had occurred to him, but that wasn't true: Yury had lived all his life without having to work, helped by his father, and he was terrified of finding himself alone without support, in an unfamiliar place among strangers. He was ashamed of this feeling and didn't admit it even to himself. But now he thought he had made the wrong choice. It was clear that his family couldn't understand or approve of what had happened to him; in addition, the material question would certainly arise—extra years as a financial burden to his father—and all this ensured that good, sincere, harmonious relations could never be established between them. Besides, it would be very boring in this little town where he hadn't lived for the last two years. Yury indiscriminately considered all the inhabitants of small provincial towns petty bourgeois, incapable not only of understanding but even of taking an interest in those philosophical and political questions that he believed were the only important and interesting part of life.

Yury got up, went to the window, opened it, and leaned out over the front garden that hugged the walls of the house. It was covered with red, blue, yellow, purple, and white flowers, all interspersed as if viewed through a kaleidoscope. A deep, dark garden lay beyond; like all gardens in this lush river town, it extended to the river, which shimmered below like pale glass among the tree trunks. The evening was quiet and clear.

Yury became sad. For too long he'd lived in large towns built of stone, and although he'd always believed that he loved nature, it remained desolate for him and did nothing to relieve his feelings, to soothe or delight him; instead, it aroused in him an incomprehensible, wistful, painful sadness.

"Aha. . . . You're up! It's about time!" said Lyalya, entering the room.

Yury came away from the window.

An oppressive feeling caused by awareness of his isolated and ill-defined position combined with a quiet melancholy aroused by the dying of the day, so that Yury was not at all pleased to see his sister so cheerful and to hear her resonant, carefree voice.

"Why are you so radiant?" he asked somewhat unexpectedly, even for himself.

"Well, how do you like that!" Lyalya exclaimed, opening her eyes wide, but immediately beginning to laugh even more cheerfully, as if her brother's question reminded her of something amusing and joyous. "Why on earth are you asking about my cheerfulness? I'm never bored. I've no time to be."

Assuming a serious look and apparently taking pride in what she was saying, she added: "This is such an interesting time that it would simply be sinful to be bored! I'm occupied with working people now, and the library takes up a great deal of my time. While you were away we organized a people's library. It's gotten off to a very good start!"

At another time this would have interested Yury and aroused his attention, but now something was bothering him.

Lyalya looked serious and, in an amusing way, waited for his approval like a young child; therefore Yury made a great effort and said: "You don't say!"

"How could I possibly be bored?" Lyalya drawled contentedly.

"Well, I'm feeling totally bored," Yury replied, again involuntarily.

"That's nice, I must say!" Lyalya feigned irritation. "You've only been home a few hours, you've slept most of those, and you're bored already!"

"What's to be done? It's my God-given fate!" Yury replied with a slight trace of complacency. He thought it was both better and cleverer to be bored than to be cheerful.

"God-given fate! God-given!" Lyalya sang out, pretending to pout, and waved her hand at him dismissively. "Ugh!"

Yury didn't notice that he was already feeling more cheerful. Lyalya's resonant voice and enjoyment of life quickly and easily banished the burdensome feeling he'd considered so serious and profound. And unconsciously Lyalya didn't believe in his melancholy, so she wasn't in the least offended by his utterances.

Yury looked her straight in the eye and said with a smile: "I'm never cheerful!"

Lyalya laughed as though he'd told her something very amusing and jolly.

"Well, that's enough, you knight of rueful countenance![5] If you say never, then it's never. Instead, let's go and I'll introduce you to a young man . . . of pleasant appearance. Let's go!"

Lyalya laughed and took her brother's hand.

"Wait a minute. And just who might this pleasant young man be?"

"My fiancé," Lyalya cried out in a loud, cheerful voice, right in Yury's face, and she danced around the room in an ecstasy of embarrassment and delight, her dress billowing out.

Yury knew from his father's letters and from Lyalya herself that a young doctor who had arrived in town not long ago was courting Lyalya, but he hadn't known that the matter was settled.

"You don't say!" he replied in surprise, and it seemed strange to him that this pure, sweet little Lyalya, whom he still thought of as a little girl, already had a fiancé and would soon get married, become a woman and a wife. He felt tenderness for his sister and a vague touch of pity.

Yury put his arm around Lyalya's waist and went with her into the dining room, where a lamp was already lit and a large, highly polished samovar stood shining. There sat Nikolai Yegorovich and an unfamiliar, solidly built young man who didn't look Russian; he had a dark complexion and alert, curious eyes.

He stood up to greet Yury in a relaxed, refined, composed manner.

"Well, let's get acquainted."

"Anatoly Pavlovich Ryazantsev," Lyalya announced in a comically exaggerated manner, extending her arm with hand upturned.

"I ask your love and indulgence," Ryazantsev added, also in a joking manner.

They shook hands in a sincere gesture of goodwill, and for a moment

---

[5] A reference to the hero of Cervantes's *Don Quixote de la Mancha* (1605).

thought about embracing each other, but did not; they merely looked each other in the eye amicably and courteously.

So that's the sort of brother she has! Ryazantsev thought in surprise, having expected that the brother of the short, spry, blonde, flourishing Lyalya would also be fair and full of joie de vivre. But Yury was tall, thin, and dark, though just as good-looking as Lyalya; his delicate, regular facial features even resembled hers.

Meanwhile, glancing at Ryazantsev, Yury reflected that here was the very man who'd come to love the grown woman in the innocent little girl Lyalya, fresh as a spring morning. He loved her, of course, in precisely the same way that Yury loved women. And for some reason he found it unpleasant and awkward to look at Ryazantsev and Lyalya, as if they could guess what he was thinking.

They felt that they had many important things to say to each other. Yury wanted to ask: Do you love Lyalya? Sincerely and earnestly? It would be pitiful and squalid if you were deceiving her. She's so pure and innocent!

And Ryazantsev would have replied: Yes, I love your sister very much, and it's impossible not to love her. Look at how pure, fresh, and pretty she is, how much she cares for me, and what lovely cleavage she shows.

But instead Yury said nothing at all and Ryazantsev asked: "Have you been banished for a long time?"

"Five years," Yury replied.

Nikolai Yegorovich, who was pacing the room, paused for a moment, but regained control of himself and continued pacing with the overly regular, measured steps of a former military man. He still didn't know the details of his son's expulsion, and this unexpected news came as quite a shock.

What the hell is going on? he thought to himself.

Lyalya understood her father's reaction and was frightened. She feared all quarrels, arguments, and unpleasant scenes, and tried to change the subject.

What a fool I am, she reproached herself mentally, not to have remembered to warn Tolya.

But Ryazantsev didn't know what all this was about, and, after answering Lyalya's question about whether or not he'd like some tea, he began to interrogate Yury once more.

"What do you intend to do now?"

Nikolai Yegorovich frowned and kept silent. Suddenly Yury perceived his father's silence and, before he could imagine the consequences, was filled with irritation and obstinacy. He replied intentionally: "Nothing for the moment."

"What do you mean, nothing? How can that be?" Nikolai Yegorovich asked, stopping his pacing. He didn't raise his voice, but a hidden reproach could clearly be heard in his tone: How can you say "nothing"? Aren't you ashamed to say that, as if I were obliged to have you hanging around my neck! How dare you forget that I'm old, that it's high time you were earning your keep? I won't say a thing; do as you wish; but how is it you yourself don't understand this? His tone implied all this.

And the more acutely he felt this, because he recognized his father's right to think this way, the more Yury was offended.

"Just so, nothing. What am I supposed to do?" he asked provocatively.

Nikolai Yegorovich wanted to say something harsh, but kept silent and, with a mere shrug began pacing again from corner to corner with his heavy, rhythmic, measured tread. His own gentlemanly upbringing prevented him from arguing with his son on the day of his arrival.

Yury followed him with his shining eyes, no longer able to restrain himself, now bristling and on guard, ready to seize upon the slightest pretext. He knew perfectly well that he was provoking a quarrel, but he could no longer control his own obstinacy and irritation.

Lyalya was almost in tears; in dismay she glanced imploringly from her brother to her father. Ryazantsev finally understood and felt sorry for Lyalya. He quickly and not very skillfully changed the subject.

The evening was tedious and drawn out. Yury didn't consider himself at fault, because he couldn't agree with Nikolai Yegorovich that political struggle was none of his business. He thought that his father didn't understand the simplest things because he was old and intellectually backward; unconsciously he blamed him for his old age and intellectual backwardness, and was annoyed. The topics raised by Ryazantsev didn't interest him; listening with only half an ear, he continued to follow his father's movements intensely and spitefully with his dark, gleaming eyes.

Novikov, Ivanov, and Semyonov arrived in time for supper.

Semyonov was a consumptive university student[6] who'd been living in town for several months, giving lessons. He was very plain-looking, gaunt, and weak; the barely perceptible but terrible shadow of imminent death could be seen in his prematurely aged face. Ivanov was a teacher at the people's school; he had long hair, broad shoulders, and an ungainly build.

They'd been strolling together along the boulevard and, learning of Yury's arrival, had dropped in to welcome him.

Things livened up after their arrival. There were witticisms, jokes, and laughter. Everyone drank at supper, Ivanov more than the rest.

In the few days that had passed since his unsuccessful declaration of love to Lida Sanina, Novikov had calmed down somewhat. He began to think that her refusal had been accidental, that he himself was to blame for it because he hadn't prepared her for it. But he still felt too ashamed and awkward to visit the Sanins. Therefore he tried to see Lida elsewhere, meeting her accidentally at a friend's house or on the street. And because Lida pitied him and felt a bit guilty, she treated him with exaggerated affection and attention; as a result, Novikov began to have hope once again.

"Here's what, ladies and gentlemen," he said, as they were about to leave. "Let's organize a picnic at the monastery. What do you say?"

---

[6] Tuberculosis was popularly known as consumption; one who suffered from tuberculosis was a consumptive.

The local monastery was the usual place for outings because it stood on a hill in a pleasant, open spot near the river, not far from town, and the road that led there was good.

Lyalya, who more than anything on earth loved all sorts of activity, outings, swimming, boat rides, and walks in the woods, seized upon the idea with enthusiasm.

"Of course, of course. But when?"

"Why, tomorrow if you like!" replied Novikov.

"Who else will we invite?" asked Ryazantsev, who also liked the idea of an outing. In the forest he'd be able to kiss Lyalya, embrace her, be in exasperatingly close contact with her body, which tempted him so intensely by its freshness and purity.

"Who else? There's the six of us. . . . We could ask Shafrov."

"Who's he?" asked Yury.

"A young studious type from around here."

"Well . . . and Lyudmila Nikolaevna will invite Karsavina and Olga Ivanovna."

"Who?" Yury asked again.

Lyalya laughed. "You'll see!" she said, kissing her fingertips in a particularly enigmatic way.

"Aha," said Yury with a smile. "We'll see, we'll see."

Novikov hesitated and then added with unnatural indifference: "We could invite the Sanins."

"Lida, absolutely!" cried Lyalya, not so much because she liked the young woman, but because she knew about Novikov's love and wanted the event to be nice for him. She was very happy in her own love and wanted everyone around her to be equally happy and content.

"Only then we'll have to invite the officers, too," Ivanov put in caustically.

"Well, what, we will. . . . The more, the merrier."

Everyone went out onto the porch.

The moon was shining brightly and evenly. It was warm and still.

"What a night," said Lyalya, inconspicuously drawing closer to Ryazantsev. She didn't want him to leave. Ryazantsev firmly pressed her warm, round arm with his elbow.

"Yes, it's a marvelous night!" he said, lending to these simple words a special meaning known only to the two of them.

"Yes, well, good for it," Ivanov said in his deep bass. "But I'm going to sleep. Good night, kind sirs."

And he strode off along the street, waving his arms like the sails of a windmill.

Then Novikov and Semyonov left. Ryazantsev took his time saying farewell to Lyalya, using the pretext of conferring about the picnic.

"Well, night-night," Lyalya said jokingly after he had gone. She stretched and sighed and with some regret took her leave of the moonlight, the warm night air, and everything to which they summoned her young, flourishing body.

Yury recalled that his father was not yet asleep and that if they were left alone, they would have to have that unpleasant conversation that would get them nowhere.

"No," he said, looking away toward the bluish mist stretching like a shroud above the river beyond the black fence. "I don't feel sleepy yet. I'll go out for a while."

"As you like," Lyalya replied in a soft, strangely tender voice. She stretched again, narrowed her eyes like a pussycat, smiled vaguely at the moonlight, and went away. Yury remained alone. For a moment he stood motionless, looking at the dark shadows of the houses and trees that seemed so deep and cold; then he shuddered and went off in the same direction as Semyonov.

The sickly student hadn't managed to get very far. He walked quietly, hunched over, coughing dryly, and his dark shadow followed him across the brightly lit ground. Yury caught up with him and immediately noticed the change that had taken place in him: all during supper Semyonov had been joking and laughing, almost more than the others, but now he was walking along gloomily, looking depressed; something awful, sad, and hopeless could be heard in his dry cough, like the illness from which he suffered.

"Ah, it's you!" he said distractedly, and, it seemed to Yury, with hostility.

"I don't feel like sleeping. So I'll walk you home," Yury explained.

"Go ahead," Semyonov agreed indifferently.

They walked on in silence for a while. Semyonov kept coughing and hunching over.

"Aren't you cold?" asked Yury, merely because this painful coughing had begun to oppress him.

"I'm always cold," Semyonov replied, seeming to be annoyed.

Yury felt awkward, as if he'd touched on a sore spot.

"Did you leave university a long time ago?" he asked again.

Semyonov didn't reply right away.

"A long time ago," he answered.

Yury began to talk about the mood of the students, what they considered most important and current. At first he spoke simply, but then he got carried away, grew livelier, and began to speak with expression and passion.

Semyonov listened and kept silent.

Then Yury shifted imperceptibly to the decline of revolutionary fervor among the masses. Clearly this subject caused him genuine pain.

"Have you read Bebel's latest speech?" he asked.[7]

"I have," Semyonov replied.

"Well, what do you think of it?"

[7] Ferdinand August Bebel (1840–1913) was the leader of a German social democratic movement and an advocate of women's rights.

In irritation Semyonov suddenly shook his stick with its large crook. His shadow also shook its arm and the movement reminded Yury of the sinister flapping wings of a black bird of prey.

"What can I say?" Semyonov began in haste and confusion. "I can tell you that I'm dying."

And he shook his stick again, and once more the black shadow of a bird of prey repeated its movement. This time Semyonov noticed it too.

"There," he said bitterly, "death is standing right behind me and watches every move I make. What do I care about Bebel? He's a babbler who babbles; another man will babble something else; it's all the same to me since I'll die tomorrow, if not today."

Embarrassed, Yury remained silent; he was depressed, pained, and offended at someone for what he heard.

"Now you think it's all so very important . . . what happens in the university or what Bebel says. But I think that when your turn comes to die, like me, and when you know for sure that you're dying, it won't even occur to you to think that some words uttered by Bebel, Nietzsche, Tolstoy, or anyone else have any meaning!"

Semyonov fell silent.

As before, the moon was shining brightly and evenly, and a black shadow followed them persistently.

"My organism is deteriorating," Semyonov said suddenly in an altogether different, weak, and pitiful voice. "If only you knew how much I don't want to die. . . . Especially on such a clear, warm night!" he said with plaintive anguish, turning his plain, haggard face with its abnormally shining eyes to Yury. "Everything's alive, but I'm dying. That seems like a trite remark to you, and so it should. But I'm dying. Not in some novel, not on any pages written 'with artistic truth,' but I really am dying, and it doesn't seem trite to me. Sometime it will happen to you. I'm dying, I'm dying, and that's that!"

Semyonov started coughing.

"Sometimes I begin thinking that soon I'll be lying in the cold ground surrounded by complete darkness, my nose eaten away, my hands rotting; meanwhile, on earth everything will be exactly as it is now while I'm alive. Why, you'll still be alive. . . . You'll be walking, looking at the moon, breathing; you'll walk past my grave and stop to relieve yourself on it, and I'll be lying there decaying. What do I care about Bebel or Tolstoy or millions of other pompous asses?" Semyonov suddenly cried shrilly and with malice.

Yury was silent, dismayed and distressed.

"Well, farewell," said Semyonov quietly. "This is where I go in."

Yury shook his hand and looked with deep pity at his sunken chest, his hunched shoulders, and his walking stick with the large crook that Semyonov had fastened to a button of his student's overcoat. Yury wanted to say something, to console and encourage him somehow, but he felt it was impossible to do so; he sighed and replied: "Good-bye."

Semyonov raised his cap and opened the gate. His steps and muffled coughing could still be heard behind the fence. Then everything fell silent.

Yury walked back. Everything that had seemed so light, bright, quiet, and peaceful half an hour ago—the moonlight, starry sky, poplar trees lit by the moon, and the mysterious shadows—now seemed deathly, sinister, and terrible, like the cold of a vast common grave.

When he arrived home he quietly made his way to his room and opened the window overlooking the garden; for the first time it occurred to him that everything he was involved in so deeply, with such confidence and self-sacrifice, was not at all what was really needed. He imagined that at some time, when he was about to die, like Semyonov, he'd feel unbearable, tormenting regret, not because people hadn't become any happier as a result of his efforts, not because the ideals he'd worshiped all his life had yet to be realized, but rather because he was dying and would cease seeing, hearing, and feeling, without having had time to enjoy everything that life could offer him.

But he felt ashamed of this thought, made a great effort, and came up with an explanation:

Life can be spent in struggle.

Yes, but for whom, if not for oneself or for one's own place in the sun? The secret thought arose gloomily within him. But Yury pretended not to heed it and tried to think about something else. But that was difficult and tedious; his thoughts kept returning to the same thing; he felt bored, pained, and wretched to the point of shedding bitter, tormenting tears.

 V

After receiving a note from Lyalya Svarozhich, Lida Sanina handed it to her brother. She thought he'd decline the invitation, and that's what she wanted him to do. She felt that on a moonlit night on the river she'd be powerfully and sweetly drawn to Zarudin, and that would be both terrifying and entertaining; and that at the same time, she'd feel embarrassed in her brother's presence, that she'd be with none other than Zarudin, whom her brother apparently despised from the depths of his soul.

But Sanin agreed immediately and willingly.

It was an absolutely cloudless day, warm, but not too hot. It was even painful to look at the sky; it shimmered from the pure air and the gleaming white-gold rays of the sun.

"By the way, there'll be some young ladies there; you can make their acquaintance," Lida said mechanically.

"Now, that is good news!" said Sanin. "And the weather's perfect. Let's go."

At the appointed hour Zarudin and Tanarov arrived in a spacious regimental carriage, drawn by a pair of large horses belonging to the regiment.

"Lidiya Petrovna, we're waiting!" Zarudin cried cheerfully, all clean and white, emitting his eau de cologne.

Lida, wearing a thin, bright-colored dress with a collar and broad waistband of pink velvet, came down the stairs and offered Zarudin her hands. For a moment Zarudin grasped them suggestively, surveying her figure with a swift, frank glance.

"Let's go, let's go," Lida cried, understanding his glance and feeling both embarrassed and excited by it.

A short time later the carriage was rolling swiftly along a little-used road through the steppe, bending the tough stems of field grass to the ground, which lashed their feet as they sprang back up. The fresh breeze gently tousled their hair and made soft waves in the grass along both sides of the road.

Just outside the town they caught up with another carriage carrying Lyalya and Yury Svarozhich, Ryazantsev, Novikov, Ivanov, and Semyonov. They were cramped and uncomfortable, and so were cheerful and in a friendly mood. Only Yury Svarozhich, after yesterday's conversation with Semyonov, felt a little uncomfortable in his presence. It seemed strange to him and even a little unpleasant that Semyonov was cracking jokes and laughing just as lightheartedly as the others. Yury couldn't understand how he could laugh after everything he'd said the day before.

Was he putting on an act, or what? Yury wondered, casting a sidelong glance at the sickly student. Maybe he's not really all that ill?

But he was embarrassed by his own thought and tried to forget it.

Witty remarks and greetings were exchanged from both carriages; Novikov, playing the fool, jumped down and ran through the grass alongside Lida. Somehow a tacit agreement had been established between them to express their friendship in an exaggerated manner. They were both extremely jocular and amicably impudent.

The hill where the shining cupolas and white stone walls of the monastery were gleaming became larger and more visible. The whole hill was overgrown with trees, and the green tops of the oaks made it look as if it were covered with curls. Those same oaks also grew on the islands; below, at the foot of the hill and among the trees, the broad river flowed by serenely.

The horses turned off the smooth road and trotted through the soft, lush grass along the riverbank, the carriage wheels and light pressure of the horses' hoofs digging deep ruts in the damp earth. There was a strong scent of river water and oak forest.

At the agreed place, a favorite one, a student and two young ladies in Ukrainian dresses who'd arrived earlier sat waiting on rugs spread out on the grass; laughing, they were preparing tea and snacks.

The horses halted, snorting and whisking away flies with their tails; the new arrivals, enlivened by the trip, the air, and the smell of river and forest, immediately jumped down from their carriages.

Lyalya exchanged loud kisses with the two young ladies preparing tea. Lida greeted them in a more restrained manner and introduced her brother and Yury Svarozhich to them. The young ladies regarded them with youthful, discreet curiosity.

"You've yet to make each other's acquaintance," Lida remembered suddenly. "This is my brother, Vladimir Petrovich, and this is Yury Nikolaevich Svarozhich."

Smiling, Sanin shook hands gently yet firmly with Yury, who paid him no attention. Sanin was interested in everyone and loved meeting new people, while Yury was convinced that there were very few interesting people and so was always indifferent to new acquaintances.

Ivanov knew Sanin vaguely and liked what he'd heard about him. He regarded Sanin with curiosity and was the first to come up and speak to him. Semyonov extended his hand apathetically.

"Well, now we can enjoy ourselves!" Lyalya cried. "We're finished with all the boring formalities!"

At first everyone felt a bit awkward because many were meeting for the first time. After they'd begun eating and the men had downed several shots of vodka while the women drank wine, the awkwardness disappeared and they became very merry. They drank a great deal, laughed, and cracked jokes, sometimes very clever ones; they chased one another and climbed the hill. The forest was so green and lovely, it was so quiet, bright, and clear all around, that no one could harbor anything dark, distressing, or evil in his soul.

"Now," said Ryazantsev, completely out of breath, "if people were to run around like this and jump up and down, nine-tenths of the world's illnesses would not exist!"

"Nor its vices either," said Lyalya.

"Well, people will always have plenty of vices," observed Ivanov; even though what he said didn't seem particularly apt or amusing, they all laughed heartily.

While they drank their tea the sun started to set, the river turned golden, and long slanting rays of reddish sunlight lengthened between the trees.

"Well, ladies and gentlemen, to the boats!" Lida exclaimed. Hoisting her skirt up high, she was the first to start running toward the riverbank. "Who's the fastest?"

While some ran, others proceeded in a more dignified manner, but everyone followed her and, with roars of laughter and many jokes, took their seats in a large, brightly painted boat.

"Cast off!" Lida cried in a youthful, reckless tone of voice.

The boat glided gently away from the bank, leaving behind it two broad furrows that spread evenly toward both sides of the river.

"Yury Nikolaevich, why are you so quiet?" Lida asked Svarozhich.

"I have nothing to say," Yury replied with a smile.

"Really?" Lida drawled, tossing her head and sensing that all the men were admiring her.

"Yury Nikolaevich doesn't like talking nonsense," Semyonov began. "And he—"

"Oh, he needs a serious subject, does he?" Lida interrupted.

"Look, there's a serious subject!" cried Zarudin, pointing to the bank.

There, under a precipice, among the gnarled roots of a crooked old oak tree, was a narrow, gloomy, black opening overgrown with tall weeds.

"What's that?" asked Shafrov, who came from elsewhere.

"A cave," replied Ivanov.

"What kind of a cave?"

"The devil only knows! They say that once there was a place for making counterfeit money near here. As usual, they were all arrested. It's really too bad about that 'as usual,' " Ivanov inserted.

"Or else you might want to open a counterfeiting operation yourself and start making twenty-kopeck pieces?" asked Novikov.

"What for? Silver coins, my friend, rubles!"

"Hmm," Zarudin said and shrugged his shoulders slightly. He didn't like Ivanov and didn't understand his jokes.

"Yes. . . . Well, they were caught and the cave was abandoned. It collapsed and no one goes in it anymore. When I was a young boy, I used to explore it. It's very interesting."

"Interesting? I should say so!" cried Lida. "Viktor Sergeevich, you go in there. You're so brave!"

Her voice had a strange tone, as if now, in the presence of other people and for all to see, she wanted to deride and repay Zarudin for that strange and frightening enchantment he had aroused when they'd been alone together the other evening.

"What for?" Zarudin asked, without understanding.

"I'll go," Yury replied and blushed, afraid that the others would think he was striking a pose.

"That's a fine idea," Ivanov said in encouragement.

"Maybe you'll go, too?" asked Novikov.

"No, I'd rather wait here."

Everyone laughed.

The boat approached the bank and now the black opening loomed just above their heads.

"Yury, please don't do anything stupid," Lyalya said, trying to dissuade her brother. "For heaven's sake, it's stupid!"

"Of course it's stupid," Yury agreed jokingly. "Semyonov, pass me a candle."

"But where will I find one?"

"Just behind you, in the basket!"

Semyonov lazily took a candle from the basket.

"Are you really going in?" asked one of the young ladies, a tall, lovely girl with a full bosom, whom Lyalya called Zina and whose surname was Karsavina.

"Of course! Why not?" Yury replied, pretending to be nonchalant, recalling how he'd tried to be just as nonchalant during all his dangerous political escapades. For some reason this recollection was unpleasant.

It was dark and damp at the entrance to the cave. Sanin glanced in and said, "Brr!"

He was amused that Yury would enter such an unpleasant, dangerous place just because other people were watching.

Yury lit the candle, trying not to look at the others. A secret thought was already tormenting him: did he look ridiculous? He felt a bit ridiculous, though at the same time it was odd because not only was he not ridiculous, he was astonishing and magnificent, arousing in women that enigmatic feeling that is both pleasant and frightening. He waited for the wick to light and then, laughing to protect himself from mockery, he went forward and disappeared at once into the darkness. Even the candle seemed to go out. Everyone became really concerned for him as well as interested.

"Watch out, Yury Nikolaevich," Ryazantsev shouted. "Sometimes wolves hide in there!"

"I have a revolver!" came Yury's muffled reply; his voice sounded somewhat strange from under the ground, as if he were dead.

He made his way forward carefully. The walls of the cave were low, uneven, and damp, like the inside of a large cellar. The floor rose up and then fell away; twice Yury almost fell into a large hole. He thought it would be best to turn back or sit down and wait a little while, and then say he'd gone deep into the cave.

Suddenly he heard footsteps behind him, someone slipping in the wet clay, as well as the sound of heavy breathing. Someone was following him. Yury raised the candle above his head.

"Zinaida Pavlovna!" he cried in surprise.

"The very one!" Karsavina replied cheerfully, lifting her skirt to jump over a hole.

Yury was pleased that it was she—a cheerful, buxom, lovely young woman. He looked at her with gleaming eyes and smiled.

"Let's go on!" the young woman urged, a bit flustered.

Yury proceeded obediently and effortlessly, no longer worrying about the danger and carefully lighting the way for Karsavina.

The walls of the cave, made of moist brown clay, at times advanced on them as if in silent threat, then retreated and gave way. In some places large piles of stones and earth had tumbled down, leaving only deep, dark cavities. The mass of earth hanging above them seemed mortifying, and there was something terrifying about the fact that it didn't come crashing down but just hung there motionless, supported by its own invisible, powerful laws.

Then all the paths seemed to converge into one large, dark cavern filled with heavy air.

Yury walked all around it, looking for a way out; he was followed by shimmering shadows and glimmers of light swallowed by darkness. But the few exits had all been blocked by earth. In one corner lay the gloomily decomposing remains of an old wooden platform, reminiscent of the abandoned planks of a rotting coffin disgorged from the ground.

"Not much of interest here!" Yury said, involuntarily lowering his voice without knowing why. He was oppressed by the large mass of earth above them.

"Oh, yes there is!" whispered Karsavina, looking around, her eyes gleaming in the candlelight. She was scared and clung unconsciously to Yury, as if seeking his protection.

Yury noticed and enjoyed this fact: it aroused a touching feeling of tenderness for the young woman's beauty and weakness.

"It's as if we were buried alive," Karsavina continued. "It seems that if we were to shout, no one would hear us!"

"Probably not," Yury said with a laugh.

And suddenly his head began to spin. He cast a sidelong glance at her ample bosom, barely covered by her flimsy Ukrainian blouse, and at her round sloping shoulders. The thought that, in essence, she was completely in his power and no one could hear anything was so strong and unexpected that for a moment everything grew dark before his eyes. But he immediately regained control of himself because he was genuinely and earnestly convinced that it was abominable to violate a woman—and for him, Yury Svarozhich, it was altogether inconceivable. And instead of doing what he wanted to do more than life itself, that which filled his whole body with strength and passion, Yury said merely:

"Let's give it a try."

The strange tremor in his own voice frightened him; it seemed to him that Karsavina might guess his thoughts.

"What?" the young woman asked.

"I'll fire my gun," he explained, pulling out his revolver.

"Won't the earth cave in?"

"I don't know," Yury answered for some reason, although he was certain that it wouldn't. "Are you afraid?"

"No. . . . Well . . . fire away," Karsavina said, drawing back from him slightly.

Yury stretched out his hand with the revolver and fired. A blazing streak flashed out, pungent, heavy smoke instantly enveloped everything, and a deafening rumble resounded gravely and angrily through the hillside. But the earth hung there as motionless as before.

"That's all there is to it," said Yury.

"Let's go back."

They started back; as Karsavina walked ahead, Yury noticed her broad, strong hips; once again the same desire took hold of him and it was difficult for him to overcome it.

"Listen, Zinaida Pavlovna," said Yury, fearing the sound of his own voice and of his question but feigning nonchalance. "Here's an interesting psychological question: Why weren't you afraid to come in here with me? You yourself said that if someone were to shout, no one would hear us. But you don't know me at all."

Karsavina blushed deeply in the darkness, but kept silent.

Yury's breathing was labored. He felt intensely pleased, as if he'd skirted some abyss, and at the same time felt intensely ashamed.

"I thought, of course, that you were a decent man," the young woman muttered weakly and unsteadily.

"But what if you'd been wrong to think that?" Yury replied, toying with the same burning sensation. Suddenly it seemed that the way he was speaking was very original and that there was something splendid about it.

"Then . . . I would've drowned myself," Karsavina answered, even more quietly, blushing even more deeply.

And, as a result of these words, Yury felt the onset of gentle compassion. Instantly his excitement vanished and he felt relieved.

What a fine girl! he thought with warmth and sincerity; and his awareness of the purity of this warmth and sincerity was so pleasant that tears welled up in his eyes.

Karsavina smiled at him happily, proud of her own reply and his silent approval.

As they made their way to the mouth of the cave, the young woman reflected with strange agitation: Why wasn't she offended or ashamed when he asked her that question? Why was she instead so intensely pleased?

 VI

Those waiting above sat down on the riverbank or stood near the entrance to the cave cracking jokes at the expense of Svarozhich and Karsavina. The men smoked cigarettes, throwing their matches into the water and watching the wide even circles spread over the surface. Lida, singing softly to herself, made her way through the grass; placing her hands on her hips, she performed some dainty dance steps with her little yellow shoes, while Lyalya picked flowers and tossed them at Ryazantsev, caressing him with her eyes.

"Isn't it time for us to have something to drink?" Ivanov asked Sanin.

"A magnificent idea!" agreed Sanin.

They got back into the boat, opened some beer, and started to drink.

"You unscrupulous drunkards, you!" Lyalya said, hurling a tuft of grass at them.

"Ex-cel-lent!" Ivanov announced with pleasure.

Sanin laughed.

"I'm always surprised when people oppose the use of alcohol, " he said in jest. "In my opinion, only a drunkard lives life as he should."

"Or like an animal," Novikov echoed from the bank.

"So what if that's true!" replied Sanin. "Nevertheless, a drunkard does whatever he wants. If he wants to sing, he sings; if he wants to dance, he dances; and he's never ashamed of his joy and merrymaking."

"And sometimes he fights," observed Ryazantsev.

"It can happen. People don't know how to drink . . . they're too embittered."

"You don't fight when you're drunk?" asked Novikov.

"No," replied Sanin. "I'm more likely to fight when I'm sober; when I'm drunk, I'm the kindest of men because I forget so many abominations."

"Not everyone's like that," Ryazantsev observed again.

"It's a pity that not everyone is. . . . But I really don't care in the least what others are like."

"One shouldn't say things like that!" said Novikov.

"Why not? Especially if it's true!"

"A fine truth, indeed!" Lyalya replied, shaking her head.

"The finest I know," Ivanov said, supporting Sanin.

Lida began singing in a loud voice and then stopped abruptly. "They don't seem to be hurrying!" she said.

"Why should they?" replied Ivanov. "It never pays to hurry."

"That Zina is a heroine without fear or reproach,"[8] Lida observed sarcastically.

Tanarov burst into loud laughter at his own thoughts and then felt embarrassed.

Lida looked at him and put her hands on her hips; her whole body swayed gracefully.

"Well, perhaps they're really having fun down there!" she added enigmatically, with a shrug.

"Shh!" Ryazantsev said, interrupting her.

A muffled roar echoed from the dark opening.

"A shot!" cried Shafrov.

"What does that mean?" Lyalya asked timidly, clinging to Ryazantsev's arm.

"Calm down, if it's a wolf, they're tame at this time of year . . . and it wouldn't attack two people," Ryazantsev said, trying to reassure her, but feeling annoyed at Yury and his childish prank.

[8] A variation on *chevalier sans peur et sans reproche* (knight without fear and without reproach), a characterization applied to Pierre Du Terrail, seigneur de Bayard (1474–1524), French hero of the Italian wars.

"Hey, of all the nerve!" Shafrov growled, he too feeling annoyed.

"Here they come, here they come! Don't worry," Lida said with a contemptuous curl of her lip.

The sound of approaching footsteps could be heard and soon Karsavina and Yury emerged from the darkness.

Yury blew out the candle and smiled at everyone in a polite yet hesitant way, because he didn't yet know how they regarded his escapade. He was completely covered with yellow clay, and Karsavina's shoulder was also very dirty where she'd brushed against the wall of the cave.

"Well, how was it?" Semyonov asked apathetically.

"Quite unusual and beautiful," Yury replied indecisively, as if trying to justify himself. "But the passageways don't lead very far; they're all blocked up. And there was some kind of wooden floor decaying."

"Did you hear the shot?" Karsavina asked with animation, her eyes flashing.

"Ladies and gentlemen, we've drunk all the beer and our souls are sufficiently invigorated!" cried Ivanov from below. "Let's go!"

By the time the boat reached a broader part of the river, the moon had already risen. The night was astonishingly quiet and transparent; the golden light of the stars was shining equally above and below, in the sky and in the water, and the boat seemed to be floating between two infinite airy depths. The forest both along the riverbank and reflected in the water was black and mysterious. A nightingale started to sing. When everyone fell silent to listen, it seemed that it wasn't really a bird singing but some happy, intelligent, pensive being.

"How lovely!" said Lyalya, raising her eyes and laying her head on Karsavina's warm, round shoulder.

Then they remained silent and listened for a long time. The nightingale's song filled the forest completely; his trill resounded over the pensive river and carried over the meadows where grasses and flowers were growing stiff in the moonlit mist, into the distance and far above, into the cold starry sky.

"What's he singing about?" Lyalya asked again, as if accidentally placing her hand, its palm turned upward, on Ryazantsev's knee, feeling how his strong, firm leg shuddered, both fearing and rejoicing at his movement.

"About love, of course!" Ryazantsev replied, half-joking, half-serious, and gently covering with his own hand her small, warm, tender palm resting innocently on his knee.

"On an evening like this, one doesn't need to think about good and evil," said Lida, replying to her own thoughts.

She was thinking about whether she was right to be enjoying this alarming and engaging game. Looking into Zarudin's face, even more manly and handsome in the moonlight, a dark brilliance shining in his eyes, she felt a familiar sweet languor and a frightening lack of will throughout her being.

"About something altogether different!" Ivanov replied to her earlier question.

Sanin smiled and didn't take his eyes off Karsavina, who was seated facing him: her prominent bosom and beautiful neck were lit by the moon.

The dark, flimsy shadow of the hill advanced and when the boat, after leaving a wake of dark-blue silvery stripes, once more emerged into an illuminated place, it seemed even brighter, broader, and freer.

Karsavina tossed aside her large straw hat and, expanding her chest even more, began to sing. She had a lovely, high voice, though not too powerful. Her song was Russian, beautiful, and sad, like all Russian songs.

"Very tender!" Ivanov muttered.

"Nice!" said Sanin.

When Karsavina finished, everyone clapped, and their applause echoed strangely and harshly through the dark forest and above the river.

"Sing another, Zinochka," Lyalya implored. "Or, even better, recite some of your own verses."

"Are you a poet too?" asked Ivanov. "How much poetry can God grant to just one of his creatures!"

"Is that a bad thing?" Karsavina asked, joking in her embarrassment.

"No, it's a very good thing," Sanin replied.

"If, let's say, the girl's young and charming, then what good is it?"

"Recite, Zinochka!" Lyalya cried, all tender and ablaze with love.

Grinning in embarrassment, Karsavina turned to look at the water and then recited in the same even, resonant, high voice:

"My dear, my dear, I won't tell you,
Won't tell you how much I love you.
I close my eyes so full of love—
They guard my secret. . . .
No one will discover this secret. . . .
Only the dreary days know,
Only the quiet blue nights,
Only the golden fires of the stars,
Only the thin, bright tracery
Of the branches in love with nighttime tales
Know everything. . . . But they won't tell, won't tell
About my secret love."

And again everyone was ecstatic and applauded Karsavina with enthusiasm, not because her verses were so fine but because they all felt good and yearned for love, happiness, and sweet sorrow.

"Oh, night, day, and dark eyes of Zinaida Pavlovna, be so kind as to tell me: am I the lucky man?" Ivanov suddenly cried so loudly and unexpectedly in a wild bass voice that everyone was startled.

"I can answer that," Semyonov replied. "You're not!"

"Woe is me!" Ivanov wailed.

Everyone laughed.

"Are my verses that bad?" Karsavina asked Yury.

Yury thought they were unoriginal and resembled hundreds of other verses, but Karsavina was so lovely and was looking at him so sweetly with her dark, bashful eyes that he made a very serious face and replied: "They seemed melodious and charming to me."

Karsavina smiled at him and was surprised that his praise pleased her as much as it did.

"You still don't know my Zinochka," Lyalya said with genuine ecstasy. "She herself is melodious and charming."

"How do you like that!" Novikov said in surprise.

"It's true," Lyalya insisted, as if justifying herself. "She has a melodious and charming voice, she herself is beautiful, and her verses are melodious and charming too . . . even her last name is melodious and charming!"

"My goodness! Let's see—style, brilliance, and gusto!" Ivanov said admiringly. "By the way, I agree with you completely."

Karsavina blushed in embarrassment and laughed, enjoying the praise.

"It's time to go home!" Lyalya said shrilly; she wasn't pleased by all this praise for Karsavina. She considered herself prettier, more interesting, and cleverer.

"Won't you sing something?" asked Sanin.

"No," Lida replied angrily, "I'm not in good voice."

"In fact, it really is time to go," agreed Ryazantsev, recalling that tomorrow he had to get up early and go to the hospital for a postmortem examination.

But everyone else was sorry to leave.

As they made their way home everyone was silent, feeling a contented, languorous exhaustion.

Once again, although now no longer visible, the steppe grasses bent under the wheels and a white cloud of dust was left behind, but soon settled back on the white road. The fields, bluish from the moon's haze, seemed flat, deserted, and endless.

 VII

About three days afterward, late in the evening, Lida returned home tired and unhappy. She was depressed and felt drawn somewhere: she both knew and didn't know where.

Entering her room, she stopped, folded her arms, and stood there for a long time, looking pale, staring at the floor.

All of a sudden Lida was horrified to realize how far she'd gone in giving herself to Zarudin. For the first time she perceived that, from that irretrievable and incomprehensible moment, the obviously fatuous and shallow officer, so far beneath her, enjoyed some kind of humiliating power over her. Now she could no longer refuse to come if he demanded it; she could no longer dally with him as she liked, either submitting to his kisses or resisting and laughing; now, without a will of her own, she must yield to his crudest caresses like a slave.

She couldn't understand how this had happened: as always, she dominated him, his caresses were under her control, and she was just as pleased, frightened, and amused; then suddenly a moment came when the fire in her body enveloped her head with a whitish haze in which everything drowned except for the burning, curious desire pushing her into an abyss. The ground swam beneath her feet, her body became powerless and submissive, and before her there remained only two dark, burning, terrifying, shameless, attractive eyes; her bare legs shamelessly and passionately shuddered from the powerful contact with the crude hands undressing her; she desired this experience all the more intensely, this shamelessness, pain, and pleasure.

Lida trembled at this recollection, shrugged her shoulders, and buried her face in her hands.

She stumbled across the room, opened the window, stared for a long time at the moon hanging right over the garden, and listened, without noticing, to a solitary nightingale singing somewhere far away in a neighboring garden. She was oppressed by melancholy. In her soul there was a strange combination of vague desire and mournful pride at the thought that she'd ruined her life for a vapid and inane man, that her fall had been stupid, sordid, and accidental. Something threatening began to rise up before her. She tried to banish this advancing, anxious foreboding of the future by stubborn and contemptible bravado.

Well, I slept with him and that's that! she thought, knitting her brows with painful pleasure as she uttered these crude words. It's all nonsense! I desired it and gave myself to him! And I still felt so happy, it was so . . . Lida shuddered and, putting out her folded hands, she stretched. It would have been absurd not to give myself to him! No need to think about it. . . . There's no going back.

With an effort she moved away from the window and began to get undressed, undoing the straps on her skirt and allowing it to slip to the floor.

After all, one has only one life to live, she thought, shivering at the cool air softly caressing her bare shoulders and arms. What would I have gained if I'd waited until I was legally married? And what good would that have been? Isn't it all the same? Am I really so foolish as to lend it special meaning? That's stupidity! Suddenly it seemed to her that all this was in fact just nonsense, that tomorrow would put an end to it all, that she'd won what was most interesting in this little game of hers, and that now she was as free as a bird, with life, interests, and happiness all ahead of her.

"If I want to fall in love, I will, and if I want to fall out of love, I will," Lida sang softly; listening to the sound of her own voice, she thought with pleasure that hers was nicer than Karsavina's was.

"It's all nonsense. If I want to, I'll give myself to the devil!" she suddenly replied to her own confused thoughts with this rude and unexpected outburst. Placing her bare arms behind her head, she straightened up so quickly and violently that her breasts shook.

"You're still not asleep, Lida?" asked Sanin's voice outside her window.

Lida shuddered with fright, then at once smiled, flung a large shawl over her shoulders, and went to the window.

"You startled me!" she said.

Sanin drew nearer and rested his elbow on the sill. His eyes were sparkling and he was smiling.

"There's no need for that!" he said cheerfully and softly. Lida looked around inquisitively.

"You looked much better without the shawl," he remarked just as softly and expressively.

Lida turned to him in perplexity and instinctively wrapped the shawl more tightly around her.

Sanin started laughing. In embarrassment Lida leaned her bosom against the windowsill and put her head out of the window. Sanin's breath could be felt on her cheek.

"You're quite a beauty!" he said.

Lida cast him a swift glance and was frightened by what she thought she saw reflected in his expression. She turned abruptly toward the garden and felt in her body that Sanin was looking at her in a very peculiar way. And this seemed so terrible and vile that she felt a chill in her breast and her heart skipped a beat. All men regarded her in exactly the same way, and that pleased her, but for some reason for him to do so was incredible and impossible. She regained control of herself and smiled.

"I know. . . ."

Sanin was silent and stared at her. When she had rested against the windowsill, her blouse and shawl had slipped down and to one side had revealed the upper part of her unbelievably tender bosom illumined by white moonlight.

"People constantly defend themselves against happiness by building a Great Wall of China around them," Sanin said; his soft, trembling voice was strange and it scared Lida even more, almost to the point of terror.

"What?" she asked faintly, without taking her eyes off the dark garden, afraid of meeting his gaze. It seemed to her that something might happen that was absolutely impossible to allow.

And at the same time she no longer had any doubts; she knew and felt horrible, hideous, and curious. Her head was on fire and she saw nothing before her; she sensed with horror, loathing, and curiosity his hot strained breath on her cheek, at which the hair bristled on her temples and shudders ran up and down her spine under the shawl.

"Nothing . . ." Sanin replied, and his voice broke off.

Lida felt as if a bolt of lightning had passed through her entire body; she straightened up swiftly and, without noticing what she was doing, leaned over the table and blew out the lamp.

"It's time to go to sleep!" she said and shut the window.

After the lamp was out, it became brighter outside; Sanin's face and figure appeared more clearly, illumined by the blue moonlight. He stood there in the deep, dew-covered grass, laughing.

Lida came away from the window and lowered herself mechanically onto the bed. Everything in her was trembling and throbbing, and her thoughts were confused. She heard Sanin's footsteps as he retreated through the rustling grass, and she pressed her hand to her pounding heart.

What's this? Am I going crazy? she wondered with loathing. How disgusting! A chance phrase, and already I . . . What is it, erotomania? Am I really so vile, so depraved? How low must I have sunk to think that . . .

All of a sudden Lida buried her face in the pillow and wept softly and bitterly.

Why am I crying? she asked herself, not understanding the reason for her tears, merely feeling unhappy, pitiful, humiliated. She cried because she'd given herself to Zarudin and because she was no longer the same proud, pure young woman she had been, and because now she felt terrible and shameful in her brother's eyes. She thought that before he never could have looked at her this way and that now it was all because she'd fallen so low.

But one feeling was stronger, more galling, and more comprehensible to her: it was painful and shameful that she was now a woman, and that as long as she was young, strong, healthy, and beautiful, her best powers would go to giving herself to men, providing them with pleasure, and the more pleasure she gave them and herself, the more they would despise her.

For what? Who gave them that right? After all, I'm just as free as they are, Lida thought, gazing intently into the dreary darkness of her room.

Will I never really see a different life, a better life?

Her entire young, strong body told her powerfully that she had the right to take from life all that was interesting, pleasant, and necessary, and that she had the right to do anything she wanted with her own magnificent, strong, vital body, which belonged to her alone.

But this thought was tangled in confusing webs, struggling as if in a vise, and it was feebly and miserably lost to oblivion.

 VIII

Yury Svarozhich had taken up painting some time ago; he liked it and devoted all his free time to it. At one time he had dreamed of becoming an artist, but at first his lack of money and later his party activities blocked his way; now he painted only occasionally and with no specific goal.

And because he had no definite training or goal, his painting brought him little welcome enjoyment; it aroused heartbreak and disappointment. Each time his work didn't go well, Yury became annoyed and suffered; when it did go well, he sank into quiet and dreamy contemplation, brought on by the troubled awareness that it was all in vain and would result in neither success nor happiness.

Yury was really taken by Karsavina. He liked such tall, beautifully firm, ample women, with their lovely voices and tender, slightly sentimental eyes. Everything he thought about her attractiveness, purity, and spiritual depth was conveyed through her physical beauty and tenderness, but for some reason Yury didn't admit this to himself; he tried to convince himself that he found the young woman attractive not because of her shoulders, bosom, eyes, or voice but rather because of her chastity and purity. And it seemed easier, nobler, and better for him to think that way, even though it was precisely her purity and chastity that aroused him, inflaming his blood and exciting his desire. From the very first evening he experienced a vague but familiar feeling, although he wasn't fully aware of it at the time: a cruel desire to deprive her of her purity and innocence; this insatiable desire usually arose in the presence of beautiful women.

Since his thoughts were now preoccupied by this lovely, healthy young woman, so full of joyous, sunny life, Yury decided to capture life in his painting. As usual, he was easily roused to enthusiasm and became ecstatic about his idea; it seemed to him that this time he would definitely bring his task to a successful conclusion.

Having prepared a large canvas, Yury set to work on the picture with feverish speed, as if afraid to delay. When he daubed on the first colors and only beautiful, lush spots appeared on the canvas, everything inside him trembled with ecstasy and strength; his future painting easily and appealingly arose before him in all its details. But the further the work progressed, the more technical difficulties arose that Yury was unable to overcome. What in his imagination seemed bright, powerful, and magnificent appeared on the canvas as flat and impotent. Details no longer fascinated him, but confused and irritated him. He stopped hesitating and began to paint in a broad, careless manner, but then, instead of bright, powerful life, there emerged pretentiously and carelessly a picture of a hastily drawn, crude woman. There seemed to him nothing original or magnificent about it; everything was stale and trite. Then Yury realized that his picture was unoriginal, that he was simply imitating sketches by Mucha,[9] and that the very idea of his painting was banal.

---

[9] Alphonse Mucha (1860–1939), Czech painter and designer, active in France, who became best known for his Art Nouveau posters.

Yury felt oppressed and gloomy, as usual.

If for some reason he hadn't thought it shameful to cry, he'd have burst into tears, buried his face in the pillow, whined, and complained to someone about something, but not about his own inadequacy. Instead, he sat before his picture sullenly and reflected that life in general was boring, confusing, and futile, and that there was nothing left that he, Yury, could possibly take an interest in. He imagined with horror that he still had many years left to live, perhaps right here in this little town.

Then—death! Yury thought, his forehead cold as ice.

Suddenly he decided to portray death. He took a knife and with particularly severe malevolence began scraping off his painting of life. It irritated him that something he'd worked on with such enthusiasm was so difficult to erase. The paint came off reluctantly, the knife slipped, jumped, and twice cut the canvas. Then it turned out that his charcoal wouldn't show up on the painted surface and this was a source of acute suffering for Yury. He took a brush and began to make an outline in brown paint; then he began painting again slowly, carelessly, and with heavy, somber emotion. The work that he now conceived didn't suffer at all; rather it benefited from his carelessness and from the dull, heavy colors. But his original idea of death had for some reason disappeared, and Yury was now depicting old age. He painted it in the form of an emaciated, bony old woman, wandering along a well-trodden road into quiet, sad twilight. The last ray of sunlight had died out on the horizon; black crosses and indistinct, dark silhouettes could be glimpsed in its greenish glow. On the old woman's back lay a heavy, black coffin of great weight, pressing down on her bony shoulders. And her expression was lackluster and joyless; one of her feet was poised on the edge of a black abyss. The whole picture was murky, gloomy, and foreboding.

Yury was called to dinner, but he didn't go and kept on painting. Then Novikov arrived and began to tell him something or other, but he didn't listen or reply.

Novikov sighed and sat down on the sofa. He was glad to be quiet and to think; besides, he'd come to see Svarozhich only because he didn't like being at home alone. His distress was desolate and painful. Lida's refusal still weighed upon him, and it was impossible to figure out whether he was ashamed or depressed. He was very forthright and slow-witted, and didn't understand all the gossip about Lida and Zarudin that was beginning to circulate in town. He wasn't feeling jealous of Lida; he merely suffered from the dashed dream that at one point had seemed so close and real that he was already feeling happy.

Novikov had begun to think that everything in life had been ruined for him; nevertheless, it never occurred to him that if this were the case, there was no point in living and he should end it all. On the contrary, he thought that now that his own life had become one of pure torment, it was his duty, since he'd stopped worrying about personal happiness, to dedicate his life to other people. He couldn't account for it, but he'd decided to give up everything and move to St. Petersburg, to revive his ties with the party, and to throw himself headlong into death. This idea seemed both magnificent and exalted to him, and his awareness of the fact that this noble and splendid idea was his own relieved his sadness and gladdened his heart. His image of himself grew in his own eyes; it was surrounded by a pleasant, bright, sad halo, and the unintentional sad reproach to Lida almost made him cry.

Then he began to feel bored. Svarozhich continued to paint and paid no attention to him. Novikov stood up and walked toward him.

The painting was unfinished, but that was precisely why it produced the impression of a powerful hint. For the time being, Yury was unable to finish it.

The painting seemed wonderful to Novikov. His jaw dropped slightly and he looked at Yury with naive, childlike delight.

"Well, what do you think?" asked Yury.

It seemed to Yury that although the painting did, of course, possess some defects, and that these might even be obvious and considerable, it was still more interesting than any painting he'd ever seen. He was unable to explain why this was so, but if Novikov said it was a bad painting, he'd be genuinely offended and embittered. But Novikov said softly and ecstatically:

"Ve-ry nice!"

Yury felt as if he were a genius despising his own creation. He sighed meaningfully, tossed his brush aside, smearing paint on the corner of the couch, and walked away, without even glancing at his painting.

"Hey, my friend!" he said.

He almost confessed to himself and to Novikov that vague feeling occasioned by the joy of victory—that is, that he was totally incapable of making anything out of this auspicious sketch. But instead, he reflected and said aloud:

"There's no point in it at all!"

Novikov thought Yury was striking a pose, but his own disappointed distress immediately pierced his heart and he thought: That's true. But after a short silence he replied: "What do you mean, there's no point in it at all?"

Yury couldn't precisely answer this question and remained silent. Novikov looked at the picture a little longer, then lay down on the sofa.

"My friend, I read your article in the journal *Country*," he began again. "Well done!"

"To hell with it!" Yury replied in annoyance, not really sure why, but recalling Semyonov's words. "What good can come of it? They'll go on executing, robbing, and raping all the same. One must do more than write articles! I'm sorry I wrote it. . . . What of it? Maybe two or three idiots will read it, if that. In the end, what business is it of mine? Why, I ask, should I bang my head against a wall?"

Yury saw passing before his eyes the first years of his involvement in party activity: conspiratorial meetings, propaganda, risk and failures, his own enthusiasm, and the total apathy of those he wished to save. He paced the room and waved his arm dismissively.

"From that point of view it's not worth doing anything," Novikov drawled; and, remembering Sanin, he added: "You're all egoists, that's all there is to it!"

"It's not worth it," Yury said heatedly and sincerely, under the influence of the same recollections and the twilight that had begun to make everything in the room look pale. "If one speaks about humanity, what good are all our efforts, constitutions, and revolutions when we can't even imagine the impending prospects awaiting it? Perhaps the seeds of destruction lie in the very freedom we dream of, and once man has achieved his ideal, he'll revert and once more crawl around on all fours. . . . In order to start all over again? And even if I think only about myself, what can I achieve? At best, I can win fame by utilizing my own talents, I can nourish myself on the admiration of those beneath me, those less important—that is, precisely those I can't respect and whose admiration shouldn't really matter to me. And then live, live until I die . . . and no longer! Ultimately the crown of laurels would fit so snugly on my bald head that even I'd become fed up with it!"

"All this is about yourself!" Novikov muttered, feigning mockery. "So!"

But Yury didn't hear him and went on, listening to himself with grief and painful pleasure; his words seemed dismal and eloquent, and aroused in him a feeling of elevated self-esteem.

"In the worst case, I'll be an unacknowledged genius, a ridiculous dreamer, the subject of humorous sketches . . . absurd, of no use to anyone."

"Aha!" Novikov interrupted him in triumph, and even stood up. " 'Of no use to anyone'—that means you realize it yourself!"

"You're a strange fellow," Yury said; now it was his turn to interrupt. "Do you really think I don't know what to live for and what to believe in? Perhaps I might even submit joyfully to crucifixion if I believed my death would save the world! But I don't believe that: whatever I do, in the end it won't change the course of history, and the good I can accomplish will be so small, so insignificant, that if it didn't exist at all, the world would be not one iota worse off. Meanwhile, for this amount smaller than one iota, I must live and suffer and grievously await death!"

Yury didn't notice that he was talking about something else now, replying not to Novikov's words but to his own strange, oppressive feelings. All of a sudden he stopped short, unexpectedly remembering Semyonov, and felt a despicable, cold, terrifying shiver run down his spine.

"You know, this inevitability torments me," he said softly and confidentially, gazing unwittingly out of the darkened window. "I know it's natural and I can't do anything about it, but it's horrible and hideous!"

Novikov knew it was all true, and felt sad and afraid, but still he replied: "Death is a necessary physiological phenomenon."

What a fool! thought Yury with rage, and replied in annoyance: "Oh, my

God! What difference does it make to us if our death serves any purpose or not!"

"What about your crucifixion?"

"That's another thing altogether," Yury said indecisively, after a momentary pause.

"You're contradicting yourself," Novikov observed with a feeling of superiority, avoiding Yury's eyes in a gesture of generosity.

Yury caught his tone and was very annoyed. He ran his fingers through his unruly black hair and grew angry.

"I never contradict myself. It's entirely understandable that if I were to die as a result of my own desire . . ."

"It's all the same," continued Novikov in the same tone, not yielding. "You all merely want fireworks, applause. . . . It's all egoism!"

"So what? It doesn't change matters."

The conversation became confused. Yury felt it had taken a wrong turn and couldn't catch the thread that only a few minutes ago had seemed so clear to him. He paced the room, gasping angrily; trying to soothe himself, he thought, as he usually did in such circumstances:

Occasionally it happens that I'm not in good form . . . sometimes I speak so clearly, as if I could see everything before my own eyes; at other times I become so completely tongue-tied . . . everything comes out clumsily . . . stupidly. . . . This can happen!

They remained silent. Yury paced the room, stopped near the window, and picked up his cap.

"Let's go for a stroll," he said.

"Let's go," Novikov agreed, with the secret hope, fear, and joy that they might accidentally meet Lida Sanina.

 IX

They walked up and down the boulevard once or twice, meeting no one they knew; they listened to the music being played in the garden, as usual. It was discordant and out of tune, but from a distance it sounded tender and melancholy. They kept encountering men and women flirting with each other. Their laughter and loud, excited voices didn't blend with the soft, sad music and the soft, sad evening; that irritated Yury. At the very end of the boulevard they met Sanin, who greeted them cheerfully. Yury didn't like him very much, and as a result the conversation didn't go well. Sanin laughed at everything they happened to see; then he met Ivanov and set off with him.

"Where are you going?" asked Novikov.

"I want to treat my friend!" replied Ivanov, who took a bottle of vodka from his pocket and displayed it triumphantly.

Sanin laughed merrily.

The vodka and laughter struck Yury as unnatural and vulgar; he turned away in disgust. Sanin noticed it, but said nothing.

"Thank you, Lord, so to speak, that I'm not like this publican!" Ivanov said in a deep voice, smiling ambiguously.

Yury blushed.

He cracks jokes, too! he thought contemptuously, shrugged, and walked away.

"Novikov, you comatose Pharisee, come with us!" Ivanov cried.

"What the hell for?"

"To drink vodka!"

Novikov glanced wistfully down the boulevard, but Lida was nowhere to be seen.

"Lida's at home repenting of her sins," Sanin remarked with a smile.

"What nonsense," Novikov muttered in an offended tone. "I have a patient waiting."

"Who'll die without your help," Ivanov rejoined. "By the way, we can also finish the vodka without your assistance."

Should I get drunk, or what? Novikov wondered gloomily, and said: "Well, all right . . . let's go!"

They set off, and for a long time Yury could hear Ivanov's rude bass voice and Sanin's carefree, merry laugh.

He walked along the boulevard again. Some women's voices called out to him. Zina Karsavina and the teacher Dubova were sitting on one of the benches along the boulevard. It was already quite dark and he could scarcely make out their figures in their dark dresses; they weren't wearing hats and were holding books in their hands. Yury went up to them quickly and eagerly.

"Where've you come from?" he asked in greeting.

"We were in the library," Karsavina replied.

Dubova quietly moved aside, making room for Yury; although he really wanted to sit next to Karsavina, he felt awkward and sat down instead next to the unattractive teacher.

"Why do you look so gloomy?" asked Dubova, curling her thin, dry lips sarcastically, as she usually did.

"Why do you think I look gloomy? I'm very cheerful. But to tell the truth I'm a bit bored."

"Obviously, you have nothing to do," Dubova replied derisively.

"While you yourself have something to do?"

"Yes, and no time to weep."

"I'm not weeping."

"Well, you're whining," Dubova joked.

"My life is such that I've forgotten how to laugh."

Such a bitter note had sounded in his voice that everyone unwittingly fell silent. Yury remained quiet and smiled.

"One of my friends has said that my life's instructive," he added, even though no one had ever told him that.

"In what sense?" inquired Karsavina cautiously.

"In the sense of how not to live."

"Well, tell us all about it. Perhaps we can derive some benefit from your example," Dubova suggested.

Yury regarded his life as a complete failure and considered himself a totally unhappy man. He took some gloomy satisfaction in this and found it pleasant to complain about his life and other people. He never spoke to men about this, instinctively sensing that they wouldn't believe him; but to women, especially beautiful young women, he willingly talked about himself at great length. He was handsome and spoke well, and women always felt affection and pity for him.

On this occasion, too, having begun with a joke, Yury quickly assumed his usual tone and spoke at length about his life. According to him, he was a man of enormous power, consumed by his surroundings and circumstances, misunderstood by the party; the fact that he'd become just another student, exiled for something insignificant, instead of a leader of the people, was due to the vagaries of fate and human stupidity; he himself was not to blame. As to all people of great pride, it never occurred to him that this fact didn't demonstrate his exceptional strength, and that every man of genius was surrounded by just such circumstances and people. It seemed to him that only he himself was pursued by such an oppressive and invincible fate.

Since he spoke so eloquently, energetically, and candidly, it sounded very much like the truth; the young women believed him, pitied him, and grieved with him. The music continued out of tune, but plaintively; the evening was dark and meditative, and they all felt sad and dreamy. When Yury fell silent, Dubova, reflecting on the fact that her own life was boring and monotonous, and that she'd soon grow old without ever having experienced happiness or love, asked softly:

"Tell me, Yury Nikolaevich, have you ever considered the idea of suicide?"

"Why do you ask?"

"Just to know."

They were both silent.

"You were on the party committee, weren't you?" Karsavina asked with interest.

"Yes," Yury replied curtly and as if unwillingly, but he found it pleasant to admit it because he thought it aroused some obscure interest in this pretty young woman's eyes.

Then Yury escorted them home. They talked and laughed a great deal along the way, and it was no longer so dreary.

"What a fine fellow he is," said Karsavina after Yury had left.

"Be careful you don't fall in love with him!" Dubova said, wagging her finger.

"Don't be silly!" Karsavina exclaimed with secret, instinctive fear.

Yury returned home in an excited and happy frame of mind. He looked at the picture he'd begun, but didn't feel anything, and went to sleep feeling satisfied. But that night he saw voluptuous and radiant images in his dreams, as well as beautiful young women.

 X

The next evening Yury returned to the place where he'd met Karsavina and Dubova. All day he'd found it pleasant to recall the evening spent with them; he wanted to meet them again, talk with them about the same things, and see once more the expression of affection and sympathy in their affable, gentle eyes.

The evening was perfectly clear, quiet, and warm. A fine, dry dust hung in the air above the streets, and there was no one on the boulevard except for a few random passers-by.

Yury shook his head angrily at the feeling of annoyance rising within him, as if someone had offended him; he walked slowly along the boulevard, his eyes fixed on the ground.

How boring, he thought. What can I do?

Suddenly the student Shafrov appeared, quickly striding toward him, swinging his arms and smiling to him courteously from afar.

"Why are you hanging around here?" he asked amicably, stopping and extending his large, broad hand to Svarozhich.

"I'm bored and have nothing to do. Where are you off to?" Yury asked in an offhand, disdainful manner. As a former member of the committee, he always talked to Shafrov like this because he'd always regarded him as a naive student who was just toying with the idea of revolution.

Shafrov smiled happily and contentedly.

"We're having a reading today," he said, showing him a pile of assorted thin pamphlets.

Yury mechanically picked one up, opened it, and read the long, dry title of a popular article on a social issue, one that he'd read a long time ago and completely forgotten.

"Where's your reading?" Yury asked with the same disdainful smile, handing back the pamphlet.

"In the local school," Shafrov replied, mentioning the school where Karsavina and Dubova both worked.

Yury recalled that Lyalya had mentioned these readings before, but then he hadn't paid any attention to them.

"Can I come along?" he asked Shafrov.

"Please do," Shafrov agreed at once, smiling happily.

He viewed Yury as a genuine activist and, exaggerating his role in the party, held him in esteem so high that it bordered on devotion.

"I'm very interested in this subject," Yury considered it necessary to add, thinking it nice that he'd be occupied that evening and might even get to see Karsavina.

"Yes, please do," Shafrov said again.

"Well, let's go."

They walked quickly along the boulevard, turned onto the bridge with its fresh, humid smell rising from both sides, and entered the two-story school building, where people were already gathering.

In a large, quiet, dark room set with even rows of chairs and benches, a white screen for a magic lantern was barely visible, and one could hear the sounds of restrained but animated laughter. Near a window, through which one could see both the darkened sky and the tops of dark-green trees, stood Lyalya and Dubova. They greeted Yury with rapturous exclamations.

"It's so good of you to come!" said Lyalya.

Dubova shook his hand vigorously.

"Why don't you start?" Yury asked, glancing furtively around the dark room but not seeing Karsavina. "Doesn't Zinaida Pavlovna attend these readings?" he asked, sounding uncertain and disappointed.

But at that very moment on the speaker's platform, right next to the screen, a match was struck and Karsavina appeared as she lit the candles. Her lovely, fresh face was brightly illuminated from below and she was smiling cheerfully.

"To think I don't attend these lectures!" she exclaimed clearly, leaning over to shake Yury's hand.

Yury was heartened but silent as he took her hand, while she, leaning on him a little, easily jumped down from the platform. Yury caught the strong scent of her robust health and freshness.

"It's time to begin," Shafrov said, coming in from the other room.

The night watchman, treading heavily in his large boots, went around the room lighting the lamps one after another, and the hall was soon illuminated with bright, cheerful light. Shafrov opened the door to the corridor and announced loudly:

"Ladies and gentlemen, this way, please!"

At first one could hear the sound of hesitant footsteps, then it became more pronounced as people began coming in through the door. Yury regarded them with curiosity; his customary perspicacious interest as a propagandist was aroused. There were old people and young, as well as children. Nobody sat down in the first row, but then some ladies unknown to Yury, the portly school director, and some familiar male and female teachers from the primary school took up their places there. The rest of the hall was filled by people in jackets and coats, soldiers, peasants, old women, and many children in assorted shirts and dresses.

Yury sat down at a table next to Karsavina and began to listen as Shafrov read quietly but poorly a paper on the right of universal suffrage. His voice was muffled and monotonous, and everything he read sounded like a statistical table; but people listened attentively. Only the intellectuals in the first row soon began whispering and fidgeting. Yury got annoyed with them and felt sorry that Shafrov was reading so poorly. When the student got tired, Yury said softly to Karsavina:

"Shall I continue reading?"

Karsavina glanced at him tenderly from under her eyelashes and said: "What a good idea! Yes, do read."

"It won't seem awkward?" he asked his confederate with a smile.

"Not at all! Everyone will be delighted."

And, taking advantage of the break, she told Shafrov. He was tired and depressed by the fact that he read so poorly; not only did he agree, he was even glad.

"Please do, please do," he repeated, as was his custom, and gave up his place.

Yury liked to read and was good at it. Without looking around, he climbed onto the platform and began in a strong, resonant voice. Once or twice he glanced at Karsavina, and both times met her bright, expressive gaze. Smiling at her in embarrassment and joy, he turned back to the book and read in an even louder and more expressive voice; he felt as if he were performing some incomprehensibly fine and interesting task for her.

When he finished, the people in the first row began to clap. Yury bowed gravely and, leaving the platform, smiled broadly at Karsavina, as if wishing to say to her, That was for you!

The audience, stamping their feet, exchanging comments, and pushing back their chairs, began to disperse, but Yury stayed behind to make the acquaintance of two ladies who said a few nice words to him about his reading.

Then they began putting out the lights and it became darker in the room than before.

"Thank you," said Shafrov warmly, squeezing Yury's hand. "If people would only read like that all the time!"

Reading was Shafrov's job and consequently he considered himself obliged to Yury as if for a personal favor, even though he said he was thanking him in the name of "the people." Shafrov uttered this word steadfastly and confidently.

"There are few among us who do anything for the people," he said, looking as if he were letting Yury in on a big secret. "And if they do, it's done . . . halfheartedly. It really seems strange to me: to entertain a group of bored gentlemen, they hire dozens of first-rate actors, singers, and readers, while for the people someone like me sits down to read." Shafrov waved his arm with good-natured irony. "And everyone's satisfied. What more do they need?"

"That's true," said Dubova, "it's revolting to see: whole columns in the newspapers are devoted to describing how marvelous actors are, while here . . ."

"But what good work this is!" Shafrov said enthusiastically, and began gathering his pamphlets together lovingly.

Blessed naiveté! thought Yury, but Karsavina's presence and his own success made him good and kind; this simplicity even moved him somewhat.

"Where are you off to now?" asked Dubova when they'd reached the street.

It was much brighter outside than back in the room, even though stars had just begun to appear in the sky.

"Shafrov and I are going to the Ratovs'," said Dubova. "You can walk Zina home."

"With pleasure," Yury said sincerely.

They went their separate ways.

Karsavina shared an apartment with Dubova in the small wing of a house set in a large but poor garden. All the way there Yury and Karsavina talked about their impressions of the reading; it seemed more and more to Yury that he'd done something significant and good.

At the gate Karsavina said, "Would you like to come in?"

"I would," Yury agreed cheerfully.

Karsavina opened the gate and they entered a small courtyard overgrown with grass, beyond which stood the dark garden.

"Go into the garden," said Karsavina with a laugh. "I'd invite you into our rooms, but I'm afraid I haven't been home since morning so I don't know whether it's neat enough to receive guests!"

She went inside while Yury slowly made his way to the fragrant, verdant garden. He didn't go far, but stopped on the path and looked with anxious curiosity at the open, dark windows of the apartment; it seemed to him that something special, beautiful, and mysterious was happening in there.

Karsavina appeared on the porch and Yury could scarcely recognize her: she'd taken off her black dress and put on a thin, short-sleeved Ukrainian blouse with a low neck and a blue skirt.

"Here I am," she said, smiling in embarrassment for some reason.

"I see," Yury replied with a mysterious expression that she understood.

She smiled and turned gracefully, and they walked along the path among low green lilac bushes and high grass.

There were large and small cherry trees with the strong odor of sap on their new leaves. Behind the garden there was a meadow covered with flowers and tall uncut grass.

"Let's sit here," Karsavina said.

They sat down on a ramshackle wattle fence and gazed across the meadow at the translucent setting sun.

Yury reached for a branch of lilac and they were showered with little dewdrops.

"Would you like me to sing for you?" asked Karsavina.

"Of course I would," Yury replied.

Just as she had done by the river, Karsavina thrust out her chest, clearly outlined beneath her thin blouse, and began to sing: "Oh, luxuriant star of love . . ."

Her voice rang out smoothly, naturally, and passionately in the evening air. Yury fell silent, hardly breathing or taking his eyes off her. She felt his gaze, closed her eyes, lifted her chest higher, and sang even better and louder. Everything seemed to fall silent in order to listen to her; Yury recalled the rapt and mysterious silence that reigns when a nightingale sings in the forest at springtime.

When she fell silent after a high silvery note, it seemed to become even quieter. The sunset had faded entirely and the sky had grown deeper and darker. The shimmering leaves were barely visible or audible; the grass rustled and something tender and sweet-smelling like a sigh floating in air came wafting from the meadow and spread through the garden. Karsavina glanced at Yury, her eyes gleaming in the twilight.

"Why are you so quiet?" she asked.

"It's very beautiful here!" Yury whispered. Once again he took hold of a branch and showered them with dewdrops.

"Yes, it is!" Karsavina replied dreamily. "It's good to be alive!" she added, then fell silent.

In Yury's mind a familiar, deceptively somber thought began to rise, but it didn't take shape and vanished.

Two shrill whistles came from the other side of the meadow and then all became quiet again.

"Do you like Shafrov?" Karsavina asked unexpectedly, then began laughing at her own question.

A feeling of jealousy stirred in Yury's breast, but he replied in earnest, forcing himself somewhat.

"He's a fine fellow."

"He's so very devoted to his work!"

Yury was silent.

A light, whitish mist began to rise above the meadow, turning the grass white with dew.

"It's getting damp," Karsavina said with a slight shrug.

Yury glanced unwittingly at her round, soft shoulders and was embarrassed; she caught his glance and was embarrassed too, but felt cheerful and secure.

"Let's go."

With regret they made their way back along the narrow path, brushing gently against each other. The garden was empty and dark; when Yury looked around, it seemed to him that some entirely private, mysterious life must now be beginning there: shadows would steal among the low trees and over the dewy grass, the twilight would fade, and silence would fall with its own inaudible, greenish voice. He said all this to Karsavina. The young woman glanced around and gazed into the dark garden with thoughtful, shining eyes. Yury thought that if suddenly she were to throw off her clothes and then, bare, light, and gay, run through the dewy grass into the mysterious green grove, it wouldn't be at all strange, but splendid and natural; instead of destroying the verdant life of the dark garden, it would only enhance it. Yury wanted to tell her this too, but he didn't dare; instead, he began talking about the reading and the people. But the conversation didn't go well and he fell silent, as if they were talking about something other than what needed to be said. So they walked as far as the gate in silence, smiling at each other and brushing the wet, dewy bushes with their shoulders. It seemed that everything had become quiet and was as meditative and happy as they were.

As before, the courtyard was deserted and still, and the white wing of the house with its open windows could be seen in the darkness. But the gate to the street had been left open and hurried footsteps could be heard in the rooms, and the sounds of drawers being opened and closed.

"Olya's back," said Karsavina.

"Zina, is that you?" Dubova asked from inside, and by her voice it was clear that something terrible had happened.

She came out onto the porch looking distraught and pale.

"Where've you been? I've been looking for you. Semyonov's dying," she said hurriedly, gasping for breath.

"What?" Karsavina asked in horror, taking a step toward her.

"Yes, he's dying. His throat filled with blood. Anatoly Pavlovich says he's done for. They've taken him to the hospital. It was so strange, so unexpected . . . we were sitting having tea with the Ratovs. He was so cheerful, arguing with Novikov about something or other; then suddenly he started coughing, stood up, staggered, and blood spurted out . . . right onto the tablecloth, into a little bowl of jam . . . all thick and dark!"

"And does he . . . know?" Yury asked with uncanny curiosity, instantly recalling that moonlit night, the black shadow, and Semyonov's irritatingly mournful, weak voice saying, "You'll still be alive . . . you'll walk past my grave and stop to relieve yourself on it, and I'll . . ."

"He seems to know," Dubova replied, wringing her hands nervously. "He looked at us and said, 'What's this?' Then, shaking from head to foot, he added, 'Already?' Oh, how hideous and terrible it is!"

Everyone was silent.

It had grown completely dark, and even though everything was as translucent and beautiful as before, it now seemed dreary and gloomy.

"Death's a horrible thing!" Yury said, turning pale.

Dubova sighed and looked down. Karsavina's chin was trembling and she was smiling sorrowfully and guiltily. She couldn't feel the same dejection as the others because life filled her whole body and wouldn't allow her to concentrate on death. Somehow she couldn't believe or even imagine that on such a lovely summer evening, just when she was feeling so happy and full of light and joy, anyone could be suffering and dying. It was only natural, but for some reason it felt wrong to her. Ashamed of her own feelings, she tried unconsciously to suppress them and to muster others; as a result she expressed her sympathy and anxiety more than the rest.

"Oh, the poor man! will he . . . ?"

Karsavina wanted to ask, Will he die soon? but she choked on the words and annoyed Dubova by asking senseless, pointless questions.

"Anatoly Pavlovich said he'd die tonight or tomorrow morning," Dubova replied indistinctly.

Karsavina said timidly and softly, "Shall we go to see him? Or perhaps that's unnecessary? I don't know."

The same question occurred to them all: was it necessary to see Semyonov die, and would it be a good thing or a bad thing? They all wanted to go but were afraid of what they would see; it seemed like a very good idea, but also a very bad one.

Yury shrugged indecisively.

"Let's go. Perhaps we won't have to go in, and perhaps . . ."

"Maybe he wants to see someone," Dubova agreed with relief.

"Let's go," Karsavina said decisively.

"Shafrov and Novikov are there," Dubova added, as if to justify herself.

Karsavina ran into the house for her hat and coat, and everyone, gloomy and despondent, set off through town to a large, gray, poorly plastered three-story hospital, where Semyonov lay dying.

It was dark in the corridors with their low, resonant ceilings, and there was a strong smell of carbolic acid and iodoform. As they passed the psychiatric ward they heard someone speaking quickly and angrily in a strangely strident voice, and because no one was visible, it seemed very eerie. They glanced apprehensively at a small, dark square window. An old gray-haired man with a long white beard like a bib, wearing a long white apron, met them in the corridor, shuffling in his large boots.

"Whom do you wish to see?" he asked, stopping.

"A student was brought here . . . Semyonov . . . today," said Dubova.

"In the sixth ward. Upstairs, please," the attendant said and walked away. They heard him spit noisily on the floor and rub the spot with his foot.

It was brighter and cleaner upstairs and the ceilings weren't vaulted. A door with a little sign saying "Doctor's Office" was ajar. Inside a lamp was lit and someone was clinking glass bottles.

Yury glanced inside and spoke.

The bottles stopped clinking and Ryazantsev came out, looking fresh and cheerful as always.

"Ah!" he said loudly and cheerfully, obviously accustomed to the surroundings that the others found so oppressive. "I'm on duty today. Greetings, ladies!"

And then immediately, arching his brows, he announced in an entirely different voice, gloomy and portentous: "It seems he's already unconscious. Go in. Novikov and the others are there."

As they walked in single file along the corridor that was excessively clean and deserted, past large white doors with black numbers on them, Ryazantsev said:

"We've already sent for a priest. It's astonishing how fast he was finished! Even I was surprised. Recently he's been getting colds, and in his condition that was the last straw. He's in here."

Ryazantsev opened a large white door and went in. The others collided in the doorway; they pushed one another awkwardly and then followed him in.

The ward was large and clean. Four beds were empty and covered identical with coarse gray blankets neatly tucked in; for some reason they resembled coffins. On one bed sat a small, wrinkled old man in a robe, fearfully eyeing the newcomers; on the sixth bed, stretched out beneath the same kind of coarse blanket, lay Semyonov. Next to him, hunched over on a chair, sat Novikov, while Ivanov and Shafrov stood by the window. Everyone felt uneasy and awkward greeting each other and shaking hands in the presence of the dying Semyonov, but for some reason it was just as awkward not to do so, as if underscoring the proximity of death; consequently, there was a pause. Some exchanged greetings, others didn't. Everyone remained standing in the same place, looking at Semyonov with timid, fearful curiosity.

Semyonov was breathing slowly and with difficulty. He bore little resemblance to the Semyonov they all knew. In general, he didn't look at all like a living being. Although he still had the same facial features as when he was alive and the same limbs as other people had, it now seemed as if both his features and his body were somehow special, terrifying, and immobile. What animated and moved the bodies of other people so simply and comprehensibly seemed not to exist for him. Somewhere in the depths of his strangely immobile body something swift and horrible was happening, as if hastening to accomplish some essential and inevitable task; all the life remaining in him was directed there, seemingly watching this task and listening to it with strained, inexplicable attention.

The lamp hanging from the middle of the ceiling clearly and distinctly illumined his motionless, blind, and deaf features.

Everyone stood there staring in silence, unable to avert their eyes, holding their breath, as if afraid to disturb something majestic; and in that silence the sound of Semyonov's monstrous, whistling, and arduous breathing was terribly conspicuous.

The door opened and they could hear the staccato steps of an old man. A small, corpulent priest had arrived together with a gaunt, swarthy man who recited psalms. Sanin came in with them too. The priest, coughing occasionally, greeted the doctors and bowed politely to them. They replied in unison to his greeting with extreme alacrity and exaggerated civility, and then fell silent. Sanin, without greeting anyone, sat down on the windowsill and began looking with interest at Semyonov and those assembled here, trying to understand what he and they were feeling and thinking.

Semyonov's breathing continued as before and he didn't move.

"Is he unconscious?" the priest asked softly, addressing no one in particular.

"Yes," Novikov replied rapidly.

Sanin emitted some unintelligible sound. The priest glanced at him questioningly, but, hearing nothing, turned away, rearranged his hair, put on his stole, and began to read in a high-pitched, sugary tenor with great expressiveness, as befitted the death of a man professing the Christian faith.

The psalm reader turned out to have a hoarse, unpleasant bass, and as these two dissimilar voices converged and diverged, they sounded sad and strange in their dissonance under the high ceiling.

When the loud, shrill lamentation began, all those present glanced with involuntary fright at the face of the dying man. It seemed to Novikov, who was standing the closest, that Semyonov's eyelids fluttered a little and his sightless eyes turned slightly in the direction of the voices. But the others thought he remained just as strangely motionless as before.

At the first notes Karsavina started weeping softly and mournfully; she didn't wipe away the tears streaming down her beautiful, young face. Everyone glanced at her and then Dubova began crying too; even the men felt tears welling up in their eyes and clenched their teeth, trying to restrain them. Every time the chanting became louder, the young women's weeping increased; meanwhile Sanin frowned and squared his shoulders in annoyance, thinking that if Semyonov could hear, it would be intolerable for him to listen to this chanting, so painful even for healthy people who are far from death's door.

"Not so loud," he said angrily to the priest.

At first the priest leaned forward politely to hear his comment, but after doing so, he began to chant even louder. The psalm reader glared sternly at Sanin, while everyone else looked at him apprehensively, as if he'd said something inappropriate and wrong.

Sanin waved his hand in annoyance and fell silent.

When everything was done and the priest had wrapped the cross in his stole, the atmosphere became even more oppressive. Semyonov remained motionless as before.

Then the same terrible but undeniable idea occurred to all of them: they wanted everything to end quickly and Semyonov to die. With a feeling of shame and horror they tried to conceal and suppress this shared desire, afraid even to exchange glances.

"If only it were over," Sanin said softly. "It's a nasty business!"

"Hmm, yes!" Ivanov replied.

They spoke softly, and although it was obvious that Semyonov could hear nothing, the others still stared at them in indignation.

Shafrov wanted to say something, but at that moment a new, inexpressibly piteous, sad sound made them all shudder painfully.

"Ugh . . . ugh-ugh," Semyonov moaned.

And then, as if finding what was needed instead of lapsing into silence, he began to draw out this long, moaning sound, interrupted only by his own hoarse, labored breathing.

At first those around him seemed not to understand what was happening, but then Karsavina, Dubova, and Novikov began weeping. The priest slowly and solemnly began to recite the prayer for the dying. His plump, good-natured face expressed tenderness and sublime grief. Several minutes elapsed. Semyonov suddenly fell silent.

"It is finished," the priest muttered.

But at that moment Semyonov slowly and with considerable effort moved his tightly compressed lips, his face contracted as if in a smile, and everyone heard his hollow, incredibly weak, horrible voice; it seemed to come from somewhere deep within his chest, as if from under the coffin lid:

"What a windbag!" he uttered, looking directly at the priest.

Then he shuddered, opened his eyes wide with an expression of insane terror, and stretched himself out full length.

Everyone heard his words, but no one stirred; the expression of sublime grief instantly disappeared from the priest's sweaty, reddish face. He glanced around timidly, but no one was looking at him; only Sanin smiled.

Semyonov moved his lips again, but there was no sound; one side of his thin, fair mustache drooped. Then he stretched out again and became even longer and more appalling.

There was not another sound, not another movement.

This time nobody cried. The gradual approach of death was more terrible and sorrowful than its immediacy. Everyone even felt rather strange that this exhausting, tormenting affair had ended so quickly and so simply. They remained standing next to the bed, staring at the dead man's pointed features, as if expecting something more to happen, trying to summon up pity and fear; they watched with strained attention as Novikov closed Semyonov's eyes and crossed his arms on his chest. Then they began to file out of the room, shuffling their feet in a reserved way. Lights had already been lit in the corridor and things out there were so simple and familiar that everyone breathed more easily. The priest went first. He took tiny, mincing steps; trying to say something nice to console the young people, he sighed and said softly:

"I feel sorry for the young man, all the more because he died, apparently, without having repented. But God is merciful, you know."

"Yes . . . of course!" replied Shafrov out of politeness; he was standing closest to the priest.

"Does he have any family?" asked the priest, feeling bolder.

"I really don't know," Shafrov replied, finding himself at a loss.

Everyone exchanged glances and it seemed odd and even indecent that no one knew whether Semyonov had any relatives and where they lived.

"His sister's a student in high school somewhere," Karsavina observed.

"Ah! Well, then, good-bye!" said the priest, tipping his hat with his chubby fingers.

"Good-bye!" they replied in unison.

On reaching the street they sighed with relief and halted.

"Well, where to now?" asked Shafrov.

At first they all shuffled indecisively, but then somehow all at once began to take their leave and headed off in different directions.

 XI

When Semyonov saw his own blood and felt the ominous emptiness around and within him, and when later they lifted him up, carried him away, put him to bed, and did everything for him that he used to do for himself, he understood that he was dying and felt strange that he wasn't afraid of death in the least.

When Dubova referred to his fear, she'd reached that conclusion because she herself was afraid; fear in a healthy person confronted by death convinced her that a dying person must fear it infinitely more. She, like all the others, interpreted Semyonov's pallor and wandering gaze—actually resulting from his weakness and loss of blood—as an indication of his fear. But that wasn't really the case, just as the question posed by him to the doctor, "Already?" wasn't really the case either.

Semyonov had always feared death, especially since learning that he had consumption. When he first found out, his condition was terribly tormenting; in all likelihood, it resembled that of a man with no hope of reprieve from a death penalty.

It almost seemed to him that the world had ceased to exist from that moment; everything he'd previously found so beautiful, pleasant, and cheerful had disappeared irrevocably; everything was dying and in a state of insufferable agony, which right now, any minute or any second, must be resolved by something unbearably horrible, yawning like a black abyss.

It was precisely in the form of a huge, round, totally black abyss that Semyonov imagined death. Wherever he went, whatever he did, this round black void stood before him; all sounds, colors, and sensations were lost and vanished in its black emptiness.

This was a terrible frame of mind, but soon it began to diminish. The more time passed and the closer Semyonov got to death, the further away from it he felt and the less intelligible and distinct it became to him.

Everything around him, all sounds, colors, and sensations remained exactly as he had always known them.

The sun shone just as brightly, people went about their business in the same way, and Semyonov himself had both important and unimportant things to do. Just as before, he got up in the morning, carefully washed himself, had dinner at noon, found tasty things good to eat and nasty things not so good; just as before he enjoyed seeing the sun and moon, and was angry at the prolonged rain and slush; as before, he played billiards with Novikov and others in the evening, read books and couldn't help finding some of them important and interesting, others boring and foolish. At first it seemed strange, insulting, even disturbing that everything around him remained as before, not only in nature and in the people surrounding him but in himself as well. He tried to change all this, to force everyone to take an interest in him and his death, to comprehend the full horror of his predicament, to realize that everything was over. But when he talked about it to his acquaintances, he saw that it wasn't right to do so. At first his acquaintances were surprised; then they didn't believe it, although they expressed their sympathy and their disbelief in the doctor's grim prognosis; then they tried to banish the unpleasant impression by talking insistently about something else; and a minute or two later Semyonov himself, without noticing it, was talking with them not about death but about life. All his efforts to involve the whole world in what was happening to him turned out to be entirely ineffectual.

Then he tried to withdraw, become introspective, and suffer all alone the complete and invincible awareness of the full horror of his death. But it was precisely because everything remained the same all around him and in his own life that it seemed absolutely absurd to imagine that it could be otherwise and that he, Semyonov, wouldn't always exist in exactly the same way as he did now. And the thought of death, at first piercing his heart sharply, began to grow less acute and to release his constricted soul. Moments of complete oblivion began to occur more and more frequently, and once again life became richer with its colors, movements, and sounds.

A sense of the proximity of the round, black abyss came only in the late evenings when he was alone. When he put out the light, it seemed to him in the darkness that something formless and faceless rose slowly above him and whispered inexorably: Sh . . . sh . . . sh. . . . And to this soundless, ceaseless whispering in the darkness something from within him replied in another miserable, horrible whisper. Then he felt as if everything were merging more and more into this whisper, this emptiness, this darkness, and that his own body was quivering in this chaos of whispers, emptiness, and darkness like a slender, pathetic splinter of wood, ready to disintegrate at any moment and disappear without a trace.

Then he took to sleeping with the lamp still lit. In its light the whisper became inaudible, the darkness receded, and the sense of all-enveloping emptiness disappeared because it was filled by thousands of details of daily life, all very ordinary and understandable: the chairs, the light, the inkstand, his own feet, an unfinished letter needing to be finished, an icon with a lamp he'd never lit, boots he'd forgotten to leave outside the door, and other items and cares surrounding him.

Yet even then the whisper was heard in those corners where the lamplight didn't reach: the darkness grew thicker there and the same all-enveloping emptiness yawned like a bottomless pit. Semyonov was afraid to look into the darkness and to think about it. All he had to do was remember the darkness and emptiness, and they rose up from all corners and filled the room, surrounded him, extinguished the lamp, drowned out his cares, and sealed the world off from him with an impenetrable shroud of ghastly, cold mist. This was inexpressibly horrible and tormenting. At such moments he wanted to cry like a little boy and bang his head against the wall.

But with every passing day, as Semyonov's life dwindled, these sensations became more and more routine. They erupted with terrible new strength only when some word, gesture, or the sight of a funeral, graveyard, or coffin reminded him that he was really dying. He avoided these reminders, no longer taking those streets that led past the cemetery and never going to sleep on his back with his arms crossed on his chest.

It was as if two lives had taken shape in him: his former extensive and observable life that couldn't accommodate the idea of death, forgot all about it, went about its business, and hoped to live forever, no matter what; and the other life, secret, elusive, hidden like a worm in an apple, which like black darkness filtered through his first life and, like venom, poisoned it with unbearable, inevitable torment.

There was something special about this double life: when Semyonov finally stood face to face with death and understood that his life was finished, he experienced hardly any fear.

"Already?" he asked, only so as to know for sure.

After realizing from the faces of those around him that "already" was the right answer to his question, Semyonov was merely surprised that it was all so simple and natural, like the end of a difficult task that had exhausted him by requiring more strength than he possessed. But he understood right away with a special new inner awareness that it couldn't be otherwise because death comes only when the organism lacks the strength to go on living.

He merely felt sorry that he would never get to see anything again. As they took him off to the hospital in a cab, he looked around silently, his tearful eyes wide open, trying to take everything in with one glance, and suffering because he couldn't retain the whole world in his memory to the very last detail, with its sky, people, verdure, and its spacious light-blue vistas. He found equally precious and dear all those little things he'd never noticed before, as well as those he'd always considered important and beautiful: the translucent darkening sky with its golden stars, the gaunt back of the cabman in his shabby blue jacket, Novikov with his sad, frightened face, the dusty road, the houses with bright lights in their windows, the dark trees receding quietly behind them, the sound of the wheels, the warm evening breeze—everything that he saw and heard and felt.

Afterward, in the hospital, he hurriedly and greedily ran his eyes over the ward, followed and remembered every movement, every face, and every object, until his physical suffering began to displace his surroundings and envelop him in loneliness. All his sensations moved to somewhere deep within his breast, to the source of his suffering. Gradually he began to withdraw from life. When something appeared before him, it already seemed alien and unnecessary. The final struggle between life and death had begun; it filled his entire being, creating its own special, lonely world of vacillation, glimmers of life, downturns, declines, and desperate efforts.

Sometimes he'd experience a moment of clarity; the torments eased, his breathing became deeper and calmer, and images and sounds appeared more or less clearly through the white shroud. But they seemed insignificant and weak, as if they came from far away.

Semyonov heard sounds clearly, but it was as if he didn't really hear them properly, and figures around him moved noiselessly, as though in a motion picture projector; at times familiar faces would appear in his field of vision, but it was as if they were unknown to him, and didn't trigger any recollections.

Near his neighbor's bed sat a man whose face was strangely clean-shaven, reading a newspaper aloud, but it never occurred to Semyonov to think about why he was reading aloud or to whom. He distinctly heard that the elections in parliament had been postponed, that an attempt had been made on the life of the Grand Prince, but the words were somehow empty, rising and bursting in a void, like bubbles, then disappearing without trace or sound. Lips moved, concealing and revealing teeth, round eyes rolled, sheets of paper rustled, the lamp shone on the ceiling evenly, as if large, ominous black flies were circling it incessantly and noiselessly.

Then something was born in his brain, glimmered like a bright spot, and began to flare up, illuminating more and more all around. Suddenly, with complete clarity and consciousness, Semyonov understood that everything was unnecessary for him now, that all the hustle and bustle of the world couldn't add even one more hour to his life because he had to die.

Once more he sank into rolling waves of dark mist, and the silent mortal battle began again between two terrible, secret forces trying to destroy one another with their imperceptible efforts, but enveloping his whole world in convulsions.

The second time he returned to life was when they began weeping and chanting over him; all this was totally unnecessary and had no connection whatsoever with what was happening within him. But once again for a brief moment it produced in him a bright spot, fanned it, and he saw and understood completely the sublimely sad face of the man who meant nothing to him and to whom he meant nothing either.

This was his last sign of life; it was followed by something completely incomprehensible and unimaginable for living human beings.

 XII

"Let's go back to my place; we'll hold a wake for the dear departed soul!" Ivanov said to Sanin.

Sanin nodded in silence.

They stopped at a shop for vodka and snacks and continued on their way, catching up with Yury Svarozhich, who looked despondent as he walked along the boulevard.

Semyonov's death had made a bewildering and painful impression on Yury, who found it both necessary and yet impossible to make sense of it.

"Well, it's all very simple." Yury tried to draw a straight, short line in his mind. "A person doesn't exist before he's born, and that doesn't seem terrible or incomprehensible. And a person no longer exists after he's dead, and that's just as simple and comprehensible. Death, like the complete collapse of a machine that produces the life force, is entirely understandable, and there's no horror in it. Once there was a lad named Yura, who went to school, broke his enemies' noses in the second grade, and cut down nettles; he had his own special, surprising, complicated, entertaining life. Then this Yura died, and instead of him, there's someone entirely different, the student

Yury Svarozhich, who walks and thinks. If they were ever to meet, Yura would never be able to understand today's Yury Svarozhich, and therefore might even hate him as a person who, for all one knows, might become his tutor and create considerable unpleasantness for him! In other words, there's a gap between them; in other words, the lad Yura really died. Yura died; I myself died and didn't notice it until now. That's what happened. It's simple and natural! Yes. . . . Otherwise, what do we lose in dying? What, exactly? In life, in any case, more bad happens than good. Nevertheless, joy still exists and it's hard to lose it, but the relief provided by death from the large mass of evil must still be seen as a great plus. Yes, it's very simple and not in the least bit terrible!" Yury said aloud with a sigh of relief, but immediately pulled himself up with a feeling of acute spiritual pain: "No! The fact is the whole world, alive, extremely subtle and complex, in one instant turns into nothing, into a clod, a despicable lump. This isn't the rebirth of the lad Yura into Yury Svarozhich; it's absurdly and sickeningly revolting, and therefore incomprehensible and terrible."

A light film of cold sweat covered Yury's forehead.

He started to muster all his mental powers to understand the condition that everyone finds impossible to bear but that everyone has to bear, just as Semyonov had recently done.

He didn't die in fear! Yury thought to himself, smiling at the strangeness of his thought. On the contrary, he was still mocking us, with the priest, the singing, and the tears. . . .

It seemed that there was a certain point that, if suddenly grasped, would illumine everything. But it was as if a thick, impregnable wall stood between his soul and that point. His mind glided over an imperceptibly smooth surface, and just when it seemed that meaning was near, his thought turned out to be at the bottom again, where it was before. In whatever direction he spread this net of subtle thoughts and ideals, invariably the very same flat and painfully unsatisfying words came back to him: incomprehensible and terrible! His thoughts went no further; indeed, it seemed they could go no further.

This was excruciating and sapped his mind, soul, and entire body. Grief invaded his heart, his thoughts became vapid and pallid, his head ached, and he wanted to sit down right there on the boulevard and give up on everything, even life itself.

How could Semyonov laugh, knowing that in a few moments everything would end? What is he—a hero? No, this isn't a question of heroism. Can it be that death isn't as terrible as I think?

At that moment Ivanov loudly and unexpectedly called out to him.

"Ah, so it's you! Where are you going?" Yury asked with a shudder.

"To a wake for our dear departed friend!" Ivanov replied coarsely and cheerfully. "Come along with us. Why do you always dawdle around alone?"

It must have been because Yury was feeling so frightened and dejected that Sanin and Ivanov didn't seem as unpleasant as usual.

"All right, let's go!" he agreed, but immediately remembered his superiority over them and said to himself: What on earth will I do with them? Drink vodka? Talk vulgar nonsense?

He was just about to turn down the invitation, but his whole being instinctively resisted the loneliness, so he went along.

Ivanov and Sanin were silent, so they reached Ivanov's house in silence.

It was already totally dark; they could scarcely make out on a bench near the gate the figure of a man holding a thick stick with a crooked handle.

"Ah, it's my uncle, Peter Ilich!" Ivanov cried joyfully.

"It is," the man replied in a low bass, his powerful voice resounding authoritatively in the night air

Yury recalled that Ivanov's uncle was an elderly, drunken member of the church choir. He had a gray mustache like a soldier at the time of Nicholas I, and his well-worn black double-breasted jacket always had a nasty smell.

Boo-oom, boo-oom! His voice sounded like something striking against a barrel when Ivanov introduced him to Yury.

Yury shook his hand clumsily and didn't know what to say or how to behave with such a fellow. But he recalled at once that for him, Yury Svarozhich, all men must be treated equally, so he walked along with the old singer, trying to let him go first.

Ivanov lived in a place that more resembled a storeroom than living quarters because there was so much dust, trash, and disorder. But when his host lit the lamp, Yury saw that all the walls were decorated with prints and paintings by Vasnetsov,[10] and the piles of trash turned out to be stacks of books.

"Do you like Vasnetsov?" asked Ivanov and, without waiting for an answer, went to fetch some plates.

Sanin told Peter Ilich that Semyonov had died.

"May he rest in peace!" The barrel resounded once again; and after falling silent for a moment, Peter Ilich added: "Well, then . . . it's a good thing. Everything's been completed."

Yury looked at him thoughtfully and suddenly took a liking to the old singer.

Ivanov came back bringing some bread and pickles on a plate, and some glasses. Setting all this on a table covered with a sheet of newspaper, he picked up a bottle and with a swift, almost imperceptible movement removed the cork without spilling a drop.

"What skill!" said Peter Ilich approvingly.

"It's immediately apparent which of us knows what he's doing!" Ivanov joked smugly, pouring the light-greenish liquid into the glasses. "Well, gen-

[10] Viktor Mikailovich Vasnetsov (1848–1927), Russian painter, was an outstanding representative of Slavic revival, using fairy tales and folk epics for his subject matter.

tlemen," he said, picking up his glass and raising his voice, "to the repose of the departed, etc., etc.!"

They began eating snacks, then drank again and again. They talked very little and continued to drink. It soon became warm and stuffy in the little room. Peter Ilich lit a cigarette and at once the air was filled with the blue fumes of cheap tobacco smoke. Yury began to feel dizzy from all the vodka, smoke, and heat. He remembered Semyonov again.

"Death is a very nasty business!"

"Why?" asked Peter Ilich. "Death? Oh! But it . . . it's inevitable! Death! And if one were to live forever? Oh! Beware of talking like that. Eternal life! What on earth?"

Yury suddenly wondered what it would be like to live forever. He imagined some endless gray ribbon extending aimlessly and exhaustingly into the void, as if carried along from one wave to the next. All conception of colors and sounds, the depth and fullness of experience were somehow swept away and rendered pale, merging into gray obscurity, flowing without course or movement. This was no longer life; it was also death.

Yury grew really frightened. "Yes, of course," he muttered.

"Obviously, it's made a big impression on you," Novikov observed.

"Who wouldn't be impressed by it?" Yury asked, instead of replying.

Ivanov nodded vaguely and began telling Peter Ilich about Semyonov's last moments.

It had now become unbearably stuffy in the room. Yury watched mechanically as the vodka, glistening in the lamplight, was transferred to Ivanov's thin red lips; he felt that everything around him was beginning to spin and swim.

"Ah-ah-ah-ah," a faint, mysteriously sad voice sang into his ear.

"No, death is a terrifying thing!" he repeated, without noticing it himself, as if replying to that mysterious voice.

"You're much too nervous about it!" Ivanov said condescendingly.

"And are you ready for it?" Yury asked mechanically.

"Me? Well, no! Of course I don't want to die: it's a futile task; it's much more amusing to live . . . but if one has to die, it's better to do it instantaneously and without any idle chatter.

"You haven't died so you don't know," Sanin said with a smile.

"That's certainly true!" Ivanov agreed with a laugh.

"All this has been said before," Yury remarked suddenly with desolate rancor. "You can say what you want, but death is still death! It's horrible both in and of itself, and a person who . . . well, a person who's aware of life must find that this inevitable, violent end will destroy any joy in life! What's the sense?"

"This has also been said before," Ivanov interrupted with a grin, he too with unexpected irritation. "You all think that only you . . ."

"What's the sense?" Peter Ilich repeated his question thoughtfully.

"There isn't any!" cried Ivanov, with the same incomprehensible rancor.

"No, that's impossible," Yury objected. "Everything's too wise and . . ."

"In my opinion, there's nothing good," Sanin added.

"What do you mean? What about nature?"

"What about nature?" Sanin said with a faint smile, waving his hand dejectedly. "It's merely customary to say that nature's perfect. But to tell the truth it's just as bad as man: each of us, even without any special effort of the imagination, can imagine a world a hundred times better than this one. Why don't we have perpetual warmth, light, and an abundant garden, always green and delightful? What's the sense?—There is sense, of course . . . it must exist simply because a goal determines the course of things; without one there can only be chaos. But this goal lies outside our lives, in the foundations of the whole world. . . . This is understandable. We can't be its beginning, and consequently we can't be its end. Our role is merely subsidiary and, obviously, passive. Our purpose is accomplished by the fact that we live. . . . Our life is necessary, and consequently our death is necessary too."

"For whom?"

"How should I know?" Sanin said with a laugh. "What business is it of mine? My life consists of pleasant and unpleasant sensations; as to what lies beyond its limits—to hell with it! Whatever hypothesis we advance, it will remain a mere hypothesis; and it would be foolish to build one's life upon it. Let whoever wants to worry about it do so, while I live my life."

"Let's all drink to that!" Ivanov proposed.

"And do you believe in God?" Peter Ilich asked, turning his lackluster eyes to Sanin. "These days no one believes . . . not even in the possibility of belief."

"I do believe in God," Sanin said with another laugh. "A belief in God has remained with me since childhood, and I see no reason either to struggle against it or to reinforce it. This is the most advantageous situation: if God exists, I offer him my sincere faith; if He doesn't, then all the better for me."

"But life is built on a foundation of faith or lack of faith," Yury observed.

"No," Sanin said, shaking his head, his face displaying a nonchalant, lighthearted smile. "I don't build my life on that foundation."

"Well, on what, then?" Yury asked lackadaisically.

Ah-ah-ah . . . I shouldn't drink any more, he thought drearily, wiping his hand across his cold, clammy forehead.

Sanin may or may not have said anything in reply, but Yury didn't hear it. His head was spinning and for a moment he felt faint.

"I believe there is a God, but faith exists in me of its own accord," Sanin continued. "He exists or He doesn't, but I don't know Him or know what He requires of me. How could I possibly know this, even if I possessed the most ardent faith? God is God, not a human being, and it's impossible to apply human standards to Him. His works that we behold encompass everything: good, evil, life, death, beauty, ugliness ... everything ... and since all certainty, all meaning disappear in it, and chaos emerges, then, as a result, its meaning isn't the same as human meaning, and its good and evil aren't the same as human good and evil. Our conception of God will always be a form of idol worship, and we'll always bestow on our fetish the physiognomy and clothing suitable to local climatic conditions. What absurdity!"

"So it is!" Ivanov cried. "Right you are!"

"Then why go on living?" asked Yury, pushing his glass away in disgust.

"And why die?"

"I know one thing," replied Sanin. "I live life and I don't want it to be miserable. For that, first and foremost, it's necessary to satisfy one's natural desire. Desire is everything: if desire dies in a person, life dies; and if he kills desire, he kills himself."

"But can desires be evil?"

"Perhaps."

"What then?"

"It's all the same," Sanin replied sympathetically, and turned his bright, unblinking eyes to look into Yury's face.

Ivanov arched his eyebrows, glanced at Sanin incredulously, and remained silent. Yury was also quiet and found it frightening to stare into those bright, clear eyes; yet for some reason he tried not to avert his gaze.

For a few moments it was quiet and one could distinctly hear a solitary moth desperately beating its wings against the inside of a windowpane. Peter Ilich shook his head gloomily and lowered his drunken face toward the dirty, stained newspaper. Sanin kept smiling.

Yury was both irritated and attracted by this constant smile.

What crystal-clear eyes he has! he thought to himself.

Sanin suddenly stood up, opened the window, and let the moth out. An astonishingly pleasant wave of cool, fresh air swept lightly through the room like a large, soft wing.

"Yes," Ivanov said, responding to his own thoughts. "There are all sorts of people; let's drink to that."

"No." Yury shook his head. "I won't drink any more."

"Why not?

"I'm not much of a drinker."

Yury's head was already aching from the vodka and the heat, and he wanted to get some fresh air.

"Well, I'm going," he said, getting up.

"Where to? Let's have some more to drink!"

"No, really, I have to ..." Yury answered absent-mindedly, looking for his cap.

"Well, good-bye!"

As Yury was closing the door, he heard Sanin reply to Peter Ilich:

"Yes, if you don't behave like children, but children don't distinguish good and evil; they're sincere in their . . ."

Yury closed the door and it became quiet again.

The moon was high in the sky, light and bright. Yury was fanned by a breeze, cool and moist from the dew. Everything was woven together by the moonlight, splendid and dreamy. As he walked alone through streets that all looked alike in the moonlight, Yury found it difficult and strange to think that somewhere there was a silent, black room where, sallow and stiff, Semyonov was lying on a table dead.

But for some reason he couldn't recall those painful, terrible thoughts that had so recently burdened his soul, enveloping his whole world in a black mist. He felt only still and sad, and didn't want to avert his gaze from the distant moon.

Walking across the empty square, seemingly so broad and smooth in the moonlight, Yury began to think about Sanin.

What sort of man is he? he wondered, feeling deeply perplexed.

He wasn't pleased that a person had turned up whom he, Yury, couldn't define immediately; as a result, he absolutely wanted to define him in an unflattering way.

A phrasemonger, he thought with malicious enjoyment. At one time people posed as if they were disgusted with life and possessed sublime, obscure spiritual needs; now they pose as animalists.[11]

Having polished off Sanin, Yury began thinking about himself, how he wasn't posing as anything, and that everything about him, his suffering and his thoughts, all were original, unlike anyone else's. That was fine, but something was missing, and Yury began to recall the late Semyonov.

He felt sad to realize that he'd never see the sick student again and that Semyonov, whom he'd never really liked all that much, had become close and dear to him to the point of tears. Yury imagined him lying in a grave with his face rotting, his body full of maggots slowly and sickeningly swarming in a decomposing mass, under his greenish, damp, greasy uniform.

"You'll walk past my grave and stop to relieve yourself on it. . . ."

But this is all people! Yury thought in horror, staring fixedly at the thick dust on the road. I'm walking and trampling over brains, hearts, eyes . . . ugh!

He felt a wretched weakness in his knees.

I too will die. . . . I'll die and people will walk over me and will think just what I'm thinking now. . . . Yes, while it's still not too late, one must live and live! And live well, and in such a way that not one moment of my life will be wasted. But how do I do that?

It was deserted and bright in the square; a delicate, enigmatic moonlit silence had settled over the whole town.

---

[11] Animalism is a theory that regards human beings basically as brutes and little or nothing more. It is characterized by an extreme preoccupation with the satisfaction of physical desires.

"And the loud strings of Boyan will say nothing about him . . ." Yury sang softly.[12]

"Dreary, gloomy, terrible!" he said aloud, as if complaining, but he was afraid of the sound of his own voice and looked around to see if anyone else had heard him.

I'm drunk, he thought.

The night was bright and still.

 XIII

While Karsavina and Dubova were away somewhere on a visit, Yury Svarozhich's life continued smoothly and monotonously.

Nikolai Yegorovich was busy with his household or his club, while Lyalya and Ryazantsev were so obviously burdened by anyone else's presence that Yury found it awkward to be with them. Of its own accord it became his practice to go to bed early and get up late, just before dinner. He spent the whole day sitting either in the garden or in his room, brooding intensely and waiting for a powerful burst of energy to undertake some great task.

Every day this "great task" assumed a new form: it was either a painting or a series of articles that, without Yury's awareness, would demonstrate to the whole world how serious a mistake the Social Democrats had made in not offering Yury Svarozhich the leading role in their party;[13] sometimes it was forging links with the people and dynamic, spontaneous work with them; but it was always something important and effective.

But the day ended just as it had begun, and brought with it nothing but boredom. Once or twice Novikov and Shafrov came to see him, or Yury attended a reading or went out visiting, but all this seemed extraneous to him, unfocused, and bore no relation to what was languishing within him.

One day Yury went to visit Ryazantsev. The doctor lived in a large, roomy apartment and had numerous items intended to amuse a strong, healthy man: gymnastic equipment, dumbbells, rubber resistance bands, fencing foils, fishing rods, nets for catching quail, cigarette holders, and pipes. Everything proclaimed healthy, masculine physicality and self-satisfaction.

[12] Boyan was a bard of ancient times whose songs are referred to in the medieval epic "The Song of Igor's Campaign."

[13] The Russian Social Democratic Labor Party, formed in 1898, united orthodox Marxists, revisionists, and trade unionists; it split into two factions in 1903, formally reunited, and then split into more factions after 1905.

Ryazantsev greeted him cordially and informally, showed him all his things, laughed, told stories, offered him a smoke and a drink, and finally invited him to go hunting.

"I don't have a gun," Yury said.

"Take one of mine: I've got five," Ryazantsev replied.

He viewed Yury as Lyalya's brother and wanted to get to know him better and to be liked by him. Therefore he warmly and insistently offered Yury his guns, cheerfully and willingly brought them all in, took them apart, explained their mechanisms, and even fired at a target in the courtyard; finally even Yury felt a desire to laugh just as heartily, to set off and go hunting; so he agreed to take a gun and cartridges.

"Well, that's splendid," Ryazantsev rejoiced sincerely. "It just so happens that I'm planning to hunt quail tomorrow. Now we can go together, right?"

"With pleasure," Yury agreed.

After returning home, Yury, without even noticing, spent over two hours fiddling with his gun, examining it, and adjusting the strap to his shoulders; he grasped it by the butt, took aim at a lamp, and then carefully oiled his old hunting boots.

The next day, toward evening, a cheerful and fresh-faced Ryazantsev arrived to fetch him in a racing carriage pulled by a well-fed bay horse.

"Ready?" he called through Yury's window.

Yury, who'd already fastened on his gun, cartridge belt, and game bag, and was awkwardly tangled up in all of them, smiled in embarrassment and came out of the house.

"Ready, ready," he said.

Ryazantsev was comfortably and lightly dressed, and looked at Yury's outfit with some astonishment.

"It's going to be difficult for you wearing all that," he said, smiling. "Take it all off and put it over here. When we get out there, you can put it all back on."

He helped Yury take off his gear and stow it under the carriage seat. Then they set off briskly, as fast as the good horse could gallop. The day was drawing to a close, but it was still hot and dusty. The wheels jolted the cart vigorously, and Yury had to hold on to the seat. Ryazantsev talked and laughed all the time, while with good-natured enjoyment Yury looked at his broad back covered in a tussah jacket with sweaty stains under the armpits and involuntarily imitated his laughter and jokes. When they emerged into a field and the stiff grass brushed lightly against their legs, it became cooler, easier, and the dust subsided.

When they reached an endless flat field covered with white watermelons, Ryazantsev stopped his sweating horse; cupping his hands around his mouth, he cried in his modulated baritone:

"Kuzma-a-a. . . . Kuzma-a-a. . . ."

Some tiny people, barely visible at the other end of the watermelon field, raised their heads and gazed at the source of this sound for a long time; then one figure moved away from the rest and walked along the rows until it became clear that it was a tall, gray-haired old man with a bushy beard, his arms dangling clumsily in front of him.

Slowly he approached; smiling broadly, he said:

"You certainly know how to shout, Anatoly Pavlovich."

"Hello, Kuzma, how are you? Can I leave the horse with you?"

"You certainly can," the old man said calmly and politely, taking hold of the horse by the bridle. "Going hunting? And just who might this be?" he asked, glancing kindly at Yury.

"Nikolai Yegorovich's son," Ryazantsev replied cheerfully.

"Ah. . . . Now I can see, he looks just like Lyudmila Nikolaevna. Yes, indeed."

Yury felt pleased somehow that this affable old man knew his sister and had mentioned her so simply and affectionately.

"Well, let's go," Ryazantsev said cheerfully and excitedly, getting his gun and bags from the front of the carriage and putting them on.

"All the best," Kuzma said as they left. They could hear how he coaxed the horse as he led her toward his hut.

They had to walk about a verst to the marsh;[14] the sun had long since set when the ground became soggy and covered with fresh swamp grass, sedge, and reeds. The water shimmered; it smelled damp and began to grow dark. Ryazantsev stopped smoking, planted his feet wide apart, and suddenly became completely serious, as if about to undertake a very important and demanding task. Yury moved away from him to the right, trying to find a less boggy and more comfortable place to stand beyond the reeds. Directly in front of him lay the water, pure and deep from the bright twilight reflected in it; beyond it lay the other bank, merging into a black stripe.

Almost immediately, rising unexpectedly from somewhere and flapping their wings with difficulty, groups of two or three ducks took flight. They'd appeared suddenly from behind the reeds and, turning their heads to and fro, were clearly visible against the bright sky over the men's heads. Ryazantsev fired first and was successful. A wounded drake fell from the air and plopped down clumsily somewhere to one side, splashing into the water and loudly crushing the reeds.

"Happy hunting!" Ryazantsev shouted in satisfaction and then burst out laughing.

He's really a splendid fellow! thought Yury for some reason.

Then Yury fired, also successfully, but the duck he shot fell somewhere far away; he couldn't find it, even though he scratched his hands on the sedge and waded out into the water up to his knees. But his failure merely encouraged him: now anything that happened seemed fine.

---

[14] About 3,500 feet, or a little more than a kilometer.

The gun smoke smelled especially sweet in the cool, clear air above the river, and the little bursts of light from the gunshots flashed brightly and beautifully amid the darkened landscape. Wounded ducks whirled gracefully against the pale green sky where twilight was fading and the first dim little stars were weakly shining. Yury felt an unusual surge of strength and joy; it seemed to him that he'd never experienced anything more interesting and exciting.

Then the ducks took flight less and less often; it became harder to aim in the deepening twilight.

"Hey!" cried Ryazantsev. "It's time to head home!"

Yury was sorry to leave, but he came to join Ryazantsev; he was no longer able to make out the water, so he splashed through pools and got tangled in the reeds. They met, their eyes gleaming; both were breathing quickly, though easily.

"Well, then," asked Ryazantsev. "Any luck?"

"I'll say!" Yury replied, showing his full game bag.

"You're a better shot than I am!" Ryazantsev said, as though rejoicing.

Yury enjoyed this praise even though he'd never accorded any special significance to physical strength and agility.

"Well, not really better," he replied complacently. "Just lucky."

It was completely dark when they reached the hut. The watermelon field had disappeared in the blackness, and only the closest rows of small melons, casting long, flat shadows, reflected the light of the fire. The invisible horse snorted near the hut; a small but bright and lively fire of dried steppe grass crackled; the spirited sound of men's talk and women's laughter could be heard, as well as the sound of someone's smooth, cheerful voice that Yury recognized.

"Why, it's Sanin," Ryazantsev said with surprise. "How did he wind up here?"

They approached the campfire. Gray-bearded Kuzma, sitting in a circle of light, raised his head and nodded to them affably.

"Any luck?" he asked in a deep bass that came from under his mustache.

"Just a little," Ryazantsev replied.

Sanin, sitting on a large pumpkin, also raised his head and smiled at them.

"How did you wind up here?" Ryazantsev asked.

"Kuzma Prokhorovich and I are old friends," Sanin explained, smiling even more broadly.

Kuzma contentedly bared the yellow stumps of his decayed teeth and slapped Sanin good-naturedly on the knee with his firm, rough hand.

"Yes, yes," he said. "Sit down, Anatoly Pavlovich, "have some watermelon. And you, young sir . . . what's your name?"

"Yury Nikolaevich," he replied, smiling courteously.

He felt awkward, but really liked this peaceful old man with his affectionate way of speaking, half-Russian, half-Ukrainian.

"Yury Nikolaevich, yes. . . . Well, let's get acquainted. Sit down, Yury Nikolaevich."

Yury and Ryazantsev brought up two large, firm pumpkins and sat down by the fire.

"Well, show me, show me what you shot," Kuzma said with interest.

A heap of dead birds spilled out of the game bags, staining the ground with blood. In the flickering light of the fire they had a strange and unpleasant look. Their blood appeared black, while their twisted feet seemed to stir.

Kuzma picked up a drake and felt under its wings.

"That's a fat one," he said approvingly. "You might give me a brace, Anatoly Pavlovich. What will you do with so many?"

"Take all mine," Yury exclaimed excitedly and then blushed.

"Why! See how generous he is," said the old man with a laugh. "But I'll take a brace so no one'll be offended."

Some other peasants and old women came up to have a look. But glancing up from the fire, Yury couldn't quite make them out. First one face, then another emerged from the darkness into the bright light, then disappeared.

Wincing, Sanin looked at the dead birds, drew back, and stood up quickly. He found it unpleasant to see such beautiful, strong birds lying there covered in dust and blood, their feathers smashed and broken.

Yury watched everything with curiosity, hungrily biting off pieces of ripe, juicy watermelon that Kuzma had cut for him with a folding pocketknife that had a handle of yellow bone.

"Eat, Yury Nikolaevich, it's good melon. . . . I know your sister Lyudmila Nikolaevna and your father, too. . . . Eat to your heart's content!"

Yury liked everything here: the peasant smell that resembled sheepskins and bread combined, the lively crackling of the fire, the pumpkin on which he was sitting; the fact that when Kuzma looked down, you could see his whole face, and when he raised his head, it disappeared into the darkness and only his eyes shone; and the fact that the darkness seemed to hang right above his head, lending a cheerful comfort to the illumined place. When Yury looked up, at first nothing at all was visible; then suddenly the high, majestically peaceful dark sky appeared with its distant stars.

But at the same time he was feeling somewhat awkward and didn't know what to talk about with the peasants.

The others—Kuzma, Sanin, and even Ryazantsev—without apparently having to choose subjects for conversation, were chatting so simply and freely about everything imaginable that Yury could only marvel.

"Well, what's happening with the land?" he asked when everyone had fallen silent for a moment; he himself felt that his question was forced and inappropriate.

Kuzma looked at him and replied: "We wait and then we wait some more. Perhaps something will come of it."

Once again they started talking about the melon field, the price of watermelons and other things; then Yury felt even more awkward and even more pleased to sit there and listen.

They heard footsteps. A small reddish dog with a curly white tail appeared in the circle of light, wagged its tail, sniffed Yury and Ryazantsev, and began to rub against Sanin's knees as he stroked its rough, full coat. A little old man appeared behind them, white in the firelight, with a straggly, shaggy beard and small eyes. In his hand he held a rusty, single-barreled gun.

"It's our watchman, Grandpa," said Kuzma.

The old man sat down on the ground, put his gun to one side, and looked at Yury and Ryazantsev.

"Been out hunting . . . yes . . ." he mumbled, showing his bare, shriveled gums. "Hey, Kuzma, it's time to boil up the 'taters, eh?"

Ryazantsev picked up the old man's gun and with a laugh showed it to Yury. It was a heavy, rusty percussion musket held together with wire.

"It's a flintlock rifle!" he said.

"How is it, old man, you're not afraid to fire it?"

"Hey . . . Almost shot myself once. Stepan Shapka told me it'd fire without caps. Yes, without caps. Said if any sulfur was left, it'd fire without a cap. So one time I laid the gun down on my knee, the trigger cocked . . . the trigger cocked, and I fired like this, with my finger. What a roar it made! Almost shot myself! Hey, the trigger cocked, and it made such a roar . . . almost shot myself, I did."

Everyone laughed; Yury found the old man's story so touching that tears welled up in his eyes—this old man with his small shaggy gray beard and his mumbling speech. The old man laughed too, his little eyes shining with tears.

"Almost shot myself!"

In the darkness, beyond the circle of light, they could hear the laughter and voices of girls, fearful of the strange men. A few feet away, not at all where Yury imagined him to be, Sanin lit a match, and when its pink flame flared, Yury could see his calm, affable eyes and another young face gazing at Sanin cheerfully and naively with her dark eyes from under black brows.

Ryazantsev winked in that direction and said, "Hey, Grandpa, you'd better keep an eye on your granddaughter, eh?"

"What's the use?" old Kuzma said, gesturing with good-natured hopelessness. "Youth is youth!"

"You can say that again!" echoed the little old man, snatching a burning coal from the fire with his bare hands.

Sanin laughed merrily in the darkness. But the woman must have been embarrassed, because they moved away and their voices became barely audible.

"Well, it's time to go," said Ryazantsev, getting up. "Thank you, Kuzma."

"For what?" asked Kuzma, using his sleeve to brush away the black watermelon seeds that had stuck to his gray beard.

He offered his hand to Yury and Ryazantsev. Once again Yury felt it both awkward and pleasant to shake his stiff, rough hand.

When they'd moved away from the fire, it was easier to see. Cold stars glittered above, and everything there seemed astonishingly beautiful, peaceful, and infinite. The people sitting near the fire, the horses, and the silhouette of the cart with its load of watermelons appeared darker against the light. Yury tripped over a round pumpkin and almost fell over.

"Careful . . . over here," said Sanin. "Good-bye."

"Good-bye," replied Yury, turning to look at his tall, dark figure; it seemed to him that the tall, lovely woman had nestled closer to Sanin. Yury's heart sank and ached sweetly. He suddenly remembered Karsavina and he felt envious of Sanin.

Once again the wheels of the carriage rattled and the good, well-rested horse snorted. The fire was left behind; the sounds of conversation and laughter died away. It became quiet. Yury slowly raised his eyes to the sky and saw the enormous tracery of diamond-like glittering stars.

When the fences and lights of the town became visible and the dogs started barking, Ryazantsev said, "That Kuzma's quite a philosopher, isn't he?"

Yury looked at the back of Ryazantsev's head and made an effort to shift from his own pensive and tenderly melancholy thoughts to understand what he was saying.

"Ah. . . . Yes," he replied after a pause.

"I didn't know Sanin was such a fine fellow!" Ryazantsev said with a laugh.

Yury came fully to his senses and imagined Sanin together with what seemed to him a woman's astonishingly delicate and lovely face lit by the flame of a match. Once again he felt unconscious envy, and as a result suddenly recollected that Sanin's behavior with regard to that young peasant girl must be squalid.

"I didn't know either," he said ironically.

Ryazantsev didn't catch Yury's tone, and remaining silent, urged on his horse, and then indecisively but tastefully remarked, "A pretty girl, wasn't she? I know her. She's the old man's granddaughter."

Yury said nothing. His overflowing and happily dreamy enchantment was quickly dissipated, and his former self knew clearly and firmly that Sanin was a repulsive, vulgar man.

Ryazantsev shrugged his shoulders, tossed his head in a strange way, and blurted authoritatively, "Oh, hell. . . . What a night, eh? It's even gotten to me! You know what? Maybe we ought to go back, eh?"

Yury didn't understand immediately.

"Those are lovely girls. Let's go back, eh?" Ryazantsev continued with a snigger.

Yury blushed deeply in the darkness. A forbidden feeling stirred within him with its animal appetite; unusual and awe-inspiring pictures penetrated his excited brain, but he gained control of himself and replied dryly, "No. It's time to go home." Then he added maliciously, "Lyalya's waiting for us."

Ryazantsev suddenly shrank back, as if withdrawing into himself, and seemed to grow smaller.

"Well, yes . . . of course . . . it's really time . . ." he muttered hastily.

Clenching his teeth in malice and loathing, staring with hatred at the broad back in the white jacket, Yury said, "In general I'm not a devotee of such adventures."

"Hmm, yes . . . ha, ha, ha . . ." Ryazantsev said with a halfhearted, hostile laugh, and fell silent.

Oh, hell. It ended awkwardly, Yury thought.

They drove home in silence; the road seemed endless.

"Will you come in?" asked Yury, without looking at Ryazantsev.

"No. You know, I have to see a patient. Besides, it's late, isn't it?" Ryazantsev replied indecisively.

Yury climbed down from the carriage and didn't even want to take his gun and game. Everything that belonged to Ryazantsev now seemed repulsive. But Ryazantsev said, "What about the gun?"

Against his will Yury came back, collected his gear and game with disgust, shook hands awkwardly, and then left. Ryazantsev drove on quietly a short distance, then suddenly turned into a narrow little street, and the wheels of his carriage rolled off in the opposite direction. Yury listened with contempt and secret, unconscious envy.

"What a lout!" he muttered, and felt sorry for his sister Lyalya.

 XIV

After carrying his things inside and not knowing what to do with himself, Yury quietly went out onto the steps leading to the garden.

It was as dark as a chasm and strange to see the sky above with its gleaming stars.

Lyalya was sitting on the steps leading to the garden, lost in thought; her small figure showed dimly in the darkness.

"Is that you, Yury?" she asked.

"Yes, it is," Yury replied. Making his way carefully, he sat down next to her. Lyalya dreamily rested her head on his shoulder. Yury smelled the fresh, clean, warm scent of her hair. It was a woman's scent, and Yury breathed it with unconscious but nervous enjoyment.

"Did the hunting go well?" Lyalya asked affectionately, and after a pause added softly and tenderly: "But where's Anatoly Pavlovich? I heard you drive up."

Your Anatoly Pavlovich is a filthy beast! Yury wanted to cry out in a sudden burst of rage, but instead he replied unwillingly: "I really don't know . . . he went to see a patient."

"A patient," Lyalya repeated mechanically and fell silent, gazing at the stars.

She wasn't annoyed that Ryazantsev hadn't come in to see her: the young woman wanted to be alone so that his presence wouldn't hinder her from pondering the mysterious and momentous feeling, so dear to her, that filled her youthful body and soul. It was the feeling of a desired and inevitable though frightening turning point, after which her entire previous life would fall away and something new would begin. It would be so new that Lyalya herself would have to become entirely different.

Yury felt strange seeing his usually cheerful and merry sister so quiet and pensive. Because he himself was filled with irritating and depressing feelings, everything—Lyalya, the distant, starry sky, the dark garden—everything seemed sad and cold to him. Yury didn't realize that this mute, still pensiveness concealed not grief but rich life: an unknown, immeasurably powerful force surged in the distant sky, the dark garden absorbed vital juices from the earth with all its might, and the gentle Lyalya's bosom was filled with such complete happiness that she feared that at any movement, any impression might destroy this enchantment and muffle that resplendent music—as dazzling as the starry sky, as alluring and mysterious as the dark garden— that music of love and desire that resounded so profoundly within her soul.

"Lyalya . . . do you love Anatoly Pavlovich very much?" Yury asked softly and carefully, as if afraid to rouse her.

How can he ask that? Lyalya felt rather than thought, but she came to her senses immediately and snuggled up to her brother gratefully because he'd begun talking not about something unnecessary and irrelevant for her now but rather about the man she loved.

"Very much," she said so softly that Yury guessed rather than heard her reply; she made a courageous attempt to use her smile to restrain the tears welling up in her eyes.

But Yury detected a melancholy note in her voice and so felt even more pity for her and contempt for Ryazantsev.

"Why?" he asked involuntarily, feeling frightened at his own question.

Lyalya looked at him in astonishment, but couldn't see his face and began laughing softly.

"Silly! Why? Because . . . Haven't you ever been in love? He's so good, kind, honest. . . ."

Handsome, strong! Lyalya wanted to add, but she blushed to tears in the darkness and didn't say it.

"Do you know him well?" asked Yury.

Hey, I shouldn't have asked that, he thought with sadness and irritation. Why? Naturally, he seems better to her than anyone on earth!

"Anatoly doesn't conceal anything from me!" Lyalya replied with timid triumph.

"Are you sure about that?" Yury asked with a wry smile, feeling that he could no longer stop himself.

In Lyalya's voice there was a note of uneasy bewilderment when she replied: "Of course. Why shouldn't I be?"

"No reason. I just . . ." replied Yury, startled.

Lyalya fell silent. It was impossible to understand what was going on within her.

"Perhaps you know something . . . about him?" she suddenly asked; the strange, painful sound of her voice struck Yury and frightened him.

"No. I was only asking. What could I possibly know, especially about Anatoly Pavlovich?"

"No. Then you wouldn't have said that!" Lyalya insisted in a ringing voice.

"I just wanted to say that in general . . ." Already frozen in embarrassment, Yury became muddled. "We men are generally such a depraved lot, all of us."

Lyalya was silent and suddenly started to laugh with relief. "Well, that I do know."

But her laughter seemed completely inappropriate to Yury.

"It's not as easy as it seems to you," he replied with annoyance and wicked irony. "And you can't possibly know everything. You can't even imagine all the vile things in life. You're still too pure for that!"

"Yes, indeed," Lyalya laughed, feeling flattered. But then, placing her hand on her brother's knee, she said seriously: "Do you think I haven't thought about that? I have, a great deal, and it was always painful and shameful: why do we value our purity, our reputation so highly? Why are we afraid to take a step lest we fall, while men consider it almost a heroic feat to seduce a woman? It's terribly unjust, isn't it?"

"Yes," Yury replied bitterly, castigating with enjoyment his own recollections and at the same time realizing that he, Yury, was really different from other men. "That's one of the greatest injustices in the world. Ask any of us: Would you marry" a prostitute, he wanted to say, but he laughed and said instead, "a courtesan, and everyone will say no. But really and truly, is a man any better than a courtesan? At least she sells herself for money, to earn a living, while the man simply . . . becomes dissipated and depraved, always in the same vile, perverted way."

Lyalya was silent.

An invisible bat flew swiftly and timidly under the balcony, twice brushed its rustling wings against the wall, and then, with a faint sound, fluttered away again. Yury fell silent, listening to this mysterious sound of nocturnal life, and then began talking again, becoming more and more irritated and carried away by his own words.

"The worst thing of all is that everyone not only knows it and keeps quiet, as if that's what they're supposed to do, but they even act out complicated tragicomedies. They sanctify marriage. They lie, as they say, before God and man! And it's always the purest, holiest young women," he added, thinking about Karsavina and feeling jealous of her, "who fall to the most depraved, filthiest, sometimes even contaminated men. The late Semyonov once said that the purer the woman, the filthier the man who possesses her. And that's the truth!"

"Really?" Lyalya asked in a strange tone.

"Oh, I'll say!" Yury said with a bitter smirk.

"I don't know," Lyalya said suddenly, and there were tears in her voice.

"What?" Yury asked, not hearing what she said.

"Is it possible that Tolya is just like all the rest?" Lyalya asked. It was the first time she'd referred to Ryazantsev that way to her brother; suddenly she burst into tears. "Well, of course he is!" she said with tears in her eyes.

Yury took hold of her hand with apprehension and anguish.

"Lyalya, Lyalechka . . . what's wrong? I didn't mean to . . . My dear . . . please stop, don't cry!" he repeated incoherently, pulling her moist little hands away from her face and kissing them.

"No. I know . . . it's true," Lyalya repeated, gasping from her tears.

Although she said that she'd thought about it before, it only seemed that way to her; in fact, she'd never conceived of Ryazantsev's private life. Of course, she knew that she was not his first love, and she understood what that meant, but. that awareness had never managed to become a clear concept; it had merely skimmed the surface of her soul.

She felt that she loved him and he loved her, and that was the main thing; nothing else really mattered. But now, because her brother had spoken with such shrill condemnation and contempt, it seemed that an abyss was opening up before her, that it was monstrous and irreparable, that her happiness had plunged into it irretrievably and forever, and that she could no longer love Ryazantsev.

Yury, almost in tears himself, tried to cajole her; he kissed her, smoothed her hair, but she kept on crying, bitterly and desperately.

"Oh, my God, my God!" Lyalya repeated, sobbing like a child; because it was so dark, she seemed small and pitiful, and her tears were so helpless and bitter that Yury felt overwhelming compassion.

Pale and hysterical, he ran into the house, knocked his head painfully on the door, and came back carrying a glass of water, spilling it on the floor and on himself.

"Lyalechka, stop it. How can you carry on like this? What's the matter? Perhaps Anatoly Pavlovich is better than all the rest. Lyalya!" he repeated in despair.

Lyalya was shaking with sobs and her teeth rattled weakly on the rim of the glass.

"What on earth is all this?" asked the maid, who appeared at the door in alarm. "What's wrong, miss?"

Lyalya, leaning on the railing, stood up; still weeping, shaking, and shuddering, she went to her room.

"Oh dear, what is it, miss? Shall I call the master? Yury Nikolaevich!"

Nikolai Yegorovich emerged from the study with his firm and measured tread and stopped in the doorway, looking at the weeping Lyalya with amazement.

"What's happened?" he asked.

"Nothing . . . mere trifles," Yury replied, forcing a smile. "I was talking about Ryazantsev. It's all nonsense!"

Nikolai Yegorovich looked at him inquisitively, thought of something, and then suddenly there appeared on the elderly face of this former gentleman a look of disgust.

"What the devil's going on?" he cried, shrugging his shoulders abruptly and then, turning to the left, went out of the room.

Yury blushed terribly, wanted to say something rude, but felt excruciatingly ashamed and afraid. Filled with outraged malice toward his father, bewildered pity for Lyalya, and painful contempt for himself, he went out quietly onto the porch, down the steps, and out into the garden.

A small frog croaked fitfully and darted beneath his feet; it was crushed and burst like an acorn. Yury slipped, gave a shudder, cried out, and jumped to one side. For a long time he kept wiping his shoe on the wet grass; he felt a nervous shiver of disgust run up and down his spine.

The anguish in his soul and the foul, squeamish feeling in his foot made him grimace in pain. Everything seemed tedious and hideous. In the darkness he groped his way toward a bench and sat down; he directed his anxious, dry, and mean gaze into the garden, and saw nothing there except indistinct patches of blackness. Difficult and dismal thoughts swarmed in his head.

He looked at the place where, in the dark grass, the small frog he'd stepped on was dying or perhaps suffering horribly. A whole world had ended there, full of individual and independent life, yet its appalling, unimaginably painful conclusion was neither seen nor heard.

Somehow imperceptibly Yury found himself thinking a new and tormenting thought—that everything filling his life, even the most important ideas, for whose sake he loved one thing and hated another, rejected one desire and accepted another against his will, all this—both good and evil—was merely an obscure cloud of mist surrounding him alone. For the world in its huge totality, all his most agonizing and heartfelt sufferings didn't even exist, just like the unknown suffering of this small creature. Imagining that his suffering, his intellect, and his concept of good and evil were terribly important to someone besides himself, he had deliberately yet senselessly woven an intricate fabric connecting himself and the world. Only the moment of death would tear this net apart and leave him alone, without reward or result.

Once again he remembered Semyonov and the late student's indifference to his most cherished thoughts and goals, those that had affected him, Yury, so deeply, as well as millions of others just like him; suddenly his innocent and candid admiration of life was profoundly eclipsed by pleasure, by women, by the moon, and by the nightingale's song—all of which had so struck him and painfully wounded him the day after his despondent conversation with Semyonov.

At that time he didn't understand how Semyonov could attribute importance to such trifles as a boat ride or to women's lovely bodies after he had consciously rejected these same profound thoughts and elevated concepts; but now Yury easily understood that it couldn't be otherwise. All these trifles constituted life—real life, full of enthralling experience and overwhelming enjoyment, and all great concepts were merely empty, determining nothing in the inscrutable mystery of life and death, a mere combination of words and thoughts. As important and conclusive as they might seem, afterward there would come—there couldn't help but come—other words and thoughts no less meaningful and definitive.

This conclusion was so uncharacteristic of Yury and had so unexpectedly emerged from his reflections on good and evil that it dismayed him. A great void opened before him, and for one second there dawned on him such an intense sensation of clarity and freedom, like the feeling of floating in air while asleep, that he wanted to take wing. But Yury felt alarmed. With all his might he collected his customary thoughts and concepts about life, and the bold sensation that had so frightened him disappeared. Everything became obscure and complicated again.

For a moment Yury was willing to admit that the meaning of real life lay in the realization of freedom; that it was natural and consequently good to live only for pleasure; and that even Ryazantsev's point of view regarding the unity of a lower order, aspiring to as many sexual pleasures as possible as the most urgent of life's sensations, was more integral and logical than his own. But, according to this argument, he had to admit that his concepts of debauchery and purity were like dry leaves covering the young, fresh grass, and that even the most romantic, chaste young women, even Lyalya and Karsavina, had the right to plunge freely deep into the stream of sensual pleasures. Yury was frightened by this idea, regarded it as obscene and blasphemous, was horrified that it aroused him, and banished it from his mind and heart with his customary oppressive, stern words.

Hmm, yes, he thought, gazing up at the infinite, dazzling sky, strewn with stars. Life is sensation, but people aren't irrational beasts; they must direct their desires toward the good, and not allow those desires to gain control over them. . . . What if there's a God above the stars? Yury recalled, and a terrifying feeling of vague reverence held him to the earth. Without tearing himself away, he gazed at the large shining star in the tail of the Great Bear and involuntarily recalled how the peasant Kuzma in the watermelon field had referred to this constellation as the "cart."

For some reason, once again involuntarily, this recollection seemed inappropriate and even somewhat offensive. He started to gaze at the garden, which, after the starry sky, now seemed totally black, and once again he thought: If the world were to be deprived of female purity, which resembles the first flowers of spring, still so timid yet grand and touching, what would remain that is still sacred to mankind?"

He imagined thousands of fair, chaste young women, like spring flowers in the sunlight under blossoming trees. Their undeveloped breasts, rounded shoulders, supple arms, and graceful hips, bending timidly and mysteriously, flashed before his eyes, and his head began to swim in sweet ecstasy.

Yury slowly drew his hand across his forehead and suddenly came to his senses.

My nerves are strained. I must get some sleep.

Feeling unsatisfied, distraught, and still languishing over his voluptuous vision, Yury, his soul filled with undirected malice, headed home, all his movements jerky and abrupt.

Lying in bed and trying in vain to fall asleep, he remembered Ryazantsev and Lyalya.

Why precisely am I so upset that Lyalya isn't Ryazantsev's first and only love?

This question didn't yield an answer, but the image of Zina Karsavina floated before his eyes, stirring gentle tenderness and soothing his overheated brain with inexpressible kindness; however much he tried to obscure this feeling, it became clear to him just why he needed it: she was pure and unsullied.

And I do love her! Yury thought for the first time; this idea suddenly banished all others and brought tears of tenderness to his eyes at this new feeling. But by the next minute Yury was asking himself with bitter sarcasm: Yet haven't I loved other women before her? True, I didn't know of her existence, but then Ryazantsev didn't know about Lyalya either. Back then, at that time, each of us thought the woman we wished to possess was the "real one," the most necessary and appropriate choice. We were mistaken then, but perhaps we're also mistaken now! That means either we preserve our chastity perpetually or allow ourselves absolute freedom . . . and, of course, allow women to enjoy love and passion. But really . . . Yury interrupted his own thought. With Ryazantsev . . . It's not so bad that he loved before, but that now he wants to go on enjoying several women. I'm not like that!

This thought filled Yury with a feeling of pride and purity, but only for an instant; the next moment he remembered the feeling that had overwhelmed him at his vision of thousands of nubile, chaste young women permeated by sunlight, and he was ashamed of his absolute inability to control himself and cope with this turmoil of feelings and thoughts.

Yury felt uncomfortable lying on his right side, so he turned over clumsily.

The fact is, he thought, none of the women I've known could satisfy me for my whole life. . . . So what I call real love is unrealizable; it's simply foolish to dream about it!

Yury grew uncomfortable on his left side and, getting his sticky, sweaty body all tangled up in the warm sheet, he turned over again. He felt hot and uncomfortable. His head began to ache.

Chastity is an ideal, but mankind would perish in the realization of that ideal. The thought occurred to him unexpectedly. That means it's absurd. But . . . then all life's absurd! Yury almost said it aloud, clenching his teeth with such malice that gold circles spun before his eyes.

And until early morning, lying in a painful, uncomfortable position, with the dull ache of despair in his soul, Yury turned these weighty, contradictory thoughts over in his mind.

At last, in an effort to extricate himself, he began to persuade himself that he was a bad, excessively voluptuous, egotistical man, and that his doubts were simply the result of his hidden lust. But this idea merely oppressed his soul even more, and gave rise in his mind to a multitude of disparate thoughts; his tormented state was finally ended by the question:

Why, in the final analysis, am I tormenting myself like this?

And with a feeling of disgust for the very process of any and all self-examination, Yury fell asleep in a dull state of nervous exhaustion.

 XV

Lyalya wept in her room until, her face buried in the pillow, she finally fell asleep. She awoke the next morning with a headache and swollen eyes.

Her first thought was that she shouldn't cry because Ryazantsev was coming for dinner later that day and he wouldn't want to see her looking so unattractive after her tears. But she recalled that it didn't make any difference now because everything was over between them and she could no longer love him; she felt both acute pain and ardent love, and began crying once more.

"How vile, how despicable!" she whispered, feeling that she was choking from the endless stream of bitter tears. "Why? Why?" she repeated; in her soul she felt endless grief that happiness had eluded her once and for all.

She was surprised and disgusted that Ryazantsev could lie to her so easily and consistently.

And it wasn't only him; they all lied, she thought in bewilderment. Everyone, absolutely everyone, was delighted at the prospect of our marriage and told me that he was a fine, upstanding man! No, as a matter of fact, they weren't lying; they merely didn't think it . . . wrong. How revolting!

Lyalya found it repulsive to view her customary surroundings, filled as they were with people who now disgusted her. She leaned her face against the windowpane and through tears looked out into the garden.

It was gloomy outside and rain was falling steadily. Large drops were beating loudly against the glass and running down it quickly; Lyalya found it hard to tell whether it was her tears or the raindrops obscuring her view of the garden. It was damp out there; the wet, drooping leaves looked pale and shuddered despondently. The tree trunks looked black from the rain; the wet grass was flattened and lay strewn across the muddy ground.

It seemed to her that her entire life was miserable, her future bleak, her past dismal.

The maid came in to summon her to tea, but for a long time Lyalya was unable to understand her words. Then, in the dining room, she was embarrassed when her father began talking to her. He seemed to be addressing her with special pity, as if everyone already knew that her beloved had deceived her so obscenely and horridly. She heard this offensive pity in each of his words and then went back to her room. She sat down again at the window; and staring out into the weeping, gray garden, she began to think:

Why did he dissemble? Why did he hurt me? Does it mean he doesn't love me? No, Tolya loves me . . . and I love him! So what's the problem? But he did deceive me; he's loved all sorts of nasty women before! And they loved him. . . . As much as I do? Lyalya asked herself with naive, ardent curiosity. What nonsense! What does that have to do with me? But he deceived me about them, and now everything's finished! Poor, unhappy me! But no, it does affect me: he was deceiving me! What if he'd confessed? It wouldn't matter! It's vile . . . he's already caressed other women like me, perhaps done even more. . . . It's terrible! How unhappy I am!

A little frog hops along the path, his tiny legs outstretched! Lyalya sang to herself silently, as she spotted a small, gray ball hopping timidly along the slippery, wet path.

Yes, I'm unhappy, and everything's finished! she thought again when the frog had disappeared into the grass. It was so wonderful for me, so nice, but for him it was just an old habit. That's why he always avoided talking about his past! That's why he always appeared to be thinking about something else. . . . He was thinking: I know all this, I know everything. I know just what you're feeling. I know exactly what you'll do next. Meanwhile, I . . . How shameful, disgusting. . . . Never, never will I love anyone ever again.

Lyalya wept and passed her head against the cold windowsill, watching through tears the clouds drifting across the sky.

And Tolya's coming for dinner today! she suddenly recalled with a shiver and jumped up from her seat. What will I say to him? What does one say in such circumstances?

Lyalya opened her mouth and directed her frightened, uncomprehending gaze at the wall.

I must ask Yury! she thought and then calmed down.

Dear Yury! He's so honest and good, she thought with tender tears in her eyes; and then, just as impetuously as ever, without delay she set off to find him.

But Shafrov was with him and they were talking about some business or other. Lyalya stood in the doorway, unsure what to do.

"Hello," she said dreamily.

"Hello," said Shafrov, returning her greeting. "Come and join us, Lyudmila Nikolaevna. We're talking about something where your help is very much needed."

Lyalya, her face still uncomprehending, sat down at the table and automatically began leafing through the green and red pamphlets spread out on it.

"You see, this is the point," Shafrov said, turning to her with a look indicating that he was about to launch into a long explanation. "Our comrades in Kursk find themselves in a desperate financial situation . . . and we must provide them with immediate assistance. So I've come up with the idea of organizing a concert . . . eh?"

At the addition of this familiar "eh?" Lyalya suddenly remembered why she'd come. She glanced over toward Yury with trust and hope.

"Why not?" she replied mechanically. "It's a very good idea," she said, surprised that Yury wasn't returning her glance.

After Lyalya's tears the day before and his own late-night reflections, Yury felt crushed and unprepared to answer her. He had expected that his sister would come to seek his advice, but he was completely incapable of arriving at any satisfactory solution. Just as he couldn't take back his words, dissuade Lyalya, and urge her back to Ryazantsev, so he couldn't inflict the decisive blow on her innocent, childlike happiness.

"So we've decided," continued Shafrov, moving closer to Lyalya, as if the matter were becoming more complicated and involved, "to invite Lida Sanina and Zina Karsavina to sing. At first they'll perform solos, then a duet. One's a contralto, the other a soprano, so it'll be very nice. Then I'll play the violin. Then Zarudin will sing while Tanarov accompanies him."

"Will the officers really participate in that kind of concert?" Lyalya asked just as mechanically, thinking about something quite different.

"Oh, yes, they will!" cried Shafrov with a wave of his arm. "If Sanina agrees, the others won't be left behind. Besides, Zarudin's glad to perform anywhere as long as he can sing. That will attract other officers, and we'll draw a full house."

"Invite Zina Karsavina," advised Lyalya, glancing at her brother with melancholy bewilderment. He can't have forgotten, she thought. How can he go on about this stupid concert, while I . . .

"That's just what I said!" replied Shafrov in astonishment.

"Oh, yes!" said Lyalya, smiling weakly. "Well, what about Lida Sanina? But you've mentioned her, too."

"Yes, of course I have," said Shafrov, nodding his head. "But who else is there, eh?"

"I don't know," replied Lyalya absent-mindedly. "I have a bit of a headache."

Yury threw her a quick glance; then, with compassion, he turned back to his pamphlets. With her pale little face and her large darkened eyes, she seemed surprisingly frail and sad to him.

Why, oh, why did I say all that to her? he wondered. I don't understand it myself, and it's an infernal problem for everyone, but for her gentle soul . . . Why did I say it?

He was ready to tear his hair out.

"Miss," said the maid from the doorway. "Anatoly Pavlovich is here."

Yury glanced apprehensively at Lyalya once more, and, meeting her frozen gaze so full of suffering, turned to Shafrov and said absent-mindedly:

"Have you ever read Charles Bradlaugh?"[15]

"Yes, I have. I read some of his works with Dubova and Karsavina. Quite interesting."

"Yes. . . . Have they come back?"

"Yes."

"When?" asked Yury with hidden agitation.

"The day before yesterday."

"Really?" asked Yury, watching to see what Lyalya would do. He felt excruciatingly ashamed and afraid, as if he'd deceived her.

Lyalya stood there for a moment, fiddled with something on the table, then moved indecisively toward the door.

What have I done? Yury wondered with sincere emotion, listening to her unusual, uneven footsteps.

Lyalya went into the living room, feeling that everything inside her had frozen in anxious and grievous bewilderment. It was as if she'd gotten lost

---

[15] Charles Bradlaugh (1833–91), English social reformer, freethinker, and radical member of Parliament, was notorious for his atheism, republicanism, and advocacy of birth control.

in a deep, dark forest. On the way she glanced into a mirror and caught a glimpse of her darkened, agonized face.

Well, so what? Let him see! she thought.

Ryazantsev was standing in the middle of the dining room, saying to Nikolai Yegorovich in his cheerful, aristocratic, self-assured manner:

"It's a strange thing, of course, but totally harmless."

At the sound of his voice Lyalya winced and felt as if something had snapped inside her. When Ryazantsev saw her, he abruptly broke off what he was saying, went up to her, and stretched out both arms, as if wanting to embrace her, but he did it so that she alone understood his intention.

Lyalya glanced up at his face; her lips were trembling. She withdrew her hand in silence and with some effort; then she went through into the living room and opened the glass door onto the balcony. Ryazantsev watched her with serene surprise.

"My Lyudmila Nikolaevna seems to be angry about something," he said with jocular tenderness to Nikolai Yegorovich.

Nikolai Yegorovich burst out laughing.

"Well then, go and make up with her!"

"There's nothing else to be done!" said Ryazantsev with a comic sigh, and followed Lyalya out onto the balcony.

It was still raining and a faint dripping sound filled the air. But the clouds were thinning above and the sky was brightening.

Resting her cheek against a cold, wet wooden pillar, Lyalya stretched her head out in the rain and her hair quickly became soaked.

"My princess is angry. . . . Lyalechka!" said Ryazantsev and drew her to him, pressing his lips into her fragrant wet hair.

Because of this contact, so familiar and delightful, everything melted in Lyalya's heart; before she had managed to understand anything, almost involuntarily her arms wound around Ryazantsev's strong neck and, between prolonged, intoxicating kisses, she said:

"I'm terribly angry with you . . . you vile man!"

And it was even strange to her that now nothing was terrible, painful, or irreparable; in the final analysis, what business was it of hers? She merely wanted to love and be loved by this big, tall, handsome man.

But during dinner she was embarrassed to look at Yury, who was staring at his sister in perplexity; seizing the moment, she whispered to him imploringly, "I'm a vile woman."

Yury smirked. In the depths of his soul he felt glad that everything had ended so fortuitously, but he tried to foster in himself contempt for this philistine tolerance and philistine happiness. He retired to his room and sat there alone almost until evening; at twilight, when the sky grew brighter and cleared, he took his gun and went out hunting, to the place where he'd been with Ryazantsev the day before. He tried not to think about what had happened.

After the rain the marsh had come alive. He could hear a variety of new sounds; first here, then there, the grass stirred as if it were alive with the mysterious life hidden within it. Frogs croaked in a friendly chorus with all their might, and a bird sang some uncomplicated, squeaky notes sounding like trrr . . . trrr. . . . Ducks quacked boisterously nearby in the wet sedge, but didn't come into range. Yury really didn't feel like shooting. He tossed the gun over his shoulder and returned home, listening to the crystal-clear sounds and gazing at the deep colors of the evening, first dark, then light.

Good, he thought. Everything's good, only man is abominable.

From afar he noticed a little fire burning near the watermelon field and the illuminated figures of Kuzma and Sanin once again, sitting near the fire.

Does he live here or what? Yury wondered with surprise and curiosity.

Kuzma was saying something and laughing, waving his arms around. Sanin was also laughing. The fire, still pink, not yet red as at night, was burning like a little candle; overhead the sky was strewn with stars twinkling serenely and softly. There was a smell of fresh earth and rain-soaked grass.

For some reason Yury was afraid he'd be noticed and felt sad that he couldn't simply join them; between them and him there stood something incomprehensible, unreal, and empty, but absolutely insurmountable, like space devoid of air.

He felt completely alone. The world, with all its evening colors, little fires, stars, people, and sounds, so airy and bright, stood apart from Yury, who felt small and dark inside, like a dark room in which something was pining and weeping. A feeling of lonely anguish so overwhelmed him that when he walked past the watermelon field, the hundreds of melons gleaming white in the twilight reminded him of human skulls strewn across a plain.

## XVI

Summer was at its peak, overflowing with warmth and light; a golden haze seemed to flow and quiver between the dazzling blue sky and the earth, exhausted by the intense heat. Trees stood sleepily in the warm haze, languishing from the heat, their motionless leaves drooping; their short, feeble shadows fell helplessly on the warm, dusty earth.

But it was cool inside. Light from the garden reflected on the ceilings was a soft green; the curtains swayed slightly at the windows and appeared strangely alive while everything else was motionless in the hot stillness.

Zarudin, his white, high-collared jacket unbuttoned, was smoking a cigarette with a special, carefully cultivated, easygoing indifference, displaying his large white teeth. Meanwhile Tanarov, soaked with perspiration, wearing only a shirt and riding breeches, reclined on a sofa and furtively followed Zarudin's every movement with his small black eyes. He was badly in need of 50 rubles and had already asked Zarudin twice for that amount; he didn't want to ask him a third time and waited anxiously to see if Zarudin would remember.

Zarudin did remember, but in the course of the last month had lost 700 rubles and begrudged him the money.

He already owes me 250 rubles as it is, he thought without looking at Tanarov, gradually growing more irritated by the heat and his annoyance. It's odd, upon my word! Of course, we maintain good relations, but isn't he ashamed of himself? If he'd just apologize for owing me so much money! I won't give him another kopeck! he added mentally, with cruel delight.

The orderly, a small, freckled man, came into the room, his clothes covered with bits of down. He stood to crooked, limp attention and without glancing at Zarudin, announced: "Y'excellency, allow me to inform you: you asked for beer, but there's none left."

Zarudin glanced involuntarily at Tanarov with increased irritation.

Well, that's that! he thought. Damn it. This is really becoming intolerable! . . . He knows I haven't a kopeck to spare, yet he still orders a beer!. . .

"The vodka's running out too," the orderly added.

"Well, go to hell. . . . You have two rubles left in there; go buy what we need." Zarudin dismissed him with growing annoyance.

"That's impossible. There's no money left."

"What? You're lying!" exclaimed Zarudin, and he stopped pacing.

"Since your honor ordered me to pay the laundress, I gave her one ruble seventy. I left thirty kopecks on the table in the study, y'excellency."

"Oh, yes," Tanarov replied with feigned indifference, blushing and becoming flustered. "Yesterday I told him to . . . it was so awkward, you know. . . . The old woman's been waiting a whole week. . . ."

Red blotches appeared on Zarudin's close-shaven cheeks and his cheekbones moved menacingly beneath his thin skin. He paced the room in silence and suddenly stopped before Tanarov.

"Listen," he said in a most offensive tone, his voice trembling strangely. "I'd like to request that you allow me to run my own financial affairs. . . ."

Tanarov reddened and grew agitated.

"I don't understand . . . such a trifle . . ." he muttered in an offended tone, shrugging his shoulders.

"It's not a matter of trifles," Zarudin replied with cruel enjoyment, as if taking revenge. "It's the principle of the thing. . . . Why, tell me, please!"

"I . . ." Tanarov was about to begin.

"No, I must ask you to let me run my own affairs!" Zarudin interrupted him insistently in the same threatening tone. "You could've told me. . . . This is now very inconvenient!"

Tanarov moved his lips helplessly and looked down, nervously fingering his mother-of-pearl cigarette holder. Zarudin waited a little longer for an answer, then turned sharply, rattled his keys, and reached into a drawer.

"Here, go buy what you need," he said to the orderly angrily, but in a calmer tone, handing him 100 rubles.

"Yes, sir," the man answered and, turning to his left, withdrew from the room.

Slowly, with emotion, Zarudin locked the cash box with his keys and closed the drawer. Tanarov managed to catch a glimpse of this box containing the 50 rubles he needed; he watched with his timid, mournful eyes and then, with a sigh, modestly began to light a cigarette. He felt terribly insulted and at the same time was afraid to express this feeling lest he make Zarudin even angrier.

What's two rubles to him, he thought, when he knows how much I need the money?

Zarudin paced the room, his heart pounding with irritation, but little by little he began to calm down. When the orderly brought in the beer, Zarudin himself drank a glass of the icy, foamy brew with enjoyment, and, licking the ends of his mustache, said as if nothing had happened:

"Lidka came to see me again yesterday. She's an interesting woman, you know! What fire!"

Tanarov, still offended, said nothing.

Zarudin took no notice and continued to pace the room, his eyes laughing merrily at some private recollection. His healthy, strong body was overcome by the heat, and he was aroused by ardent, exciting thoughts. All of a sudden he stopped and burst into loud laughter, as if he were neighing.

"You know, yesterday I wanted to . . ." He uttered a special obscene word, terribly demeaning to women. "At first she resisted. You know, sometimes her eyes fill with such proud fire. . . ."

Tanarov, feeling his own body tensing swiftly and greedily, involuntarily relaxed his face into an unseemly lecherous grin.

"But then it was . . . I was almost overcome with spasms of delight!" Zarudin concluded, shuddering at the painfully clear recollection.

"You're a lucky bastard, damn it all!" Tanarov exclaimed enviously.

"Zarudin, are you home?" called Ivanov's booming voice from the street. "May I come in?"

Zarudin was startled by the unexpectedness of it; as always, he was afraid that someone might have overheard his story about Lida Sanina. But Ivanov had called from the lane beyond the fence and couldn't even be seen.

"Yes, I'm home!" cried Zarudin through the window. The sound of voices and laughter could be heard in the hallway, as if a large crowd were invading the house. Ivanov, Novikov, Captain Malinovsky, two other officers, and Sanin had all arrived.

"Hurrah!" cried Malinovsky deafeningly, crossing the threshold sideways, his crimson face glowing with ample, quivering jowls and a bushy mustache looking like two sheaves of rye. "Greetings, boys!"

Oh, hell. Here goes another twenty-five rubles! Zarudin thought with irritation, blinking his eyes. But more than anything he feared that someone might not regard him as a most generous, congenial, affluent man; so he smiled broadly and cried:

"Where on earth are you all coming from? Welcome! . . . Hey, Cherepanov! Bring us some vodka and whatever else there is! Run down to the club; tell them to send us a case of beer. You do want beer, don't you, gentlemen? It's so hot!"

When the vodka and beer arrived, the noise grew even louder. They guffawed and roared with laughter, carried away by their rowdy merrymaking, and they all drank and shouted. Only Novikov remained gloomy, and something unpleasant kept flaring up on his usually gentle and easygoing face.

Yesterday he'd become aware of something he hadn't known before, even though the whole town was already talking about it, and a feeling of unbearable injury and bitter, jealous humiliation had overwhelmed him at first.

It can't be! That's nonsense! Mere gossip! he thought at the outset, and his brain refused to imagine the proud, unapproachably beautiful Lida, with whom he was so innocently and reverently in love, engaged in disgracefully filthy intimacy with Zarudin, whom he'd always considered infinitely lower and duller than he was. But then ferocious, bestial jealousy arose from the bottom of his soul and drove everything else out. He felt a moment of bitter despair, then a terrible, almost elemental hatred of Lida and even more of Zarudin. This feeling was so unusual for his gentle, flaccid soul that it proved unbearable and demanded an outlet. All night he hovered on the morbid edge of tormenting self-pity and dark thoughts of suicide; toward morning he somehow calmed down and was left with only a bizarre, malicious desire to set eyes on Zarudin again.

Now, amid the noisy shouting of drunken voices, he sat off to one side, mechanically drinking beer after beer and with every ounce of his strained consciousness following every movement Zarudin made, as if he were a wild beast encountering another in the woods, pretending he had noticed nothing but prepared to spring.

Everything—the smile with its display of white teeth, the good looks, the laughter and Zarudin's voice—struck with sharp blows against the torment that suffused Novikov's entire being.

"Zarudin," said the tall, skinny officer with exceptionally long arms dangling in front of him, "I've brought you a book."

Through the noise and commotion Novikov instantly caught Zarudin's name and voice. As if everyone else had fallen silent, he alone spoke:

"What book?"

"Tolstoy's *About Women*,"[16] replied the tall officer precisely and with pride, as if delivering a military report. It was clear from his long, colorless face that he was glad to be reading and discussing Tolstoy.

"So you read Tolstoy?" asked Ivanov, observing his proud, naive expression.

"Von Deitz is a Tolstoyan!" exclaimed the drunken Malinovsky and then burst out laughing.

Zarudin picked up the slim red volume, flipped through a few pages, and asked, "Is it interesting?"

"You'll see!" Von Deitz replied, transported with delight. "He's got a head on his shoulders, I tell you! It seems as if I knew it all myself. . . ."

"But why, tell me, should Viktor Sergeevich read Tolstoy when his own views about women are already so fully formed?" Novikov asked in a low voice, without raising his eyes from his glass.

"How did you reach that conclusion?" Zarudin asked cautiously, instinctively sensing an attack but not yet sure about it.

Novikov was silent for a while. Everything in him was straining to cry out and to smash Zarudin's handsome, self-satisfied face, to knock him off his feet, to kick him in a wild burst of anger, thus allowing his malice free reign. But the words failed to leave his mouth; feeling that he was saying things he shouldn't, and suffering and agonizing even more at this awareness, Novikov smirked and said:

"It's enough to take one look at you to reach that conclusion."

The strange, menacing sound of his voice cut through the general commotion and at once everything fell silent, as it does just before a murder. Ivanov realized what was happening.

"It seems to me that . . ." Zarudin began coldly, his expression changing slightly, but he immediately regained control of himself, as if mounting a familiar horse.

"Come, gentlemen, gentlemen. . . . What's all this about?" asked Ivanov.

"Leave them alone; let them fight it out!" interjected Sanin, smiling.

"It doesn't seem like that to me, but that's the way it is," Novikov said, still not raising his eyes from his glass and maintaining the same tone of voice.

But a living wall of shouts and waving arms, of unnaturally broad grinning faces and imprecations, rose up between them. Zarudin was pushed back by Von Deitz and Malinovsky, Novikov by Ivanov and the other officer. Tanarov began to fill empty glasses and to shout something, addressing no one in particular. There arose a false, artificially merry hubbub, and Novikov suddenly felt that he lacked the strength to go on. He smirked foolishly, glancing at the faces of Ivanov and the officer trying to distract him with conversation, and then thought in dismay:

What am I doing? I should strike him! Walk right up to him and hit him!

---

[16] He is probably referring to chap. 40, "On Men's and Women's Work," of Tolstoy's didactic essay *What Then Must We Do?* (1882).

Otherwise I'll be left looking foolish. Everyone's already guessed that I was looking for a quarrel.

But instead of doing that, he listened with feigned attention to what Ivanov and Von Deitz were saying.

"As far as his view of women is concerned, you know, I'm not entirely in agreement with Tolstoy," the officer said smugly.

"In the first place, woman is the female of the species!" Novikov replied. "For every thousand men you can find at least one who deserves to be called a human being; whereas among women . . . there's not even one! They're just naked, pink, plump monkeys without tails. That's all there is to it!"

"Well said!" Von Deitz observed with pleasure.

And true! Novikov thought bitterly.

"Hey, dear friend!" Ivanov replied, waving his arm in front of Von Deitz's nose. "Tell folks this: 'I say unto you that any woman who looks at a man with lust has already committed adultery with him in her heart.'[17] Many will think they're hearing a very original pronouncement."

Von Deitz burst into hoarse laughter, sounding like a barking hunting dog, and looked at Ivanov with envy. He didn't really understand the joke: he was merely envious because he hadn't said anything as clever.

Novikov unexpectedly extended his hand to him.

"What?" Von Deitz asked in surprise, glancing at the outstretched hand with curiosity and anticipation.

Novikov made no reply.

"Where are you off to?" Sanin asked.

Novikov was still silent. He felt that in another moment the sobs mounting in his chest would burst out.

"I know what's wrong with you. To hell with it!" said Sanin.

Novikov glanced at him with pitiful eyes, his lips trembling; then, with a dismissive wave of his arm, he left without saying good-bye. He felt agonizingly impotent, like a man who doesn't understand his own torment; to comfort himself he thought: Well, what of it? What would I have proved by smashing that scoundrel in the face? It'd only have led to a vulgar fight. It wouldn't even have been worth getting my hands dirty!

But the feeling of unrequited jealousy and revolting impotence didn't pass; Novikov returned home in deep anguish, buried his face in the pillow, and lay there most of the day, suffering because he could do nothing else.

"Do you want to play macao?"[18] asked Malinovsky.

"Why not?" Ivanov agreed.

The orderly set up the card table; the green felt cover smiled at them merrily. Concentrated animation took hold of them; tapping his short hairy fin-

---

[17] Ivanov has reversed the terms of Matt. 5:28: ". . . whosoever looketh on a woman to lust after her hath committed adultery with her already in his heart."

[18] Macao was a card game of Hungarian origin.

gers smartly, Malinovsky began to deal. The colorful cards were gracefully distributed in regular circles around the small green table, silver rubles rang out with a resonant clink hand after hand, and from all sides fingers pounced on them like greedy spiders, gathering in the money. Only brief words and monotonous exclamations could be heard, expressing either studied vexation or pleasure. Zarudin didn't have much luck. He stubbornly staked 15 rubles on each hand and lost every time. Sinister blotches of random irritation appeared on his handsome face. During the last month he'd already lost 700 rubles and now he didn't even want to calculate his losses. His mood spread to the others. Von Deitz and Malinovsky exchanged harsh words.

"I staked on the side," Von Deitz said in an irritated but restrained tone of voice, sincerely surprised that the tipsy, coarse Malinovsky would dare argue with so clever and decent a man as he, Von Deitz.

"What are you saying?" Malinovsky cried rudely. "The hell you did! When I win, you always say you staked on the side, but when I lose . . ."

"Well, excuse me!" Von Deitz said in bad Russian, as he always did when he was upset.

"I won't excuse anything. Take it back! Go on, take it. . ."

"But I'm telling you!" Von Deitz cried in a thin voice.

"Gentlemen! What the hell is going on here?" Zarudin burst out suddenly, flinging down his cards.

But he was immediately frightened by his own shrill shouting, the drunken, brawling men, the cards, and the bottles—by all the circumstances of a vulgar army drinking bout—because a new face had appeared in the doorway.

A tall, thin gentleman in a loose-fitting white suit and a very high, tight collar paused on the threshold in astonishment, searching for Zarudin with his eyes.

"Ah, Pavel Lvovich! What brings you here?" the flushed Zarudin exclaimed, rising hastily to greet the newcomer.

The gentleman entered the room hesitantly; everyone noticed first how his very white shoes stepped into the swamp of beer puddles, corks, and crushed cigarette butts. He was dressed entirely in white, clean and scented; amid the clouds of tobacco smoke and drunken red faces he would have looked like a lily in the marsh if he hadn't been so helplessly frail, so enduringly cunning, and if he hadn't had such a tiny face with a puny mustache and bad teeth.

"Where have you been? Just come from ole Piter?"[19] Zarudin asked with excessive solicitude, wondering timidly whether it was all right to say "Piter," and grasping his hand firmly.

"I got here only yesterday," the man in white replied at last; his voice was self-assured but weak, like the crowing of a cock being strangled.

---

[19] "Piter" was an affectionate nickname for St. Petersburg used by its inhabitants.

"My colleagues," Zarudin introduced the rest, "Von Deitz, Malinovsky, Tanarov, Sanin, Ivanov. . . . Gentlemen, Pavel Lvovich Voloshin."

Voloshin bowed slightly.

"We'll make a note of that," the tipsy Ivanov replied, much to Zarudin's horror.

"Over here, Pavel Lvovich. . . . Would you like some wine, or perhaps some beer?"

Voloshin sat down gingerly in an armchair; his white form looked feeble against the harsh, checkered upholstery.

"I've come for only a few minutes. Don't go to any trouble!" he replied with a squeamish chill, surveying the company.

"No, that's impossible. I'll send for some white wine. You like it, do you?"

Zarudin rushed out into the hallway.

Why did this swine have to pick today? he wondered in annoyance, instructing his orderly to fetch some wine. Now Voloshin will tell all his buddies in Piter such tales that I'll never be allowed into any decent house again!

Meanwhile Voloshin, without concealment, as if feeling immeasurably superior to everyone else, continued to examine the company. The glassy gaze of his gray eyes was blatantly inquiring, as if he were observing some strange little beasts. Sanin's height, the obvious strength of his muscular shoulders, and his clothes attracted Voloshin's attention.

An interesting type. He must be very strong! he reflected with the genuine deference that all small, weak men feel when confronted with large, strong men, and he wanted to speak to him.

But Sanin, leaning his chest against the windowsill, was gazing into the garden.

Voloshin choked on his words; the thin, disjointed sound of his own voice embarrassed him.

What hooligans! he thought.

At that moment Zarudin returned.

He sat down next to Voloshin and began asking him about Petersburg and Voloshin's factory, so that the others would understand how wealthy and important a man this guest was. An expression of strange, petty self-satisfaction was reflected on the handsome face of this large, strong animal.

"Everything's the same as always, as you see," Voloshin said offhandedly. "And how've you been?"

"Me? Just vegetating," said Zarudin, sighing mournfully.

Voloshin was silent and looked disdainfully at the ceiling, on which green reflections of the garden were silently moving.

"We've always had only one form of recreation here," Zarudin continued, deftly including with a broad gesture the bottles, cards, and his guests.

"Yes-s-s . . ." Voloshin drawled indistinctly; in his tone Zarudin heard: And you're just the same!

"Well, I must be going. . . . I'm staying in the hotel on the boulevard. We'll see each other again, won't we?" Voloshin said, changing his tone and standing up.

Just then the orderly came in, stood lamely to attention, and announced, "Y'excellency, a young lady's come."

"What?" Zarudin asked with a shudder.

"Yes, sir."

"Oh, yes. . . I know," Zarudin said hastily, his eyes wandering awkwardly, feeling a momentary presentiment of something unpleasant grip his heart.

Could it be Lidka? he wondered in surprise.

Voloshin's eyes flared with greedy, curious fire, and his feeble body became agitated under his loose-fitting white suit.

"Yes. . . . Well, good-bye!" he said with emphasis, baring his teeth in a grin. "You haven't changed a bit!"

Zarudin smirked complacently but apprehensively.

Escorted by Zarudin, Voloshin left the room quickly, his white shoes flashing and his sharp eyes darting around.

Zarudin returned.

"Well, gentlemen. . . . How's the game going? Tanarov, take over for me; I'll be right back," he said hurriedly, his eyes still wandering.

"Lies!" the bovine-looking Malinovsky replied, now completely intoxicated. "We'll see what sort of woman you have here!"

But Tanarov took him by the shoulder and forcibly sat him back down at the table. The rest of them sat down quickly too, trying for some reason to avoid looking at Zarudin. Sanin sat down too, chuckling in earnest.

He guessed that Lida had come to see Zarudin, and a vague feeling of jealous pity for his lovely and now obviously unhappy sister arose within him.

## XVII

Lida Sanina sat sideways on Zarudin's bed, absent-mindedly twisting and crumpling her kerchief.

Even Zarudin was struck by the changes her appearance had undergone: not a trace remained of the proud, elegant, strong young lady of before; before him sat a stooped, hysterical, painfully weak woman. Her face had grown thin and pale; her dark eyes wandered from side to side in agitation.

When Zarudin entered, she raised her eyes quickly to meet his, then looked down again; he felt instinctively that she was afraid of him. A feeling of completely unexpected malice and extreme irritation arose within him.

He locked the door firmly and walked rudely and directly over to her, not at all as he had done previously.

"You're an astonishing person," he began, hardly controlling himself; for some reason he felt a powerful desire to strike her. "I have a houseful of people. Your brother's here. Couldn't you have picked a better time? I swear to God . . ."

She raised her dark eyes with a strange flash and, as always, Zarudin grew frightened of his own harshness; he bared his white teeth in an obsequious grin, and, taking Lida by the hand, sat down next to her.

"Well, it doesn't really matter. It's just that I'm afraid for you. I'm glad to see you. I've missed you."

Zarudin raised her slightly damp, warm hand with its subtle and exquisite perfume and kissed it just above her glove.

"Is that true?" Lida asked with an expression he didn't understand; once again she raised her eyes to his with a look that said, Is it true that you love me? You see how pitiful I am, how unhappy. . . not at all like I was before. I'm afraid of you and I'm aware of the full horror of my present humiliation, but I have no one else to rely on.

"Do you doubt it?" Zarudin replied uncertainly; a slight trace of coldness, difficult even for him to discern, touched these words. He raised her hand again and kissed it.

He experienced a strange, complex mixture of feelings and thoughts. Only two days ago, on this same white pillow, Lida's dark tresses had been spread and her pliant, warm, resilient body had been enveloped in a fit of passion; her lips were aflame, her whole being was overcome with the dark fire of inordinate pleasure. At that moment the whole world, thousands of women, all pleasures and all life merged for him in a desire to torment that burning, demanding, submissive body more voluptuously, more tenderly and brutally, more shamelessly and cruelly; and now suddenly he found her repulsive. He wanted to leave, push her away, no longer see or hear her. This desire was so great and inexorable that it even became painful for him to sit there. But at the same time a dark, aimless fear of her deprived him of his will and kept him there. With all his being he was aware that he wasn't bound to her; he controlled her by her own consent; he had promised her nothing and had given back what he'd received; meanwhile it seemed that he'd become deeply and hopelessly entangled in some sticky substance against which he was incapable of struggling. He was waiting for Lida to demand something of him; then either he'd have to agree to it or he'd do something revolting, difficult, and sordid. Zarudin felt completely powerless, as if all the bones had been removed from his arms and legs and as if he had a wet rag in his mouth instead of a tongue. This offended and infuriated him. He wanted to shout and tell her once and for all that she had no right to demand anything of him; but instead, his heart cringed in cowardly fashion and he uttered something he knew was foolish, unexpected, and totally inappropriate to the present situation:

" 'Ah, women, women,' as Shakespeare once said."[20]

Lida looked at him in fear. Suddenly a bright, merciless insight dawned upon her. In an instant she understood that she was lost: that she had given away the immense, pure, great gift she could bestow on a man who no longer existed. Her splendid life, irretrievable purity, and audacious pride had all been tossed at the feet of a vile, cowardly little beast who'd taken them without a word of gratitude for the delight and pleasure they had brought him and merely disgraced them in acts of dark, brutal lust. There was a moment when a fit of despair almost knocked her to the floor with uncontrollable weeping and wringing of hands, but with painful swiftness this despair was replaced by a surge of vengeful, bitter malice.

"Don't you see how stupid you are?" she said sharply and quietly through clenched teeth, leaning toward him.

These harsh words and her burning, malicious look were so unexpected coming from the elegant, feminine Lida that Zarudin even took a step back. But he didn't understand the full significance of her look and tried to make light of it.

"What a way to put it!" he said, astonished and humiliated, with eyes wide, and shrugged.

"I don't care how I put it!" Lida replied bitterly, wringing her hands help-lessly.

"Well, why such tragic emotion?" Zarudin asked with a frown. With sud-denly awakened passion, he unconsciously followed the curve of her round, finely molded hands and sloping shoulders.

This display of her despair and helplessness once more confirmed the cer-tainty of his own superiority.

It was as if they stood on a pair of scales and when one side descended, the other rose immediately. With poignant pleasure Zarudin felt that this young woman whom he'd unconsciously considered above him and whom he'd instinctively feared even during their voluptuous caresses was now act-ing, according to his understanding, a pitiful, ignominious role. He found this agreeable and comforting. Tenderly he took hold of her limp, powerless arms and almost drew her to him, now feeling aroused and beginning to breathe more heavily.

"Well now, that's enough. Nothing terrible happened!"

"You think so?" Lida asked ironically, growing stronger and staring at him with strange intensity.

"Yes, of course!" Zarudin answered. He tried to embrace her in a special, shamelessly arousing way, the power of which he knew well.

But she emanated coldness and his embrace slackened.

---

[20] Cleopatra's poignant exclamation over Antony's body in *Antony and Cleopatra* (1606–7), Act IV, sc. xv, l. 89: "Ah, women, women! come; we have no friend / But resolution, and the briefest end."

"Well, it'll be all right. What are you so angry about, my little kitten?" he asked with gentle reproach in his voice.

"Let me go. Here I . . . Leave me alone!"

With a fierce effort Lida tore herself away from his embrace.

Zarudin was mortally offended that his surge of passion was to no avail. Dammit all! he thought. So much for getting involved with women!

"What's the matter?" he asked her with irritation. Red blotches appeared on his cheeks.

It was as if this question clarified something for Lida: she suddenly covered her face with her hands and, completely unexpectedly for Zarudin, burst into tears. She wept the way old peasant women weep, burying her face in her hands, leaning her body forward, and emitting prolonged sobs. Locks of her long hair hung down over her moist face and she looked very unattractive. Zarudin was bewildered. Smiling and fearing that his smile might offend her, he tried pulling her hands away from her face, but Lida stubbornly and insistently resisted and kept on crying.

"Good Lord!" Zarudin exclaimed.

Once again he wanted to shout at her, seize her hand, say something harsh.

"Why on earth are you howling? So we had sex. So what? Is that so terrible? Why are you so upset now? Stop it!" he cried in a shrill voice and yanked at her arm.

Lida's head with its wet face and disheveled hair was jolted by his movement, and she suddenly fell silent, lowered her hands, folded them, and looked up at him with childish fear. The insane thought that now anyone could strike her suddenly flashed through her mind. But Zarudin grew weak once more and said in an insinuating, uncertain manner:

"Come on now, Lidochka. That's enough! You're the one to blame. Why make such scenes? So you've lost a great deal; on the other hand, you've enjoyed much happiness too. We'll never forget those . . ."

Lida started crying again.

"Stop it right now!" Zarudin shouted.

He paced the room, pulling at his mustache above his quivering lips.

It was quiet and the slender green branches of a tree swayed just outside the window, as if disturbed by a bird. With difficulty Zarudin regained control of himself, went up to Lida, and embraced her cautiously. But she freed herself immediately and with her protruding elbow accidentally struck him on the chin so hard that his teeth rattled.

"Oh, hell!" he exclaimed, rankled by the pain and even more by the fact that the sound was so unexpected and ridiculous.

Although she didn't notice the sound, she instinctively felt that Zarudin was ridiculous and, with her feminine cruelty, took advantage of it:

"What a way to put it!" she said, mimicking him.

"That's enough to drive anyone crazy!" Zarudin replied with apprehensive indignation. "If only I could find out what's really the matter!"

"You still don't know?" Lida drawled with the same irony.

There was a pause. Lida stared at him stubbornly, her face on fire. Suddenly Zarudin began to pale rapidly and evenly, as if his face were being covered in a gray coating.

"Well, now what? Why are you so silent? Say something. Console me!" Lida said, her voice swelling to a hysterical cry, frightening even her.

"Me?" Zarudin uttered, his lower lip trembling.

"Nobody else! You, unfortunately!" Lida almost shouted, choking on her rancorous and desperate tears.

A veneer of politeness, beauty, and gentleness seemed to fall from both him and her, and a wild, lacerating beast emerged more clearly from beneath.

A series of possibilities flashed like lightning through Zarudin's mind, as if a group of busy mice were scurrying around inside. His first thought was to break off with Lida as soon as possible, give her money for an abortion, and be done with it. But even though he considered this best for himself and absolutely essential, he didn't say so to her.

"I really never expected . . ." he muttered.

"Never expected!" she cried ferociously. "How did you dare never to expect it?"

"Lida . . . I never said I . . ." Zarudin replied, afraid of what he wanted to say and feeling that he might really say it.

Lida understood him without words. Her lovely face was distorted by the horror of despair. She let her arms drop limply and sat down again on the bed.

"So what shall I do now?" she asked with strange pensiveness, as if talking to herself. "Drown myself or what?"

"Come now! Why say that?"

"You know, Viktor Sergeevich," she said slowly, suddenly looking him right in the eye, "you wouldn't even object if I did drown myself!"

In her eyes and her lovely quivering mouth there was something so sad and terrible that Zarudin unintentionally looked away.

Lida stood up. She suddenly felt appalled and revolted that she could ever have conceived of him as her savior, or thought about spending her whole life with him. For some reason she wanted to shake her fist at him, express her contempt for him, take revenge for her humiliation; but she felt that if she were to start speaking, she'd burst into tears and humiliate herself even more. Her last ounce of pride, a vestige of the beautiful, strong, former Lida, restrained her; instead, in a controlled but clear and expressive manner, unexpected for both herself and Zarudin, she said:

"You—pig!"

She rushed out of the door, catching and tearing her lace sleeve on the handle.

The blood rushed to Zarudin's head. If she'd shouted "scoundrel" or "villain," he'd have taken it calmly, but the word "pig" was so hideous and so contradicted his image of himself that he was flabbergasted. Even the whites of his handsome, prominent eyes turned red. He smiled distractedly, shrugged, buttoned and then unbuttoned his jacket, and felt genuinely miserable.

But at the same time somewhere within his body a feeling of freedom and joy had begun to take root—that one way or another, everything was finished. The dastardly thought occurred to him that he might never meet another woman like Lida. For a moment he was annoyed that he'd lost such a lovely, luscious mistress, but then he ceased caring.

"To hell with her. There's plenty of others!"

He adjusted his jacket, lit a cigarette in his still trembling lips, and, successfully summoning up a nonchalant expression, returned to his guests.

 XVIII

The only gambler who was still paying attention to the game was the drunken Malinovsky.

Everyone else was extremely curious to find out who the woman was who'd come to see Zarudin and why she'd come. Those who guessed it was Lida Sanina were unconsciously jealous; their imagination prevented them from playing cards, as they pictured to themselves her unseen nakedness and her intimacy with Zarudin.

Sanin didn't sit there for long; he got up and said, "I don't want to play anymore. Good-bye."

"Wait a moment, my friend. Where are you off to?" asked Ivanov.

"I'm going to see what's going on in there," Sanin replied, pointing to the locked door.

Everyone burst out laughing at what they took to be a joke.

"That's enough clowning around! Sit down and have something to drink!" Ivanov said.

"You're the real clown," Sanin replied indifferently and left the room.

Emerging into the narrow lane where nettles grew in rich profusion, Sanin figured out where the windows in Zarudin's apartment must face, and, carefully tramping down the nettles, made his way to the fence and easily climbed it. At the top he nearly forgot why he'd climbed it because it was so pleasant to look down at the green grass and lush garden, and to feel in all his muscles, straining with the effort, the fresh, gentle breeze blowing freely through his thin shirt and cooling his warm body.

Then he jumped down into the nettles on the other side, rubbed the place where he'd been stung, and set off through the garden. He reached the window just as Lida was saying, "You still don't know?"

Immediately, from the strange expression in her voice, he realized what had happened. Leaning his shoulder against the wall, he stared into the garden and listened with interest to the unsteady, distraught, excited voices. He felt sorry for the lovely, humiliated Lida with her splendid looks, not at all in keeping with the coarse, bestial, agonizing word "pregnant." But even more than the conversation, he was intrigued by the strange, absurd contrast between the ferocious, hateful voices of the people in the room and the luminous silence in the green garden that was bestowed by nature on these very same people.

A white butterfly, soaring and dipping, fluttered lightly above the grass, basking in the sunny air; Sanin followed its flight just as carefully as he followed what was being said inside.

When Lida cried "Pig!" Sanin laughed good-naturedly, pushed himself away from the wall, and, not even worrying whether he could be seen from the window, made his way slowly through the garden.

A lizard scuttled across his path and caught his attention; for a long time Sanin followed the movement of its supple grass-green body as it slithered deftly through the tall green weeds.

 XIX

Lida headed not for home but in the opposite direction.

The streets were empty and a haze hung in the hot air. Short shadows lay under the fences and walls, vanquished by the triumphant sun.

Shielding herself with her parasol only out of habit, oblivious of whether it was hot or cold, light or dark, Lida hurried along by the fences overgrown with dusty grass; she kept her head down and her dry, shining eyes fixed on her feet. Now and then she encountered some apathetic, panting, overheated pedestrians, but they were few; an after-dinner summer silence prevailed in the town.

After hurriedly and cautiously sniffing her skirt, a little white dog attached itself to her, ran anxiously ahead, then glanced back and wagged its tail, making sure they were still together. At a turn in the road stood a small boy, incredibly fat, his shirttails hanging out the back of his pants; with his elderberry-stained cheeks puffed out, he was blowing desperately into a reed pipe.

Lida waved the dog away and smiled at the lad, but all this merely skimmed the surface of her awareness, while her soul was tightly closed. The dark force that had cut her off from the whole world carried her along swiftly, alone and dead, past the greenery, the sun, and the joy of life, farther and farther toward a black void, the proximity of which she already felt in the chill, feeble anguish that gripped her heart.

An officer with whom she was acquainted rode by and, recognizing her, made his chestnut horse rear up and pull back; the horse was slightly sweaty and the sunlight gleamed on its smooth coat, producing forged golden flecks.

"Lidiya Petrovna," he cried in a cheerful, resonant voice. "Where are you going in such heat?"

Lida unconsciously ran her eyes across his small peaked cap jauntily set on his sweaty forehead, half-red and half-white; she said nothing, merely smiled coquettishly out of habit.

And at that moment she asked herself at a loss: Where to now?

She felt no malice and had no thought of Zarudin. When, not knowing why, she'd gone to see him, it seemed impossible to continue living and impossible to resolve her grief without him; but now he'd merely disappeared from her life. All that had been had died; what remained concerned only her and had to be resolved by her alone.

Her brain was working quickly and with feverish clarity. The most horrible thing was that the proud, beautiful Lida would disappear, and instead there would be left a small, persecuted, besmirched animal, who'd be mocked by everyone and completely powerless in the face of slander and disgrace. She had to preserve her pride and beauty, leave the filth behind, go where the viscous mess couldn't touch her.

As soon as she had clarified all this to herself, she immediately felt the emptiness around her; sunlight, life, and people no longer existed for her; she was all alone, had nowhere to go, had to die, had to drown herself.

This dawned on her with such final clarity that it was as if a stone circle had been erected between her and everything else that had ever been and could ever be. Even this inner sensation, repugnant and terrible in that it was so unnecessary and yet so inevitable, a sensation of something that was incomprehensible but already destroying her life, a sensation she had never imagined feeling from the moment she guessed she was pregnant, disappeared for a moment.

A light, colorless void formed around her in which the indifference of death reigned supreme.

How simple it all is! Nothing more is needed! she thought, glancing around and seeing nothing.

She quickened her pace, but it still seemed unbearably slow, even though she was no longer walking but almost running, getting tangled in her stylish full skirt.

Here's a house, and here's another with green shutters, and then an open space. . . .

She had no conception of the river, the bridge, or what would happen there. All she saw was a hazy, deserted place where everything would end.

But that lasted only until she reached the bridge. When she paused at the railing and looked down at the turbid, greenish water, the sensation of lightness instantly vanished and her entire being was filled with agonizing fear and a strong desire to live.

Once again she heard the sound of voices and the chirping of sparrows, she saw sunlight, white daisies in the bushy greenery along the banks, and the little white dog that had decided without doubt that Lida was its rightful mistress. The dog sat down facing her, raised a front paw, and endearingly brushed the ground with its white tail, leaving amusing little hieroglyphs in the sand.

Lida stared at the dog and almost grabbed it in a desperate, passionate embrace. Large tears welled up in her eyes. The feeling of regret for her precious, lovely, ravaged life was so great that her head began to spin and she feverishly rested her elbows on the railings warmed by the sun. With this movement she dropped one of her gloves and followed it with her eyes with mute, indescribable horror.

Spinning quickly, the glove dropped and fell inaudibly onto the smooth, somnolent surface of the water. Quickly spreading circles moved toward the banks, and Lida could see how the pale-yellow glove, now water-soaked, was turning darker and slowly sinking into the murky, greenish depths. Curiously, almost in miserable agony, it turned once or twice, then began to descend with slow circular movements. Lida strained her eyes and tried to keep it in view, but the yellow spot became harder and harder to make out in the turbid, greenish water; it appeared once, then again, and finally disappeared, without a sound. Once more before her eyes there appeared only the smooth, somnolent, murky depths.

"How could you, miss?" said a woman's voice nearby.

Lida took a step back in fear and glanced into the face of a fat, snub-nosed peasant woman who was looking at her with curiosity and pity.

And although this pity concerned only the drowned glove, it seemed to her that the fat, genial peasant knew her and felt pity for her; for an instant it occurred to her that if she told her the whole story, she'd feel much better. But at that moment she felt divided and realized that it was impossible. She blushed and hastily muttered, "It's nothing," and ran hurriedly and unsteadily off the bridge like a person who was half-drunk.

This isn't the place. They'd pull me out. The thought flashed coldly through her vacant brain.

She continued on her way down, turned left along the bank, and followed a narrow path through nettles, daisies, burdock, and bitter-smelling wormwood between the river and the overgrown wattle fence of someone's garden.

It was quiet and peaceful there, as in a country churchyard. Willows, their slender branches hanging low, gazed dreamily at the water; sunlight cast bright and dark patches and stripes on the steep green bank; the broad leaves of burdock stood quietly among the tall nettles; prickly thistles easily became tangled in the lace trimming of her dress. Some leafy grass, as tall as a tree, sprinkled her with fine white powder.

Now Lida had to compel herself to go where she was going, in spite of the great force within her that was resisting.

I must, I must, I must, I must . . . she repeated in the depths of her soul; her feet, as if breaking heavy chains at every step, carried her with difficulty farther and farther from the bridge to a place that suddenly appeared to her as the end of her journey.

When she arrived there, and when she saw the cold, black water beneath the slender, intertwining willow twigs, swirling swiftly past the overhanging bank, she realized how much she wanted to live, how terrible it would be to die, but that she had to die because it was impossible to go on living. Without looking, she tossed her other glove and parasol into the grass and turned off the path into the thick weeds.

At that moment Lida remembered and experienced a great deal: in the very depths of her soul a childish game with its naive entreaty and fear, long forgotten and suppressed by new thoughts, repeated: "Lord, save me. . . . Lord, help me." From somewhere there emerged the refrain of an aria she'd been practicing to piano accompaniment, and the whole piece flashed through her mind; she remembered Zarudin, but didn't stop to think about him; her mother's face, at that moment so infinitely sweet and dear, appeared before her, and it was that face which now urged her on toward the water. Never before and never afterward had she understood with such clarity and depth that her mother and all the other people who loved Lida had loved her in fact not so much for who she was, with all her faults and desires, as for what they wanted to see in her. And now that she'd bared herself and strayed from the path that in their opinion was the only one open to her, it was precisely those people who'd loved her so much in the past, her mother most of all, who were now the ones tormenting her the most.

Then everything became confused, as if she were in delirium: fear, the will to live, an awareness of inevitability, a lack of faith, the certainty that everything was finished, hope for something, despair, the tormenting recognition of the place where she would die, and a man resembling her brother who was climbing quickly over a wattle fence and coming toward her.

"You couldn't have thought up anything more stupid!" Sanin cried, out of breath.

By an enigmatic sequence of thoughts and sensations operating in the human mind Lida had come to precisely the spot where Zarudin's garden ended and where, against a ramshackle wattle fence, in an uncomfortable position, hidden from the moonlight by the dark shadows of trees, she'd first given herself to Zarudin. Sanin spotted her and recognized her from a distance, and guessed what she was up to. His first inclination was to leave and let her do as she wished, but her impetuous movements, obviously involuntary and excruciating, made his heart ache with pity. He ran toward her, jumping over bushes and garden benches.

Her brother's voice had a terribly powerful effect on Lida: her nerves, strained to breaking point in her inner struggle, suddenly eased; she felt light-headed and everything around her began to spin. She couldn't tell where she was, in the water or still on the bank. Sanin managed to catch her at the very edge; he was extremely pleased with his own agility and skill.

"There we are!" he said.

Then he led her to the wattle fence, sat her down on the stile, and looked around in amazement.

What do I do with her now? he wondered.

But Lida came to her senses at once; pale, distraught, and weak, as if suffering a nervous breakdown, she burst into bitter, agitated tears.

"My God, my God!" she cried, sobbing like a child.

"You silly girl!" Sanin replied tenderly and compassionately.

Lida didn't hear him, but when he moved, she clutched his arm convulsively and resolutely, and sobbed even louder.

What am I doing? she wondered in horror. I mustn't cry. I must make light of it . . . or else he'll guess!

"Well, now, why are you so upset?" Sanin asked, gently rubbing her shoulders; he was pleased to be speaking so affectionately and tenderly.

She looked up at his face timidly, like a child, from under the brim of her hat, and calmed down.

"I know all about it," Sanin said. "I've known for a long time . . . the whole story."

Although Lida knew that many people would suspect her liaison, it was nevertheless as if Sanin had struck her across the face; her supple form recoiled and she peered at her brother through wide, instantly dry eyes with the intense terror of a magnificent animal at bay.

"Well, now what is it? You're acting like I just stepped on your tail!" Sanin said with a good-natured smile; he took hold of her soft, round shoulders, trembling timidly beneath his fingers, and sat her down again on the wattle fence. She obediently reassumed her previous crushed pose.

"What is it that's distressing you?" Sanin inquired. "Oh, the fact that I know? Is it really true that, having given yourself to Zarudin, you now have such a low opinion of your act that you're afraid to acknowledge it? That I don't understand? And the fact that Zarudin won't marry you—thank heavens for that! Now you know . . . and you knew before what sort of man he is—though he's handsome and amorous, he's base and worthless. The one good thing about him was his good looks, but you've made use of that already!"

He used me, not I him. . . . Maybe I did, too. Yes! Oh, Lord, good Lord! The words rushed through Lida's feverish brain.

"And now, the fact that you're pregnant . . ."

Lida closed her eyes and hung her head down to her shoulders.

"Of course, that's bad," Sanin continued in a soft, gentle voice. "First, because to give birth to an infant is a very unpleasant, dirty, painful, ridiculous thing; and second, because—and this is the main point—people will torment you. Lidochka, you, my Lidochka!" Sanin added, interrupting himself with a strong rush of affection. "You haven't done anyone any harm, and even if you gave birth to a dozen infants, the only person who'd suffer as a result would be you!"

Sanin fell silent, chewing the ends of his mustache thoughtfully, his arms folded across his chest.

"I'd tell you what to do, but you're too weak and foolish for that. You lack boldness and daring. But it's not worth dying for. Look at how nice everything is. The sun's shining, the water's flowing. . . . Imagine that after your death people found out you were pregnant; what good would that be to you? It'd mean that you had died not because you were pregnant but because you were afraid that other people wouldn't let you live. The whole horror of your misfortune isn't that it's a misfortune but that you put it between yourself and life, and you think there'll be nothing else left. But in fact life will go on just the same. You won't fear those who don't know you; of course, you'll only fear those close to you, most of all those who love you and for whom your 'fall' was such a terrible blow simply because it took place somewhere out in the woods or on the grass, instead of in a conjugal bed. But they won't give up until they punish you for your sin, so what good will they be to you? In other words, they're stupid, cruel, and trivial. Why do you suffer and want to die for the sake of such stupid, trivial, and cruel people?" Lida slowly raised her large inquisitive eyes and looked at him; in them Sanin saw a little spark of comprehension.

"What shall I do? What?" she asked in anguish.

"You have two choices: either get rid of this child that nobody needs and whose birth, as you see, will bring nothing but grief to everyone in the world . . ."

Dark fear appeared in Lida's eyes.

"To murder a being that already knows the joy of life and the fear of death is cruel, but to kill a fetus, an unconscious mass of flesh and blood . . ."

Lida experienced a strange feeling: first of all, acute shame, as if she'd been stripped bare and all the secret places of her body were being probed by crude fingers. She was horrified to look at her brother, fearing they'd both be mortified with shame. But Sanin's gray eyes didn't flinch; his look was clear and steady; his voice was calm and didn't waver, as if he were saying the simplest things, no different from any others. Her shame dissipated under the steadfastness of his words, lost its power, even its meaning. She discerned the profundity of his words and no longer felt either shame or fear. Then, frightened at her own thoughts, she grasped at her temples in despair, setting the sleeves of her dress flapping like the wings of a frightened bird.

"I can't do it . . . I can't!" she cried. "Perhaps it's true, perhaps . . . But I can't do it. It's too horrible!"

"Well, so you can't. So what?" Sanin said, going down on his knees before her and gently prying her hands away from her face. "Then we'll conceal it. I'll arrange for Zarudin to leave, and you . . . you'll marry Novikov and be happy. I know that if that handsome young stallion of an officer had never appeared, you'd have fallen in love with Novikov. That's exactly where things were heading."

At the mention of Novikov's name something radiant and agreeable flashed like a bright ray of light through Lida's soul. Whether it was because Zarudin had made her so miserable and because she felt Novikov wouldn't, it seemed to her for a moment that all this was such a simple and rectifiable mistake; there was nothing terrible about it; she'd stand up at once, start walking, say something, smile, and once more life would unfold before her in all its sunny colors. She'd be able to live again, love again, but this time in a much better, stronger, purer way. But then suddenly she remembered that this was impossible, that she was already defiled, soiled by unworthy, senseless debauchery.

An extremely coarse word, one she hardly knew and had never before uttered, entered her mind. With painful enjoyment she stigmatized herself with the word, like a brutal slap across the face, and then she felt frightened.

My God. Can it really be so? Is that what I am? Well, yes, yes . . . it is. I am. So there!

"What're you saying?" she whispered to her brother in despair, tormented and ashamed by her own resonant voice, enchanting as usual.

"What of it?" Sanin asked, looking down at her lovely, tousled hair over her white neck on which light golden flecks of sunlight filtered through the leaves.

Suddenly he was afraid that he might not succeed in convincing her, and that this beautiful, sunny young woman, capable of bestowing happiness on so many people, would disappear into a senseless void.

Lida was unable to speak. She was trying to suppress in herself that beloved hope which, against her own will, was taking possession of her entire trembling body. It seemed to her that after all that had happened it was shameful not only to go on living but even to want to live. But her strong young body, so full of sunlight, repelled these monstrous, unwholesome thoughts like poison, not wishing to acknowledge them as its crippled offspring.

"Why are you so quiet?" Sanin asked.

"It's not possible. It'd be vile. I . . . ."

"Please don't talk nonsense," Sanin replied with displeasure.

Lida glanced at him once again with her lovely eyes, so full of tears and secret desire.

Sanin was silent, picked up a twig, and snapped it in two, then tossed it away.

"Vile, vile," he continued. "You were so struck by what I said. . . . Why? Neither you nor I can answer that question definitively. And if we try, it won't be the right answer! A crime? What constitutes a crime? If a mother's life is threatened during childbirth and the living infant, just about to be born, is torn apart or quartered, its head crushed by the steel forceps—that's not a crime! It's merely unfortunate necessity. But to terminate an unconscious, physiological process, something that doesn't yet exist, some sort of chemical reaction—that's called a crime, a horrible deed! Horrible, even though the mother's life may depend on it, and even more than her life—her happiness! How so? No one knows, but everyone shouts 'Bravo!'" Sanin said with a sarcastic smile. "Oh, people, people . . . they create phantoms for themselves, conditions, mirages, and then they suffer. They shout: 'Man is majestic, significant, and inscrutable! Man is tsar!' Tsar of nature who never actually reigns: everyone suffers and fears his own shadow!"

Sanin was silent for a moment.

"Yes, but that's not really the point. You say it's vile. I don't know . . . it may be. But just remember, if you tell Novikov about your fall, he'll stage a terrible scene, perhaps even shoot himself, but he won't stop loving you. And he'll be the guilty one because he'll be struggling with the same prejudices that he doesn't officially accept. If he were really clever, he'd pay no attention to the fact that you had slept with someone, forgive me for the crude expression. Neither your body nor your soul is any the worse as a result of that act. Good Lord, why, he might even marry a widow, for example! Obviously, facts aren't the main point here: it's all that nonsense filling your head. And you . . . If a person's supposed to fall in love only once, then the attempt to love a second time wouldn't work out; it'd be painful, revolting, uncomfortable. But that's not what happens. It's just as pleasant and joyful. You'll come to love Novikov. And if you don't, you'll come away with me, Lidochka! We can live anywhere!"

Lida sighed, trying to push away some heavy burden.

"Perhaps everything will be all right again. Novikov . . . he's likable, a nice fellow. He's even good-looking. . . . No, yes . . . I don't know."

"Well, and what would happen if you drowned yourself? Good and evil would suffer no loss or gain. Your bloated, disfigured corpse would be covered with silt, then fished out of the water and buried. That's all!"

The sinister green depths rose before Lida's eyes; slimy threads, streaks, and bubbles extended their slow serpentine movements, and she suddenly felt terrified and disgusted.

No, no, never! I'd rather bear the shame, have Novikov, anything at all—but not that! she thought, turning pale.

"See how overwhelmed you are by fear?" Sanin said with a laugh.

Lida smiled through her tears, and this accidental smile, as if showing that she could laugh again, warmed her own heart.

No matter what, I'll go on living! she thought with a passionate, almost triumphant burst of feeling.

"Well now," Sanin said joyfully, and stood up abruptly and cheerfully. "Nothing's so sickening as the thought of death, but if one's shoulders can bear the burden and if one can go on hearing and seeing life, then live on! Right? Come, give me your little paw!"

Lida extended her hand: there was childish gratitude in her timid, feminine gesture.

"Well, that's fine. You have such lovely little hands!"

Lida smiled and said nothing.

It was not Sanin's words that had influenced her. There was within her a huge, stubborn, bold sense of life; the moment of silence and weakness had merely stretched her taut, like a string. A little more pressure and the string would have broken, but this hadn't happened, and her soul rang out with more harmonious and resonant daring, thirst for life, and reckless strength. With enthusiasm, astonishment, and unfamiliar assertiveness Lida looked and listened, perceiving with every ounce of her being the powerful, joyous life going on around her in the sunlight, in the green grass, in the flowing water permeated by light, in her brother's serene, smiling face, and within herself. It seemed to her that she was seeing and hearing all this for the first time.

To live! a voice cried out jubilantly and deafeningly within her.

"Well, that's fine," said Sanin. "I've helped you in your struggle at a difficult moment; so now, since you're such a beauty, give me a kiss."

Lida smiled silently; her smile was enigmatic, like that of a wood nymph. Sanin put his arms around her waist, and feeling her supple, warm body stretch and quiver in his muscular arms, he pressed her to him boldly and firmly.

Something strange transpired in Lida's soul, but something inexpressibly pleasant: everything in her was alive and greedily wanted even more life; without realizing it, she slowly wrapped her arms around her brother's neck and, closing her eyes partway, pursed her lips for a kiss. She felt unrestrained happiness when Sanin pressed his warm lips painfully against hers for a prolonged kiss. At that moment she didn't care who was kissing her, just as a blossom warmed by the sun doesn't care what's warming it.

What's the matter with me? she wondered with joyful surprise. Oh, yes . . . for some reason I wanted to drown myself. How stupid! What for? Ah, this is so nice. It doesn't matter who it is. Just to be alive!

"Well now," said Sanin, releasing her. "All's well that ends well . . . and one needn't attach any more significance to it!"

Lida slowly rearranged her hair, looking at him with a happy, foolish grin. Sanin handed over her parasol and glove. At first Lida was surprised by the absence of the other one; then she remembered and laughed softly, recalling how momentous and sinister the drowning of her glove had seemed to her at the time; now it meant nothing at all.

Well, that's that! she thought, walking with her brother along the bank and feeling the warm sunlight on her prominent bosom.

 XX

Novikov himself opened the door to Sanin and frowned at seeing him. He found everything painful that reminded him of Lida and of the incomprehensibly splendid vision that had been shattered in his soul like a delicate vase.

Sanin noticed this and entered with a conciliatory and sympathetic smile. Novikov's room was dirty and in disarray, as if a whirlwind had blown through it, scattering papers, straw, and other rubbish across the floor. Books, underwear, medical instruments, and suitcases were strewn on the bed, on chairs, and in open drawers of the dresser.

"Where are you off to?" Sanin asked in amazement.

Novikov, trying not to look at him, shuffled through a few items on the table.

"I'm heading out to where there's a famine. I've received my orders," he replied awkwardly, annoyed at himself for being like this.

Sanin looked at him, then at the suitcase, then again at him, and suddenly smiled broadly. Novikov was silent, mechanically wrapping up a pair of boots together with some test tubes. He felt anguish and utter, miserable loneliness.

"If you pack like that," Sanin observed, "you'll arrive with neither instruments nor boots."

"Ah . . ." said Novikov, glancing quickly at Sanin, his eyes full of tears, and said: "Leave me alone. You can see how painful this is for me!"

Sanin understood and was silent.

Dreamy summer twilight was already visible through the window, and the pure, crystal-clear sky was fading above the light-green garden.

"In my opinion," Sanin began, then paused, "instead of heading to the devil knows where, you ought to stay here and marry Lida!"

Novikov turned toward him unnaturally quickly and suddenly began trembling all over.

"I must ask you to . . . stop making such stupid jokes!" he cried in a ringing voice.

The sound of his voice drifted away into the dreamy, cool garden and echoed strangely under the quiet trees.

"Why are you so furious?" Sanin asked.

"Listen . . ." Novikov said hoarsely, his eyes very round, and his face not at all like the good, kind face Sanin knew so well.

"Are you going to argue that marrying Lida won't make you happy?" Sanin asked, only the corners of his eyes laughing merrily.

"Stop it!" Novikov screeched, swaying like a drunkard; then, rushing at Sanin, he grabbed one of his own dirty boots and brandished it over Sanin's head with unexpected strength.

"Quiet, you devil!" Sanin said angrily, retreating involuntarily.

Novikov tossed the boot aside in disgust and stood facing him, breathing heavily.

"You were going to take that old boot to me?" Sanin said, shaking his head in reproach. He felt sorry for Novikov and was amused by everything he did.

"You're the one to blame," Novikov replied, weakening immediately and becoming embarrassed.

Suddenly he felt tenderness and confidence in Sanin. He was so large and serene, while Novikov was like a little boy who wanted to come closer and complain about how he was being tormented. Tears even welled up in his eyes.

"If only you knew how painful it all is!" he said in a broken voice, making an effort with his throat and mouth not to start crying.

"Yes, my friend, I know everything," Sanin answered affectionately.

"No, you can't!" Novikov replied trustingly, sitting down next to him mechanically. His situation seemed so exceptionally agonizing that no one could possibly understand.

"Yes, I do know," said Sanin. "If you like, I'll swear I do! And if you promise not to attack me again with that old boot, I'll prove it to you. Well, do you promise?"

"Yes. . . . Forgive me, Volodya," Novikov muttered in embarrassment, calling Sanin by his first name, something he had never done.

Sanin liked that; as a result, his wish to help and be reconciled became even stronger.

"Listen, my friend. Let's talk frankly," he said, affectionately placing his hand on Novikov's knee. "You're planning to leave merely because Lida refused you and because later, at Zarudin's, you thought she'd come to see him."

Novikov hung his head. It seemed that Sanin was reopening a fresh, extremely painful wound.

Sanin looked at him and thought, Oh, you kind, dumb creature.

"I won't try to convince you," he continued, "that Lida wasn't involved with Zarudin. I don't really know. I don't think so," he added hurriedly, noticing the look of intense suffering that crossed Novikov's face just like the shadow of a passing cloud.

Novikov stared at him in vague hope.

"Their relations began so recently," Sanin explained, "that nothing serious could've occurred. Especially if you consider Lida's character. Why, you know Lida."

Before Novikov's eyes there rose an image of the Lida he knew and loved: a proud, shapely woman, with large eyes, not exactly tender or menacing but cool and pure, as if surrounded by an icy halo. He shut his eyes and believed Sanin.

"And even if some perfectly ordinary spring flirtation occurred between them, now it's all obviously finished. Besides, what do you care about the insignificant attraction of a young woman who's still free and seeking happiness, while you yourself, without having to search your memory, can recall dozens of such escapades, some even much worse."

Novikov turned to face him; as a result of the confidence filling his soul, his eyes became bright and transparent. Within him a vital seedling was sprouting—so fragile that it was ready to vanish at any moment; and he himself was afraid of destroying it by a careless word or thought.

"You know, if I . . ." Novikov didn't finish because he couldn't formulate what it was he wanted to say, but he felt sweet tears of tenderness welling up in his throat and easing his grief and emotion.

"Well, if you what?" Sanin asked triumphantly, his voice raised, his eyes gleaming. "I can tell you only one thing: there is not and has never been anything between Lida and Zarudin!"

Novikov looked at him distractedly.

"I thought," he said in horror, feeling as if he didn't believe Sanin.

"You thought nonsense," Sanin replied with sincere irritation. "You don't understand Lida: if she hesitated for so long, what sort of love could it really be?"

Novikov grabbed his arm, looking at him ecstatically.

Suddenly Sanin was filled with terrible malice and loathing. For a while he stared into the face of this man so enraptured by the idea that the woman with whom he wanted to copulate had not done so previously with anyone else. Undisguised animal envy, trivial and mean as a snake, emanated from these human eyes, now transformed by sincere grief and suffering.

"Oho!" Sanin exclaimed ominously and stood up. "Well then, here's what I have to tell you: not only did Lida fall in love with Zarudin, but she also had an affair with him, and now she's even carrying his child!"

There was dead silence in the room. Novikov, smiling strangely, stared at Sanin and wrung his hands. His lips trembled and stirred. Only a faint cry emerged and then faded away. Sanin stood over him and looked him in the eye; a cruel, menacing wrinkle formed on his lower jaw and in the corners of his mouth.

"Well, why don't you say something?" asked Sanin.

Novikov raised his eyes quickly to look at him, then lowered them just as quickly, remaining silent as before and grinning distractedly.

"Lida's endured a terrible ordeal," Sanin began softly, as if talking to himself. "If chance hadn't been guiding me, she might not be alive today; what was yesterday a beautiful, healthy young woman might now be lying naked and hideous, somewhere in the slime along the riverbank being devoured by crayfish. The point isn't that she would've died—everyone has to die, but with her all the immense joy she brings to the lives of others would have vanished too. Lida . . . she's not alone, of course, but if all feminine vitality were to perish, life on earth would become as gloomy as the grave. And when a lovely young woman is so senselessly mistreated, I personally conceive a desire to kill someone! Listen, it's all the same to me whether you marry Lida or whether you go to hell, but I want to say one thing: you're an idiot! If even one sound, unsullied thought stirred within your thick skull, would you suffer like this? Would you make yourself and others so unhappy merely because an unattached young woman, having chosen a mate, made a mistake, and now she's free again after engaging in a sexual act, rather than before? I tell you, you aren't alone. You idiots have made life an impossible prison, without sunshine and joy—there are millions of you! As for you, how many times have you wallowed on some prostitute's belly and there, all drunk and filthy, writhed in lust like a dog? In Lida's fall there was passion, there was poetry and power, while you? What right do you have to turn away from her, you, who consider yourself a clever, intelligent man, someone who knows no conflict between intelligence and life? What do you care about her past? Is she any the worse? Will she provide you with less enjoyment? Did you want to be the one to deprive her of her innocence? Well?"

"You know that's not the case," Novikov uttered, his lips trembling.

"Yes, it is the case!" Sanin cried. "If not, then what is?"

Novikov was silent.

His soul was empty and dark; only like a lighted window in a dark field far, far away there glimmered the agonizing happiness of forgiveness, sacrifice, and heroic achievement.

Sanin looked at him and seemed to catch the direction of the twisted thoughts going through his mind.

"I can see," he began again in a quiet but sharp voice, "you're thinking about self-sacrifice. A loophole has even occurred to you: you'll condescend, protect her from the rabble, and so on. You're already growing in your own eyes, like a worm in carrion! No, you're lying! There isn't a trace of self-abnegation in you. If Lida had been disfigured by smallpox, then you might actually have performed a heroic deed; but a few days later you'd destroy her life; entreating fate, you'd either abandon her or torment her, having agreed to such a feat with despair in your heart. And now you gaze at yourself as if you were an icon! I should say so: your face radiates holiness, everyone will say you're a saint, and you won't have lost a thing! Lida has the same arms, legs, bosom, the same passion and life! It's nice to enjoy yourself, knowing that you're performing a holy act! I should say so!"

As a result of these words the poignant self-love that had begun to blossom in Novikov's soul shrank pathetically into a little ball, like a crushed worm, and his gentle soul offered a new feeling, simpler and more sincere than the former.

"You think me worse than I really am," he said with a sad reproach. "I'm really not as dumb as you say. Perhaps . . . I won't deny that I do have strong prejudices, but I love Lidiya Petrovna . . . and if I knew she loved me, would I really have to ponder this for long?"

He uttered the last words with an effort; this effort to say what he believed caused him great suffering.

Sanin suddenly cooled down. He thought for a while, paced the floor, stopped by the window looking onto the garden at dusky twilight, and said softly, "Now she's unhappy; she's not thinking about love. Who knows whether she loves you or not? I simply think that if you go to her and become the second person in the world who doesn't punish her for her careless moment of happiness, then . . . who knows?"

Novikov gazed before him pensively. He felt both sadness and joy; his sad joy and joyful sadness together created in his soul a sense of poignant happiness, glowing like a dying summer evening.

"Let's go and see her," said Sanin. "Whatever happens, it'll be easier for her to see a human face among the masks hiding all those brutish mugs. You, my friend, are rather foolish, it's true, but in your own foolishness, you have something that others lack. Just think, for a long time the world has built its happiness and hopes on this foolishness. Let's go."

Novikov smiled timidly. "I will. But will she want to see me?"

"Don't think about that," Sanin said, placing his hands on Novikov's shoulders. "If you think you're doing the right thing—do it, and you'll see what happens.

"Well, let's go!" Novikov said decisively.

He stopped in the doorway; then, glancing straight into Sanin's eyes, he said with particular emphasis, "You know, if it's possible, I will make her happy. It sounds banal, but I can't express my feelings any other way."

"Never mind, my friend," Sanin replied warmly. "I understand what you mean!"

## XXI

The heat of summer lay upon the town. At night the round bright moon rode high in the sky; the air was warm and thick, and together with the fragrance of gardens and flowers it aroused powerful, languorous feelings.

People worked by day, engaging in politics and art, implementing various ideas, eating, drinking, bathing, and conversing; but as soon as the heat passed, as soon as the oppressive, all-enveloping dust settled and from behind a distant grove or close rooftop the rim of the round, mysteriously bright moon appeared over the dark horizon, shedding its cold enigmatic light on the gardens, everything came to a halt; as if shedding some multicolored apparel, everyone began to live real life more freely and easily. The younger the people, the fuller and freer this life. Gardens resounded with the singing of nightingales; grasses, brushed by flimsy women's dresses, waved their little heads mysteriously, shadows lengthened, an amorous torpor hung in the air, eyes flashed and then clouded over, cheeks grew flushed, and voices became cryptic and inviting.

And new generations came into being in the cold moonlight on the succulent, matted grass, in the cool shadows of silent trees.

Like Shafrov, Yury Svarozhich was interested in politics and self-improvement circles, and was reading the latest books; he imagined that in these pursuits lay real life, as well as the resolution and mitigation of all his anxieties and doubts. But no matter how much he read and how much he organized, everything still bored and exhausted him, and there was no spark in his life. He was on fire only at those times when he felt healthy and strong, and was in love with a woman.

At first all women, young and beautiful, seemed equally appealing to him and aroused him equally; then one among them began to stand out and gradually assumed all their colors and charms; she stood before him magnificent and lovely, like a young birch on the edge of a forest in spring.

She was very pretty, tall, shapely, and strong; at every step her lovely, high chest was prominent; atop her strong white neck she held her head high; she laughed loudly, sang beautifully, and although she read a great deal, she appreciated clever thoughts and her own verses; but her entire being experienced full enjoyment only when she had to exert herself, press her resilient bosom against an object, grasp something with all her strength, plant her feet, laugh, sing, and gaze at strong, handsome men. Sometimes, when the sun gleamed and powerfully burned everything till dark, or when the moon shone in the dark sky, she felt like taking off all her clothes, running through the green grass, throwing herself into the cold, heaving water, watching and waiting for someone, summoning him with a sonorous call.

Her presence troubled Yury, inspiring in him unknown and still untested powers. His tongue spoke more clearly in her presence, his muscles became more powerful, his heart beat stronger, and his mind was suppler. He thought about her all day and in the evening went to find her, concealing it even from himself.

But there was something disconnected, annoying in his soul, something that was blocking the way and going against his will. He paused on every feeling aroused in him and cross-examined it; then the feeling faded, withered, and lost its petals, like a blossom in the frost. When he asked himself what was drawing him to Karsavina, he replied: sexual attraction and nothing more. Although he himself didn't know why, these straightforward words aroused in him a brusque and painful feeling of contempt.

Meanwhile, a mysterious bond was gradually developing between them without a single word, and, as if in a mirror, each of his movements was reflected in hers and hers in him.

Karsavina didn't think about what was happening but reveled in her feeling, feared it, desired it, and hoped to conceal it from others so that it would remain intact and belong to her alone. It tormented her that she was unable to understand everything that was happening in the body and soul of this nice, handsome man so dear to her. At times it seemed to her that there was nothing between them; then she suffered, wept, and pined, as if she'd lost a treasure. Nevertheless, the attentions of other men who approached her and regarded her with strange, comprehensible, and incomprehensible looks in their eyes couldn't help but gratify and disturb her. Therefore, especially when Karsavina was sure that Yury loved her and she was blossoming like a bride to be, the secret of her avid desires shocked her and those around her.

She felt a particularly disturbing surge of emotion when Sanin drew near, with his broad shoulders, serene gaze, and self-assured manner. Catching herself with this secret agitation, Karsavina was frightened; she considered herself immoral and depraved, but she still returned Sanin's gaze with interest.

On the evening of the day when Lida experienced her own painful drama, Yury and Karsavina met in the library. They merely exchanged greetings and each went about his business: Karsavina selected books while Yury skimmed the Petersburg newspapers. But it happened that they left together and walked along the deserted, bright, moonlit streets.

The air was unusually still; the only sounds that could be heard, softened by the distance, were the night watchman's rattle and a small dog's bark coming from far away. Along the boulevard they encountered a group of people sitting in the shadows under some trees.

Animated voices could be heard; mustaches and beards could be glimpsed momentarily lit by glowing cigarettes. As they walked past, a distinct and spirited male voice was singing:

"The heart of a maiden
Is like a breeze in the fields!"[21]

Before they reached Karsavina's apartment, they sat down on a bench near a gate in the dark shadows; from there they could see the wide, evenly moonlit street, and at one end the white fence around the church and dark lime trees above which a cross gleamed coldly in the sky like a star.

"Look how lovely it is!" Karsavina said melodiously, gesturing at the scene.

Yury glanced around and admired her full white shoulders, shimmering brightly through the wide collar of her Ukrainian blouse; he felt an irresistible urge to embrace her, kiss her luscious, full lips, now parted because his own were so close to hers. He suddenly felt he had to do so, and that she was waiting, both fearing and desiring it.

But instead, he allowed the moment to pass; losing heart, he twisted his mouth and laughed sarcastically.

"What are you laughing at?" Karsavina asked.

"Nothing, nothing special," Yury replied, restraining the passionate tremor in his legs. "It's just a bit too lovely!"

They were silent for a while, listening attentively to the distant sounds that reached them from the dark gardens and moonlit roofs.

"Have you ever been in love?" she asked suddenly.

"Yes," he replied slowly. What if I tell her? he thought with a sinking heart. "I'm in love right now," he said.

"With whom?" she asked wincing, full of fear and certainty.

"With you, of course!" he replied, and tried to make light of it but couldn't carry it off. He leaned forward and looked into her eyes, shining strangely in the shadows.

She glanced at him quickly and apprehensively; her fearful, blissful face filled with expectation.

Yury wanted to embrace her. He could already feel her soft, cool shoulders and her supple bosom beneath his hands, but he was frightened. Once again the moment passed; lacking the strength and unable to do what he wanted, he pretended to yawn in embarrassment.

He's teasing! Karsavina thought painfully; suddenly she cooled completely, feeling both downhearted and offended. She thought she might start crying soon and clenched her teeth with a feverish effort to hold back her tears.

"What nonsense!" she muttered in a different tone of voice, rising hastily.

"I'm being quite serious!" Yury said in an unnatural voice, already against his will. "I love you, believe me, I do—very passionately!"

Without replying, Karsavina collected her books.

[21] An inexact translation of the first two lines of the aria "La donna e mobile" from Giuseppe Verdi's opera *Rigoletto* (1851). A closer rendering would be: "The lady is fickle / As a feather in the wind."

Why? What for? she wondered with a pang, and suddenly thought in horror that she'd betrayed herself and he now despised her.

Yury picked up a book that had fallen to the ground.

"It's time to go," she said softly.

Yury felt truly sorry that she was leaving, and at the same time all this seemed to be ending in a very original, artistic way that was far from vulgar. He replied enigmatically, "Good-bye."

But when Karsavina extended her hand, Yury leaned over and, against his will, kissed her soft, warm palm, inhaling her gentle, tender scent. She pulled her hand away at once with a faint cry.

"What are you doing?"

But the momentary sensation of contact of his soft lips with her cool, virginal body was so strong that Yury's head began to spin; he could only smile blissfully and foolishly, listening to the sound of her footsteps as she hurried away.

Soon the gate creaked and Yury, still smiling, headed home, inhaling the fresh air deeply and feeling strong and happy.

 XXII

But, after experiencing the expanse and coolness of the moonlit night, back in his room, stuffy and cramped like a prison cell, Yury began to think once more about how boring it was to go on living, how petty and vulgar everything was.

I stole a kiss from her! What happiness, what a feat, just think! How admirable and poetic: moonlight, the hero seduces the maiden with fiery speeches and kisses. . . . Ugh! What vulgarity! A person imperceptibly becomes trivial in this accursed, out-of-the-way place!

So just as when he lived in a big town Yury supposed that all he had to do was go to the country, become engrossed in simple rural life with its work, its genuine, natural toil, its fields, sunshine, and peasants, for his life finally to acquire real meaning, now he thought that if it were not for this godforsaken place, if he were to be transported to the capital, his life would proceed along its true path.

There's bustle in the capital, orators hold forth! Yury told himself with a dreamy expression and unconscious pathos.

But immediately catching himself in such boyish enthusiasm, he waved his arm dismissively.

But what could come of that? It wouldn't make any difference! Politics, science . . . all that looks impressive from a distance, ideally, in general; but in the life of an individual they're merely professions like the rest! Struggle, titanic efforts, yes. . . . But that's impossible in contemporary life. What then? I suffer earnestly, struggle, overcome . . . and then? In the final analysis? The goal of the struggle lies outside my life. Prometheus wanted to give men fire and he did—that's a triumph. What about us? We merely toss a few chips on the blaze ignited and extinguished by others.

Suddenly it occurred to him that this was because he, Yury, was no Prometheus. This idea was not very pleasant, but he nonetheless seized upon it with painful self-flagellation:

What sort of Prometheus am I? I see everything in personal terms—me, me, me! All for me, all for me! I'm just as weak and insignificant as all those other small fry I regard with such contempt!

This parallel was so tormenting that Yury became confused and for a while stared blankly into space, searching for some justification.

No, I'm not like others! he thought with relief. The fact that I'm even thinking about it makes me different. Ryazantsev and all the Novikovs and Sanins of this world can't even think about it. They're far removed from tragic self-flagellation; they're as content as triumphant swine. Zarathustras![22] Their whole life is contained within their own microscopically small ego; and they're even infecting me with their vulgarity. He who keeps company with wolves learns to howl like a wolf! It's only natural!

Yury began to pace the room and, as often happens, this change of position produced a change in his thoughts.

Well, fine. It's so, but there's still much to ponder. What kind of relations do I have with Karsavina? It doesn't matter whether I love her or not; what can come of it? If I were to marry her or simply become involved with her for a while, would that make me happy? To deceive her—that would be a crime, and if I do love her, then . . . Well, fine. She'll bear children, Yury thought rashly, blushing for some reason. There's nothing bad about that, but still, it'll bind me to her and deprive me of my freedom forever! Family happiness—that's a philistine joy! No, that's not for me!

One, two, three . . . he thought, automatically trying to move in such a way as to step across two floorboards at once and plant his foot on the third. If one could know for sure that there wouldn't be children . . . Or if I could come to love my children so much that I could devote my life to them . . . No, that's vulgar too. Ryazantsev will love his offspring. In what way would I be different from him? To live and sacrifice! That's genuine life! Yes. . . . But sacrifice for whom? How? Whatever path I choose, whatever goal I set myself, where's that pure and unquestionable ideal that would be worth dying for? I'm not the one who's weak: it's that life isn't worth the sacrifice and love. And, if that's so, then life's not worth living either!

This conclusion had never occurred to Yury before with such clarity.

---

[22] Here a derogatory epithet; see n. 4 above.

A revolver always lay on his table, and now, each time he passed it on his way to the table and back, its brightly polished metal caught his eye.

He picked it up and examined it carefully. The revolver was loaded. He cocked the trigger and put it to his temple.

Like this, he thought. Once and for all? Is it stupid or clever to shoot oneself? Suicide is cowardice. . . . Well then, that means I'm a coward.

The cautious contact of the cold metal against his warm temple was pleasant yet frightening.

What about Karsavina? the question occurred to him unconsciously. So I'll never get to enjoy her and will leave that pleasure to someone else?

At the thought of Karsavina everything voluptuously and tenderly quieted down. But by his own will power, Yury forced himself to think that all this was insignificant, nothing in comparison with those thoughts that were now filling his head, thoughts that seemed to him important and profound. But this required great effort; and this forced emotion took vengeance on him with its unsatisfied longing and a lack of desire to go on living.

Why not do it? he asked himself with a sinking heart.

Once again, and now with a deliberation in which he didn't believe and at which he laughed bashfully, he placed the revolver against his temple and, without thinking what he was doing, pulled the trigger.

Something sharp and cold jerked in him with wild horror. There was a ringing in his ears and the whole room seemed to spin. But there was no shot—only the faint sound of the metallic click of the trigger.

Overcome with weakness from head to toe, he slowly lowered the revolver. Everything in him shook and ached, his head was spinning, and his mouth had gone completely dry. When he put the gun down, his hand trembled and knocked it against the tabletop several times.

A fine fellow! he thought. Regaining control of himself, he went to the mirror and glanced at its dark, cold surface.

Am I a coward, then? No. The answer flashed proudly through his mind. I'm not a coward! I actually tried it and it's not my fault the gun misfired!

The same face as always stared back at him from the dark mirror, but it seemed uncompromising and triumphant. With pleasure, however, he tried to convince himself that he attached no significance to this act of self-control; he stuck his tongue out at himself and walked away from the mirror.

"So it's not to be!" he said aloud, and these words comforted and encouraged him.

What if someone saw me? he wondered with timid embarrassment at the same moment and instinctively glanced around.

But everything was quiet. Nothing was stirring behind the locked door. It seemed as though nothing existed beyond the confines of the room, and that Yury was living and suffering alone in an endless void. He blew out the lamp and was surprised that the pale pink light of morning was already showing through his shutters.

He lay down to sleep and dreamed that someone ponderous and solid was sitting on top of him, exhaling an ominous red light.

It's the devil! the thought occurred to him with sudden horror.

Yury made a feverish effort to free himself. But the Red Figure didn't leave, didn't speak, didn't laugh; it merely made a strange clicking sound with its tongue. It was impossible to make out whether this sound was meant to be sarcastic or sympathetic, and that was tormenting.


## XXIII


Softly and warmly, breathing the fragrance of grasses and flowers, dusk floated in through the open window.

Sanin sat at the table; in the last shades of daylight he was reading a story he'd read many times before, about how a tragically lonely old bishop was dying, surrounded by people, adoration, and the smoke of burning incense, decked in golden raiment and diamond crucifixes, enveloped in universal respect.

It was just as cool and fresh inside as it was out, and the light breath of evening wafted freely around the room, filling Sanin's chest, rustling his soft hair, and caressing his broad shoulders as he was seriously attending to the volume.

He read, thought, moved his lips, and looked like a large lad who was engrossed in a book. The more he read, the stronger and deeper were the gloomy thoughts aroused in him about how much horror there is in human life, how stupid and coarse people are, and how distant he felt from them. He thought it would have been a good thing if he'd known that bishop, and that the old bishop's life wouldn't have been so lonely.

The door to his room opened and someone came in. Sanin turned around.

"Ah! Hello," he said, putting the book aside. "Well, what's new?"

Novikov shook his hand weakly and laughed with a pale, sad grimace.

"Nothing. Everything's just as awful as before!" he replied with a wave of his hand and went over to the window.

From where Sanin sat only Novikov's large, handsome silhouette could be seen, softly outlined by the fading light of the evening sky. Sanin looked at him closely for a long time.

When for the first time he'd taken the embarrassed, suffering Novikov to his pitiful, hysterical sister Lida, who was now not at all like the beautifully bold, proud young woman she'd been not long before, they didn't exchange a word about what had permeated their souls so deeply. Sanin realized they'd be unhappy if they talked about it but twice as unhappy if they didn't. He felt that they could discover what was so clear and simple to him only by groping, passing through suffering; he hadn't interfered, but he realized that these two people had withdrawn into a closed circle and that their meeting was inevitable.

Well, so be it, he thought. Let them suffer. They'll become gentler and purer as a result of their suffering. So be it!

But now he felt the time had come.

Novikov stood before the window and stared silently into the darkening sky. He was filled with a strange feeling in which longing for what had been irretrievably lost was subtly merged with a tremor of impatient expectation of new happiness. In this soft, sad twilight he could more clearly imagine Lida as timid, unhappy, insulted, and humiliated by everyone; it seemed to him that if he had the strength, he would fall to his knees before her, warm her cold fingers with kisses, and kindle new life in her by his great, all-forgiving love. Everything in him burned with a thirst for this feat, with tender emotion for himself and loving compassion for Lida, but he lacked the strength to go to her.

Sanin understood this too. He stood up slowly, shook his head, and said, "Lida's in the garden. Let's go."

Wistfully and happily, Novikov's heart tightened with a painful, pitiful feeling. A slight shudder passed across his face and disappeared. As he twirled his mustache it was clear that his fingers were trembling.

"Well then? Shall we?" Sanin repeated; his voice was imposing and serene, as if he were about to undertake some important but comprehensible task.

From his tone Novikov realized that Sanin understood everything occurring within him; he felt both enormous relief and naive, childlike apprehension.

"Let's go, let's go," Sanin continued softly; he took Novikov by the shoulders and pushed him toward the door.

"But . . . I . . ." Novikov muttered, suddenly feeling sweet tenderness and a desire to kiss Sanin. But he didn't; instead, he merely looked him in the face with his deep, tearful eyes.

It was dark in the garden and there was a smell of warm dew. Greenish shafts of twilight stood between the tree trunks like Gothic windows. The first mist of evening hovered lightly over the pale meadows. It seemed that something quiet and invisible was walking along the deserted paths among the silent trees, and that the dozing grasses and flowers were softly shuddering at its approach.

It was brighter on the bank and twilight filled half the sky beyond the river, gliding luminously through dark meadows. Lida was sitting there, very close to the water, her slender, sloping silhouette showing white against the grass, like a mysterious spirit grieving over the water.

The bright, bold mood that had taken possession of her under the influence of her brother's serene voice had disappeared just as quickly as it had come. Once again that dismal duo returned—shame and fear hovered over her and instilled in her the idea that she had no right not only to any new happiness but also to life itself.

For days at a time, book in hand, she sat in the garden because she couldn't look her mother in the eye. Thousands of times everything in her became indignant, thousands of times she told herself that her mother's distress would be nothing compared to her own life, but each time her mother drew near, Lida's voice faltered, losing its resonance, and a guilty, timid look came into her eyes. Her embarrassment, blushes, uncertain tone, and awkward glance troubled her mother. Annoying questions, anxieties, and agonizing, searching looks tormented Lida, so she began to keep her distance.

Thus she was sitting that evening, drearily watching the twilight fading on the dark horizon and thinking her own painful, inescapable thoughts.

She was reflecting on the fact that she didn't understand life. Something incomprehensibly huge and hidden, as tenacious and powerful as an octopus, was rising before her.

From the list of books she'd read, a series of great, liberating ideas passed through her mind, and she saw that her action was not only natural but also even good. It harmed no one and provided enjoyment to her and another person. Without this enjoyment she'd have had no youth and her life would be as depressing as a tree in autumn after losing all its leaves. The idea that religion hadn't sanctified her union with a man was ridiculous to her: the entire foundation of that idea had been long since undermined and destroyed by man's free thinking. Really, then, she should rejoice in the way a flower does on a sunny morning after being pollinated with new life, but she suffered and felt as if she were at the bottom of an abyss, beneath everyone else, the last of the last. No matter how many noble ideas and invincible truths she summoned up, they all melted away like wax near heat before the disgrace awaiting her tomorrow. Instead of trampling underfoot those whom she despised for their stupidity and limitations, she thought only about how to save herself and how to deceive them.

When she wept alone, hiding her tears from others, when she deceived them with her feigned cheerfulness, or when she sank into dull despair, she felt attracted only to Novikov, as a flower turns toward sunlight. The idea that he would save her seemed criminally disreputable to her; at times her indignation was aroused that she could depend on his forgiveness and love; but stronger than her convictions and stronger than her protest was the awareness of her own impotence and her longing to live. Instead of feeling indignant at people's stupidity, she trembled; instead of looking Novikov right in the eye, she was as timid in his presence as a slave. In this agitated young woman there was something pitiful and helpless, like a bird whose wings have been clipped and that will never be able to fly again.

At times when her torment became unbearable, Lida would always think of her brother: her soul would be filled with naive astonishment. It was clear that he held nothing sacred, that he looked at her, his own sister, with the eyes of a male of the species, that he was egotistical and immoral, but at the same time he was the only person with whom she felt at ease, with whom she could speak freely about the most precious secrets of her life. In his presence everything seemed so simple and trivial: she was pregnant, yes, but so what? She had had an affair, yes, but she had enjoyed it so much! Others would despise and humiliate her—what of it? Life lay before her, sunshine and open space, and there were people everywhere. Her mother would suffer—but that was her own choice! Lida hadn't been around to see her mother's youth, and her mother wouldn't be around to pursue her after she died; having met by chance on the road of life, having traveled together for part of the way, they couldn't and shouldn't now put obstacles in each other's path.

Lida saw that she herself would never become as free as her brother; in so thinking, she was merely submitting to the charms of that composed, determined man, but she continued to regard him with the same amazement and enraptured tenderness. Strange, freethinking thoughts wandered through her mind.

What if he were a stranger instead of my brother? she thought indecisively and apprehensively, trying to destroy this shameful but attractive idea.

Once again her thoughts turned to Novikov and, like a slave, she timidly awaited and hoped for his forgiveness and his love.

Thus was this enchanted circle completed; Lida was struggling within it helplessly, using up the last strength and brilliance of her bright young soul.

She heard steps and turned around.

Novikov and Sanin were coming toward her in silence, stepping over the tall grass. It was impossible to make out their faces in the pale evening twilight, but for some reason Lida at once felt that the terrible moment was imminent. She became pale and weak, as if life itself had abandoned her.

"Well now," said Sanin. "I've brought Novikov to see you. He'll tell you what he wants himself. Sit here for a while and I'll go and have some tea."

He turned sharply and walked away, stepping briskly across the grass.

For a few moments longer his white shirt was visible, gradually merging with the darkness; then it disappeared behind the trees, and it became so quiet that it was hard to believe he'd gone and wasn't standing there in the shadows of the trees.

Novikov and Lida followed him with their eyes; both understood from this shared gesture that everything had already been said and that all they had to do now was to repeat it aloud.

"Lidiya Petrovna," Novikov said quietly; the sound of his voice was so sad and touchingly sincere that Lida's heart tightened tenderly.

He's unassuming and pathetic too, and he's good, the young woman thought with dismal delight.

"I know everything, Lidiya Petrovna," Novikov continued, feeling that tender emotion was rising within him as he faced this challenge, as well as pity for her melancholy, timid figure. "But I love you just as I did before. Perhaps you'll come to love me sometime. Tell me . . . do you want to be my wife?"

There's no need to say anything about *that,* he thought. Let her never know the sacrifice I'm making for her.

Lida was silent. It was so still that swift splashes of water in the stream could be heard rushing toward the willow bushes.

"We're both unhappy," Novikov said suddenly and unexpectedly from the depths of his soul. "But perhaps together it'll be easier for us to go on living!"

Warm tears of gratitude and tenderness welled up in Lida's eyes. She raised her face to his and said, "Yes . . . perhaps!"

Her eyes said: As God as my witness, I'll be a good wife and will always love and comfort you!

Novikov felt this glance; he quickly and abruptly sank to his knees beside her and began kissing her trembling hand, himself trembling with tender emotion and suddenly awakened joyous passion. This passion was so distinctly and profoundly conveyed to Lida that her painful, pitiful feelings of timidity and shame vanished.

Well now, it's all over. I'll be happy once again. My dear, my poor dear! she thought, weeping tears of happiness without removing her hands, and kissing Novikov's soft hair, which she'd always liked. The memory of Zarudin flashed through her mind but it disappeared immediately.

Having decided that enough time had elapsed for their declarations, when Sanin arrived Lida and Novikov were holding hands, talking softly and trustingly. Novikov was saying that he'd never stopped loving her, while she was saying that she loved him now. And this was the truth, because Lida wanted love and happiness; she hoped to find them in him and loved this hope of hers.

It seemed to them that they'd never been so happy. Seeing Sanin, they fell silent and looked at him with their embarrassed, joyful, trusting eyes.

"Well, I understand!" Sanin said meaningfully, after glancing at them. "Thank heavens! May you both be happy!"

He wanted to add something but sneezed very loudly instead.

"It's damp. . . . Don't catch cold!" he added, wiping his eyes.

Lida laughed gaily, and her laughter once again carried over the river, enigmatically and beautifully.

"I'm going!" Sanin declared after a brief silence.

"Where to?" Novikov asked.

"Svarozhich has come for me with that officer—the one who likes Tolstoy. What's his name? That thin German!"

"Von Deitz!" Lida put in, laughing for no reason.

"That's him. They came to invite us all to some meeting. But I told them you weren't home."

"Why?" Lida asked, still laughing. "Maybe we would've gone along."

"Stay here," Sanin replied. "I'd sit here, too, if I had someone to sit with!"

And again he left, this time for good.

Evening set in. Stars twinkled in the dark, flowing stream.

 XXIV

The evening was dark and dense. Above the tops of the black, motionless trees clouds swirled heavily and hurriedly, as if hastening to some invisible goal, racing across the sky. Pale stars twinkled and faded in the greenish openings. Above, everything was filled with constant, malevolent motion, while below everything had become anxious expectation.

In this stillness the voices of people arguing sounded extremely harsh and shrill, like the screeching of small irritated animals.

"No matter what you say," Von Deitz cried, stumbling clumsily along on long legs like a crane's, "Christianity's given mankind an indestructible treasure as the only complete, comprehensible humanitarian doctrine there is!"

"Well, yes," Yury replied from behind, tossing his head stubbornly and staring angrily at his back. "But in the struggle with animal instinct, Christianity's proved just as powerless as every other."

"What do you mean proved?" Von Deitz exclaimed in annoyance. "The future belongs to Christianity; to talk about it as if it were all in the past . . ."

"Christianity has no future!" Yury interrupted, glaring with unprovoked hostility at the moving shape of the officer's military jacket. "If Christianity couldn't conquer humanity at the time of its most intense development and fell helplessly into the hands of scoundrels as a tool of shameless deception, then now, when even the word 'Christianity' has become insipid, it's absurd and ridiculous to expect a miracle. History doesn't forgive: what has once passed from the scene can never again return!"

The wooden track was barely visible beneath their feet; when it was pitch dark under the trees the possibility of stumbling over wooden stumps along the way became painfully real; their voices seemed unnatural because their faces were invisible.

"Christianity? passed from the scene?" cried Von Deitz, exaggerated astonishment and indignation in his voice.

"Of course it has," continued Yury stubbornly. "You seem so surprised, as if it were even inconceivable. Just as the Law of Moses passed from the scene, just as Buddha died and the Greek gods passed away, so too Christ is dead. It's the law of evolution. What is it about that that frightens you? After all, you don't believe in the divinity of his teachings, do you?"

"Of course not!" snorted Von Deitz in an offended manner, responding not so much to the question as to Yury's offensive tone.

"So how can you even allow for the possibility that man can create eternal laws?"

What an idiot! thought Yury about Von Deitz at this moment; and an invincible, most agreeable certainty that this man was infinitely less intelligent than he, and that he'd never be able to understand what was as clear as day and simple to him, combined in Yury's head with an annoying desire to persuade him no matter what and to win the argument.

"Let's assume it's so," the lanky officer replied, now agitated and irritated too. "But Christianity is the foundation of the future. It hasn't perished; it's fallen into the earth like a seed, and will bring forth fruit."

"That's not what I'm talking about," answered Yury, a little confused and therefore even more exasperated. "I wanted to say . . ."

"No, allow me," Von Deitz interrupted him triumphantly, fearing to lose the advantage, and once again glancing around and stumbling on the path. "That's precisely what you said."

"If I say it's not so, then it's not so. How odd!" Yury cut him off with shrill malice at the thought that the ignorant Von Deitz could think, even for one moment, that he was smarter than he was. "I wanted to say . . ."

"Well, perhaps. Excuse me if I misunderstood!" said Von Deitz with a condescending smirk and a shrug of his narrow shoulders, in no way concealing the fact that he'd caught Yury, and that whatever he might say now would only be a belated retreat.

Yury understood him and felt such hostility and offense that he almost choked.

"In no way am I denying the enormous role played by Christianity."

"Then you're contradicting yourself!" chortled Von Deitz with new triumph, rejoicing that Yury was incomparably less intelligent than he; apparently he hadn't even the remotest conception of what was laid out so elegantly and beautifully in Von Deitz's mind.

"It may seem to you that I'm contradicting myself, but as a matter of fact . . . on the contrary, I . . . my thinking is absolutely logical, and it's not my fault that you . . . you've no desire to understand me," Yury cried in a shrill voice, now sounding somewhat inconsistent and agonized. "I'm saying and have said before that Christianity's outlived its usefulness and that it's no longer possible to expect salvation from it."

"Well, yes, but do you reject the beneficial influence of Christianity—that is, its role in the foundation—" said Von Deitz, also raising his voice and hastening to grab his thought before it escaped at this point in the conversation.

"I do not reject that."

"But I do!" Sanin spoke up humorously from where he'd been walking along in silence. His voice was cheerful and serene, and in strange contrast to the strident tone of the conversation.

Yury fell silent. This calm voice and plainly good-natured sarcasm offended him, but he could think of nothing to reply. He always felt awkward and uncomfortable arguing with Sanin, as if all the words he was accustomed to use were not those he needed when he talked to Sanin. And he always had the feeling that he was trying to topple a wall while standing on slippery ice.

But Von Deitz, stumbling along, with his spurs jangling loudly, cried in a high-pitched, nasty voice, "Allow me to ask why this is so?"

"It just is," Sanin replied with an elusive expression.

"How can that be? If you say things like that, you have to prove it!"

"Why do I have to prove it?"

"What do you mean, why?"

"I don't have to prove anything. It's my own conviction; I haven't the least desire to convince you, and there's no need to."

"If that's what you think," said Yury with restraint, "then one should cross off all literature."

"No, why?" Sanin replied. "Literature's a great and important thing. Literature! Genuine literature, as I understand it, doesn't polemicize with any sluggard who just happens by, who has nothing to do and wants to convince everyone that he's so clever. Literature reconstructs the whole of life, enters into the lifeblood of humanity from generation to generation. If you destroyed literature, life would lose most of its color, it would fade."

Von Deitz stopped, let Yury get ahead, and then, drawing level with Sanin, said, "No, please go on. I find the question you've just broached extremely interesting."

"My idea's very simple," Sanin said with a laugh. "If you like, I can explain it to you. In my opinion, Christianity's played a sad role in the life of mankind. At a time when things became really unbearable for human beings and people were at their wits' end, when the oppressed and dispossessed had come to their senses and with one blow had overturned the impossibly severe and unjust order of things, simply destroying everything that lived off the blood of others, at that moment gentle, humble Christianity appeared, full of promise. It condemned strife, promised inner bliss, plunged man into sweet sleep, offered a religion of nonresistance to evil, and, to make a long story short, allowed all the steam to escape! Those colossal figures who'd been brought up amid age-old insults went, like complete idiots, into the arena and there, with a courage worthy of infinitely better devotion, practically tore off their flesh with their own hands! Their enemies, of course, could hope for nothing better! Now centuries will be needed, centuries of endless humiliation and oppression, to arouse the spirit of indignation once more. Christianity's covered over the human personality, which is too in-domitable to become a slave, with a detestable mantle and has concealed be-neath it all the colors of the free human spirit. It has deceived the strong who could take happiness into their own hands right now, today, and it has transferred the center of gravity of their life into the future, to a dream about something unreal, something none of them will ever see. All the beauty of life has disappeared; boldness has vanished; only obligation remains and a senseless dream of the future golden age . . . a golden age for others, of course! Yes, Christianity's played a disgraceful role, and for a long time Christ's name will be the scourge of all mankind!"

Von Deitz suddenly came to a halt; in the darkness his long arms could be seen waving up and down.

"Well, I say!" he said in a strange voice, full of apprehension and incom-prehension.

A complex feeling arose in Yury's soul, as if there were nothing special in Sanin's words and as if he, too, just like Sanin, could say everything he thought and wanted to say; but the shadow of enormous fear before the Unknown, a fear whose existence Yury had forgotten in his own soul and didn't want to think about, oppressed his thoughts. Yury felt this secret ap-prehension and was ashamed of it.

"Can you imagine the bloody chaos that would've burst upon mankind if Christianity hadn't forestalled it?" he asked with a feeling of strange, ner-vous animosity toward Sanin.

"Nope!" said Sanin with a gesture of disdain. "First of all, during the reign of Christianity the arenas were drenched with the blood of martyrs; people were killed, locked up in prison, confined to madhouses. Day after day more blood was shed than could ever be lost in any major world up-heaval. And worst of all, people still bring about any improvement in their lives through bloodshed, revolution, and anarchy, while they continue to make humanitarianism and the love of one's neighbor the foundation of their lives. The result is stupid tragedy, hypocrisy, and lies—neither fish nor fowl! I'd prefer worldwide catastrophe immediately rather than dull and senselessly stupid life for the next two thousand years!"

Yury fell silent for a while. It was strange that his mind paused not on the meaning of the speaker's words but on Sanin's personality. His obvious self-confidence struck him as extremely offensive, even completely insufferable.

"Tell me, please," he said suddenly, not anticipating what he would say but giving way to a strong desire to offend Sanin. "why do you always speak as if you were lecturing young children?"

Von Deitz was surprised and embarrassed; he muttered something, jan-gling his spurs in a conciliatory manner.

"Well, how do you like that!" said Sanin with annoyance. "Why are you so resentful?"

Yury felt that his words were inopportune and that he should stop, but deep-seated irritation and his own wounded self-respect had taken hold of him.

"That's really an unpleasant tone!" he replied in a stubborn, threatening voice.

"It's my usual tone," said Sanin with a strange expression of annoyance and a desire to calm him down.

"It's not always appropriate," Yury continued, raising his voice unintentionally and making it shrill. "I don't know where you get all that self-confidence."

"Probably from the knowledge that I'm more intelligent than you are," Sanin replied, more calmly now.

Shuddering from head to foot like a taut string, Yury paused momentarily.

"Listen here!" he said in a ringing voice; although his face wasn't visible, one could sense that he'd turned pale.

"Don't get angry," Sanin said affectionately. "I don't want to offend you; I merely express my sincere opinion. It's just what you think of me, what Von Deitz thinks of the two of us, and so on and so forth. . . . It's only natural."

Sanin's voice was so sincere and affectionate that it was somehow strange to go on shouting, and Yury fell silent for a moment. Von Deitz, obviously suffering on his account, was quietly jangling his spurs and breathing heavily.

"But I don't say it to your face," Yury muttered.

"That's a mistake. I was listening to your argument, and the same affront was obvious in every word. It's all a question of form. I say what I think, while you don't say what you think. That's not interesting at all. If we were more candid, it'd be much more enjoyable!"

Von Deitz suddenly started laughing shrilly.

"That's original!" he cried, choking on his laughter.

Yury fell silent. His rage subsided and he even began to feel cheerful; but he was upset that he'd conceded and he didn't want to show it.

"That would be much too simple!" declared Von Deitz pompously after he stopped laughing.

"You prefer it to be intricate and complicated?" Sanin asked.

Von Deitz shrugged and became thoughtful.

 XXV

They left the boulevard; it was brighter in the bare, empty streets farther away. The dry planks of sidewalks shone white against the black earth, while in the broad, pale sky filled with puffy clouds, a few stars twinkling through loomed unusually large.

"Here," said Von Deitz. Opening a low gate, he vanished into the darkness.

Immediately a rasping old dog started barking and someone shouted from the porch, "Down, Sultan!"

An enormous deserted courtyard opened out before them. At one end stood the dim, dark shape of a steam mill with its thin black chimney, sadly and mournfully rising toward the distant clouds; black sheds surrounded it; there were no trees, only a small garden under the windows of one wing of the house. A window was open and its bright light streamed out into the dusky darkness, illuminating the translucent green leaves.

"What a dismal place!" said Sanin.

"How long is it since the mill closed down?" asked Yury.

"Oh, a long time," replied Von Deitz. Glancing through the lighted window in passing, he said in a tone of strange satisfaction: "Oho! Quite a few people have gathered already."

Yury and Sanin also glanced across the front garden. Through the inviting, bright rectangular window they could see heads moving in a cloud of blue tobacco smoke. Someone leaned out of the window into the darkness: a broad-shouldered man with a halo of curly hair blocked their view.

"Who's there?" he asked loudly.

"Friends," replied Yury.

They climbed onto the porch and encountered a man who immediately started shaking their hands in a friendly, hasty fashion.

"I'd begun to think you weren't coming!" he said cheerfully with a thick Jewish accent.

"Soloveichik, this is Sanin," said Von Deitz, introducing them and amicably shaking the invisible Soloveichik's cold, trembling hand.

Soloveichik laughed nervously in embarrassment.

"Pleased to meet you. I've heard so much about you, and you know, it's very . . ." he said in confusion, stepping back, even though he was still holding Sanin's hand.

He bumped into Yury and trod on Von Deitz's foot.

"Forgive me, Yakov Adolfovich!" he cried, letting go of Sanin's hand and grabbing hold of Von Deitz.

As they were all crowding into the dark hallway, it took a long time to find the door and each other.

In the entrance hall, on nails methodically and purposefully hammered into the wall by Soloveichik for this evening, were hanging hats and caps; the whole window was filled with numerous dark-green beer bottles.

In the light Soloveichik turned out to be a youthful Jew with dark eyes, curly hair, and a handsome slender face with bad teeth constantly displayed in his obsequious, humble grin.

Those entering were met with a chorus of animated, noisy greetings.

First of all Yury saw Karsavina sitting on the windowsill; everything before his eyes immediately took on a joyful appearance, as if he hadn't come to a stuffy, smoke-filled room but had arrived at a spring festival in an open meadow in the forest.

Karsavina smiled at him cheerfully but in embarrassment.

"Well, ladies and gentlemen, it seems that everyone's here now," Soloveichik shouted, trying to speak loudly and cheerfully but straining his weak voice painfully and unsteadily, and gesturing strangely with his hands. "Excuse me, Yury Nikolaevich, I seem to keep pushing you," he said, interrupting himself, bending forward and grinning broadly.

"Never mind," said Yury, taking hold of his arm cheerfully.

"Not everyone's here—but to hell with the others!" a portly, handsome student replied, and from his ample but strong merchant's voice it was clear that he was very confident and accustomed to telling people what to do.

Soloveichik jumped over to a table and suddenly rang a small bell, cheerfully and cunningly smiling at his own idea, thought up that very morning.

"Hey, stop it!" the portly student cried in anger. "You always cook up such stupid things! That's a completely unnecessary formality!"

"It's nothing. I just . . ." Soloveichik said with an embarrassed giggle, and hid the bell in his pocket.

"I think we could move the table to the middle of the room," said the student.

"Right away," Soloveichik said hurriedly, grabbing hold of one edge of the table ineffectually.

"Watch out . . . don't knock the lamp over!" cried Dubova.

"Hey, who asked you to poke your nose in?" the student said with irritation, banging his fist on his knee.

"Let me help you," Sanin offered.

"Please," Soloveichik replied so quickly that it came out sounding more like "pis."

Sanin moved the table to the center of the room, and as he did so, for some reason everyone stared at his back and shoulders, which were easily visible beneath his thin shirt.

"Now then, Gozhienko, as the initiator of this meeting, it's fitting for you to have the first word," said the pale Dubova; from her intelligent, unattractive eyes it was difficult to tell whether she was speaking in earnest or mocking the portly student.

"Ladies and gentlemen," Gozhienko began in a deep though pleasant-sounding baritone, raising his voice. "Of course, everyone already knows why we're gathered here, so we can proceed without a formal introduction."

"I, for one, don't know why I came, but so be it," Sanin replied with a smile. "I heard there'd be beer."

Gozhienko glanced at him brusquely through the light and continued: "The aim of our circle is, through mutual readings, discussion of those readings, and independent synopses, to . . ."

"What do you mean by 'mutual' readings?" asked Dubova, and once again it was hard to tell whether she was being serious or sarcastic.

The portly Gozhienko blushed slightly. "I meant to say 'joint' readings. Thus the aim of our circle, while fostering the development of our members in the process, is to clarify individual views and to encourage the emergence in our town of a party circle that will be sympathetic to the program of the Social Democrats."

"Aha!" Ivanov drawled, scratching the back of his head quizzically.

"But that's for later. To begin with, we won't set such broad goals for ourselves."

"Or such narrow ones," Dubova prompted him in a peculiar tone of voice.

"Such broad goals," Gozhienko continued, pretending not to hear her. "We'll begin by drafting a program of readings; I propose that we devote this evening's meeting to that task."

"Soloveichik, are your workers coming?" asked Dubova.

"But of course!" Soloveichik jumped up from his seat as if he'd been stung. "We've gone to fetch them!"

"Soloveichik, don't squeal!" Gozhienko said, interrupting him.

"Here they come," Shafrov said seriously and thoughtfully, listening to what Gozhienko was saying as if performing a religious ritual.

The creaking of the gate could be heard through the window, as well as the husky barking of a dog.

"They're coming," cried Soloveichik with extraordinary excitement; he rushed headlong out of the room.

"Sultan, down!" he shouted loudly.

They could hear heavy footsteps, voices, and coughing. A smallish student from the technical school entered, resembling Gozhienko except that he was dark and unattractive; he was followed by two embarrassed and awkward men with blackened hands, wearing short jackets over their dirty red shirts. One was very tall and thin with a clean-shaven, ashen face on which prolonged malnutrition, endless worry, and persistent spite concealed in the depths of his oppressed soul had left their dark, pale imprint. The other resembled an athlete—broad-shouldered, curly-haired, and handsome like a peasant lad come to town for the first time and finding himself in a strange, still somewhat amusing setting. Soloveichik followed them in, walking sideways.

"Gentlemen, here are . . ." he began triumphantly.

"That'll do," Gozhienko said, interrupting him as usual. "Greetings, comrades."

"Pistsov and Kudryavyi," said the student from the technical school, introducing them.

It seemed odd to everyone that Pistsov turned out to be the bearded, handsome athlete and Kudryavyi the thin, pale worker.[23]

---

[23] Pistsov means "scribe"; Kudryavyi means "curly."

Stepping cautiously and heavily, they made their way around the room, stiffly shaking the hands extended to them in a particularly courteous way. Pistsov smiled in embarrassment, while Kudryavyi moved his long, thin neck in a curious way, as if choked by his shirt collar. Then they sat down next to the window near Karsavina, who was perched on the windowsill.

"Why didn't Nikolaev come?" the disgruntled Gozhienko asked.

"He couldn't," Pistsov replied courteously.

"Nikolaev's dead drunk," Kudryavyi interrupted glumly and abruptly, with a jerk of his neck.

"Ah . . ." Gozhienko said, nodding his head awkwardly.

For some reason his awkwardness struck Yury Svarozhich as disagreeable; he immediately felt that this portly student was his personal enemy.

"He chose the better path," Ivanov observed.

The dog began barking in the courtyard.

"Someone's here," said Dubova.

"Could it be the police?" Gozhienko said with feigned indifference.

"You really want it to be the police, don't you?" Dubova added at once.

Sanin looked into the intelligent eyes in her unattractive face—though they were nicely set off by the blonde braid falling over her shoulder—and thought, What a splendid young woman!

Soloveichik jumped up to rush outside, but recovered himself in time and pretended he was getting a cigarette from the table.

Gozhienko noticed his movement and instead of replying to Dubova he said, "You're such a pest, Soloveichik!"

Soloveichik blushed deeply and blinked his eyes, which for a moment became downcast and pensive, as if the thought had finally occurred to his unassuming, uncertain mind that his desire to serve everyone and to help really didn't deserve such sharp rebukes.

"Leave him alone!" said Dubova in annoyance.

Novikov came into the room quickly and noisily.

"Well, here I am!" he said, smiling cheerfully.

"So I see," Sanin replied.

Novikov smiled in embarrassment and, shaking his hand, whispered hurriedly, as if in justification, "Lidiya Petrovna had guests."

"Ah!"

"Well then, have we come here to talk or what?" asked the technical student glumly.

"Let's begin."

"So you haven't started yet?" Novikov asked excitedly, shaking hands with the workers who stood up hurriedly to greet him.

They found it awkward that here the doctor who condescended to them when he treated them at the hospital was extending his hand as a comrade.

"Is it possible to start on time with the likes of you?" said Gozhienko disagreeably through clenched teeth.

"Well then, ladies and gentlemen, of course we all wish to broaden our general outlook, and since we find that the best means of self-education and self-development is systematic reading together and the exchange of opinions about our reading, we have decided to establish a small circle."

"Indeed," Pistsov said with a sigh, cheerfully surveying everyone with his sparkling dark eyes.

"The question now is this: What exactly should we read? Perhaps someone will suggest a provisional program?"

Shafrov adjusted his glasses and, notebook in hand, stood up slowly.

"I think," he began in a dry monotone, "that our readings should be divided into two parts. Undoubtedly any form of development consists of two components: the study of life in its evolutionary aspect and the study of life as it is."

"Shafrov, be more specific," countered Dubova.

"The first aim is achieved by reading books of a scholarly, historical kind; the second, by reading literary texts that direct us inward, toward life."

"If we go on like this, everyone's going to fall asleep," Dubova said unrelentingly, with a gentle twinkle in her eyes.

"I'm trying to speak so that everyone will understand," Shafrov replied meekly.

"Have it your own way. Speak in any way you can," said Dubova with a dismissive gesture.

Karsavina also began laughing affectionately at Shafrov; tossing back her head, she displayed her ample white neck. Her laughter was sonorous and deep.

"I have drawn up a program but it might be tedious to read it out aloud," Shafrov said hurriedly, glancing at Dubova. "Therefore I propose that we start with *The Origin of the Family*[24] and read Darwin alongside it, and from literature, Tolstoy—"

"Tolstoy, of course!" agreed the lanky Von Deitz smugly and he began to light a cigarette.

For some reason Shafrov paused a moment until the cigarette was lit, then continued methodically.

"Chekhov, Ibsen, Knut Hamsun . . ."[25]

"But we've read all that already!" Karsavina exclaimed in surprise.

Yury listened to her resonant voice with enamored delight and said, "Of course! Shafrov's forgetting that he's not at some Sunday reading group. Besides, what a strange combination—Tolstoy and Knut Hamsun!"

Shafrov calmly and tediously offered several arguments in defense of his proposal, but no one could understand what he wanted to say.

---

[24] *The Origin of the Family, Private Property, and the State* (1884), by Friedrich Engels (1820–95), ranks among the fundamental works of Communist literature and profoundly influenced Lenin.

[25] Knut Hamsun (1859–1952), Norwegian novelist, was awarded the Nobel Prize for Literature in 1920. His works stressed individualism.

"No," replied Yury loudly and decisively, delighted that Karsavina was looking at him. "I don't agree with you."

He began to expound his own views; and the more he said, the more he tried to win Karsavina's approval. He felt that he was succeeding and attacked Shafrov mercilessly, even on those points where he agreed with him.

The portly Gozhienko began to object. He considered himself more educated, smarter, and more eloquent than everyone else; and having organized this circle, he was determined to play the leading role. Yury's success wounded him and goaded him into action. He hadn't been familiar with Yury's views before and was therefore unable to argue with him tooth and nail; so he merely seized on some weak points and refused to let go.

A lengthy and seemingly interminable argument followed. The technical student, Ivanov, and Novikov took part in it, and soon their irritated faces glowered in the tobacco haze and their words became tangled in a confused, formless chaos in which nothing could be understood.

Dubova sank into thought and stared silently at the lamp, while Karsavina, no longer listening, opened the window onto the front garden and, folding her ample arms on her chest, leaned the back of her head against the window frame and gazed dreamily into the dark night.

At first she could see nothing; then from the black darkness there emerged dark trees, the illuminated fence of the front garden, and behind them a shimmering, dim pool of light falling on the path leading through the grass. A gentle, steady breeze enveloped her shoulder and arm and lightly ruffled separate strands of hair on her temples. She raised her head and in the gently glowing darkness could discern dimly a constant, strangely agitated procession of dark clouds. She was thinking about Yury and her love; thoughts both sweetly sad and sadly sweet, alarming and soothing, filled her young woman's mind. It was so good to sit there, yielding her whole body to the cool darkness and listening to one agitated male voice in particular, the loudest of all that resounded in the general din.

There was a general commotion in the room and it became increasingly clear that each person there thought himself cleverer than the rest and wanted to enlighten all the others. There was something unpleasant and painful about this that embittered even the most peaceable among them.

"Yes, if you talk like that," said Yury stubbornly, becoming tense, his eyes flashing, and afraid to concede before Karsavina, who was listening only to the sound of his voice, not to his words, "one must return to the source of all ideas."

"Then, in your opinion, what should we read?" Gozhienko asked in a hostile, sarcastic tone.

"What? Confucius, the Gospels, Ecclesiastes . . ."

"The Psalms and Lives of the Saints!" put in the technical student with ridicule.

Gozhienko laughed maliciously, failing to recall that he himself had never read any of these works.

"What on earth!" Shafrov drawled in disappointment.

"Just like church!" Pistsov said with a giggle.

Yury blushed angrily. "I'm not joking! If you want to be logical . . ."

"But what did you just say to me about Christ?" Von Deitz interrupted him triumphantly.

"What did I say? If one wants to study life, to formulate a definitive worldview that consists entirely of a person's relationship with others and with himself, then isn't it best to reflect on the extraordinary work of those people who represent the best models of mankind, and who first and foremost tried during their own lives to apply the most practicable, most complicated, and most intelligible relations to mankind—"

"I don't agree with you!" said Gozhienko, interrupting.

"And I do," said Novikov, interrupting the student.

Once again a chaotic and confusing uproar ensued in which it was impossible to identify either the beginning or the end of any opinion.

As soon as everyone started talking, Soloveichik immediately fell silent, sat down in the corner, and listened. At first the expression on his face was one of rapt, heartfelt, even somewhat childlike attention, but then unmistakable traces of incomprehension and suffering began to appear in the corners of his mouth and eyes.

Sanin sat there in silence, drinking beer and smoking. There was a look of boredom and irritation on his face. When amid the din he began to detect shrill notes of dissension, he stood up, put out his cigarette, and said, "You know, this is becoming tiresome!"

"Extremely tiresome!" Dubova echoed.

"Vanity of vanities and vexation of spirit!" said Ivanov in a voice indicating that he'd been thinking this for some time and was just waiting for a chance to employ it.

"How so?" asked the dark-haired technical student nastily.

Sanin paid no attention to him; turning to Yury, he said, "Do you really think in all seriousness that one can develop a worldview just by reading some books?"

"Of course I do," Yury said, looking at him in astonishment.

"You're wrong," replied Sanin. "If that were true, one could transform all mankind according to one model by giving them books to read that are all based on the same assumptions. A worldview is provided by life itself, in its entirety, in which literature and human thought are only an insignificant part. A worldview isn't a theory of life; rather it's the disposition of an individual human personality, variable at that, as long as a person's soul is still alive. So there can never be any definitive worldview such as the one you're working toward."

"What do you mean, never?" Yury cried angrily.

Once again a look of boredom appeared on Sanin's face. "No, of course not. If a worldview were possible as a finished theory, human thought would cease altogether. But it doesn't: each moment of life offers its new word . . . and each of us must hear this word and apprehend it without setting limits or boundaries for ourselves beforehand.

"But what's the use of talking about it?" Sanin interrupted himself. "Think whatever you like. I'd merely like to ask you one thing: Why have you, after reading hundreds of works, from Ecclesiastes to Marx, not yet formed your own worldview?"

"What do you mean, 'not yet formed'?" Yury replied with acute sensitivity, his dark eyes flashing menacingly. "I have one. Perhaps it's mistaken, but it exists!"

"So what are you planning to formulate?"

Pistsov giggled.

"You . . ." Kudryavyi growled at him with contempt, his neck swaying.

"He's so clever!" Karsavina thought to herself about Sanin with naive admiration.

She looked at him and at Svarozhich, and felt thoroughly embarrassed, elated, and confused: it was as if these two men were arguing not between themselves but only over her, to win her over.

"So it turns out," said Sanin, "that you really have no need for what it is you've all met to discover. I understand and see clearly that everyone here merely wants to force others to accept his own opinion, and most of all fears he'll be disabused of his own views. Speaking frankly, that's boring."

"Excuse me!" Gozhienko objected, raising his husky voice noticeably.

"No," replied Sanin in dissatisfaction. "You have the most splendid worldview and you've read a lot of books, that's immediately apparent, but you're annoyed that not everyone thinks the way you do; besides, you're offending Soloveichik, who's done you absolutely no harm."

Gozhienko fell into astonished silence and looked at Sanin as if he'd said something absolutely extraordinary.

"Yury Nikolaevich," Sanin said cheerfully. "Don't be angry with me for speaking somewhat harshly to you. I can see the real conflict in your soul."

"What conflict?" asked Yury, blushing, not knowing whether to be offended. Just as it had done on the way to this meeting, Sanin's tender, serene voice moved him now.

"You yourself know," replied Sanin, smiling. "You shouldn't give a damn about this childish undertaking, otherwise it'll end badly."

"Listen here," said Gozhienko, now flushed. "You're taking far too many liberties!"

"No more than you."

"What?"

"Just think about it," Sanin said cheerfully. "There's much more that's impolite and unpleasant in what you say and do than in what I say."

"I don't understand you!" Gozhienko exclaimed bitterly.

"Well, that's not my fault!"

"What?"

Without saying another word, Sanin picked up his hat, then declared, "I'm leaving. This is too tiresome!"

"Right you are! And there's no more beer!" Ivanov said in agreement and went out into the hall.

"Yes, it's clear nothing will come of this," said Dubova.

"Walk me home, Yury Nikolaevich," called Karsavina. "Good-bye," she said to Sanin.

Their eyes met for a moment, and for some reason Karsavina found it both frightening and enjoyable.

"Alas!" Dubova said, leaving. "Our circle has withered before it ever blossomed."

"But how did it happen?" Soloveichik asked suddenly, in a downhearted, absent-minded tone of voice, getting in everyone's way.

Only now did they remember about him, and many were struck by the strange, confused expression on his face.

"Listen, Soloveichik," Sanin said thoughtfully. "I'll come and chat with you sometime."

"Please do," Soloveichik said hurriedly and happily, standing up straight.

Outside, after the bright room, it was so dark they couldn't even see who was standing next to whom; only loud voices could be heard.

The workers walked apart from the others; after they'd withdrawn into the darkness, Pistsov said with a chuckle:

"Look . . . it's always like that: they gather together to do something and then each goes off on his own! I only liked that big strapping one!"

"A lot you understand when educated folks get together to have a discussion," Kudryavyi said, twisting his neck as if he were being suffocated, his voice bitter and blunt.

Pistsov whistled smugly and sarcastically.

 XXVI

For a long time Soloveichik stood quietly in the courtyard looking up at the dark, starless sky and rubbing his cold hands.

Beyond the black storehouses, whistling around their metal roofs, the wind bent the treetops as they huddled together like ghosts; meanwhile, as if powered by some invincible force, the clouds raced by overhead. Their dark masses stood silently on the skyline, climbing and reaching unattainable heights, while multitudes of them rolled into the abyss over the new horizon. It seemed as if innumerable regiments were awaiting them impatiently beyond the edge of the black earth and, one after another, with dark banners unfurled, were marching boisterously into mysterious combat. From time to time the restless wind brought the din and clamor of distant battle.

Soloveichik looked up with childlike anxiety; he had never felt as clearly as he did that night how small he was, how frail, as if he didn't exist at all amid the infinitely enormous, swirling chaos of the sky.

"Oh, God, God!" he said with a sigh.

When faced with the sky and the night, he was not the same man he was in the presence of other people. The anxious obsequiousness that distorted his gestures vanished; his decaying teeth, resembling the ingratiating, bared grin of a mangy hound, were covered by this Jewish youth's thin lips; his dark eyes looked sad and serious.

He slowly returned to the room, extinguished an unnecessary lamp, clumsily put the table back in its place, and arranged the chairs neatly. Waves of tobacco smoke swirled through the air, the floor was covered with rubbish, crushed cigarette butts, and burned matches. He quickly picked up a broom and swept the floor, with a strange, dreamy fondness trying as always to make the place where he lived more beautiful and elegant. Then he fetched an old slop bucket from the storeroom, broke some bread into it, and, hunching over, made his way across the courtyard, taking very small steps and waving one arm.

He set a lamp in the window so that it would be brighter, but it was still deserted and eerie outside, and he was glad when he reached Sultan's kennel.

Invisible in the darkness, the shaggy, warm Sultan came out to meet him, wheezing; his iron chain rattled incongruously and mournfully.

"Ah, Sultan. Here, boy!" Soloveichik cried, trying to reassure himself with the sound of his own loud voice. In the darkness Sultan thrust his cold, wet nose into his hand.

"Here, here . . ." said Soloveichik, putting down the bucket.

Sultan sniffed the offering and then munched noisily, while Soloveichik stood over him and smiled glumly into the darkness.

What can I do? he wondered. Can I force people to think another way? I thought others would tell me how to live and what to think! God didn't give me the voice of a prophet! What can I accomplish?

Sultan growled contentedly.

"Go ahead, eat. Go on!" Soloveichik said. "I'd let you off your chain to run around a little, but I don't have the key and I'm feeling too weak."

They're such grand, clever people. They know so much and profess Christ's teaching, while I . . . Perhaps I'm to blame myself: I should've said something, but I didn't know what!

In the distance, beyond the town, someone gave a prolonged, mournful whistle. Sultan lifted his head and listened. Large drops could be heard falling from his muzzle into the bucket.

"Eat, go on, eat. That's the sound of the train!" said Soloveichik, guessing the reason for the dog's apprehension.

Sultan sighed heavily.

"I wonder if people will ever live like that. Or perhaps they can't," Soloveichik said aloud, shrugging gloomily.

In the darkness he imagined limitless infinity, a sea of people emerging from the darkness and then returning to it. A succession of centuries without beginning or end, a chain of suffering without a ray of hope, without meaning or completion. And there, above, where God was, only eternal silence.

Sultan's collar rattled against the empty bucket, and then he overturned it and wagged his tail, making the chain jingle slightly.

"Finished, eh? Well . . ."

Soloveichik stroked Sultan's rough shaggy coat and for a minute felt beneath his hand the dog's warm body respond affectionately to his touch; then he headed toward the house.

Somewhere behind him Sultan's chain rattled; it was brighter somehow in the courtyard, but as a result the huge dark mass of the mill seemed even blacker and more terrible, with its chimney reaching to the sky and its narrow storehouses resembling coffins. A long band of light stretched from the window across the front garden; in it one could see the motionless, mysterious little heads of lovely, frail flowers shrinking apprehensively beneath the stormy black sky, its countless dark banners unfolding malevolently.

Overcome by grief, terror, loneliness, and a feeling of irreparable loss, Soloveichik returned to his room, sat down at the table, and began to weep.

## XXVII

A dissipated human body, like the raw edge of an exposed nerve honed to the point of pain by violent pleasures, reacted painfully to the very word "woman." Immutably naked, immutably available, she stood before Voloshin at every moment of his life; every woman's dress, draped around the lithe, full figure of a female body, aroused him to a state in which his knees began to tremble dreadfully.

When he left Petersburg, where he'd relinquished a large number of luscious, sleek women who tormented his body nightly with frenzied, naked caresses, and when he had to attend to a complicated, important matter on which the lives of many people who worked for him depended, Voloshin was preoccupied by the unconcealed fantasy of young, fresh females reared in the provincial wilderness. He imagined them as shy, frightened, and as firm as forest mushrooms; even from a distance he could detect the enticing fragrance of their youth and purity.

Despite the fact that the thought of Zarudin's company seemed shocking to Voloshin, as soon as he had liberated himself from those hungry, dirty, secretly irate people, he freshened up his thin, flabby body with cologne and the snow-white cleanliness of a light suit, took a cab, and, trembling with impatience, set off to find Zarudin.

The officer was sitting before his window looking into the dark garden, drinking cold tea and trying to enjoy the gentle, cool evening air wafting in.

"A lovely evening!" he was repeating, but his mind was far away; he felt awkward, frightened, and embarrassed.

He was afraid of Lida. He hadn't seen her since the day of their last conversation and now pictured her quite differently from the way she was when she gave herself to him.

Whatever happens, this affair isn't over yet! One way or another we have to get rid of the infant. Or else forget about it? Zarudin asked himself timidly.

What's she doing now?

Before his eyes rose the beautiful but threatening and vengeful face of a young woman with tightly clenched thin lips and enigmatic dark eyes.

What if she suddenly does something stupid? That sort of woman doesn't just turn her back! Somehow I'll have to . . ."

The vision of an unforeseen but horrible scandal rose hazily before Zarudin's eyes, and his cowardly heart sank.

But what exactly could she do to me? he asked himself at times; then it occurred to him, so very simple and not at all burdensome: Perhaps she'll drown herself? Well, to hell with her. I didn't make her do it! She'll say she was my mistress. So what? That merely proves I'm an attractive man. I never promised to marry her! It's odd, really! he thought with a shrug, but at the same moment he felt a dark, dreadful weight pressing down on him again. Rumors will circulate and I won't be able to show my face anywhere! he thought; with a trembling hand he mechanically brought the glass of cold, overly sweetened tea to his lips.

He was just as clean, sweet-smelling, and handsome as ever, but it seemed that all over him, on everything—his face, his snow-white jacket, his hands, and even his heart—there lay some filthy stain that was spreading.

Hey, it will all pass. It's not the first time! he kept reassuring himself, but something inside him didn't want to believe it.

Voloshin entered, shuffling his feet casually and grinning condescendingly; at once the whole room was filled with the smell of cologne, tobacco, and musk, replacing the odor of the cool air and green garden.

"Ah, Pavel Lvovich!" said Zarudin, jumping up rather startled.

Voloshin greeted him, sat down by the window, and lit a cigar. He was so self-assured in Zarudin's opinion, so elegant and clean, that the officer felt a tinge of envy and tried his utmost to assume the same carefree, self-assured look. But his eyes continued to wander nervously: since Lida had called him a pig to his face, it seemed to him that everyone must know about it and be laughing at him behind his back.

Smiling and self-assured but with ineffectual wit, Voloshin began chatting about trifles; but it was hard for him to maintain that tone. An impatient desire to discuss the theme of women quickly began to force its way into his witticisms and anecdotes about Petersburg and the strike at the factory.

Taking advantage of the moment when he lit another cigar, he fell silent and looked intently into Zarudin's eyes.

From his look something furtive and shameless penetrated the officer's gaze and they understood each other. Voloshin adjusted his pince-nez and smiled, baring his teeth. This smile was immediately reflected on Zarudin's handsome, now impudent face.

"I assume you're not wasting your time here?" asked Voloshin slyly, squinting knowingly.

Zarudin replied with a boastfully disdainful shrug, "Oh, more or less as usual. What else is there to do?"

They laughed and fell silent for a while. Voloshin greedily awaited details; a little vein beneath his left knee throbbed convulsively. But before Zarudin flashed momentarily the details of something else—not what Voloshin wanted to hear but of the thing that had been tormenting him of late.

He turned slightly toward the garden and drummed his fingers on the windowsill.

But Voloshin waited quietly and Zarudin felt the need to strike the necessary tone.

"I know," he began with feigned self-assurance, "that for you residents of the capital, the local women must seem very special. You're sadly mistaken! It's true, they do have freshness, but they lack style. No, how can I put it? There's no art to their loving!"

Voloshin momentarily came to life; his eyes sparkled and his voice changed.

"Yes, of course. But after a while all this becomes so boring. Our Petersburg women have no bodies. Do you understand? They're bundles of nerves, not female bodies, while here . . ."

"That's true," Zarudin agreed, becoming more animated; he began twirling his mustache contentedly.

"Remove the corset from the most stylish lady of the capital and you'll see. Here's something for you—have you heard the latest story?" Voloshin suddenly interrupted himself.

"No, I haven't," said Zarudin, leaning forward with eager interest.

"Well, it's very typical. A Parisian coquette . . ." Voloshin skillfully recounted in exquisite detail a shameless story in which naked lust and a woman's paltry breasts were intertwined in such an obnoxious, nightmarish manner that Zarudin began to laugh nervously and twitch as if he were being stung.

"Yes, the most important thing in a woman is her breasts! For me a woman with a bad figure doesn't even exist," Voloshin concluded, rolling his eyes, which were coated with a white film.

Zarudin recalled Lida's breasts, so tender, rosy-pink, well-rounded, firm, resembling bunches of a splendid unfamiliar fruit. He remembered how much she liked it when he kissed her breasts; suddenly he felt awkward talking about this with Voloshin, and painfully sad at the realization that all this had passed and would never again be repeated.

But this feeling, he thought, was unworthy of a man and an officer; making a great effort, he replied with unnatural exaggeration, "To each his own! For me the most important thing in a woman is her back, the sinuous curves . . ."

"Yes!" Voloshin drawled nervously. "You know, some women, especially very young ones . . ."

Treading heavily in his peasant boots, the orderly came in to light the lamp; while he fussed at the table, rattling the glass and striking matches, Zarudin and Voloshin were silent. Only their sparkling eyes and glowing cigarettes were visible in the growing light.

After the orderly had gone, they resumed their talk: the word "woman," naked and obscene, in distorted and almost meaningless form, hung in the air. Zarudin was overcome by the male instinct to boast; tormented by an unbearable desire to surpass Voloshin and brag about the magnificent woman who'd given herself to him, Zarudin began talking about Lida, revealing the inner secrets of his desire more clearly with every word.

She arose before Voloshin's eyes completely naked, shamelessly exposed in the most profound mysteries of her body and passion, debased like some animal to be traded at a fair. Their thoughts crawled all over her, licked her, mauled her, mocked her body and her feelings; a stinking poison trickled onto this splendid young woman, who was capable of giving pleasure and love. They didn't love the "woman," they weren't grateful to her for the pleasures she afforded; they tried to humiliate and insult her, to cause her the vilest, most indescribable pain.

It was stuffy and smoky in the room. Their sweaty bodies exuded a demented, heavy, unhealthy smell; their eyes shone dully; their voices sounded disconnected and stifled, like the cries of frenzied animals. Outside the window a clear, quiet moonlit night had fallen; but the whole world, with all its colors, sounds, and riches, had receded, vanished; only a naked woman remained before them. Soon their imaginations became so powerful and demanding that they absolutely had to behold this Lida whom they now referred to not as Lidiya or even Lida, but Lidka.[26]

---

[26] Lidiya is the full form of her name; Lida is the simple diminutive; Lidka is normally a condescending diminutive, but among close friends the form can be used as a sign of affection.

Zarudin ordered his horses to be harnessed and they set off for the outskirts of town.

## XXVIII

A letter sent the next day by Zarudin to Lida Sanina in which he asked permission to see her, cryptically and awkwardly hinting that it might still be possible to remedy the situation, fell into Marya Ivanovna's hands because the maid had left it on the table in the kitchen.

From the pages of this letter a dirty, sinister shadow crept appallingly across the pure image of her daughter, so full of tender sanctity. Marya Ivanovna's first reaction was painful incomprehension. Then she recalled her own youth, its love and betrayal, and the difficult dramas played out during her disappointing marriage. A series of enduring sufferings intertwined with life, based on strict laws and rules, stretched on into her old age. It resembled a long gray stripe with dark patches of boredom and grief, and frayed edges of unbridled desires and dreams—something that could be recalled only as an unbroken succession of days.

But awareness that her daughter had burst through the sturdy wall of this stale, gray life and had perhaps already fallen into a striking, stormy whirlpool where joy and happiness were chaotically interwoven with suffering and death seized the old woman with terror.

And this terror turned into rage and anguish. If she could have done so, she would have grabbed Lida by the neck, pushed her down to the ground, and shoved her back into the gray stone corridor of her life, where the sunny world penetrated only through secure little windows barred with iron grates, and would have forced her to begin again the life she'd lived so far.

What a vile, worthless, loathsome girl! Marya Ivanovna thought, her hands falling despondently into her lap.

But the simple, small, comforting thought occurred to her that all this had gone no further than accepted harmless limits. Her face assumed a vacant, sly look. She set about reading and rereading the note, but could extract nothing from its affected, cold style. Then, feeling her own impotence, she wept bitter tears, then adjusted her headdress and asked her maid, "Dunka, is Vladimir Petrovich home?"

"What?" Dunka replied loudly.

"You fool, I'm asking if the master's at home."

"He just went to his study. He's writing a letter!" Dunka reported cheerfully, as if this letter afforded her the greatest enjoyment.

Marya Ivanovna looked her straight in the eye; a dull, evil expression appeared in her kind, faded pupils. "And you, you miserable creature, if you ever carry notes again, I'll give you a lesson you'll never forget."

Sanin was sitting there and writing. Marya Ivanovna was not used to seeing him writing, and despite her grief, she was interested.

"What are you writing?"

"A letter," Sanin replied, raising his buoyant, calm face.

"To whom?"

"An editor I know. I'd like to work for his newspaper again."

"Are you a writer?"

"I do everything," Sanin said with a smile.

"Why do you want to work there?"

"I'm bored with living here, mama," he answered with a sincere grin.

Marya Ivanovna was mildly offended. "Thank you," she said with irony.

Sanin looked at her attentively; he wanted to say that she wasn't such a fool as not to understand that a person couldn't remain in one place with nothing to do without getting bored, but he kept silent. It annoyed him to have to explain such a simple matter to her.

Marya Ivanovna took out her handkerchief and for a long time sat quietly crumpling it with the slender old fingers of a decrepit aristocrat. If it hadn't been for Zarudin's note and the fact that she was now plunged into a chaotic state of doubt and fear, she would have rebuked her son bitterly and at length for his rudeness; but now she limited her response to a tragically pitiful contrast.

"Yes," she said. "One sneaks out of the house like a wolf, while the other . . ." She gestured in resignation.

Sanin raised his head with curiosity. Obviously the old, everyday drama was beginning to unfold further.

"What do you know?" he asked, putting down his pen.

Suddenly Marya Ivanovna felt ashamed that she'd read her daughter's letter. A dark-red flush colored her old cheeks and she replied unsteadily but angrily, "Thank God, I'm not blind! I can see."

Sanin thought for a while.

"You don't see a thing," he said. "To prove it I can congratulate you on the lawful marriage of your daughter. She wanted to tell you herself, but it doesn't really matter."

He felt sorry that one more torture was interfering in Lida's lovely young life—an elderly parent's tiresome love, capable of tormenting with the most refined, cruel suffering.

"What?" Marya Ivanovna asked, drawing herself up.

"Lida's getting married."

"To whom?" the old woman cried in joyful disbelief.

"To Novikov, of course."

"But . . . what about . . ."

"To hell with him!" cried Sanin with sudden vexation. "What difference does it make to you? Why meddle in someone else's affairs?"

"No, it's just that I don't understand, Volodya," she said in embarrassed indecision, trying to justify herself. Meanwhile, her heart sang an incomprehensibly joyful refrain: "Lida's getting married, Lida's getting married!"

Sanin shrugged sternly.

"What is there not to understand? She was in love with one man, then fell in love with another, and tomorrow she'll love a third. God bless her!"

"What are you saying?" Marya Ivanovna cried indignantly.

Sanin stood with his back to the table and folded his arms. "Were you in love with one man your whole life?" he asked angrily.

Marya Ivanovna stood up; stone-cold pride shone from her dull, elderly face. "That's no way to talk to your mother!" she cried shrilly.

"Who?"

"What do you mean, who?"

"Who shouldn't talk like that?" Sanin asked, looking at her sullenly.

He looked at his mother and for the first time noticed how dumb and vacant was the look in her eyes, how ridiculous was the cap that perched on her head like a cock's comb.

"No one should talk like that!" she said dully, in a lifeless voice.

"Well, I do. And that's that," Sanin replied, suddenly growing calm and reverting to his usual mood. He turned and sat down. "You've taken what you could from life; and so you have no right to stifle Lida," he said rather indifferently, without turning around and resuming his writing.

Marya Ivanovna was silent and looked Sanin straight in the eye; her cock's comb stood up on her head even more ridiculously. Instantly suppressing all recollection of her own past life, those voluptuous nights of her youth, she closed her eyes and thought only one thing: How dare he speak to his mother like that? She didn't know what else to do.

But before she could decide, Sanin turned serenely, took her by the hand, and said affectionately, "Leave all this alone. And send Zarudin away, or he'll really play some dirty tricks."

A gentle wave passed through Marya Ivanovna's heart.

"Well, God bless you," she said. "I'm glad. I've always liked Sasha Novikov. Of course we can't receive Zarudin, even if only out of respect for Sasha."

"Out of respect for Sasha," Sanin agreed, laughing only with his eyes.

"But where's Lida?" Marya Ivanovna asked, now with placid joy.

"In her room."

"And Sasha?" the mother added, pronouncing Novikov's name with tenderness.

"I really don't know. He went to . . ." Sanin began, but just at that moment Dunka appeared at the doorway and said:

"Viktor Sergeevich has come . . . with another gentleman."

"Ah. Throw them out on their ears," Sanin advised.

Dunka giggled in embarrassment. "Oh, sir, how can we?"

"Of course we can. What the hell are they doing here?"

Dunka covered her face with her sleeve and went out.

Marya Ivanovna drew herself up and seemed to become younger, but her eyes acquired an even duller, more bestial expression. Instantly, with astonishing ease and clarity, as if she'd shrewdly cheated at cards, a complete change took place in her: as warm as she'd felt toward Zarudin before when she thought the officer intended to marry Lida, so she became inimically cold toward him now it was clear that another man would become her husband and that he, Zarudin, could be nothing but her lover.

As his mother turned to go, Sanin looked at her stony profile with its gray, malevolent gaze, and thought: There's a beast for you!

Then he folded his piece of paper and followed her. He was most curious to see how this new, difficult, and confusing situation in which people had put themselves would take shape and be resolved.

Zarudin and Voloshin stood up to greet the old woman with exaggerated politeness, Zarudin lacking the freedom he had previously allowed himself in the Sanins' household. Voloshin felt somewhat awkward because he'd come with the specific idea of taking a look at Lida, and now it was necessary for him to conceal that thought. But this feeling of awkwardness merely excited him further.

On Zarudin's face, through his assumed nonchalance and impudence, one could clearly see his timid anxiety. He knew he shouldn't have come: he was ashamed and afraid; he couldn't imagine how he could meet Lida, and at the same time he wouldn't have revealed these feelings to Voloshin for anything on earth, wouldn't have undermined his image of himself as a self-assured, fearless man who could do just as he liked with a woman. At times he even hated Voloshin, but he followed him as if he were attached to him, lacking the strength to show his real feelings.

"Dear Marya Ivanovna," Zarudin began, baring his white teeth unnaturally. "Permit me to introduce my good friend Pavel Lvovich Voloshin."

With these words and an imperceptible wink in the corners of his eyes and lips, he smiled obsequiously at Voloshin.

Voloshin bowed, replying to Zarudin with the same smile but more noticeably and almost brazenly.

"Very pleased," said Marya Ivanovna coldly.

Her look of concealed hostility lighted coolly on Zarudin, and the cautious officer noticed it immediately. Instantly his last trace of self-assurance vanished, and their behavior, now definitely deprived of playful amusement, began to appear impossible and preposterous to him.

Hey, we shouldn't have come! he thought. And for the first time he clearly recalled what he'd forgotten in the excitement aroused by the unattainable impressiveness of Voloshin's company: Lida could come in at any moment!

Why, it was the selfsame Lida who'd had an affair with him, who was pregnant by him, the mother of his unborn child who one way or another would very soon be born! What on earth would he say to her and how would he look at her? His heart sank timidly and a heavy weight pressed down on him.

What if she knows already? he wondered in horror, now unable to look at Marya Ivanovna. He began to fidget and tremble; he lit a cigarette, shrugged, shifted his legs, and glanced from side to side.

Hey, we shouldn't have come, he thought again.

"Will you be staying here long?" Marya Ivanovna asked Voloshin in a cold, aloof voice.

"Oh, no," Voloshin replied lightheartedly, looking sarcastically at this provincial lady, turning his hand and cleverly positioning his cigar in the corner of his mouth so that the smoke would rise directly into her face.

"It must seem so boring to you here, after Petersburg."

"Oh, no, not at all. I like it here a great deal; it's such a patriarchal little town, don't you think?"

"You should visit the outskirts; we have some splendid places to see.[27] For swimming, boating . . ."

"Oh, absolutely, ma'am!" Voloshin exclaimed, sarcastically emphasizing the "ma'am"; he was already feeling rather bored.

The conversation wasn't going well; it was labored and ridiculous, like a smiling cardboard mask behind which hostile and bored eyes were lurking. Voloshin began glancing at Zarudin, and the meaning of his glances was understood not only by the officer but also by Sanin, who was carefully observing them from behind the corner.

The thought that Voloshin might cease to view him as a clever, witty, brazen fellow, capable of anything, proved stronger than Zarudin's secret fear.

"And where might Lidiya Petrovna be?" he asked with selfless effort, his body once again unaccountably beginning to move.

Marya Ivanovna looked at him with surprise and enmity. What business is it of yours, since you're not going to marry her? her eyes said.

"I don't know. Probably in her room," she replied coldly.

Voloshin shot Zarudin another knowing look. Can't she summon Lidka immediately, because this old woman's not very interesting! he said to himself.

Zarudin opened his mouth and twirled his mustache helplessly.

"I've heard so many flattering things about your daughter," Voloshin began, and baring his rotten teeth and leaning forward politely, he rubbed his hands. "I hope to have the honor of making her acquaintance."

Marya Ivanovna cast a glance at Zarudin's face, which had changed imperceptibly; she instinctively understood what it was that this putrid, insolent little man might have heard about her crystal-pure and tenderly holy

---

[27] Brothels were generally located on the outskirts of town.

Lida. This thought was so intense that for a moment she had a terrible premonition of Lida's fall and was overcome with helpless horror. She was dismayed, and at the same time her eyes became softer and more human.

If we don't get rid of them, Sanin thought at this moment, they'll cause even more grief for Lida and Novikov.

"Did I hear you'll be leaving?" he asked suddenly, staring pensively at the floor.

Zarudin was surprised that such a simple and convenient thought hadn't occurred to him.

Ah! To take a month's vacation, or even two . . . flashed through his mind, and he replied hastily:

"Yes, I'm planning to . . . I need some rest, a change of scene. You know, one grows moldy being in one place too long!"

Sanin suddenly started laughing. This entire conversation, not one word of which expressed what people were really feeling and thinking, with all its deceit that fooled nobody, and the fact that everyone, seeing clearly that nobody believed anything, continued to deceive each other—all this struck him as amusing. An unambiguous, buoyant feeling swept through his soul in a great wave.

"Good riddance!" he said—it was the first thing that came into his head.

It was as if a stiff, starched suit had suddenly fallen away from them and all three men were instantly transformed. Marya Ivanovna turned pale and seemed smaller; a primitive, cowardly feeling flashed through Voloshin's eyes; Zarudin stood up from his place slowly and uncertainly. A shiver ran through the room.

"What?" asked Zarudin in a muffled tone; his voice couldn't help but show his character.

Voloshin's laugh was timid and trite and his frightened eyes searched the room for his hat. Sanin, without replying to Zarudin, with a cheerful and wicked expression found Voloshin's hat and handed it to him. Voloshin opened his mouth and out came a thin, muffled sound resembling a pitiful squeak.

"How am I to take that?" Zarudin cried in despair, no longer on firm ground. What a scandal! the thought flashed through his inert mind.

"Any way you like!" said Sanin. "You're utterly superfluous here and you'd bring everyone great pleasure if you cleared off."

Zarudin took a step forward. His face was hideous, his white teeth bared ominously and savagely.

"Aha. So that's how it is," he muttered, breathing hard.

"Get out of here," Sanin replied firmly and abruptly, with contempt.

His tone of voice contained such a steely, menacing threat that Zarudin took a step back and fell silent, his eyes rolling wildly in a ridiculous way.

"Who the hell knows what's going on?" Voloshin muttered in a dull voice; lowering his head, he hurried toward the door.

But there in the doorway stood Lida.

Never, neither before nor after, had she ever felt so humiliated, just like a naked slave girl over whom two aggressive males were squabbling at the market. At first, when she learned of Zarudin's arrival with Voloshin and understood instantly the purpose of their visit, her feeling of physical humiliation was so strong that she burst into hysterical sobs and fled into the garden, down to the river; once again the idea of suicide occurred to her.

What on earth is this? Isn't it over yet? Did I really commit such a horrible crime that it'll never be forgiven? Will everyone always have the right to . . . ? she nearly screamed, holding her head in her hands.

But it was so bright and clear in the garden, the colorful blossoms, the bees, and the birds were all so serene, the sky was so blue, the water glistened near the sedge, and Mill, the fox terrier, was so pleased to be on an outing that Lida came to her senses. Suddenly she recalled instinctively that men had always pursued her eagerly and greedily; she remembered the energy her entire body felt under the gaze of these men; then the idea of pride and propriety arose in her consciousness.

Well then, she thought. What do I care? So it's him. I loved him once and now we've separated. No one can ever dare despise me!

She turned abruptly and returned to the house.

Lida's appearance in the doorway was very different from the way people were accustomed to seeing her. Instead of her usual stylish and mannered coiffure, a thick, sumptuous braid hung delicately down her back; instead of her customary elegant and refined clothes, a simple, neat blouse covered her bosom and shoulders, innocently displaying her magnificent, liberated body; all in all, in this sweet, simple domestic guise there was something unexpectedly charming and lovely.

Smiling strangely—with a smile that made her look like her brother—Lida stepped calmly over the threshold and in a resonant, pleasant voice said in a particularly sweet, girlish tone, "Here I am. Where are you going? Viktor Sergeevich, put down your cap!"

Sanin fell silent; His eyes wide, he gazed at his sister with attentive rapture. What's all this? he wondered.

An inner strength, awesome, agreeable, insuperable, and tenderly feminine, entered the room. It was as if an animal tamer had entered a cage of enraged wild beasts. The men suddenly became gentle and submissive.

"You see, Lidiya Petrovna," Zarudin began in embarrassment.

As soon as he started to speak, a sweetly pitiful, helpless expression spread across Lida's face. She threw him a swift glance and suddenly felt unbearably disconcerted. A painfully delicate twinge of physical tenderness awoke in her and desperately wanted to rely on something. But this desire was momentarily replaced by the acute, primitive need to demonstrate to him how much he'd lost and how splendid she really was, in spite of the misfortune and humiliation he'd caused her.

"I don't want to see anything!" Lida said powerfully and somewhat theatrically, almost closing her lovely eyes.

Something terrible happened to Voloshin: this charming warmth emanating from a scarcely concealed, tender feminine body, displayed in unexpected, sweet domestic beauty, crushed his entire being. His sharp little tongue instantly licked his dry lips, his small eyes narrowed, and his whole body, beneath its light, loose-fitting suit, swelled in involuntary physical excitement.

"Do introduce us," Lida said, turning her large attractive eyes, made even more prominent by her eyelashes, to look at him over her shoulder.

"Voloshin, Pavel Lvovich," muttered Zarudin.

To think that such a beauty was my mistress! The thought occurred to him with genuine enthusiasm, and with it he felt a desire to brag to Voloshin and a slight twinge of awareness of his irrevocable loss.

Lida turned slowly to her mother. "Mama, someone wants to see you," she said.

"I don't care," Marya Ivanovna began.

"I said . . ." Lida interrupted, her voice sounding unexpectedly tearful.

Marya Ivanovna stood up hastily. Sanin looked at Lida; his nostrils inflated broadly and powerfully.

"Gentlemen, let's go into the garden. It's so hot in here!" said Lida, and as before, without looking to see if anyone was following, she went out onto the balcony.

The men trailed after her as if hypnotized; it looked as if she'd ensnared them with her long braid and was forcibly leading them wherever she wished. Voloshin went first, enthralled and excited, having forgotten about everything else on earth except her.

Lida sat in a swing under a linden tree and stretched her little feet clad in black openwork stockings and pale yellow shoes. It was as if there were two creatures within her: one languishing from shame, insult, and anguish, the other stubbornly assuming consciously provocative poses, each more attractive and accommodating than the last. The first creature regarded herself, men, and all of life with loathing.

"Well, Pavel Lvovich. What sort of impression does our provincial town make on you?" she asked, her eyelids drooping.

Voloshin quickly folded and rubbed his fingers. "Probably the same as any man would feel coming upon a splendid flower in the midst of the deep forest!" he replied.

Between them there ensued a light, vacuous, and thoroughly artificial conversation in which everything that was uttered was a lie and everything that remained unspoken was the truth. Sanin was quiet and listened closely to the silent, genuine conversation that passed wordlessly across their faces, hands, and feet, through intonations and gestures. Lida was suffering. Voloshin was taking tormented and unsatisfied delight in her beauty and fragrance. Meanwhile Zarudin had begun to hate her and Sanin and Voloshin and the whole world; he wanted to leave, but didn't; he wanted to do something rude and smoked cigarette after cigarette. For some reason the unbearable need to portray Lida to everyone as his mistress oppressed him with unrelieved malice.

"So you like it here and don't regret leaving Petersburg?" Lida inquired.

Perhaps this torture was the most tormenting of all for Lida; she found it strange that she didn't stand up and leave.

"*Mais au contraire!*"[28] Voloshin protested, spreading his hands flirtatiously and fixing his gaze on Lida's bosom.

"No speeches!" Lida said with a coquettishly imperious gesture; once again two beings were struggling within her: one brought a blush to her face, the other displayed her bosom even more prominently and imperceptibly moved it more shamelessly in the direction of his devouring gaze.

You think I'm miserable—that I'm crushed! Well then, just have a look! That's what you are—well, this is what I am! she said silently to Zarudin through the tears inside her.

"Oh, Lidiya Petrovna!" Zarudin replied with hatred. "What on earth do you mean by that?"

"Did you say something?" Lida asked coldly; then quickly altering her tone, she turned to Voloshin.

"Tell me about life in Petersburg. Here we have no life; we merely vegetate."

Zarudin felt that Voloshin was almost grinning at him and doubting whether Lida had ever been his mistress.

Aha, aha! Well, all right, then! he said to himself with implausible spite.

"Our life? Oh, that well-known 'Petersburg life'!"

Voloshin chattered easily and quickly and gave the impression of a small, foolish monkey, chattering in its own vacuous, incomprehensible tongue.

Who knows? he thought with secret hope, gazing at Lida's face, bosom, and broad hips.

"I give you my word of honor, Lidiya Petrovna, our life is very dull and boring. But until today I thought that all life was boring, no matter where a person lived—in the capital or the countryside."

"Really?" said Lida, batting her eyes.

"What really makes life interesting is a beautiful woman! As for the women in big towns—oh, if only you could see them! You know, I'm convinced that if anything can save the world, it's going to be beauty!" Voloshin added suddenly, but considered his remark very appropriate, articulate, and witty.

His face was ridiculously flushed and he jabbered in a broken voice, constantly returning to the same theme, women, about whom he spoke as

28 "But on the contrary!" (French).

if he were incessantly undressing and violating her. Noticing this expression, Zarudin suddenly felt a vague jealousy. He blushed and then turned pale; he was unable to remain still and paced back and forth, up and down the path.

"Our women are all alike; they're so affected and trite! To find someone capable of eliciting the genuine adoration of beauty—not that narrow feeling, you know, but really pure, sincere adoration, the kind you feel standing before a statue—that's impossible in our big towns! For that one must resort to the backwoods, where real life still survives—virgin soil capable of producing lavish blooms!"

Sanin unwittingly scratched the back of his head and crossed his legs.

"But what good is it if they blossom here when there's no one to pluck them?" Lida replied.

Aha! Sanin thought with attention. So that's where she's heading!

He was very interested in this lewd, subtle play of feeling and desire that was unmistakably yet imperceptibly unfolding before him.

"You don't say?"

"Yes, indeed I do! Who's there to pick our forlorn flowers? Who are these people we set up as our heroes?" Lida uttered with absolute sincerity, in a touchingly sad voice.

"You show us no mercy!" Zarudin responded unintentionally to Lida's concealed implications.

"Lidiya Petrovna's right!" Voloshin exclaimed with enthusiasm, but he hesitated immediately and glanced apprehensively at Zarudin.

Lidiya laughed aloud, and her eyes, burning with revenge, shame, and anguish, were aimed in a threatening, sorrowful way at Zarudin's face. Meanwhile, Voloshin kept yammering on; his words rained down, bounced around, and smashed to pieces, like a pack of ludicrous monsters assembled from God knows where.

Now he was saying that a woman with a splendid body could, without arousing any obscene desire, appear naked on the street; it was clear that he wanted this woman to be Lida and that he wanted her to appear naked for him.

Lida laughed and interrupted him; in her high-pitched laughter could be heard embarrassment and tears of insult and anguish.

It was hot and the sun beat down on the garden; leaves rustled softly, as if agitated by the burning but constrained indolence of desire. Beneath these leaves an attractive, pregnant young woman, with concealed tears and torments, was trying to take revenge for her profaned passion; she felt that she wasn't succeeding, and she suffered with impotent shame. Alone, one weak-willed, cowardly male endured torments of aroused and concealed voluptuous desire, while the other suffered from jealous and humiliating rancor.

Sanin sat to one side in the soft green shade of a linden tree, observing them calmly.

"It's high time we were going," Zarudin said at last, unable to restrain himself. Without knowing why, he felt in everything, in her laughter, her eyes, her trembling fingers, concealed blows to his face; he was tormented by feelings of ill will toward her, jealousy toward Voloshin, and the physical pain of irretrievable loss.

"So soon?" asked Lida.

Voloshin, squinting sweetly, smiled and ran his little tongue over his lips.

"It can't be helped. Viktor Sergeevich, apparently, isn't feeling well," he said sarcastically, imagining himself the victor.

They began to take their leave. When Zarudin bowed to kiss Lida's hand, he suddenly whispered, "Farewell!"

He himself didn't know why, but he'd never loved and hated her so much as he did at that moment. In response something in Lida's soul began to tremble and subside in a desire to bid farewell with sad and tender gratitude—without retribution, rancor, or revulsion—for the enjoyment they'd shared. But she repressed this feeling and replied in a pitilessly loud voice:

"Farewell! Bon voyage! Don't forget us, Pavel Lvovich!"

As they left, Voloshin remarked in a voice louder than necessary, "What a woman! She's as intoxicating as champagne!"

They left, and when the sound of their footsteps had died away, Lida sat down in the rocking chair, but not at all as she had done before: now she was hunched up and trembling all over. She was shedding mild, peculiarly poignant, maidenly tears. For some reason Sanin dwelled on the touching, thoughtful image of a young Russian woman with her long braid, her cheerless life, and the muslin sleeve with which that spring she'd wiped away a flood of tears in secret. The fact that this ancient, innocent image wasn't at all characteristic of Lida as she usually was—with her fashionable hairdo and elegant lace-trimmed dresses—was especially poignant and pathetic.

"What's all this?" asked Sanin, going up to her and taking hold of her hand.

"Leave me alone. Life's so awful," Lida said, and she leaned forward, burying her face in her hands. Her soft braid slipped gently over her shoulder and hung down.

"Shame on you!" Sanin replied angrily. "Crying over such trifles!"

"Are there really no . . . other, better people?" she began again.

"Of course not," said Sanin with a smile. "Man's depraved by nature. Don't expect any good to come from him, and then the evil he does won't cause you so much grief."

Lida raised her head and looked at him with her beautiful, tear-stained eyes.

"Don't you expect anything from him?" she asked in a calmer, more thoughtful way.

"Of course not," Sanin replied. "I live alone."

 XXIX

The next day Dunka, with bare head, bare feet, and a fixed expression of fear in her vacant eyes, came running up to Sanin as he was clearing a path in the garden. Obviously repeating someone else's words, she announced: "Vladimir Petrovich, those off-i-sirs have come and wish to see you."

Sanin was not surprised: he'd been expecting some sort of challenge from Zarudin.

"Are they very eager to see me?" he asked Dunka jokingly.

But Dunka apparently knew something terrible, and instead of hiding her face in her sleeve, in her usual way, she looked him directly in the eye with an expression of frightened sympathy.

Sanin put down his spade, tightened his belt, and walked toward the house with his usual springy step.

What fools they are! What idiots! he thought of Zarudin and his seconds with annoyance; this was not a form of verbal abuse—it was rather his sincere opinion.

As he made his way through the house, Lida emerged from the door to her room and stood on the threshold. Her face was ashen and apprehensive, her eyes full of suffering. She moved her lips but said nothing. At that moment she felt that she was the most unhappy and most culpable woman in all the world.

Marya Ivanovna sat helplessly in an armchair in the living room. She too had a frightened, forlorn expression, and her cock's comb was drooping in dismay. She too glanced at Sanin with imploring, anxious eyes, and moved her lips without saying anything.

Sanin smiled at her, was about to pause, but changed his mind and continued on his way.

Tanarov and Von Deitz were seated in the drawing room on chairs near the window closest to the door; they were seated not in their usual way—their legs were drawn up and both were sitting up straight, as if terribly uncomfortable in their white military jackets and tight blue riding breeches. At Sanin's entrance they stood up slowly and indecisively, obviously not knowing what to do next.

"Greetings, gentlemen," Sanin said loudly, going up to them and extending his hand.

Von Deitz hesitated for a moment, but Tanarov bowed quickly and in such an exaggerated way as he shook hands that the closely cropped hair at the nape of his neck flashed before Sanin's eyes.

"Well, what's going on?" asked Sanin, noticing Tanarov's peculiarly obliging willingness, and feeling surprised at how skillfully and confidently this officer was performing the ridiculous formalities of artificial ceremony.

Von Deitz straightened up and lent a frosty appearance to his equine countenance, but soon became embarrassed. It was odd that the usually reticent and bashful Tanarov began speaking so bluntly and assuredly.

"Our friend Viktor Sergeevich Zarudin has done us the honor of requesting that we raise a certain matter with you," he said distinctly and coldly, as if a machine were set in motion inside him.

"Aha!" Sanin uttered, opening his mouth wide with comic gravity.

"Yes, sir," Tanarov continued stubbornly and deliberately, lowering his brows. "In his opinion, your behavior concerning him was not quite . . ."

"Well, yes. . . I understand," Sanin interrupted, quickly losing patience. "I tossed him out on his ear, if that's what you mean by 'not quite . . .' "

Tanarov made an effort to understand, failed, and went on: "Yes, sir. He demands that you take back your words."

"Yes, yes," for some reason the lanky Von Deitz thought it necessary to add; he shifted from leg to leg like a crane.

"How can I take them back? 'Words are not like birds: out you let them, back you never get them!' " *Sanin replied, only his eyes laughing.

Tanarov stood there in silent bewilderment, looking Sanin straight in the eye.

What evil eyes he has! Sanin thought to himself.

"We have no time for jokes," Tanarov said suddenly in an angry, brusque tone, as if finally understanding something and turning red. "Are you willing to take back your words or not?"

Sanin was silent. What a first-class idiot! he thought, not without sorrow; he took a chair and sat down.

"I might be willing to take back my words in order to satisfy Zarudin and appease him," he began earnestly. "All the more so since doing it really wouldn't make any difference to me. But in the first place, Zarudin is stupid and wouldn't understand the way it was meant, and instead of being appeased, he'd gloat; in the second place, I really don't like Zarudin at all, and given the circumstances, it really isn't worth taking back my words."

"Very well, sir," Tanarov hissed maliciously.

Von Deitz looked at him fearfully and the last traces of color disappeared from his elongated face. It became yellow and wooden.

"In that case," Tanarov began, raising his voice and assuming a menacing tone.

Sanin glanced at his narrow forehead and tight breeches with surprising contempt, and interrupted him: "Yes, and so on and so forth. I know. But I won't fight a duel with Zarudin."

Von Deitz turned swiftly. Tanarov drew himself up and, assuming a disdainful look and emphasizing each syllable, he asked: "And—why—not?"

Sanin burst out laughing; his hatred vanished as quickly as it had appeared. "Well, because, in the first place, I don't want to kill Zarudin; and in the second and even more, I don't want to die."

---

* Popular Russian saying.

"But . . ." Tanarov began with a sneer.

"I won't and that's all there is to it!" Sanin said, rising. "I don't feel like explaining it to you. There's no need. I don't want to. So there you are."

The most profound contempt for a man who refuses to fight a duel was combined in Tanarov with the invincible conviction that no one but an officer is capable of being sufficiently courageous and chivalrous to fight. So he was not in the least surprised; on the contrary, he was even overjoyed.

"That's your business," he said, no longer concealing but now even exaggerating his contemptuous expression. "But I must warn you that—"

"Yes, I know that too," Sanin said with a laugh. "But I would advise Zarudin not to . . ."

"Not to what, sir?" the grinning Tanarov repeated, picking up his cap from the windowsill.

"I would advise Zarudin not to touch me, or I'll give him a beating he'll never forget!"

"Look here!" Von Deitz cried out suddenly. "I can't allow this. You're making fun of us! Don't you realize that refusing to accept a challenge is . . . why, it's . . ."

He turned as red as a brick; his dull eyes protruded ferociously yet foolishly from their sockets, and there were traces of foam on his lips.

Sanin looked at his mouth with curiosity and said, "And this man still considers himself a follower of Tolstoy!"

Von Deitz threw his head back and winced.

"I must ask you!" he screamed, terribly embarrassed that he was shouting at a close acquaintance with whom he'd recently discussed many important, interesting questions. "I must ask you to desist. It bears no relation to the matter at hand!"

"On the contrary," replied Sanin, "it's closely related."

"And I must ask you," Von Deitz cried, now almost hysterical and spewing saliva, "it's absolutely . . . in a word, it's . . ."

"To hell with you!" Sanin said, drawing back in distaste from the spray from his mouth. "Think whatever you like, but tell Zarudin he's an ass."

"You have no right!" cried Von Deitz in a desperate whine.

"Very well, sir, very well," Tanarov said with satisfaction. "Let's go."

"No," Von Deitz cried in the same plaintive voice, waving his long arms fatuously. "How dare he! It's just . . . it's . . ."

Sanin looked at him, made a dismissive gesture, and started to walk out.

"We'll convey this message to our friend," Tanarov called after him.

"You do that," Sanin replied, without even turning round.

What a fool he is, but when he gets on his hobby horse, he becomes so controlled and coherent! Sanin thought, listening as Tanarov was trying to mollify the overwrought Von Deitz.

"No, it can't be left like this!" cried the lanky officer, realizing with sadness that as a result of this incident he'd lost an interesting acquaintance.

Having no idea how to repair the damage, he was even more embittered; obviously he had ruined everything once and for all.

"Volodya," called Lida softly from the doorway.

"What?" Sanin paused.

"Come here. I want to talk to you."

Sanin went into Lida's little room, where the light was faint and greenish from the trees shading the window and where it smelled of perfume, powder, and a woman.

"How nice it is in here!" Sanin said with a deep sigh of relief.

Lida stood with her face to the window; greenish reflections from the garden lay softly and beautifully on her shoulders and cheeks.

"Well, what would you like?" Sanin asked tenderly.

Lida was silent and breathing heavily.

"What's the matter?"

"You're not going to . . . fight a duel, are you?" Lida asked in a husky voice, without turning round.

"No," Sanin replied curtly.

Lida was silent.

"Well, so what then?"

Her chin began to tremble. She turned round quickly and, gasping for breath, muttered incoherently, "I can't . . . I can't understand how . . ."

"Ah," Sanin replied, frowning. "I'm very sorry you don't understand!"

Wicked, blind human stupidity surrounding him on all sides, coming equally from evil people and from good, from handsome people and from ugly, exhausted him. He turned around and left the room.

Lida watched him go; then she took her head in her hands and collapsed on the bed. Her long, dark braid, like a soft, fluffy tail, looked splendid on the clean white blanket. At that moment she was so lovely, so strong, and so resilient that despite her despair and tears she looked astonishingly alive and young; the green garden, permeated by sunlight, glanced in at her window; her little room was bright and cheerful. But she saw none of it.

 XXX

It was one of those special evenings that rarely occur on earth; it seemed to have descended from the transparent, majestically beautiful blue sky above. The low, late-summer sun had already set, but it was still quite light and the air was astonishingly clear and calm. It was dry, but in the gardens a heavy dew had appeared from God knows where; the dust was rising with difficulty and stood in the air long and lazy; it was close and already cool. All sounds were carried swiftly and easily, as if on wings.

Sanin, without a hat, in his wide blue shirt somewhat faded at the shoulders, made his way along a dusty street and a long lane overgrown with nettles, to the house where Ivanov lived.

Ivanov, broad-shouldered and sedate, his long hair straight as straw, sat at a window looking onto the garden, where heavy dew was settling and reviving the greenery that had become so dusty during the day; he was methodically stuffing tobacco into cigarette papers, so that you felt like sneezing if you came within two yards of him.

"Hello," said Sanin, resting his elbows on the windowsill.

"Greetings."

"I've been challenged to a duel," said Sanin.

"A fine thing!" Ivanov replied, unperturbed. "By whom and for what?"

"Zarudin. I threw him out of the house, so he took offense."

"So," said Ivanov "does that mean you're going to fight? If so, I'll be your second. You'll shoot your friend's nose off."

"Why? The nose is a noble part of the body. I'm not going to fight!" Sanin said with a laugh.

"Good for you!" Ivanov nodded his head. "Why fight? One shouldn't fight."

"But my little sister Lida is of a different opinion," Sanin said with a smile.

"Then she's a ninny!" Ivanov replied with conviction. "There's so much foolishness in each and every one of us!"

He rolled his last cigarette, lit it immediately, then gathered up the rest and put them away in a leather case; after blowing the remaining tobacco off the windowsill, he climbed out of the window.

"What shall we do?" he asked.

"Let's go and see Soloveichik," Sanin proposed.

"To hell with him!" Ivanov said, frowning.

"What do you mean?"

"I don't like him! He's a sluggard!"

"No worse than all the rest," Sanin said with a dismissive gesture. "Never mind . . . let's go."

"Well, fine, what the hell!" Ivanov agreed as quickly as he always did with whatever Sanin said.

They made their way along the streets, two robust, tall men with broad shoulders and cheerful voices.

But Soloveichik wasn't at home. His wing of the house was locked; the courtyard was dreary and deserted, with only Sultan growling on his chain near the storehouse, barking at these strangers who'd entered the yard for some reason or other.

"What a dismal place," said Ivanov. "Let's stroll along the boulevard."

They left, shutting the gate; Sultan barked a few more times and then sat down in front of his kennel and stared sadly into the empty courtyard at the deserted mill and the narrow, crooked white paths winding across the low, dusty grass.

Music was playing as usual in the municipal garden. It was already quite cool and light along the boulevard. There were lots of people out for a stroll and the dark crowd looked like a field of tall weeds topped by flowers, scattered with women's dresses and hats, waving back and forth, flowing first toward the dark garden, then away from its stone gates.

Arm in arm, Sanin and Ivanov entered the garden. In the first avenue they met Soloveichik, who was pacing pensively beneath the trees, his arms behind his back and his eyes downcast.

"We just came from your place," Sanin said.

Soloveichik smiled timidly and said, as if he were at fault, "Oh, I beg your pardon. I didn't know you were coming. I would've waited. I decided to go out for a walk." His eyes were fiery and forlorn.

"Come with us," Sanin continued, reaching for his arm affectionately.

Soloveichik gladly extended his arm, feigning good cheer, then shifted his cap unnaturally to the back of his head and set off looking as if he weren't holding merely Sanin's arm but a precious object. His mouth was wide open from ear to ear.

Amid the soldiers, their faces red from blowing so deafeningly loud into brass trumpets, stood a scrawny army conductor, twirling and, obviously putting on airs, waving his baton and looking like a sparrow. Crowded around them were members of the general public: clerks, young students, boys in boots, and girls in bright kerchiefs; along the avenues, as if in an endless quadrille, colorful groups of young ladies, students, and officers were mingling in confusion.

They soon ran into Dubova with Shafrov and Svarozhich. They exchanged smiles and bows. Sanin, Soloveichik, and Ivanov circled the entire garden and then met them again. This time Karsavina was with them too, tall and graceful, wearing a light dress. From a distance she smiled at Sanin, whom she hadn't seen for a while, and her eyes gleamed with an expression of flirtatious friendliness.

"Why are you walking all alone?" asked the gawky, stooped Dubova. "Join us."

"Let's turn down a side lane; it's too crowded here," suggested Shafrov.

The large, cheerful group of young people turned into the semidarkness of a shady, quiet lane, filling it with their merry, resonant voices and their rich, unprovoked laughter.

They walked to the far end of the garden and were planning to turn back when suddenly Zarudin, Tanarov, and Voloshin appeared from behind the gate.

Sanin noticed immediately that the officer hadn't been expecting this meeting and became flustered. His handsome face flushed deeply and his entire body stiffened. Tanarov grinned dismally.

"Is that little runt still here?" Ivanov asked in surprise, indicating Voloshin with his eyes.

Without looking at them or turning around, Voloshin glanced at Karsavina as she went past.

"Right here!" Sanin said with a laugh.

Zarudin thought this laughter was directed at him and that struck him like a blow. He became furious. Gasping for breath and seized by a powerful force, he left his group and walked in his polished boots directly up to Sanin.

"What do you want?" Sanin asked, suddenly becoming serious and looking carefully at the slender riding crop that Zarudin was holding unnaturally in his hand.

Oh, what an ass! he thought with anger and pity.

"I have a few words to say to you," Zarudin uttered hoarsely. "Did you receive my challenge?"

"Yes," Sanin said with a slight shrug, still following carefully every movement of the officer's hand.

"And do you absolutely refuse to . . . to act as any decent man would, to accept my challenge?" Zarudin asked in a muffled tone but somewhat louder, now not even recognizing his own voice, afraid of it and of the cold handle of the riding crop he suddenly felt with particular intensity in his sweaty fingers; but he no longer had the strength to turn from the dreadful path before him. Suddenly it seemed impossible to breathe in the garden.

Everyone stood still and listened with a terrible sense of premonition, not knowing what to do.

"Now what . . ." Ivanov said, trying to come between Sanin and Zarudin.

"Of course I refuse," Sanin said in a strangely calm voice, fixing his keen, all-seeing gaze on Zarudin.

The officer drew a deep breath, as if lifting a heavy weight. "Once more. . . . You refuse?" he asked even louder; his voice had a hollow, metallic ring.

Oh, no. He's going to hit him. Oh, that's not good. Oh, dear! Soloveichik didn't think but felt, turning pale.

"Hey, once said . . ." he muttered, twisting his whole body and trying to shield Sanin.

Zarudin had hardly noticed him when he so rudely and easily pushed him off the path. He saw only Sanin's serene, somber eyes before him.

"I've told you already," Sanin replied in his previous tone of voice.

Everything began to spin around Zarudin; hearing hurried footsteps and women's voices behind him, with something akin to the desperate feeling of a person plunging headlong into the abyss, with a convulsive movement he clumsily raised his riding crop far too high.

But at that moment, flexing his muscles with terrible force, Sanin struck him swiftly and abruptly right in the face with his fist.

"So there!" cried Ivanov involuntarily.

Zarudin's head recoiled limply to one side; something warm and dark, instantly penetrating his eyes and brain with sharp needles, filled his nose and mouth.

"Oh. . . ." An anguished, frightened sound came from him; dropping his riding crop and cap, Zarudin fell to his hands and knees, seeing nothing, hearing nothing, aware of nothing except the irreparable finale and a dull, burning pain in his eye.

In the quiet, shaded lane there was unruly, appalling confusion.

"Oh, oh!" cried Karsavina in a piercing voice, grabbing her temples and shutting her eyes in terror. Yury, with the same feeling of terror and loathing, glanced at Zarudin, who was still down on all fours, and rushed toward Sanin together with Shafrov. Voloshin, dropping his pince-nez and getting tangled in the bushes, ran hurriedly out of the lane and straight across the wet grass; his white trousers soon turned black up to the knees. Tanarov, gritting his teeth and narrowing his pupils ferociously, hurled himself at Sanin, but Ivanov grabbed him by the shoulders from behind and pushed him away.

"Never mind, never mind. Let him," Sanin said softly with disgust and in a maliciously merry tone, planting his feet wide apart and breathing deeply. Large drops of heavy perspiration stood out on his forehead.

Zarudin got to his feet, staggering and emitting incoherent, pitiful sounds from his swollen, trembling moist lips. These sounds contained unexpected, inappropriate, and somehow absurdly repellent threats against Sanin. The whole left side of his face was bloated, his eye was closed, blood was oozing from his nose and mouth, his lips were trembling, and he himself was shaking all over, as if feverish, not at all the handsome, elegant man he had been just a few moments ago. The terrible blow seemed to have robbed him of everything human and turned him into something pitiful, deformed, and frightened. He felt the desire neither to run away nor to defend himself. Rattling his teeth, spitting blood, brushing sand obliviously from his knees with trembling hands, he began to sway and fell down again.

"How horrible, how horrible!" repeated Karsavina, trying to get away from the place as soon as she could.

"Let's go," Sanin said to Ivanov, glancing up, since he felt both revolted and distressed looking at Zarudin.

"Let's go, Soloveichik."

But Soloveichik didn't move. With his deadly pale eyes wide open he stared at Zarudin, the sand and blood strangely staining his white shirt, shaking and moving his lips feebly.

Ivanov tried to drag him off in anger, but Soloveichik pulled away with unnatural force, held onto a tree with both hands, as if they were trying to haul him away; then he suddenly burst into tears and began shouting, "Why did you? Why?"

"How despicable!" cried Yury Svarozhich hoarsely right in Sanin's face.

Sanin was already in control of himself and, without glancing at Zarudin, smiled scornfully and said, "Yes, despicable. Would it have been better if he'd struck me?"

He waved his arm dismissively and walked quickly along the wide lane. Ivanov looked at Yury with contempt and, lighting a cigarette, slowly followed Sanin. Even his wide back and straight hair made it evident how contemptuous he was of the entire episode.

"Man's capable of such wickedness and stupidity!" he said.

Sanin turned to look at him in silence and then walked faster.

"Like beasts!" said Yury with sorrow, leaving the garden and turning to gaze at its dark mass. The garden looked the same as it had so many times before—otherworldly and lovely; but now, after what had happened, it seemed cut off from the rest of the world; it had become grotesque and repugnant.

Shafrov sighed deeply and in confusion, glancing nervously over his spectacles, as if he expected an assault or violence from anywhere.

 XXXI

In an instant the appearance of Zarudin's life had changed dramatically. As easygoing, comprehensible, and nonchalantly pleasant as it had been before, now it had become just as unbelievably horrible and oppressive. It was as if it had thrown off a bright, smiling mask and revealed beneath it the vicious and terrible face of a wild beast.

As Tanarov was taking him home in a droshky,[29] Zarudin tried to exaggerate the pain and weakness he felt so as not to have to open his eyes. Somehow it helped him avoid the shame of the thousands of eyes he felt were trained on him, all the people waiting to encounter his gaze and then run after him, hooting, making faces, poking their fingers into his face.

In everything, in the skinny blue back of the droshky driver, every passerby, the windows behind which maliciously inquisitive faces appeared, even Tanarov's own arm supporting him around the waist, the beaten and bruised Zarudin imagined silent but manifest contempt. And this sensation was so unexpected and brutally tormenting that at times he felt really sick.

---

[29] A low, open, four-wheeled carriage in which passengers straddle a long, narrow bench.

Then it seemed that he was losing his mind; he wanted either to die or to wake up.

His brain refused to accept what had happened; it seemed that it couldn't be true, that there was some sort of mistake, that there was something he didn't understand, and that this something would make everything totally different, much less terrible and irreparable. But the clear and unalterable fact stood before him, and his soul was buried more and more deeply in the darkness of despair.

Zarudin knew that he was being supported, that he was feeling pain and discomfort, that his hands were covered with dust and blood, yet it seemed strange that he could feel anything at all, that his body hadn't been completely destroyed and was continuing to follow its own worthless, impotent course, when everything that had seemed so splendid, fashionably self-confident, and cheerful to him had disappeared once and for all, without trace.

At times when the droshky turned at a corner, he opened his eyes slightly and through murky tears recognized familiar streets, houses, churches, and people. Everything was just the same as always, but now it seemed infinitely remote, alien, and hostile. Passersby stopped and stared; he closed his eyes again quickly, almost losing consciousness from shame and despair.

The road wound on endlessly and it seemed as if there'd be no end to this torture.

Faster, faster! The word flashed drearily through his mind, but when he imagined the faces of his servant, landlady, and neighbors, it seemed better to keep on going, to drive on forever and never have to open his eyes.

Meanwhile Tanarov, terribly ashamed of Zarudin, and looking straight ahead, tried his utmost, drawing on an incomprehensible reserve of composure, to show everyone they met that he really had nothing to do with the whole affair and that he wasn't the one who'd suffered a beating. In a cold sweat, he was flushed and distraught. At first he mumbled something or other, expressing annoyance and insincere consolation; then he fell silent and merely urged the driver on through clenched teeth. As a result of this and the unsteady arm with which he was partly supporting, partly repelling him, Zarudin guessed his feelings, and the fact that now the paltry Tanarov, previously so far below him, suddenly had the right to be ashamed of him added the final and decisive straw to his awareness that everything was now at an end.

Zarudin couldn't walk across the courtyard alone; he was practically carried by Tanarov and by the frightened orderly who came running out to meet them, his hands shaking. Zarudin didn't notice whether or not others were present. They laid him on a sofa and at first didn't know what to do; they stood around foolishly in a crowd, thus causing him incredible suffering. Then the orderly suddenly recovered, began to bustle about, brought some warm water and a towel, and carefully washed Zarudin's face and hands. Zarudin was afraid to look him in the eye but the orderly's face wasn't at all malicious, contemptuous, or mocking, merely frightened and sympathetic, like that of a kind old woman.

"How could this happen, your Excellency? Oh, my God! How on earth!" he wailed softly.

"Well . . . it's none of your business!" Tanarov hissed, turning crimson, and then for some reason glanced around timidly.

He walked over to the window and reached mechanically for a cigarette, but unsure whether he should smoke in Zarudin's presence, he inconspicuously slipped the cigarette case back in his pocket.

"Should I call a doctor?" asked the orderly, standing to attention as usual and not at all put off by Tanarov's rude remark.

Tanarov spread his fingers in bewilderment. "Oh . . . I really don't know," he replied in a very different tone and once again glanced around.

But Zarudin heard and was appalled to think that the doctor would also see his battered face.

"Never mind. There's no need," he said in an unnaturally weak voice, still trying to convince himself that he was dying.

Now, after they'd washed the blood and dirt off his face, he didn't look so terrible—merely disfigured and distressed. With animal curiosity, Tanarov glanced at him quickly and immediately looked away. This almost imperceptible gesture, like all those that now surrounded Zarudin, was extremely painful for him to witness and he was almost choked by despair. He suddenly screwed up his swollen eye and cried in a shrill, strained voice, "Leave me . . . leave me alone!"

Tanarov glanced up at him, looked askance, and was suddenly filled with profoundly contemptuous spite.

He's still shouting! Well, I'll be damned! he thought maliciously.

Zarudin fell silent and lay motionless, his eyes closed. Tanarov quietly drummed his fingers on the windowsill, twirled his mustache, turned and looked out of the window again, feeling a nagging, cold desire to escape.

This is so awkward, damn it! Should I wait till he falls asleep or what? Then I can . . . he thought with bitter boredom.

A quarter of an hour passed but from time to time Zarudin stirred. Tanarov felt unbearably uncomfortable. At last Zarudin became completely still.

He seems to have fallen asleep, Tanarov thought insincerely, glancing imperceptibly at him. He's asleep.

He moved slowly, barely jingling his spurs. At once Zarudin opened his eyes. Tanarov hesitated for a moment, but Zarudin understood his intention and Tanarov realized that he understood. Then something strange and eerie passed between them: Zarudin quickly shut his eyes and pretended to be asleep, while Tanarov, convincing himself that he believed this act, and at the same time obviously realizing that both knew what was really going on, stooping awkwardly, tiptoed from the room with the feeling of a convicted traitor, filled with uncertainty and shame.

The door closed quietly and something between them that had seemed so sturdy, affectionate, and constant suddenly disappeared forever: both Zarudin and Tanarov felt that an unbridgeable gulf now separated them once and for all, and that among all men that lived, neither of them meant anything to the other anymore.

But in the next room Tanarov could breathe more comfortably; he was once more at ease and free. He felt neither compassion nor regret that everything had ended between him and Zarudin, a man who'd been his friend for so many years now.

"Listen, you," he said quickly to the orderly, glancing from side to side and hurrying as if to carry out a last formality. "I'm going now. But if something happens, then you should . . . You hear?"

"Yes, sir!" the soldier answered apprehensively.

"Well, then. In there . . . change his compresses frequently."

He hurried down the steps and sighed again with relief, walking out of the gate into the empty, broad street. It was already twilight and he was glad that his flushed face couldn't be seen by passersby.

What if it turns out that I'm implicated in this dreadful affair? he thought with a sudden chill in his heart as he crossed the boulevard. But what have I got to do with it? he thought, consoling himself, and trying to forget that he'd thrown himself at Sanin and that Ivanov had pushed him away so forcefully that he'd nearly fallen over.

Oh, damn it all! What a foul business! Tanarov thought, screwing up his whole face as he walked on. All because of that fool! he thought of Zarudin with malice. Why on earth did I ever get mixed up with that rascal? Oh, what a lousy business!

The more he thought about how disgusting and base it all was, the more his ordinary little figure with its prominent shoulders and chest, its tight-fitting breeches, foppish boots, and jacket shining white in the twilight instinctively straightened up; his shoulders and head took on a menacing look.

He scanned each passerby for signs of mockery; had he detected even the slightest trace, he would have reached for his sword and hacked the offender to death. But there were few passersby, and the ones there hurried by, their flat silhouettes sliding over the fences along the dark boulevard.

Back home and beginning to calm down, Tanarov once again recalled how Ivanov had pushed him away.

Why didn't I smash him in the face? I should have hit him! Pity my sword wasn't drawn! I'd have done him in! But I had a pistol in my pocket! Here it is: I could've shot him like a dog. Hmm. . . . I forgot about the pistol."

Of course I forgot, or I would've shot him on the spot like a dog! Oh, maybe it was a good thing I forgot. If I'd killed him—a trial! Perhaps one of them had a pistol, too. The devil knows what would've happened! Now no one knows I had a pistol and . . . it will all gradually blow over.

He looked cautiously from side to side, then pulled the pistol from his pocket and put it in a drawer of the table.

I must call on the colonel today and explain that I had nothing to do with it, he decided as he locked the drawer loudly.

But stronger than this intention, there suddenly appeared a nervous, insurmountable, and even somehow boastful desire to go to the club and, as an eyewitness to the events, tell everyone.

The agitated and vociferously indignant officers had gathered in the brightly lit club in the middle of town. They already knew about the incident in the garden and secretly rejoiced at Zarudin's misfortune, since he'd always annoyed them with his polish and style. They greeted Tanarov with great curiosity. Tanarov, feeling himself the hero of the evening, described the entire scene in great detail. In his voice and dark, narrow eyes there stirred a restrained and unconscious feeling of revenge: the oppression he'd suffered from his former friend, the matter of the money, his offhand treatment of him, his superiority—all made Tanarov retaliate by endlessly repeating and savoring the details of Zarudin's beating.

Meanwhile Zarudin lay there all alone on the sofa in his room, forsaken by the entire world.

Having found out what had happened, the orderly brought in the samovar with the same expression of a frightened, sympathetic old woman; he ran to fetch some wine and chased the energetic, affectionate setter out of the room—the dog was so excited that Zarudin had come home. Then he tiptoed back in to see his master.

"Your Excellency. . . . You should drink some wine," he said barely audibly.

"Huh? What?" Zarudin asked, opening and then closing his eyes immediately; and in what seemed to him a humiliating way, but in fact only pitifully, he frowned and hissed with difficulty through his swollen lips, "A mirror. Give me . . ."

The orderly sighed; he obediently brought a mirror and lit a candle. What's there to look at? he thought in disapproval.

Zarudin looked in the mirror and gave an unintentional moan. From the dark surface of the glass, lit by crimson light from the side, there stared at him a one-eyed, puffy, black-and-blue face with its blond mustache ridiculously tangled.

"Oh! Here, take it away," he mumbled and suddenly let out a hysterical sob. "Water. Give me . . ."

"Your Excellency, there's no need to cry! It'll heal," the orderly said sympathetically, offering him some water in a sticky glass that smelled of cold sweet tea.

Zarudin didn't drink it; he merely put his lips to the rim of the glass and spilled water on his chest.

"Go away!" he said.

It seemed to him that his orderly was the only person in the whole world who pitied him, but his warm feeling for the soldier was overshadowed by the unbearable awareness that now even an orderly had the right to pity him.

Blinking his eyes, with his clear desire to cry, the soldier went out onto the porch and sat down on a step; with a sigh he began stroking the soft, wavy coat of the dog who'd come running over. The setter rested his handsome, slobbering snout on his lap and looked up at him with dark, uncomprehending, though somehow expressive eyes. Bright, silent stars were shining above the garden. The soldier felt sad and afraid for some reason, as if expecting a terrible, irrevocable misfortune.

Hey, what a life, what a life! he thought bitterly, and his thoughts went back to his own village.

Zarudin turned over abruptly to face the back of the sofa and lay still, not noticing that the warm, wet compress had slipped from his face.

It's all over! he repeated, sobbing, to himself. What's over? Everything, my whole life. Everything. Life's finished. Why? Because I've been shamed, because . . . I've been beaten like a dog! A fist in the face! I can't stay in the regiment!

He recalled with unusual clarity being down on all fours in the middle of the lane, senselessly muttering impotent threats, so pitiful and petty. He kept reliving that terrible moment over and over again, and it appeared even more vividly and mortifyingly before his eyes. He recalled all the details as if illumined by electric light, and for some reason his ridiculous threats and Karsavina's white dress flashing before him just as he was uttering those threats were the most tormenting details of all.

Who lifted me up? he wondered, trying not to think, intentionally muddling his own thoughts. Tanarov? Or that little Yid who was with them? Tanarov? Ah! That's not the point. What is? It's that my whole life is ruined. I can't stay in the regiment. What about a duel? He still won't fight. I can't stay in the regiment!

He recalled how a military tribunal on which he had served had discharged two older married officers from the regiment because they'd refused to fight a duel.

That's what they'll do to me. Politely, without shaking hands, the same people who . . . And no one will ever be proud to walk arm in arm with me along the boulevard, no one will envy me or imitate my style. . . . But that's not the point! Disgrace, disgrace, that's the main thing! Why disgrace? Because I was hit? But they used to beat me in military school! I was smacked by that fatso Shvartz and had a tooth knocked out, and nothing ever came of it. Afterward we made up and remained the best of friends until the end of school. No one despised me! Why isn't it like that now? Isn't it the same? On that occasion I fell down and bled too. . . . Why not?

In his mind there was no answer to this question, so full of desperate misery. He merely felt that some foul, deep filth had covered his head and that now he was sinking uncontrollably to the bottom, seeing and understanding nothing around him.

If he'd agreed to fight a duel and then put a bullet in my face, that would have been even more painful and hideous than this, but no one would despise me for it and everyone would feel sorry for me. That means, between his bullet and his fist. . . But what's the difference? Why?

His thoughts were racing along. From their depths, intensified by the irreparable misery and torment he suffered, there began to emerge something new, as if it had been there before but had been forgotten during the course of his easygoing, vacuous, and boisterous life as an officer.

Not long ago Von Deitz was arguing with me; he said if someone strikes you on the left cheek, you should offer him the right; yet at the time he himself came up and shouted, waving his arms, angry that he'd refused to fight a duel! It's really others who are to blame for my wanting to hit him with my riding crop. And it's all my fault that I didn't manage to strike him! But that's ridiculous! Unfair! Still, it's a disgrace. I can't stay in the regiment!

Zarudin took hold of his head helplessly, tossing it around on the pillow, and focused mechanically on the dull, aching pain in his eye. Suddenly he felt a terrible, even tormenting surge of malice.

Get a revolver, rush out, and shoot him . . . bullet after bullet. Then, after he falls, stamp on his face . . . right on his face, his teeth, his eyes . . .

The wet compress fell to the floor with a dull thud. He opened his eyes apprehensively and saw the dimly lit room, basin of water, wet towel, and the strange dark window staring at him mysteriously like a dismal eye.

No, it's no use. It won't help, he thought, sinking into impotent despair. It doesn't matter: everyone saw how I was struck in the face and how I was down on all fours. Beaten, beaten. Right in my face. I can't go back, ever! I'll never be happy or free again.

Once more something acute and unusually clear stirred in his brain.

Have I ever really been free? I'm done for now because my life's never been free, never been my own. Would I really have gone on my own to fight a duel, would I have struck him with the riding crop? I wouldn't have been hit and everything would be fine, happy. . . . Who decided when that an insult has to be avenged with blood? It wasn't me! So I've avenged . . . it's been avenged with my blood. . . . So what? I don't know, but I have to leave the regiment!

His inept, feeble thoughts tried to rise, but plummeted like a bird with clipped wings. Wherever his mind led, it always came back to the idea that he had to leave the regiment and that he was permanently disgraced.

Once Zarudin had seen how a fly had become stuck in thick spittle, struggling helplessly on the floor, its legs and wings tangled, blinded and suffocating in the disgusting, implacable slime. It was obvious that it was all over for the fly, even though it still tried to crawl, stretching out its legs, exhausting its strength. At the time Zarudin had shuddered squeamishly and turned away; and now, even though he didn't recall it all clearly, it was as if some hidden consciousness, resembling a hallucination, reminded him of that unfortunate fly. And then he must have started hallucinating: suddenly he couldn't remember exactly or clearly that he'd seen two peasants. They were cursing and fighting; one struck the other on the ear and the older, graying one fell over; then he stood up and, wiping the blood dripping from his nose with his shirtsleeve, said with conviction, "What a fool!"

I did see that once! Zarudin recalled clearly; and again he became conscious of the semidarkened room with a candle on the table. Afterward they went and had a few drinks together at the tavern.

Then he must have dozed off again because the candle and the room vanished, but he didn't stop thinking; later, together with the candle that emerged from the darkness, he formulated his own thought: One can't go on living with this disgrace . . . that's all. So one must die! But I don't want to die, and who needs it? Not me! Reputation? What do I care about reputation? What does reputation mean if I have to die? But I have to leave the regiment. . . . How will I live afterward?

Something vague, mysterious, and bizarre appeared to him as his future, and he retreated feebly from it. Thus every time a passionate desire for life and happiness began to clarify something for him, a fog enveloped his brain and settled even lower upon it; once more he found himself facing an inescapable abyss.

It was night and an oppressive silence stood outside the window, as if Zarudin were the only person alive in the whole world and were suffering all alone.

On the table the guttering candle was still burning, and its flame, yellow and steady, rose in a deathly calm way. Zarudin looked at it, his eye gleaming in his fever and despair, but didn't see it, enveloped as he was in a dark fog of endlessly confused and paralyzed thoughts. Amid these chaotic fragments of recollections, imaginations, and feelings, one stood out more clearly than all the others and stabbed his heart with a poignant sense of sadness. It was the painful and pitiful awareness of his complete solitude. Out there, somewhere or other, millions of people were living, rejoicing, laughing, perhaps even talking about him, while he was all alone. In vain he summoned up one familiar face after another. They stood there in a pale, distant, and apathetic line, and in their cold features he could detect only curiosity and gloating. Then with timid sorrow he remembered Lida.

He imagined her as she had appeared to him the last time he saw her: with her large, serious eyes, her soft, delicate body beneath her simple blouse, and her long braid. In her face he saw neither malice nor contempt. She was looking at him with sad reproach, and something of possibility forever lost could be detected in her forlorn expression. He recalled the scene when he'd rejected her at the moment of her most extreme grief. An awareness of irrevocable loss wounded him like a knife cutting into the deepest recesses of his soul.

She must've suffered then even more than I am suffering now. I rejected her. I even wanted her to drown herself, to die!

As if to the last safe haven, his entire being reached out to her in tormented yearning for her caresses and sympathy. For a moment it occurred to him that his suffering this time must atone for the past; but he knew that she'd never come to him, that everything was finished, and that total emptiness had enveloped him in a great abyss.

He raised his hand, pressed it firmly to his head, and lay still, closing his eyes, clenching his teeth, and trying to see nothing, hear nothing, feel nothing. But he soon let his hand drop, got up, and sat down. He felt terribly dizzy, his mouth was on fire, and his arms and legs were trembling. He stood up and, swaying from the weight of his head, which had suddenly become very large and heavy, moved over to the table.

All is lost, everything. My life, Lida, everything. . . .

A bright flash of unprecedented clarity illumined his mind for a moment: he suddenly realized that there had been nothing beautiful or good or easy about the life that had just vanished; instead everything was confused, defiled, and stupid. The singular, handsome Zarudin, who had the right to enjoy everything pleasant, no longer existed; there was only a powerless, pusillanimous, dissolute body that had previously enjoyed pleasure but now felt only pain and humiliation. When the mirage of success had vanished, it left only a bare, poor image.

It's impossible to go on living, he thought clearly. In order to live again, I must discard my entire past, begin to live life in a new way, become an entirely different person, and I can't do that.

He lowered his head heavily to the table and, in the sinister light of the flickering, guttering candle, lay there motionless.

 XXXII

That same evening Sanin went alone to see Soloveichik.

The little Jew was sitting by himself on the porch of his wing of the house, staring at the dismal, deserted courtyard, where small, white, aimless paths wound tediously to and fro and the dusty grass had withered. The locked warehouses with their large rusty padlocks, the dim windows of the mill, and the vast, empty area where life seemed to have died away many years ago created a tedious, painful feeling of gloom.

Sanin was struck at once by Soloveichik's face: he wasn't grinning or displaying his little teeth as usual; instead his expression was grieved and strained. Some terrifying, wild, secret idea was perceptible in his dark Jewish eyes.

"Ah, greetings," he said apathetically; then, shaking Sanin's hand feebly, he turned his face back to the deserted courtyard and darkening sky, against which the derelict roofs of the storehouses were etched in black.

Sanin sat down on the other side of the porch railing, lit a cigarette, and stared at Soloveichik for a long time, guessing that something unusual was happening.

"What do you do here?" he asked.

Soloveichik slowly moved his sad eyes to look at Sanin.

"Well, I . . . When the mill was running, I used to work in the office. I also lived here. Then everyone else left and I stayed behind."

"Don't you find it depressing to be here all alone?"

Soloveichik was silent.

"It makes no difference," he said with a dismissive gesture.

It was quiet for a long time; in the silence the lonely rattling of the dog's chain in the kennel near the warehouse could be heard.

"It's not depressing out there," Soloveichik said suddenly in an unexpectedly loud, passionate voice, springing into action. "Not out there! But in here and in here!" He pointed to his head and his heart.

"What's wrong?" Sanin asked calmly.

"Listen," Soloveichik continued even more loudly and passionately. "Earlier today you struck a man and smashed his face . . . and may even have smashed his life. Please don't be angry with me for asking, because I've thought about it for a long time. I've been sitting here thinking and I'm feeling miserable. Please answer me!"

For a moment his face was distorted by his customary obsequious little grin.

"Ask whatever you want," Sanin said with a smile. "Are you afraid of offending me or what? You can't offend me with that. What's done is done. If I thought I'd done something wrong, I'd tell you."

"I'd like to ask you," Soloveichik began in an agitated voice. "Do you realize that you might have killed that man altogether?"

"I'm almost certain of that," Sanin replied. "It would've been difficult for a man like Zarudin to extricate himself in any other way, except by doing away with me or him. As for killing me . . . the psychological moment had been lost: now he's too badly hurt to kill me. Later on he won't have the courage. He's finished."

"And you can say that calmly?"

"What do you mean by 'calmly'?" asked Sanin. "I can't watch calmly when a chicken gets slaughtered, and here we're talking about a human being. It's painful to hit anyone. True, it's pleasant to feel one's own strength, but it's still a terrible thing. Terrible that it ended so crudely, but my conscience is clear. I'm merely incidental here. Zarudin is perishing because his whole life has been headed in that direction. What's surprising is not that only one man's been lost but that they all weren't lost. These people learn how to kill others and pamper their own bodies; they don't understand in the least what they're doing or why. It's madness; they're idiots! If we let madmen loose in the street, they'll cut each other's throats. How am I to blame if I defended myself against that sort of madman?"

"But you killed him!" Soloveichik repeated stubbornly.

"In that case he should complain to the Lord God who brought us together on a road with no room to pass."

"But you could've restrained him, grabbed his arm!"

Sanin raised his head. "In such circumstances one doesn't think rationally. Besides, what would have come of that? The law that governs his life would demand vengeance at any price. I couldn't have held his arm forever. That would've been one more insult for him, that's all."

Soloveichik spread his arms in a strange way and fell silent.

Darkness had surrounded them imperceptibly on all sides. A band of twilight, sharply outlining the edges of the dark roofs, grew even more distant and chill. Eerie black shadows crowded beneath the sheds and at times it seemed that mysterious, terrifying creatures had arrived to occupy this deserted, abandoned courtyard for the night and to share its enigmatic life. Their noiseless tread must have disturbed Sultan, because he suddenly emerged from his kennel and sat down, rattling his chain anxiously.

"Perhaps you're right," Soloveichik said drearily. "But did it have to happen at all? Perhaps it would've been better for you to have taken the blow?"

"Better? For whom?" asked Sanin. "It's always terrible to take a blow! Why should I? For what reason?"

"No, listen to me!" Soloveichik hastily interrupted him, and even stretched out his hand imploringly. "Perhaps it would've been better . . ."

"For Zarudin, of course."

"No, for you too. For you too. Just think about it."

"Ah, Soloveichik," said Sanin with slight irritation. "That's all old fairy-tale stuff about moral victory! Besides, that story's so primitive. . . . Moral victory consists not in proffering the other cheek but in being right before one's own conscience. It doesn't matter how that's achieved: it's a question of chance and circumstance. . . . There's nothing more terrible than slavery—and the most terrible slavery in the world is when a man, though totally opposed to violence, submits to it in the name of something stronger than he is."

Soloveichik suddenly grasped his head in his hands, but his expression was no longer discernible in the darkness.

"My mind is feeble," he said with a whine. "I can't understand anything anymore, and I haven't got the faintest idea how one ought to live!"

"Why do you want to know? Live the way a bird flies: if you feel like flapping your right wing, flap it; if you feel like flying around a tree, fly around it."

"That's fine for a bird but I'm a human being!" Soloveichik replied with naive earnestness.

Sanin guffawed, and for a moment his hearty, masculine laughter filled all corners of the dark wasteland with life.

Soloveichik listened to it, then shook his head.

"No," he said gloomily. "And you can't teach me how to live! No one can teach me how to live."

"That's true; no one can teach you that. The art of living is a talent too. He who lacks that talent either perishes or taints his life, transforming it into a pitiful form of existence without light or joy."

"You're so composed now and talking as if you know everything. Please, don't be angry with me . . . but have you always been like this?" Soloveichik asked with burning curiosity.

"Well, no," Sanin said, shaking his head. "It's true I've always been very composed, but there have been moments when I experienced various kinds of indecision. There was a time when I seriously considered the ideal of a Christian life."

Sanin paused to think, and Soloveichik, stretching out his neck as if expecting to hear something incredibly important, stared at him.

"It was in my first year at university and I had a friend, a student of mathematics, Ivan Lande.[30] He was an extraordinary fellow of unassailable power, and a Christian not by conviction but by nature. In his life he reflected all the essential aspects of Christianity: when he was attacked, he didn't defend himself; he forgave his enemies; he treated every man as his brother; he refrained from sexual relations with women. . . . Do you remember Semyonov?"

Soloveichik nodded with naive delight. This was unimaginably important for him: suddenly, in a familiar setting among acquaintances, an image appeared before him of which he'd had only a vague impression but one that attracted him like a moth in the darkness of night to the bright flame of a candle. He was on fire with attention and anticipation.

"Well, then. Semyonov was very ill at the time; he was living in the Crimea, where he was giving lessons. There in his loneliness, with a presentiment of death, he fell into gloomy despair. Lande found out about it, and, of course, decided he had to go and save this soul that was perishing. . . . And so he literally walked there: he had no money and no one would lend him any since he was considered such a holy fool;[31] so he set out to walk a thousand versts! He died somewhere along the way, having given his life for others."

---

[30] The eponymous hero of Artsybashev's story "The Death of Lande" (1904), which adumbrates many of the themes and characters of *Sanin*.

[31] The figure of the wise fool or a "fool for Christ's sake" has played an important role in the Russian religious tradition.

"And you . . . Please tell me!" Soloveichik cried, springing suddenly into action, his eyes blazing in ecstasy. "Do you approve of this man?"

"There were many arguments about him in his day," Sanin replied thoughtfully. "Some didn't consider him a Christian at all and rejected him for that reason. Others considered him simply a holy fool, with a certain touch of willfulness. Still others denied his power because he didn't struggle, didn't become a prophet, wasn't victorious; instead he provoked general animosity. Well, I regard him differently. At the time I was under his influence to a ridiculous extent. It went so far that once a student actually struck me in the face. At first everything began to spin around me, but Lande was there and I glanced toward him. I don't know what happened, but I merely got up silently and walked away. Well, at first I was terribly proud of what I'd done, even absurdly so; then I came to hate that student from the bottom of my heart. Not because he had struck me, that wasn't important at all; it was rather that my act had given him inordinate pleasure. Completely coincidentally I noticed what deception I was engaged in. I became absorbed in thinking about it. For two weeks I went around like a madman, and then stopped feeling proud of my specious moral victory. After his first smug taunt, I beat him to a pulp. Then a fundamental break came between Lande and me. I began to examine his life more clearly and saw that it was terribly unhappy and miserable."

"Oh, what are you saying?" cried Soloveichik. "Can you possibly conceive of the wealth of his feelings?"

"These feelings were all of one kind: the happiness of his life consisted in accepting any and all misfortune without a murmur, and the wealth consisted of even greater and deeper renunciation of all life's richness. He was a beggar by choice and an impractical dreamer, living in the name of something he knew nothing about."

"You don't know how you're tormenting me!" cried Soloveichik, abruptly wringing his hands.

"You know, Soloveichik, you've become hysterical!" Sanin observed in astonishment. "I'm not saying anything unusual. Or else this question has become very painful for you."

"Very painful! I think and think until my head aches. . . . Was this all really a mistake? I feel as if I were in a dark room . . . and no one can tell me what to do! Why does a person go on living? Tell me that!"

"Why? No one knows."

"Isn't it possible to live for the future? So that afterward people can enjoy a golden age?"

"There can never be a golden age. If life and human beings could become better instantaneously, that would constitute golden bliss, but that can never be. Improvement occurs by imperceptible steps; mankind sees only the preceding and succeeding stages. You and I haven't lived the lives of Roman slaves or primitive Stone Age people, so we can't recognize the good fortune of our own culture; similarly, in a golden age man won't perceive any difference between his own life and his father's, just as his father perceived no difference between his and his father's, and so on. Mankind stands on an endless road. Paving the way to happiness is like adding new digits to an infinite number."

"Does that mean everything's in vain? Is there nothing at all?"

"That's what I think. Nothing at all."

"Well, what about your Lande? Why, you just said . . ."

"I loved Lande and still do," Sanin replied seriously, "not because he was like that, but because he was sincere and didn't swerve from his path when faced with any obstacles, either trivial or formidable. For me Lande was worthy in and of himself, and his worth disappeared after his death."

"Don't you think that such people ennoble life? And that others will come after them?"

"Why ennoble life? That's the first question. Second, it's impossible to follow that model. You have to be born a Lande. Christ was magnificent but Christians are ineffectual."

Sanin was tired of talking and fell silent. Soloveichik was silent too, as was everything around them; it seemed that only the twinkling stars above were holding an unending, silent conversation. Suddenly Soloveichik whispered something, and his whispering was strange and uncanny.

"What's that?" Sanin asked with a shudder.

"Tell me," muttered Soloveichik, "tell me what you think. If a man doesn't know where to go, spends all his time thinking and suffering, and finds everything terrible and incomprehensible . . . is it perhaps better for him to die?"

"Well," said Sanin, frowning in the darkness, clearly and intuitively realizing what was coming from the little Jew's dark soul, "perhaps it is better to die. There's no sense in suffering, and no one's going to live forever. Only someone who finds joy in life should go on living. For those who are suffering—it's better to die."

"That's just what I thought!" cried Soloveichik with conviction, and suddenly took firm hold of Sanin's hand.

It was completely dark, and in the dusk Soloveichik's face appeared white, like that of a corpse, and his eyes resembled two empty black cavities.

"You're a dead man," Sanin said and stood up with unintentional apprehension in his soul. "And perhaps the best place for a dead man really is the grave. Farewell."

Soloveichik seemed not to hear him and sat still, like a black shadow with a deathly white face. Sanin was silent, waited a moment, and then walked away. He paused near the gate and listened. Everything was quiet, and Soloveichik was barely visible on the porch, merging with the darkness. A disagreeably tormenting presentiment crept into Sanin's heart.

It makes no difference! he thought. To live like that or to die . . . if not today, then tomorrow.

He turned quickly and, opening the creaking gate, headed out into the street.

It was just as quiet in the courtyard as before.

When Sanin reached the boulevard, he heard strange, agitated sounds in the distance. Someone was running swiftly in the darkness of night, his feet pounding loudly; he seemed to be both wailing and weeping as he ran. Sanin stopped. A black figure was emerging from the darkness, coming closer and closer. For some reason Sanin once again had an uncanny feeling.

"What's the matter?" he called loudly.

The approaching figure stopped for a moment and Sanin looked closely at the soldier's confused, frightened face.

"What's happened?" he cried uneasily.

The soldier muttered something and then ran on, his feet pounding again; he was either wailing or weeping. The night and the silence swallowed him up like a ghost.

Why, that's Zarudin's orderly! Sanin recalled; then suddenly a mighty, radiant thought flashed distinctly and definitively through his mind: Zarudin's shot himself!

Sanin felt a slight chill. For a moment or two he stared silently into the dark face of night; between the mysterious, terrible darkness and the tall, strong man with a steady gaze there was a brief silent but terrible struggle.

The town was asleep, its sidewalks white, its trees black, and its dark windows staring dully, watching the deep stillness.

Suddenly Sanin shook his head, grinned, and cast his clear gaze ahead.

"I'm not to blame in this matter," he said loudly. "One more, one less!"

And then on he went, a tall dark shadow disappearing into the night.

## XXXIII

As quickly as things become known in a small town, so everyone soon learned that two men had taken their lives on the same evening.

Ivanov brought this news to Yury Svarozhich; he went to see him the next day, just after Yury had returned from a lesson and had sat down to work on Lyalya's portrait. She was posing in a bright blouse, her bare neck and pink arms showing through the light fabric. Sunlight filled the room, its golden sparks lighting the thick hair on Lyalya's head; she was so young, innocent, and cheerful—just like a golden bird.

"Greetings," said Ivanov, coming in and tossing his hat on a chair.

"Ah. . . . Well, what news?" asked Yury, smiling hospitably.

He was in a contented, buoyant mood because he'd finally been able to arrange some lessons, no longer felt so dependent on his father, and was now standing on his own two feet; and also because of the sunshine and the closeness of the joyful, attractive Lyalya.

"Quite a lot," said Ivanov with a vague look in his gray eyes. "One man has hanged himself, another has shot himself, and a third's been possessed by the devil!"

"What do you mean?"

"I added the third for special effect, but the first two are real. Zarudin shot himself last night, and just now I heard that Soloveichik has hanged himself . . . that's what!"

"Impossible!" cried Lyalya, jumping up. She was all white, pink, and golden; her eyes looked frightened but they were shining with curiosity.

Yury quickly put down his palette in astonishment and apprehension, and went up to Ivanov.

"You're not joking?"

"Not in the least!" said Ivanov with a wave of his hand.

As usual he tried to assume an air of philosophical indifference, but it was obvious that he felt troubled and upset.

"Why did he shoot himself? Because Sanin hit him? Does Sanin know?" Lyalya asked, clutching Ivanov naively and choking with emotion.

"Apparently yes. Sanin's known since yesterday," Ivanov replied.

"What was his reaction?" Yury asked despite himself.

Ivanov shrugged. He'd already had more than one argument about Sanin with Yury, and was beginning to be annoyed.

"None whatsoever. What does he have to do with it?" he replied with rude irritation.

"Still, he's the reason for it!" said Lyalya, assuming a meaningful expression.

"Well, what of it? That fool Zarudin had no business getting involved with him. Sanin's not to blame. It's all very regrettable, but it must be ascribed entirely to Zarudin's own stupidity."

"Well, let's presume the reasons lie deeper," Yury replied glumly. "Zarudin lived within a certain set. . . ."

"And the fact that he lived within such a stupid set, and even submitted to it, provides proof that he himself was a fool!" said Ivanov with a shrug.

Yury fell silent and rubbed his hands mechanically. He found it disagreeable to be talking like this about the departed, although he really didn't know why.

"Well, fine. Zarudin—that I can understand, but Soloveichik . . . I never expected that," said Lyalya tentatively, arching her eyebrows. "Why did he do it?"

"God knows," said Ivanov. "He always seemed a bit odd."

Just then Ryazantsev drove up and Karsavina also walked in. They met at the gate; even from the porch one could hear Karsavina's high-pitched, be-wildered, disbelieving tone and Ryazantsev's playful, jocular voice that he always used when speaking to beautiful young women.

"Anatoly Pavlovich has just come from there," Karsavina said with an expression of agitated interest, coming into the room first.

Ryazantsev came in laughing as usual; he was lighting a cigarette as he did so.

"Well, I'll be damned!" he said, filling the room with his voice, vitality, and self-assured cheerfulness. "Soon there won't be any young people left in town!"

Karsavina sat down in silence, her lovely face perplexed and distraught.

"Well, tell us all about it," said Ivanov.

"Let's see, then," Ryazantsev began, arching his brows like Lyalya and laughing, but not as cheerfully as before. "I'd just left the club yesterday when suddenly a soldier comes running up. 'His Excellency,' he says, 'has shot himself.' I took a cab and headed over there. I arrive, and almost the whole regiment's there already. He's lying on his bed, jacket open."

"Where did he shoot himself?" Lyalya asked with interest, clinging to his arm.

"In the temple. The bullet pierced his skull, right here, and hit the ceiling."

"Was it a Browning?" Yury asked for some reason.

"Yes. A sordid scene. The wall was splattered with brains and blood. And of course his face was completely mutilated. Yes, what a job it did on him!"

Starting to laugh again, Ryazantsev shrugged.

"A powerful man!"

"Indeed, a sturdy fellow!" Ivanov said for some reason, nodding his head in self-satisfaction.

"How disgusting!" Yury said, frowning squeamishly.

Karsavina looked at him timidly.

"But in my opinion he's not to blame," she remarked. "He wasn't just going to wait. . . ."

"No," Ryazantsev said, knitting his brows vaguely, "but to strike him like that! Why, he was given a chance to fight a duel."

"Astonishing!" Ivanov said, shrugging in annoyance.

"No, it's true . . . a duel's a stupid thing," Yury replied prudently.

"Of course it is," Karsavina supported him swiftly.

Yury felt she was glad to have an opportunity to vindicate Sanin, and he was not pleased.

"Nevertheless, it's still . . ." he replied, not knowing what to say so as to discredit Sanin.

"Savagery, whatever you say!" Ryazantsev suggested.

Yury thought Ryazantsev himself wasn't very far from being a contented animal, but he remained silent, even feeling glad that Ryazantsev had started disagreeing with Karsavina and sharply condemning Sanin.

Karsavina, noticing the expression of displeasure on Yury's face, fell silent, although in the depths of her soul she approved of Sanin's strength and decisiveness; what Ryazantsev said about his level of culture seemed wrong to her. And, just like Yury, she felt Ryazantsev had no right to pontificate on that subject.

But Ivanov became angry and began to argue.

"Just think! A sublime level of cultivation means you shoot someone's nose off or stick a knife in his guts!"

"Is it any better to smash him in the face?"

"Yes, in my opinion it is. What's a fist? What harm can a fist do? The bruise will heal, and that's that. No one's ever suffered disaster as a result of a fist."

"That's not the point!"

"What is, then?" Ivanov asked, his thin lips curling. "In my opinion, one shouldn't fight. Why cause such a scandal? But if there must be a fight, then at least it should be without bodily injury. That's absolutely clear!"

"He almost knocked his eye out!" Ryazantsev remarked ironically. "Isn't that bodily injury?"

"His eye, of course. . . . If he knocks his eye out, then the man suffers harm; but a lost eye's still better than a knife in the guts! At least there's no loss of life!"

"But Zarudin's dead!"

"Well, that was his own choice."

Yury stroked his beard nervously.

"In fact, I can state candidly," he said, pleased to be speaking so sincerely, "that for me personally this question's still unresolved. And I don't know how I would've behaved had I been in Sanin's place. It's stupid to fight a duel, of course, but it's also unbecoming to have a fistfight!"

"But what should one do to the person who provokes it?" asked Karsavina.

Yury shrugged sadly.

"No, it's Soloveichik we ought to feel sorry for," Ryazantsev remarked after a pause, but his complacent, cheerful face was out of keeping with his words.

Suddenly they remembered that they hadn't even asked about Soloveichik, and everyone felt awkward.

"Do you know where he hanged himself? Under the shed, near the dog kennel. He let the dog off its chain and then hanged himself."

Simultaneously Karsavina and Yury seemed to hear his shrill voice crying, "Sultan, lie down!"

"And he left a note, you see," Ryazantsev continued, without concealing a cheerful twinkle in his eyes. "I even made a copy of it. A human document, right?"

He took his notebook from his side pocket.

" 'Why should I go on living when I myself don't know how to live? People like me can't make others happy,' " Ryazantsev read and unexpectedly fell uncomfortably silent.

It grew quiet in the room, as if someone's pale, sad spirit were passing overhead. Karsavina's eyes filled with large tears, Lyalya's face flushed pathetically, and Yury, smiling painfully, went over to the window.

"That's all there was," Ryazantsev added mechanically.

"What more could there be?" Karsavina asked, her lips trembling.

Ivanov stood up. Getting some matches from the table, he muttered, "What immense stupidity—that's for sure!"

"You should be ashamed!" Karsavina snapped in annoyance.

Yury glanced squeamishly at Ivanov's long, straight hair and turned away.

"Yes. So much for Soloveichik," Ryazantsev said, once again with a cheerful gleam in his eyes; he spread his hands. "I always thought he was just a poor devil and, if you'll allow me, a little Yid—nothing more! Now look at him! It turns out he wasn't even of this world. There's no higher love than the sacrifice of one's own life for others!"

"But he didn't sacrifice his own life for others!" Ivanov objected.

Why does he put on airs? He's such an animal! he thought, looking askance at Ryazantsev's contented, smooth face with enmity and contempt, and, for some reason, at his vest stretched tight over his portly belly.

"It's all the same. The impulse was clear."

"It's not the same at all," Ivanov replied stubbornly; his eyes became mean. "It's muck and mire and nothing else!"

His strange hatred for Soloveichik made an unpleasant impression on everyone. Karsavina stood up and, taking her leave, whispered intimately to Yury as if confiding in him lovingly, "I'm leaving. He makes me sick!"

"Yes," Yury said with a nod of his head. "What astonishing cruelty!"

Lyalya and Ryazantsev left after Karsavina. Ivanov became thoughtful, smoked a cigarette in silence, stared angrily into the corner, and then left too.

As he walked along the street swinging his arms as usual, he thought with annoyance and spite: These fools imagine, of course, that I don't understand what they're doing. It's astonishing! I know what they're feeling better than they do themselves! I know there's no greater love than when a man sacrifices his own life for a loved one, but to hang oneself because he's no use to other people—that's nonsense!

And Ivanov, recalling the endless series of books he'd read and the Gospels most of all, began searching for something that would explain Soloveichik's act as he would've liked. His books seemed to open obediently at the very pages he needed and to tell him in a dead language just what he needed to hear. His thoughts worked feverishly and became so intertwined with ideas derived from books that he was no longer able to distinguish what he himself thought from what he remembered from his reading.

Arriving home, he lay down on his bed, stretched out his long legs, and went on thinking until he fell asleep. He woke late in the evening.

## ▒▒ XXXIV ▒▒

As Zarudin was being borne to his final resting place to the strains of martial music, Yury watched the entire grim, stately procession from his window—the horse draped in black, the funeral march, and the solitary officer's cap placed on the coffin lid. There were many flowers, broodingly somber women, and imposingly mournful music. That night he felt particularly gloomy.

That same evening he'd had a long walk with Karsavina; he saw her beautiful, loving eyes and magnificent body reaching out to him but felt downhearted even with her.

"How strange it is and how strange to think," he said, his dark, nervous eyes looking straight ahead, "that Zarudin no longer exists. Once there was an officer, so handsome, cheerful, carefree. It seemed as if he'd live forever . . . that the horror of life with all its torments, doubts, and death couldn't exist for him, held no meaning for him. And then one fine day this man is crushed, ground to dust. He experiences a terrible private drama, and now he's gone and will never be seen again! And that cap on the coffin lid . . ."

Yury fell silent and stared despondently at the ground. Karsavina walked calmly beside him, listening attentively, and softly fingering the lace of her white parasol with her lovely ample hands. She wasn't thinking about Zarudin: her gorgeous body was rejoicing in Yury's closeness; but unconsciously deferring to him and trying to please him, she assumed a sorrowful expression and looked distraught.

"Yes, it was so sad to see! And that music!"

"I don't blame Sanin," Yury said abruptly. "He couldn't behave otherwise. The awful thing is that the paths of these two men crossed and one or the other had to give way. And the awful thing, too, is that the inadvertent victor doesn't see the horror of his victory. He wiped a man off the face of the earth, and he's still in the right."

"Yes, in the right. And so . . ." Karsavina said, not waiting for Yury to finish, growing so excited that her prominent bosom began to heave.

"No, but I say even that's awful!" Yury interrupted her, feeling a jealous hatred and casting a sidelong glance at her bust and animated face.

"Why?" Karsavina asked timidly, becoming terribly embarrassed. Somehow her eyes had lost their gleam and her cheeks were flushed.

"Because this would cause painful suffering in anyone else. Doubts, uncertainty . . . A spiritual struggle would follow; yet he behaves as if nothing has happened! I'm very sorry, he says, but I'm not to blame. Is it really only a matter of blame? Of simple right?"

"What then?" Karsavina asked unclearly and softly, lowering her head, obviously afraid of angering him.

"I don't know, exactly, but a man has no right to act like a beast," Yury cried shrilly and with suffering in his voice.

They went on walking for a long time in silence. Karsavina was suffering because she felt estranged from Yury and for a moment had lost that nice, warm, special bond with him; meanwhile he felt that what he'd said was confused and unclear, and he suffered from a heavy fog in his heart and from his vanity.

He soon headed home, leaving the young woman in a tormented state of discontent, fear, and helpless injury.

Yury noticed her dismay; but for some reason it brought him painful pleasure, as if he'd retaliated against a woman he loved because of some terrible offense.

Back at home he felt unbearably wretched.

At supper Lyalya repeated what Ryazantsev had told her—how at the mill, just as they were taking Soloveichik's body down from the noose, some local boys shouted from behind the fence, "The Yid's hanged himself! The Yid's hanged himself!"

Nikolai Yegorovich laughed heartily and made Lyalya repeat the story: "So—'The Yid's hanged himself'!"

Yury went to his room, sat down to correct his pupil's notebook, and thought with inexpressible hatred, There's so much bestiality left in people! Is it possible to suffer and sacrifice oneself for these dull-witted, stupid creatures? But then he realized that this wasn't very nice and became ashamed of his own malice. They're not to blame. "They know not what they do."[32]

But whether they know or not, right now they're still beasts and nothing more! he thought, but tried not to dwell on this idea and began thinking about Soloveichik.

Man is so lonely: the unhappy Soloveichik lived and carried within him a great heart, suffering for the entire world, prepared to make any sacrifice. But no one, not even I—the thought flashed through his mind with an unpleasant stab of pain—noticed or appreciated him. On the contrary, we almost despised him! And why? Simply because he didn't know how or was unable to express himself, because he was fastidious and a little tiresome. But in that fastidiousness and tiresomeness lay his ardent desire to get closer to everyone, to help and please everyone. He was a saint, yet we considered him a fool!

A feeling of guilt tormented Yury's soul so excruciatingly that he put his

---

[32] Luke 23:34.

work aside and paced the room for a long time, entirely under the spell of his unresolved, painful thoughts. Then he sat down at the table, picked up his Bible, opened it at random, and read a passage he'd read more often than any other; its pages were worn and ragged:

> By mere chance were we born, and afterwards we shall be as though we had never existed, for the breath in our nostrils is but a wisp of smoke; our reason is a mere spark kept alive by the beating of our hearts,
> And when that goes out, our body will turn to ashes and the breath of our life disperse like empty air.
> With the passing of time our names will be forgotten, and no one will remember anything we did. Our life will vanish like the last vestige of a cloud; and as a mist is chased away by the sun's rays and overborne by its heat, so too will life be dispersed.
> A fleeting shadow—such is our life, and there is no postponement of our end. Man's fate is sealed: no one returns.[33]

Yury read no further because then it spoke about how it made no sense to think about death and how one should rejoice in life like a youth; but he couldn't understand that part and it didn't correspond with his own agonizing thoughts.

How true, horrible, and inevitable it all is! he thought of his reading, trying to imagine how his spirit would dissipate after his death. But he couldn't.

It's horrible! I sit here, alive, thirsting for life and happiness, and I read my own inescapable death sentence. I read it and can't even protest!

He had pondered this idea many times and read it in books in exactly the same words. Wearied as he was by his own acknowledged, monotonous frailty, this idea distressed him and tormented him all the more.

He took his head in his hands; with despair in his soul he rocked from side to side, like a wild animal in a cage. With eyes closed and endless weariness in his heart, he appealed to Someone. With malice but lacking force, with hatred but without bitterness, with entreaty but without acknowledgment, he spoke:

"What has man done to You, that You should mock him in this way? Why have You, if You exist, hidden Yourself from him? Why have You made it so that even if I were to believe in You, I wouldn't believe in my own belief? If You were to answer me, how could I believe it was really coming from You, and not from within myself? If I'm right in my desire to live, why do You take away my right to do so after You Yourself gave it to me? If you require suffering—so be it! We would bear it out of love for You. But we don't even know which is more necessary—a tree or us.

"There's always hope for a tree! Even if it's chopped down, it can always grow more roots and put out new shoots, and come back to life. But man dies and disappears! I will lie down and never rise again, and no one will ever know what happened to me. Perhaps I will live again, but I don't know. If I knew that

---

[33] Wisdom of Solomon 2:2–5, Apoc.

in a billion years, a billion billion years, I would live again, I would wait patiently and without complaining in eternal darkness during all those eons."

And he began to read again:

What does anyone profit from all his labor and toil here under the sun?

Generations come and generations go, while the earth endures forever.

The sun rises and the sun goes down; then it speeds to its place and rises there again.

The wind blows to the south, it veers to the north; round and round it goes and returns full circle.

What has happened will happen again, and what has been done will be done again; there is nothing new under the sun.

Those who lived in the past are not remembered, and those who follow will not be remembered by those who follow them.

I, Ecclesiastes, ruled as king over Israel. . . .[34]

"I, Ecclesiastes, ruled as king . . ." Yury repeated loudly, even menacingly, with an anguish he himself didn't understand. But he grew frightened at the sound of his own voice and glanced round. Had anyone heard him? Then he took a piece of paper and rather mechanically, as if yielding to an unconscious necessity, began to write, thinking about what had just occurred more and more frequently:

"I begin this note that must end with my death . . ."

"Ugh, how vulgar!" he said with disgust and pushed the paper away with such force that it flew off the table and, after spinning in the air, fell to the floor.

Meanwhile Soloveichik, the puny, pitiful Soloveichik, didn't say to himself that it was vulgar when he became convinced that he couldn't understand life.

Yury didn't see that he was taking as an example a man whom he himself described as puny and pitiful.

Well, what of it? I know that sooner or later I'll end up the same way. There's no other way. Why not? Could it be because . . . ?

Yury paused; he seemed to know exactly why, and had just been thinking about it, but now couldn't find the words to answer his own question. It was as if something had suddenly grown weak within his soul. His thoughts failed and he became confused.

"Rubbish! It's all rubbish!" he said loudly and with spite.

The lamp had almost burned down; in the darkness its unpleasant light weakly illuminated a small circle around his head.

Why didn't I die when I was a child and caught pneumonia? I'd be happy now, at peace.

At that very moment he imagined himself dead and became so frightened that he shuddered.

[34] Ibid. 1:3–6, 9, 11–12.

But then I'd never have seen all that I've seen. No, that's horrible too.

He shook his head and stood up.

It's enough to make me lose my mind.

He went over to the window and pushed it, but the shutters, fastened with a bolt, didn't open. He took out a pencil and managed to free the bolt.

Something creaked loudly from outside, the shutters opened easily and gently, and fresh, cool air wafted in through the window. He looked dully at the sky and saw the light of dawn.

The morning was bright and clear. The pale-blue sky was already pink along one edge. The seven stars of the Big Dipper were becoming paler and lower in the sky; the large, light-blue, lustrous morning star quietly shed its brilliant liquid light in the pink dawn. A sharp, cool breeze rose from the east and drove the white morning mist in light, flowing streams over the dark-green, dewy grass of the garden, clinging to the tall burdocks and white clover over the transparent, lightly rippling water of the river, above the leaves of the green and white water lilies growing in such profusion along its banks. The transparent blue sky was filled with banks of airy clouds lit with pink flame; solitary pale stars drowned unnoticed and then disappeared without trace in its deep blue vault. The moist white mist kept rising slowly from the river, floating in bands over the deep, cold water, flowing among the trees into the damp green depths of the garden where the light, transparent twilight still reigned. It seemed as if a strange, silvery sound hung in the moist air.

Everything was so lovely and quiet, as if the enraptured earth, totally naked, were preparing for the immense, extravagant celebration of a mystery—the arrival of the sun, which had yet to appear but whose gentle pink light already shimmered above.

Yury lay down to sleep but the light disturbed him, his head ached, and he kept seeing something flash painfully before his eyes, ever so faintly.

 XXXV

Early in the morning, while the sun was still low and bright, Ivanov and Sanin set out from town.

The dew glimmered and sparkled in the sunlight, making it seem as if the grass in the shadows were gray. Along the edges of the road beneath the scraggy old willows pilgrims were already making their way to the monastery; their red-and-white kerchiefs, bast sandals, skirts, and blouses looked very colorful in the shafts of sunlight between the slats of the wattle fence.

The monastery bells were ringing. Their reverberation, cleansed by the fresh morning air, resounded with astonishing clarity over the surrounding steppe; it must have reached as far as the silent, dark-blue trees standing like a mirage on the rim of the horizon. Along the road the sound of a troika bell was jingling harshly and impatiently; one could hear the rough, businesslike voices of the pilgrims.

"We've come too early," Ivanov observed.

Sanin looked around boldly and merrily.

"We'll wait," he said.

They sat down under the wattle fence, right on the sand, and lit their cigarettes with satisfaction.

Peasants walking toward town behind their carts glanced up at them; old women and young girls, rattling past in empty wagons, laughed and called each other's attention to them with mocking smiles. Ivanov took no notice, but Sanin chuckled along with them; the entire road came alive with the sound of women's laughter.

The mist began to lift.

Finally, on the porch of the tavern, a small white building with a bright-green roof, the proprietor emerged, a tall man in a waistcoat. Yawning and noisily unfastening the locks, he opened the door. A countrywoman in a red kerchief came bustling out behind him.

"The way's clear!" Ivanov announced. "Let's go."

They went in to buy some vodka and, from the woman in the red kerchief, some fresh pickled cucumbers.

"Hey, my friend, you're certainly well off!" said Ivanov, when Sanin pulled out his wallet.

"I got an advance," Sanin said with a laugh. "To my mother's great shame, I've taken a position as a clerk with an insurance agent . . . and earned both money and my mother's disapproval simultaneously."

"Well, now that's much better!" said Ivanov when they'd come out onto the road again.

"Yes, indeed. Shall we take off our boots?"

"Yes, let's!"

They took off their boots and socks and went barefoot. Their feet sank into the warm, soft sand and stretched agreeably after being cramped in such narrow, heavy boots. The warm sand stuck between their toes but it soothed rather than irritated their feet.

"Nice," said Sanin with delight.

The sun beat down even harder. They'd left town and were now walking along the road. The distant horizon steamed and dissolved, blue and transparent. On the tops of the posts marking the road, the telegraph wires hummed and swallows perched in orderly fashion on the thin strands. Alongside, on the embankment, a passenger train with its blue, yellow, and green cars rumbled by, slowing down. In the windows and on the little platforms could be glimpsed the furrowed faces of sleepy passengers. They glanced out and then vanished. On the last platform stood two young women in light hats, their faces youthful, hearty, and vivacious in the morning air. They stared intently and with astonishment at the two spirited, barefoot men. Sanin laughed at them and danced a jig over the sand, his bare heels flashing in the air. Before them stretched a meadow where it was also pleasant and amusing to tramp barefoot through the thick damp grass.

"What bliss!" said Ivanov.

"Why in the world would anyone want to die?" Sanin agreed.

Ivanov stole a glance at him: for some reason it seemed to him that Sanin must have been referring to Zarudin, though a considerable time had passed since the funeral. But Sanin apparently wasn't thinking of anyone in particular; and although this was a bit odd, Ivanov was pleased.

After the meadow the road continued again with its carts, peasants, and laughing countrywomen. Trees appeared, and patches of sedge, then water gleaming in the sunlight, and the monastery hill, where the church cross shone like a golden star.

Colorful boats lined the shore and peasants sat nearby in bright shirts and vests. After long and playful haggling, Sanin and Ivanov hired a boat from them.

Ivanov took the oars, Sanin the rudder, and the boat moved swiftly and easily along the shore, passing through the shadows and light, and leaving behind it narrow, smooth ribbons of silver ripples.

Ivanov rowed quickly and vigorously with rapid, even strokes; as a result, the boat quivered and raced ahead as if it had come alive. Occasionally the oars grazed low branches that would tremble long and pensively over the dark, deep water along the bank. Sanin manned the rudder with such gusto that the water swirled and foamed with a joyful sound; he steered the boat into a narrow opening between overhanging bushes where it was dark, damp, and cool. The water was extremely clear and for a full fathom one could make out yellow pebbles on the bottom and schools of little pink fish darting here and there.

"Here's the best spot," Ivanov said, his voice ringing out merrily beneath the low branches.

With a soft crunch the boat came alongside the dark grass on the bank, from which a bird noiselessly took wing. Ivanov jumped out onto the bank.

"On earth the entire human race!" he sang in his deep bass voice, and the air rocked and rumbled.

With a laugh, Sanin leaped out after him and scrambled quickly up the high bank, sinking up to his knees in the lush, wet grass.

"There's no place better!" he cried.

"And no need to look further: it's fine anywhere under the sun," replied Ivanov from below, getting their vodka, pickled cucumbers, bread, and a parcel of snacks from the boat.

He carried everything up to a soft hillock under the trunk of a large tree and spread it out on the grass.

"Lucullus dines with Lucullus," he said.[35]

"And is happy," Sanin added.

"Not entirely," Ivanov replied with playful discontent. "They forgot to bring a glass."

"Damn," Sanin said merrily. "Well, never mind, we'll make one."

Thinking about nothing at all and merely enjoying the light, warmth, greenery, and his own swift, agile movements, he climbed a tree, chose a tender green bough, and began to saw it off with his knife. The soft, moist wood yielded easily to his efforts; soon small, fragrant white shavings and chips were scattered on the green grass. Ivanov raised his head and looked up; he found it so easy and pleasant to breathe in that position that he held it there and kept smiling joyfully.

The branch cracked and fell softly to the grass. Sanin jumped down from the tree and began carving a little goblet from the branch, trying not to pierce the bark. The goblet emerged smooth and handsome.

"Well, my friend, I'm thinking of taking a swim later," said Ivanov, looking carefully at Sanin's work.

"Good idea," Sanin agreed merrily, scraping the goblet with his knife and then tossing the finished product into the air.

They sat down on the grass and with gusto began downing vodka and eating juicy, sweet-smelling green cucumbers.

It was already noon. The sun stood high in the sky and it was hot everywhere, even in the shade.

"I can't take it," said Ivanov. "My soul longs for a swim."

He didn't know how to swim; undressing quickly, he walked into the water slowly at the shallowest, clearest place, where the bright-yellow, flat, sandy bottom was clearly visible.

"All right!" he said, jumping and splashing in the water.

Without hurrying, Sanin watched him, got undressed, ran down to the water's edge, jumped up, dove in, and took off across the river.

"You'll drown," Ivanov cried.

"No, I won't," replied Sanin, snorting and laughing.

Their cheerful voices carried a good distance along the bright surface of the river and the green meadow.

Then they came out of the water and stretched out naked in the soft, fresh grass.

"Splendid!" said Ivanov, turning his broad back, still gleaming with little drops of water, toward the sun. "Let's build two little shacks here."

"To hell with 'em!" Sanin cried cheerfully. "It's splendid even without any shacks. I've had my fill of them!"

---

[35] Lucullus (110–56 B.C.), Roman general, consul, and statesman famous for his military victories, was known also for his enormous wealth and luxurious lifestyle.

"Hey, hey! Up and away!" cried Ivanov, executing some wild, joyful leaps.

Laughing loudly, Sanin stood facing him and set about imitating his movements.

Their naked bodies gleamed in the sunlight; their muscles rippled swiftly and powerfully beneath their taut skin.

"Oh!" said Ivanov, gasping for breath.

Sanin continued dancing alone, then did a somersault.

"Come over here, or I'll drink all the vodka," Ivanov called to him.

After getting dressed, they finished the pickled cucumbers and drank the vodka.

"Some nice cold beer would be gr-r-r-reat!" Ivanov said wistfully.

"Let's go."

"All right."

They ran from the shore over to their boat and pushed off right away.

"It's steamy," said Sanin, squinting happily at the sun and sprawling in the bottom of the boat.

"It's going to rain," replied Ivanov. "Hey, you! Get up and steer!"

"You'll get us there all by yourself," Sanin answered.

Ivanov splashed with his oar, and clear, bright spray drenched in sunlight cascaded all around.

"Many thanks for that!" Sanin said.

As they were passing one of the lush islands, they heard the happy shouts, splashing, and laughter of young women. It was a holiday and many people from town had come out to stroll and swim.

"The girls are swimming," said Ivanov.

"Let's go have a look," said Sanin.

"They'll see us."

"No, we could land here and go through the reeds."

"To hell with 'em," said Ivanov, blushing slightly.

"Let's go."

"It's shameful," said Ivanov, with a playful shrug.

"What?"

"Well . . . they're girls! It's not right."

"You're a fool," Sanin said, laughing. "You'd love to see them."

"If it's a girl . . . and she is . . . then who wouldn't?"

"Well, let's go."

"Let them be."

"Damn!" said Sanin. "There isn't a man alive who wouldn't want to see a beautiful naked woman. Nor is there one who wouldn't sneak a glance just once in his life, while you . . ."

"That's true," Ivanov agreed. "Nevertheless . . . If you think like that, you'd be better off going right up to them instead of hiding."

"But it's more exciting this way, my friend," said Sanin cheerfully.

"Of course, it'd be extremely gratifying. . . . But you should refrain."

"For chastity's sake?"

"If only . . ."

"Not if only! There's no other reason!"

"Well, so be it."

"Well . . . But neither of us has any chastity."

"If thine eye offend thee, pluck it out,"[36] said Ivanov.

"Don't talk nonsense, like Svarozhich," Sanin said with a laugh. "God gave you eyes; why pluck them out?"

Ivanov grinned and shrugged.

"So, my friend," said Sanin, steering the boat toward the shore. "If the sight of naked women bathing were to arouse no feeling of desire in you whatsoever, then you could call yourself chaste. I'd be the first person to marvel at your chastity, though I wouldn't imitate it and very possibly might cart you off to the hospital. But if you have this desire within you and if it's straining to get out, while you hold it in like a dog on a chain, then your chastity isn't worth a damn."

"That's correct, but if I didn't hold it in . . . A man could get into trouble!"

"What kind of trouble? If voluptuousness sometimes leads to trouble, then it's not to blame."

"Maybe so. But don't make excuses!"

"Well, shall we go?"

"But I just . . ."

"You're a fool, that's what. Quietly!" said Sanin with a smile.

They crept along through the fragrant grass, gently parting the rustling reeds.

"Look over there, my friend!" Ivanov said excitedly.

Judging by the colorful blouses, skirts, and hats spread out on the grass, the young ladies were indeed bathing. Some were in the river, splashing, frolicking, and laughing, the water gently dripping from their soft, round shoulders, arms, and breasts. One of them, tall and slender, suffused by sunlight that made her seem transparent, rosy, and lithe, stood on the bank laughing; her pink belly and firm young breasts were quivering with her laughter.

"Oh, my friend!" said Sanin with ardent ecstasy.

Ivanov retreated in alarm.

"What's the matter?"

"Shhh. It's Karsavina!"

"Really? I didn't even recognize her. She's lovely!" Sanin said aloud.

"I'll say!" Ivanov said with an eager, broad smile.

At that moment the girls heard them and must have seen them. A cry and a laugh rang out, and Karsavinao, frightened, graceful, and supple, ran

---

[36] Matt. 18:9.

straight ahead and quickly ducked into the clear water, leaving only her rosy face and shining eyes exposed.

Happy and excited, Sanin and Ivanov beat a hasty retreat though the reeds.

"Ahhh, life is good!" said Sanin, stretching expansively. Then he sang out loudly:

> From behind the island into the channel,
> Onto the broad expanse of the river . . . [37]

Beyond the green trees the nervous, flustered, joyful laughter of the young women could still be heard; they were both embarrassed and curious.

"There's going to be a thunderstorm," said Ivanov, glancing up as they came back to the boat.

The trees had become darker and shadows were moving swiftly across the green meadow.

"We've had it, my friend. Run!"

"Where to? We can't escape it," Sanin cried cheerfully.

Without sound or wind the storm clouds were moving closer and closer and had already become the color of lead. Everything fell silent and became fragrant and darker.

"We'll get soaked to the skin," said Ivanov. "Give me a cigarette to drown my sorrows."

The small flame began to burn and there was something strange in its pale-yellow light under the leaden gloom descending from above. A gust of wind suddenly blew, whirled around, began to howl, and carried off the flame. A large raindrop hit the boat, another splashed onto Sanin's forehead, and suddenly drops rustled in the leaves and splattered on the water. At once everything grew darker; the rain came down in torrents, drowning out all other sounds with its own miraculous noise.

"Very nice, too," said Sanin, flexing his shoulders with his wet shirt clinging to them.

"Not bad," replied Ivanov, but sat there looking very glum.

The clouds didn't disperse, but the rain lessened very quickly and now splashed sporadically on the wet greenery and people; the surface of the water looked as if steel nails were bouncing on it. The air was dark and heavy; lightning was flashing beyond the woods.

"Well then . . . shall we head home?" asked Ivanov.

"Why not? Let's."

They rowed out onto the dark water, above which a low, heavy, dark cloud was swirling. The lightning became more frequent and its awesome flashes could be seen punctuating the black sky. The rain stopped altogether

---

[37] The first two lines of a famous Russian folk song, "Stenka Razin," about a Don Cossack who led a peasant revolt in 1670.

and the air became dry and smelled menacingly of thunder. Some dark agitated birds flew swiftly above the surface of the water. The trees stood dark and motionless, clearly outlined against the blue-gray sky.

"Uh-oh!" said Ivanov.

As they made their way across the sand hardened by the rain, everything became darker and quieter still.

"Here it comes!"

The storm cloud swirled lower and lower, its ominous white belly approaching the earth.

All of a sudden the wind burst forth with new strength, whirling dust and leaves to and fro, and the entire sky was rent asunder with a terrible crash, flash, and thunderclap.

"Oho-o-o!" cried Sanin, trying to outshout the deafening roar surrounding them on all sides. But he couldn't even hear his own voice.

When they reached the field, it was already dark. Only when the lightning flashed were their sharp, dark figures visible in the darkness as they inched their way across the smooth sand. Everything rumbled and roared.

"Oh . . . ah . . . oh!" cried Sanin.

"What?" cried Ivanov as loudly as he could.

The lightning flashed again and he caught a glimpse of Sanin's joyful face and gleaming eyes.

Ivanov couldn't make out what he was saying. He was a little afraid of thunderstorms.

When the lightning flashed again, Sanin, grasping life and power with all his being, spread his arms wide and, at the top of his voice, cried out happily and protractedly to the approaching thunder that was crashing with a roar and rumble all across the mighty expanse of the sky.

## XXXVI

The sun was as bright as in springtime, yet there was already something autumnal in the imperceptible, gentle stillness, in the crystal-clear air between the trees touched here and there by fading yellow colors. In that stillness the forlorn cries of birds echoed at random and the hurried buzzing of large insects could be heard hovering ominously over their dying kingdom. There were no grasses or flowers left; only the weeds still grew, tall and untamed.

Yury wandered slowly along the garden paths; with wide eyes and lost in deep thought, he looked around—at the sky, the yellow and green leaves, the quiet paths, and the clear water—as if seeing it all for the last time and trying to retain and absorb it, so that he'd never forget it.

Sorrow gently filled his heart, the reasons for it obscure. It seemed that with every passing moment something precious was moving farther away from him, something that could have been but was not and never would be. And it was painful for him to realize that it was his own fault.

Was it the youth and happiness he'd never enjoyed and that never return? Was it the momentous clandestine activity, now for some reason passing him by, though at one time he'd stood at its very center? How this had happened he didn't understand. He was convinced that in the depths of his soul he possessed the strength to topple the world's tallest cliffs and an intelligence that encompassed horizons broader than anyone else on earth. Where such certainty came from he couldn't say; he was embarrassed to proclaim it aloud to just anyone, even to his nearest and dearest. But this certainty existed, even when he plainly felt that he tired easily, didn't dare undertake many things, and could merely contemplate life, standing in the wings.

Well then, he thought, looking sadly at the water where the banks were reflected upside down as if in a mirror and decorated with yellow and red lace. "Perhaps it's all for the best, the wisest thing."

The image of a man full of intelligence and sensitivity standing pensively on the sidelines of life with an ironically sad smile and observing the absurd vanity of those condemned to death appeared to him as deceptively attractive. But there was something empty in all this; in the depths of his soul he wanted someone to see and understand how attractive he was in this pose contemplating life; soon he found that he was consoling himself and he felt bitterly ashamed.

Then, to escape this painful awareness, he began to tell himself for the thousand and first time that no matter how his life had turned out, no matter who was to blame for his mistakes, in the final analysis all its imposing and seemingly grandiose stream was emptying slowly and stupidly into the black abyss of death, where there was no evaluation of how and why a man had lived his life.

Does it make any difference whether I die as a people's tribune, the greatest scholar, the most profound writer, or merely as a loafer, a plaintive member of the Russian intelligentsia? It's all nonsense! he thought gloomily and turned toward home.

He began to feel extremely despondent in the limpid stillness of the golden day, where his own thoughts were even more audible and he felt the slow, steady flight of the past.

Here comes Lyalya, he thought, seeing something pink and cheerful appear fleetingly behind the green and yellow bushes. Lucky Lyalya! She lives like a butterfly, only in the present, needing nothing. Oh, if only I could be like that!

But the thought was merely superficial: his own intellect, sorrow, torment, and contemplation, from which he suffered so deeply, seemed so extraordinarily rare and valuable that it was inconceivable to exchange them for Lyalya's mothlike existence.

"Yura, Yura!" Lyalya cried in her musical voice, even though by now she was only a few steps away from him; concealing the smile of a playful conspirator, she silently handed him a small pink envelope.

"From whom?" Yury asked, somehow suspecting something bad.

"From Zinochka Karsavina," Lyalya announced triumphantly and at the same time mysteriously; she also wagged her finger at him.

Yury blushed deeply. It seemed to him that the delivery of a scented letter in a pink envelope by his sister was tasteless, and that he himself, as the fortunate addressee, was made to look somewhat ridiculous. He suddenly seemed to shrivel into a ball and expose his pointed quills in all directions. Meanwhile, walking next to him, Lyalya began prattling with that special rapture that sentimental sisters love to feel when marrying off their beloved brothers; she talked about how much she liked Karsavina, how happy she was, and how much happier she would be after they were married.

The unfortunate word "married" brought a deep blush and spiteful expression to Yury's face. A provincial novel, with little pink notes, sisters playing the role of confidantes, legal marriage, a household, a spouse, and children—all this rose before him with precisely that vulgar, cozy, spineless, sweet sentimentality he feared more than anything else on earth.

"Oh, leave me alone, please. What silliness!" he flung at Lyalya, brushing her off with such contempt that she was offended.

"Why are you so stubborn? So what if you're in love—what does it matter?" she asked, pouting. Then, with unwilling feminine vindictiveness, she took aim at his sore spot: "I don't understand why all of you always make yourselves out to be such great heroes!"

She swirled the pink hem of her dress, haughtily displaying her azure stockings, and headed for home, behaving like an offended princess.

Yury angrily watched her leave with harsh, dark eyes; then he tore open the envelope.

> Yury Nikolaevich:
>
> If you can and want to, come to the monastery this evening. I'll be there with my aunt. She's fasting and won't leave the church. I'm bored and would like to chat with you about several things. Do come. I may be doing a very bad thing by writing to you, but come anyway.

Forgetting everything he'd been thinking, Yury read the last sentence in a strange state of excited, physical rapture. Suddenly, in this one short sentence, this sweet young woman had revealed herself with unusual clarity, displaying her secret love so innocently and trustingly. It was as if she'd already come to him, entirely powerless, timid, and loving, no longer able to struggle, not knowing what would happen next, and placing herself entirely in his hands. The unexpected immediacy of such a result filled Yury's entire exhausted body with trembling. He sensed the woman's youthfulness so close to him and inevitable, felt her naked, still shy chaste body for the first time, the fragrance of her hair, the frightened, happy look in her eyes, and her tears, glistening like dewdrops.

He tried to smile ironically but couldn't manage it; everything was drowning in a surge of such voracious happiness that he felt as if he were a bird soaring high above the trees into the sunlit blue sky.

All day his heart was so light and he felt such strength in his body that every movement brought him fresh, pure pleasure.

Toward evening he took a cab so as not to have to walk across the sand; he made his way to the monastery in a state of unconscious confusion, smiling to himself.

At the pier he transferred to a boat; a hearty, sweaty peasant rowed him swiftly across to the hill.

Yury still couldn't understand exactly what he was feeling; only when the boat emerged from the tangle of narrow channels into the broad expanse of water and he suddenly sensed the gentle, moist air rising from the depths did he consciously realize that he was happy and that his happiness was the result of the innocent pink envelope.

So what? What difference does it make, really and truly? He thought it necessary to console himself. She's lived in such a small world. . . . A provincial romance? Well, then, let it happen!

The rhythmic ripples of the water splashed against the sides of the boat as the current flowed past; the green hill with its special atmosphere bathed in twilight and the dampness of the forest rose swiftly ahead. The sand crunched as the boat pushed noisily against the waves. Still embarrassed, Yury climbed out of the boat, handed the boatman 50 kopecks, and headed up the hill.

The calm evening was already advancing through the forest and its shadows were moving beneath the mountain. A wistful dampness was rising from the earth, yellow leaves were enveloped by twilight, and the forest once again seemed summerlike, dense, and green. Above, in the monastery grounds, it was as peaceful and quiet as in church. Poplars stood sternly in even rows as if deep in prayer and the silent evening shadows of tall monks in black robes made their way among them. Candles glimmered in the dark vault of the church doors. An imperceptibly delicate fragrance, impossible to identify, came wafting through the air: was it the odor of old incense or of the fading leaves of the poplars?

"Ah, greetings, Svarozhich!" cried someone from behind him.

Yury turned around quickly and saw Shafrov, Sanin, Ivanov, and Peter Ilich. They were making their way across the courtyard in a dark, noisy crowd. Monks in black glanced at them apprehensively; even the poplars, disturbed by the sudden noise and movement, seemed to lose their devotional tranquillity.

"We're here to . . . you know!" said Shafrov, coming up to Yury, whom he revered, and looking directly at him in a friendly fashion with his round eyes.

"That's nice," Yury muttered stiffly.

"Perhaps you'd like to join us?" Shafrov asked, coming even closer.

"No, thanks, really. I'm not by myself here," Yury said, refusing and moving away hastily.

"That's all right," replied Ivanov, grabbing hold of his arm with rough affability. "Come on!"

Yury dug in his heels aggressively, and for a moment they pulled each other in opposite directions in an amusing way.

"No, really, I can't! Perhaps I'll stop by later," Yury repeated, more resolutely; it seemed to him that this lively horseplay was completely inappropriate and humiliating.

"Well, all right." said Ivanov, and without noticing it let go of his arm. "We'll be waiting for you. So join us!"

"All right, all right."

They left the monastery grounds, laughing and waving their arms; once again everything became reverent and serene, as if in prayer. Yury took off his cap and entered the church with mixed emotions of mockery and humility.

As soon as he rounded one of the dark columns, he saw Karsavina standing in the half-light in her gray jacket and round straw hat, which lent her the look of a schoolgirl. His heart skipped a beat: the tremor resembled a bird's sense of alarm or a cat's tenseness before its spring. Everything about her seemed appealing and sweet somehow: her jacket, her hat, her dark hair twisted in a braid over the nape of her white neck, and that schoolgirl look, so attractive and alluring in such a tall, ample grown woman.

She sensed Yury's presence and turned round; her deep, dark eyes, so modest and thoughtful, reflected her demure delight.

"Hello," he said, lowering his voice but still speaking too loudly; he didn't know whether it was appropriate to shake hands in church or not.

Several worshipers standing nearby turned to look at them and Yury felt embarrassed by their dark, parchmentlike faces. He blushed, while Karsavina, as if guessing his embarrassment and coming to his rescue as a mother might, smiled faintly and rebuked him tenderly with her loving eyes. Yury smiled blissfully and fell silent.

Karsavina didn't look at him and crossed herself frequently, but Yury sensed that she was aware only of his presence; this formed a secret bond between them at which his heart pounded and shuddered and everything around him seemed miraculous and mysterious.

The dark visage of the church, with its strange voices singing and reading, candles twinkling like night lights, deep sighs, and lonely, heavy footsteps near the doors, regarded Yury with its grave, severe eyes; amidst this dark, stern silence, he distinctly heard the smooth, steady, intrepid sound of his own little heart beating.

He stood there quietly, looking at her white neck below her dark hair and at the soft outline of her figure beneath her gray jacket; at moments he felt so good that his heart was deeply touched. Then he wanted to stand so that everyone would see that even though he didn't believe in anything here—the singing, the reading, the candles—he harbored no feeling but generous kindness. He was aware of his own mood, so very different from the melancholy malice he'd felt that morning.

So it is possible to be happy? he asked, smiling to himself; at once he answered in all earnestness: Of course! Everything I thought about death, the meaninglessness of life, and the absence of rational goals and so on, all this is absolutely correct and reasonable, but it's still possible to be happy. And I am happy, all because of this astonishing young woman whom I got to know not very long ago.

An amusing idea occurred to him—that when they'd both been young, merely a funny little boy and funny little girl, they might have met somewhere, looked at each other, and then gone their separate ways, never suspecting that one day they'd bring each other the greatest gift in life, that they'd love each other, and that one day she would take all her clothes off for him.

This last thought occurred to Yury somewhat unexpectedly and he grew ashamed, but at the same time he felt so good that he blushed to the roots of his hair; for a while he was afraid to look at her.

Meanwhile, stripped bare in his thoughts, she stood there, so sweet and pure in her gray jacket and round hat, praying silently that he might love her as tenderly and passionately as she loved him.

It must have been that something purifying in her communicated itself to him, because his shameless thoughts vanished and his soul became pure and still.

Warm tears of tender emotion and love filled his eyes. He raised them, saw the gold iconostasis lit by gleams of light from the burning candles, and then looked higher still—at the cross; with a feeling that was long forgotten and a tension that was unfamiliar, he cried inwardly:

O Lord, if You do exist, make it so that this young woman continues to love me and I her as much as we do now!

He began to feel a little embarrassed at his outburst of emotion, but this time he merely smiled indulgently to himself. It's all so silly! he thought.

"Let's go," Karsavina said to him quietly, almost in a whisper that sounded like a sigh.

They left the church respectfully and went out onto the porch with stillness in their souls, as if bearing away all those voices that were singing quietly and reading loudly, as well as the glimmering candles and sighs; they passed through the grounds together and went out through the old gate leading to the cliff. There was no one nearby and the old white monastery wall with its cracked towers separated them from everyone else. At their feet along the slope they could see the tops of oak trees, the glistening river far below, and beyond it, merging with the dark horizon, the green meadows and fields.

They walked in silence to the edge of the cliff and stopped, unsure what to do next. They were afraid of something and held back. Just when it seemed they might never have the strength to say or do anything, Karsavina raised her head and then somehow, in a completely unexpected and natural way, her lips met Yury's. She became very pale; her heart raced and then stopped, while he embraced her in silence and for the first time felt her supple, warm body in his arms. It became quiet all around and it seemed to them both that the whole world stood still in solemn, strained silence.

It must have been the ringing in his ears, but Yury thought that an invisible and silent bell was loudly proclaiming the hour of their meeting.

Then she pulled away, smiled, and stepped back.

"My aunt will notice my absence. Wait a while. I'll be back."

Never afterward could Yury recall whether she'd shouted those words in a loud voice that echoed through the dark woods or whether the warm evening breeze carried her disconnected words to him as a fleeting whisper.

He sat down on the grass and ran his hand through his hair.

How good and silly it all is! he thought, smiling to himself; and closing his eyes, he shrugged as if at that moment shaking off all his previous thoughts, doubts, and sufferings.

Karsavina ran back to the gate and stopped. Her heart was pounding and her face burning. She pressed her hand firmly to the left side of her agitated chest and for a moment leaned against the wall.

Then she opened her eyes, looked round mysteriously, and, sighing lightly, gathered up her black skirt and with swift, youthful steps ran along the path to the hospice, calling from a distance to her sullen old aunt who was sitting on the porch waiting, "I'm coming, Auntie, I'm coming!"

 XXXVII

At first the distant horizon became dark, then the river grew pale in the mist; the faint neighing of horses could be heard from the green meadow below; lights along the banks flickered.

Meanwhile Yury sat by the cliff edge and waited, mechanically counting the campfires in the meadows.

One, two, three . . . No, there's another one in the far distance . . . barely visible. Just like a little star! Grown men are sitting there, peasants, keeping watch at night, boiling their potatoes, and chatting. The campfire's burning merrily, blazing and crackling; you can even hear the horses snorting. But from here it seems no more than a little spark. It may go out at any time!

He found it hard to think about anything at all, and as if in response to his own joyful happiness he couldn't hear his own thoughts. He sat still for a very long time, feeling his resilience and strength increasing as if he were preparing for something he was unable consciously to consider. He continued to be aware of his first contact with her youthful body, covered by its thin fabric, and with her half-open, fresh lips. At moments he said to himself with apprehension, She'll be right back!

His heart raced and then slowed and his body became increasingly tense, strong, vigorous, and confident.

Thus, filled with expectation, he sat above by the cliff edge, listening unconsciously to the distant neighing of horses, the cries of geese beyond the river, and the thousands of other obscure sounds coming from the forest and the evening, floating harmoniously over the earth.

When he heard uneven footsteps and the rustling of a dress, he knew without turning round that it was she; he began trembling, overcome with love, desire, and awe in anticipation of the decisive moment.

Karsavina came up and stood beside him; he could hear her heavy breathing. All of a sudden, feeling the joyful certainty that he'd do all that was needed, Yury immediately turned round and with unexpected audacity and strength lifted her up in his arms and carried her down the hill, sliding through the grass.

"We'll fall!" she whispered, gasping with embarrassment and happiness.

Once again Yury held her body in his arms: at times she seemed large and ample, like a grown woman, at others small and frail, like a little girl. His hands could feel her legs through the dress; he was even frightened by the idea that he was touching her legs.

Down below, under the trees, it was dark; only above, over the rim of the cliff edged by the bright moon, shone the pale, dusky moonlight. Yury put the young woman down on the grass and sat down; because the ground was sloping, they seemed to be lying next to each other. In the pale moonlight he found her warm, soft lips and began to press on them deliberate, demanding kisses from which white-hot, glowing iron seemed to scorch their languorous bodies.

It was a moment of total madness governed only by powerful animal instinct. Karsavina didn't resist; she merely trembled when Yury's hand tenderly yet audaciously touched her legs as no one ever had before.

"Do you love me?" she asked abruptly; the whisper of her lips invisible in the darkness was as strange as an insubstantial, enigmatic sound in the forest.

All of a sudden Yury asked himself in horror: What on earth am I doing?

An icy clarity pierced his heated brain and everything instantly became empty, pale, and light, just like a winter's day when there's neither life nor strength.

She half-opened her pale eyes and reached out to him with a puzzled, per-plexed look. But suddenly she too glanced round swiftly and widely, saw his face and herself and, overwhelmed with unbearable shame, quickly straight-ened her dress and sat up.

An excruciating turmoil of feelings overpowered Yury: it seemed impossi-ble to stop—it would've been ridiculous and repulsive. Distractedly and awkwardly he tried to continue and wanted to mount her, but she defended herself just as distractedly and awkwardly; her weak, helpless resistance overwhelmed him with a terrible, hopeless awareness of their shameful, ridiculous, and repulsive situation; it really was ridiculous and dishonor-able. Distraught and once more at the moment when her strength ebbed and she was ready to submit, he released her again. Her breathing was intermit-tent and shallow, like that of a hunted animal.

A painful, inescapable silence settled on them; then he suddenly spoke: "Forgive me. . . . I must be mad."

She was drawing ever more frequent breaths; he realized that he shouldn't have said that—it was insulting. Perspiration soaked his weakened body, and once again his tongue, as if against his will, muttered something about what he'd seen that day, about his feelings for her, then about the thoughts and doubts that constantly preoccupied him; he was distracting himself, just as he'd distracted her so often. But now everything seemed clumsy, constrained, and lifeless; his voice rang hollow. Finally he fell silent, feeling only one unexpected desire: that she would leave, and that one way or an-other this unbearably absurd situation would be terminated, at least tem-porarily.

She must have felt the same thing because she held her breath for a mo-ment, then whispered timidly and imploringly, "I have to go. It's time."

What should I do? What should I do? Yury asked himself, turning colder.

They stood up without looking at each other. In a final attempt to restore their previous intimacy, he took her in a weak embrace. Suddenly a mater-nal feeling was kindled in her again. She seemed stronger than he was; she gently enfolded him in her arms and, smiling directly into his eyes, encour-aged him with her tender smile:

"Good-bye. Come and see me tomorrow."

She kissed him so tenderly, so firmly, that his head started to spin; something like a feeling of reverence before her warmed his distraught soul.

After she'd left, he listened for a long time to the sound of her footsteps; then he picked up his cap covered with leaves and dirt, brushed it off, and put it on; then making his way down the hill, he returned to the hospice, avoiding the path that Karsavina would follow.

Well, what of it? he thought, walking through the darkness. Was it absolutely necessary to defile this pure, holy young woman? To behave like any other vulgar man would? Let her be! It would've been so repulsive; thank God I turned out to be incapable of it! It's all so vile: on the spot, almost without words, like an animal! he thought, with a fastidious feeling about what had just recently filled him with such strength and happiness.

But inside something still gnawed and tore at him in his impotent agony, causing his mute and painful shame. Even his hands and feet seemed to dangle awkwardly somehow, to no purpose, and his hat sat on his head like a dunce cap.

Am I really capable of living? he asked himself in sudden despair.

## XXXVIII

In the wide corridor of the monastery hospice there was a smell of fresh bread, samovars, and incense. An agile, burly monk went hurrying by, carrying a samovar as round and plump as a watermelon.

"Father," said Yury, unintentionally confusing his title and expecting the monk would be confused too.[38]

"What can I do for you?" asked the monk politely and calmly, peering through the cloud of steam rising from the samovar.

"Do you have a group of people here from town?"

"In room number seven," the monk immediately replied, as if he'd been expecting this question for some time. "This way, please, out onto the balcony."

Yury opened the door to room 7. It was dark inside and the room must have been completely filled with tobacco smoke. There was light coming from beyond the door onto the balcony, bottles were clinking, and people were bustling about, laughing and shouting.

"Life's an incurable disease!" Yury heard Shafrov declare.

"You're an incurable fool!" Ivanov replied in a loud voice. "Listen to him—spewing such fancy phrases!"

When Yury appeared, everyone greeted him with joyous, drunken cries. Shafrov jumped to his feet, almost dragging the tablecloth off as he stood

---

[38] The title "father" is used for an ordained priest, not a monk.

up, and shaking Yury's hand with both of his, he started muttering affectionately, "It's so good of you to come! Thank you, so help me God! Really, indeed. . . ."

Yury sat down between Sanin and Peter Ilich and glanced round. The balcony was brightly lit by two lamps and a lantern; an impenetrable black wall seemed to stand outside the circle of light. Turning away from the light, Yury could still make out quite clearly the greenish band of twilight, the hunched silhouette of the hill, the tops of the nearest trees, and, far below, the faintly glimmering, sleepy surface of the river.

Moths and insects were flying from the forest toward their lamps, circling, falling, rising, and then crawling quietly over the table before expiring in senseless, fiery death.

Yury looked at them and felt sad. People are just the same, he thought. We also fly to the flame, toward every brilliant idea, we flutter around, and die in great suffering. We think that each idea is an expression of the world will, but it's merely the fire in our brains.

"Well, shall we drink?" asked Sanin, passing him the bottle in a friendly fashion.

"Why not?" Yury agreed sadly, and wondered at once if it weren't perhaps the only thing left for him to do.

They clinked glasses and drank. Yury found the vodka repulsive, like bitter, hot poison; with a fastidious shudder shaking his whole body, he reached out for something to eat. But even the food had a lingering, repulsive taste and stuck in his throat.

No, no matter what—death, hard labor—I have to get away from here, he said to himself. But where to? It's the same everywhere, and there's no escaping from myself. Once a man rises above life, it can't satisfy him anywhere or in any form. Whether in this little town or Petersburg, it's all the same.

"And in my opinion," cried Shafrov loudly, "man in and of himself is worth nothing!"

Yury looked at his unintelligent, boring face, and his tiny, dull eyes behind his glasses, and thought that a man like him really was, both in and of himself, worth nothing.

"The individual's a nonentity!" Shafrov said. "Only those who emerge from the masses and manage not to lose their links with those masses, who don't set themselves against the crowd in the way so-called bourgeois heroes love to do, only they possess the strength."

"What kind of strength would that be?" Ivanov asked sharply, crossing his arms and leaning his elbows heavily on the table. "Is it in a struggle against the existing government? Yes! But in their struggle for personal happiness, will the masses help them?"

"Oh, yes. You're a superman! You need some special happiness! Your own! While we, mere people in the crowd, think it's precisely in the struggle for the general good that we'll discover our own happiness. The triumph of the idea—now that's real happiness!"

"What if your idea's wrong?"

"It doesn't matter." Shafrov shook his head categorically. "One only has to believe."

"Damn that," replied Ivanov contemptuously. "Everybody believes that what he's doing is the most important, necessary thing in the world. Even a ladies' tailor thinks that. You used to know that, but you've probably forgotten it. It's a friend's job to remind you."

Yury looked him straight in the eye with unreasonable hatred. Ivanov's face was pale from all the vodka he'd drunk and covered in sweat, and his large gray eyes were lifeless.

"So then where, in your opinion, does happiness lie?" he asked with a curl of his lip.

"Well, certainly not in whining all one's life and asking at every step: 'I just sneezed. Oh, was it a good thing? Did I harm anyone by doing so? With this sneeze of mine did I fulfill my mission?' "

Yury clearly saw the hatred in his cold eyes; he shuddered, thinking that Ivanov must consider himself smarter than he was and so wanted to make fun of him.

Well, we'll see about that! he said to himself.

"That's no 'program,' " Ivanov declared, his lip curling even more, trying to make each of his features display both his unwillingness to argue and his utter contempt.

"Must you have a program? I do what I want and what I can! That's my program," Yury replied.

"A fine program indeed!" Shafrov said indignantly. But Yury merely shrugged contemptuously and maintained his silence.

They drank in silence for a while; then Yury turned to Sanin and started to explain, without looking at Ivanov, yet intending him to hear, what he considered the greatest good. He thought that once he had uttered a few words in succession and managed to articulate his complete thought, no one would be able to refute him. But, to his annoyance, at his first mention of the fact that man cannot live without God, and that having overthrown one, he must now find another so that life could become more than just a meaningless existence, Ivanov said over his shoulder:

"You mean Catherine?[39] We've heard it all before."

Yury fell silent and then continued to develop his thought. Having been distracted by the argument, he didn't even notice that he was energetically defending what constituted the source of his own doubt. Earlier that morning he'd been raising questions about his faith, but now, in the heat of the

---

[39] Presumably a mutual acquaintance not mentioned elsewhere in the text.

moment, everything seemed well thought out and he was affirming it all with conviction.

Shafrov listened to him with reverence and tender joy. Sanin smiled while Ivanov looked at him with his face half-turned away; at every idea Yury considered new and original, Ivanov put in with contempt:

"We've heard that before too!"

Yury grew angry.

"Well, you know, we've 'heard that before' too! There's nothing easier than saying, 'We've heard it all before,' and then falling silent when you can think of nothing more to say! If all you can do is repeat 'We've heard it all before,' then I too have the right to say: 'You haven't heard a thing!' "

Ivanov turned pale and his expression became very vicious.

"Perhaps," he said with undisguised sarcasm and a desire to offend, "we've never heard anything before: neither tragic reflections nor the possibility of living without God nor even about naked man on the naked earth." Ivanov pronounced each phrase in a pompous way; then suddenly he shouted maliciously and abruptly, "Think up something newer!"

Yury felt there was some truth in Ivanov's mockery. He suddenly recalled the huge pile of books he'd read about anarchism, Marxism, individualism, the superman, the transfigured Christian, mystical anarchism, and many other things. In fact, everyone had "heard it all before," yet things remained the same, and he himself was experiencing a painful weariness of the spirit. Nevertheless, not for one second did it occur to him to retreat and fall silent. He spoke up shrilly, realizing that he was offending Ivanov more than he was proving his own idea.

Ivanov became furious and looked terrifying. His face grew even paler, his eyes started from their sockets, and his voice roared in a coarse, savage way.

Then Sanin intervened with an annoyed, weary look. "Enough, gentlemen. Don't you find this boring? It's impossible to hate a man because of the way he thinks."

"There's no thinking, merely lies!" Ivanov snapped. "He wants to show us he thinks more deeply and subtly than we do, but not . . ."

"What right do you have to say that? Why am I the one who wants to do that, and not you?."

"Listen!" Sanin cried loudly and authoritatively. "If you want to argue, both of you leave and go and fight it out wherever you like. You have no right to force us to listen to your foolish row!"

Ivanov and Yury fell silent. They were both flushed and agitated, trying not to look at each other. Things were awkward and quiet for a while. Then Peter Ilich began singing softly:

"Perhaps, on the silent hillside, they'll place Ruslan's quiet grave. . . ."[40]

[40] Ruslan is the hero of Pushkin's romantic poem *Ruslan and Lyudmila* (1820).

"Rest easy. They'll put it there soon enough," Ivanov growled.

"So be it," Peter Ilich said obediently, but stopped singing and poured Yury a glass of vodka.

"Enough thinking," he mumbled. "Better to have a drink!"

Hey, it's better to give it all up! Yury thought. He took the glass and downed it in one large gulp.

Strange to say, but at that very moment he felt a burning desire for Ivanov to notice what he had done and to conceive a feeling of respect for him. If Ivanov were to do that, Yury would develop a fondness for him, even tenderness; but Ivanov paid no attention to him at all. So immediately suppressing in himself this disgraceful desire, Yury frowned and was totally filled with the naked, loathsome sensation of vodka taking possession of his entire insides, right up into his nose.

"Well done, Yury Nikolaevich, really and truly!" Shafrov cried, but Yury was embarrassed that it was Shafrov praising him.

Having scarcely overcome the surge of vodka rushing through his nose and mouth, and shuddering from physical revulsion, Yury was unable to come to his senses for a while; he groped around the table, looking for and then rejecting various snacks. Everything repulsed him like poison.

"Yes. I hesitate to use the word 'people' to describe them," Peter Ilich said in his loud bass voice when Yury began looking and listening again.

"You hesitate? Bravo, old man!" Ivanov cried maliciously, and although Yury hadn't heard the beginning of the conversation, he guessed from their tone that they were talking about him and people like him.

"Yes, I hesitate. A man must be . . . a general!" Peter Ilich declared distinctly and pompously.

"That's not always possible. Why, look at you!" Yury replied with a spiteful tremor of vulnerability without looking at him.

"Me? I'm a general at heart!"

"Bravo!" Ivanov bellowed so ferociously that some nocturnal bird plunged like a stone into the nearest thicket, snapping twigs on its way.

"Only at heart," Yury replied, trying to maintain the irony, and painfully imagining that everyone was against him, trying to offend and humiliate him.

Peter Ilich looked at him gravely both from above and from one side.

"I do what I can. What about it? It's good, even if it's only at heart. Someone old, drunk, and poor like me is a general at heart, while someone else is young, strong, and a general in real life. To each his own. But as for those who whine, the cowards . . . those I hesitate to call people."

Yury made some reply but no one heard him through all their laughter and talk, though his objection seemed devastating to him. He repeated it more loudly but once again no one heard him. A venomous sense of outrage poisoned him to the point of tears and suddenly everyone seemed to despise him.

But I'm just drunk! he thought unexpectedly; at that moment he realized that he really was drunk and that he shouldn't have any more to drink.

His head was spinning silently and unpleasantly, the lights and lanterns appeared to dance before his eyes, and his field of vision was strangely narrowed. Everything that came into close range was remarkably distinct while everything else was dark. Even voices sounded strange: people spoke in deafeningly loud tones but it was impossible to understand what they were saying.

"A dream, you say?" Peter Ilich asked soberly.

"A curious dream," replied Ivanov.

"There's something in them, these dreams," the bass voice intoned pompously.

"You see," said Ivanov, "I went to bed last night. . . . Yes. I picked up a book to read before going to sleep, somehow hoping to clear my head, which was stuffed full of nonsense and torpor. I came across a little article about how, where, when, and who's been condemned at one time or another. I looked at it—it's an intelligent piece and sincere, too. I'm starting to read; I'm reading and reading, and the more I do so, the more appalling it gets. I reach the point where it says who deserves anathema and for what. And at this point, to tell the truth, I realize without surprise that they're invariably anathematizing none other than me. Having ascertained my condemnation by all the existing churches, I tossed the book away, had a smoke, and started to doze, now fully convinced about my place in the universe. As I was falling asleep, I set my mind to work on the question that if millions of people are alive and condemning me with total conviction, then I . . . But at this point I fell fast asleep and the question remained unresolved. And then I began to feel that my right eye wasn't really my eye at all but Pope Pius X,[41] while my left eye was something like the ecumenical patriarch, and each was condemning the other. Then all these strange transformations of things woke me up."

"That's all?" asked Sanin.

"What do you mean? I fell asleep again."

"Well?"

"Well, from then on there was no rest for my spirit. I thought I saw a house—it could have been ours or an altogether unfamiliar one—and then I was pacing the largest room in it from corner to corner. And you, my pal, Peter Ilich, were somewhere nearby. He went on talking and I kept listening, but it was as if I couldn't see him. 'I've often noticed,' says Peter Ilich, 'how the cook prays.' So I think to myself that in the kitchen on the stove, the cook must really be praying. She lives there and prays there. 'We dimly

[41] Pius X (1835–1914), pope from 1903 to 1914, opposed anticlerical laws in France, set up commissions to recodify canon law and retranslate the Bible, and championed social reforms for the poor.

imagine and fail to comprehend, but a person so simple at heart, you understand, so sim-ple. . . . As she's praying and remembering everyone in her prayers, nothing's happening; but when she mentions you—me, that is—and Sanin, then,' when he said this I felt that something unusual had to happen. 'After all, all simple people couldn't have been praying in vain since the day of creation!' And just imagine, most opportunely, God Himself must have appeared to the cook. Then Peter Ilich disappears completely from the scene but keeps talking: 'Supposedly an image has appeared to her.' I still didn't feel too bad, because even though I knew it wasn't really God, it was something, and that was flattering! 'An image has appeared to her, but not as an image.' After that he disappears completely. I grow alarmed: this thing, not an image, has totally destroyed my serenity. To restore it, I have to eliminate immediately whatever it was that had turned up in the corner of my room and was squeaking there. It was clear that it was only a mouse, gnawing at something and biting it in two. The mouse kept gnawing and chewing steadily, keeping time. . . . And that's when I woke up."

"If only you'd slept a little longer!" Sanin remarked.

"The same thought crossed my mind, too."

Despite Ivanov's facetious tone, the dream had clearly made a powerful impression on him, filling his soul with incomprehensible fear. He smiled wryly and reached for a beer. Everyone was silent; in that silence the darkness seemed to close in from the balcony. It had become much less cheerful, more oppressive, and eerie. The unintelligible dream, through its derision and disbelief, had released a faintly burning sensation of dismal horror in their hearts.

"Yes," Peter Ilich announced triumphantly. "You're all so clever—clever as devils—but there's something to it, there really is! You don't know it, but it's speaking to you."

Whether it was in the singer's voice, the darkness enveloping them, their brains befuddled by vodka, or the momentary glimpse of the immediate mystery of life and death, so incomprehensible and monstrous, something reverberated in the soul of every one of them.

"And what if . . . what if there's something to it?"

Sanin stood up. His face, unruffled as always, reflected boredom. He yawned and dismissed it.

"It's all fears, just fears," he said, "as if there's still anything to be afraid of. When we die, then we'll see."

He slowly lit a cigarette and went to the door.

On the balcony people were shouting and arguing again; just as before, below all the loud, drunken voices silent moths were crawling over the table and circling in torments of fiery death as they flew into the flames.

Sanin went out into the hospice courtyard. The dark-blue night gently and eagerly caressed his warm body. The moon emerged from the forest like a little golden egg; its semimagical light slipped across the dark earth. Beyond the orchard, from which the fragrance of plum and pear trees floated heavily and sweetly, the white shape of the other hospice was scarcely visible; one window peered directly at Sanin through the green leaves.

Through the darkness came the shuffling of bare feet, like that of an animal's paws; with eyes still unaccustomed to the light, Sanin could barely make out the silhouette of a boy.

"What do you want?" he asked.

"The young lady, the teacher, Karsavina," the barefoot lad replied in a thin voice.

"What for?" asked Sanin. At the mention of Karsavina's name he remembered her standing on the shore, naked and bathed in light, her youthfulness merging with the bright sunshine.

"I have a note for her," replied the boy.

"Aha. She must be in the other hospice. She's not here. Over there."

Once again, like a little animal, the lad shuffled his bare feet and swiftly disappeared into the darkness, as if going off to hide in the bushes.

Sanin followed him slowly, drinking in the orchard air, which was as thick as honey. He made his way toward the illuminated window in the other hospice, and a band of light fell across his thoughtful, serene face. In the light, amidst the dark-green leaves, large, heavy pears gleamed white. Sanin stood on tiptoe and reached for a pear; then through the window he caught sight of Karsavina.

She was visible in profile, wearing only a blouse; streaks of light slid over her round shoulders, as if on satin. She was looking down intently and thinking; whatever she was thinking must have been causing her both shame and joy because, although her eyelids were quivering, her lips were smiling. Sanin was struck by her smile: something imperceptibly tender and passionate flickered in it, as if the young woman were smiling in anticipation of an approaching kiss.

He stood there and stared, overcome by a feeling stronger than he himself was, while Karsavina thought about what had happened to her; she felt both agonizingly ashamed and agonizingly delighted.

Oh, Lord, she said to herself with unusually pure emotion, like that of a flower in full bloom. Am I really so depraved?

And for the hundredth time she recalled with the most profound rapture the incomprehensibly enticing sensation she'd experienced in submitting to Yury for the first time.

"My darling, my darling!" she said, reaching out to him in her thoughts, her emotions flaring up and then dying down; once again Sanin could see how her eyelashes trembled and her pink lips smiled.

The young woman chose not to recall the hideous and excruciatingly ridiculous scene that came afterward. Some mysterious feeling deflected her from that dark corner in which, like a tiny splinter, there lurked painful and shameful confusion.

There was a knock at her door.

"Who's there?" she asked, raising her head; Sanin could clearly make out her strong, tender white neck.

"I've got a note," the boy squeaked outside the door.

Karsavina stood up and opened the door. Barefoot and splashed with mud up to his knees, the lad entered the room and quickly removed his cap.

"It's from a young lady."

"Zinochka," Dubova wrote, "if you can, come back to town today. The inspector's arrived and will visit our school tomorrow morning. It'll be awkward if you're not here."

"What's the matter?" asked her old aunt.

"Nyuta's[42] sent for me. The inspector's come," Karsavina replied, deep in thought.

The boy scratched one foot with the other.

"She really wants you to come," he added.

"Are you going?" asked the aunt.

"How can I go alone? It's dark."

"The moon's out," replied the boy. "You can see."

"I have to go," Karsavina said hesitantly.

"Go, so there won't be any trouble."

"Yes, I will!" said the young woman, nodding decisively.

She quickly got dressed, put on her hat, and went up to her aunt.

"Good-bye, Auntie."

"Good-bye, my child. God be with you."

"Will you come with me?" Karsavina asked the boy.

He hesitated and scratched his foot again.

"I came here to see my mother. She does the washing for the monks."

"But how can I go alone, Grisha?"

"Well, let's go," he agreed, shaking his head with a decisive look.

They went out into the garden. The dark-blue night enveloped the young woman just as gently and carefully as before.

"It smells so nice," she said, and suddenly cried out, bumping into Sanin.

"It's me," he said, laughing.

In the darkness Karsavina extended her hand, still trembling at her fright.

"Hey, what a sissy!" Grisha remarked condescendingly.

She laughed in embarrassment.

"I can't see a thing," she said by way of excuse.

"Where are you going?"

"Back to town. They just sent for me."

"Alone?"

"No, with him. He's my knight in shining armor."

"Knight!" repeated Grisha with delight, shuffling his bare feet.

---

[42] An error: elsewhere her first name is given as Olga.

"What are you doing here?"

"We came to do a little drinking," Sanin explained in jest.

"We?"

"Shafrov, Svarozhich, Ivanov."

"Yury Nikolaevich is also with you?" Karsavina asked, blushing in the darkness. It was both terrifying and thrilling to utter his name: she felt as if she were hanging above a precipice.

"What of it?"

"Oh, nothing. I met him here," she replied, blushing even more deeply.

"Well, good-bye."

Sanin politely took hold of her outstretched hand.

"Why not let me row you across to the other side? Otherwise you'll have to walk all the way round."

"No, why?" she replied with unaccountable bashfulness.

"Let him row you across; it's very muddy at the dam," replied the barefoot Grisha authoritatively.

"Well, all right. You can go back to your mother."

"Aren't you afraid to cross the fields alone?" asked Grisha firmly.

"I'll escort her back to town," said Sanin.

"What about your friends?"

"They'll be here till dawn. Besides, I've had enough of them."

"Well, that's very kind of you," Karsavina said with a smile. "Go home, Grisha."

"So long, miss."

Once again the boy seemed to disappear into the bushes; Karsavina and Sanin were left alone.

"Take my arm," Sanin offered, "or you may slide down the hill."

Karsavina grasped his arm and, with a strange sense of discomfort and vague agitation, felt his muscles, hard as steel, rippling beneath his thin shirt. Constantly bumping into each other accidentally in the darkness and sensing the strength and warmth of each other's bodies, they made their way through the forest toward the river. There was total, almost constant darkness in the woods; it seemed as if there were no trees, but only pitch-blackness, silent and impenetrable, breathing warmth.

"Oh, it's so dark!"

"Never mind," Sanin whispered softly in her ear, his voice trembling a little. "I love the woods more at night. People shed their ordinary selves in the dark forest and become more mysterious, more adventurous, and more intriguing."

The earth sloped away beneath their feet and they almost fell over.

Because of the darkness, her collisions with his supple, firm body, and the proximity of a powerful man whom she'd always liked, the young woman was overcome with a sense of unfamiliar excitement. Her face became flushed in the darkness and her arm felt hot against Sanin's. She laughed frequently; her laughter was high-pitched and incongruous.

It was brighter below, and the moon shone clearly and serenely upon the river. They felt a cool breeze from the water; the dark forest seemed to recede gloomily and mysteriously into the background, as if delivering them to the river.

"Where's your boat?"

"Right here."

The boat was easily discernible, as if etched against the smooth, light surface of the water. While Sanin adjusted the oars, Karsavina, gently balancing herself with her arms, made her way to the stern and sat down. She was immediately transformed into a creature of fantasy, bathed in blue moonlight and the shimmering reflection from the water. Sanin gave the boat a push and climbed in. Rustling softly, it slid over the sand, splashed into the water, and emerged into the moonlight, leaving long, smooth ripples in its wake.

"Let me row," said Karsavina, still feeling an excited, insistent sense of power. "I like doing it myself."

"Well, sit over here," Sanin said with a laugh, standing up in the middle of the boat.

Light and lissome, she brushed the fingertips of his extended hand as she moved past him onto the seat. As she did so, Sanin glanced up at her; when her breasts passed near his face, he caught the scent of her perfume and her young woman's body.

They set off. The dark-blue sky and wistful moon were reflected in the broad water; the boat seemed to float along in a bright, peaceful expanse. Karsavina was sitting up straight, her bosom thrust forward; she pulled the oars weakly, splashing water. Sanin sat in the stern looking at her, at the bosom on which he would've liked to rest his burning head, at her supple, round arms that could so powerfully and tenderly entwine around his neck, at her body so full of languor and youth, to which he could cling so steadfastly and passionately. The moon illumined her pale face with its shining eyes and dark brows, and glided across the white blouse over her breasts and the skirt covering her plump knees. Something happened to Sanin—he felt as if he were drifting away with her further and further into a fairy-tale kingdom, away from people, from reason, and from rational human laws.

"It's a lovely evening," she said, glancing round.

"Yes, it is," Sanin replied softly.

She suddenly began to laugh.

"For some reason I want to toss my hat into the water and undo my braid," she said, feeling an instinctive urge to do so.

"Well, go ahead and do it," said Sanin, even more softly.

But she suddenly felt embarrassed and fell silent.

Once again recollections, brought by the night, the warmth, and the vast expanse, flooded the young woman's soul, and she felt both ashamed and delighted to gaze around. She thought that Sanin had to know what had happened to her and, as a result, her experience became richer and more complex. She had an irresistible but only dimly conscious desire to let him know that she was not always such a quiet, modest young woman and that perhaps she could be altogether different, perhaps naked and shameless. She felt excited and elated as a result of this unfulfilled desire.

"Have you known Yury Nikolaevich long?" she asked in a faltering voice, feeling an irresistible urge to skirt the abyss.

"No," Sanin replied. "Why do you ask?"

"No reason. Don't you think he's a fine, clever man?"

An almost childlike timidity rang in her voice, as if she were asking a favor from an older person who could either caress or punish her.

Smiling, Sanin looked at her and replied, "I do."

Karsavina guessed from his tone that he was smiling, and she blushed almost to the point of tears.

"No, really. And he's only . . . He must've suffered a great deal," she managed to say with difficulty.

"Probably. He's certainly unhappy," Sanin agreed. "Do you feel sorry for him?"

"Of course," she said in a tone of feigned innocence.

"Yes, that's understandable. But you have a strange understanding of the word 'unhappy.' You think a man who's morally discontented, who regards everything with trepidation, is not simply unhappy and pathetic but some kind of special, sublime, even perhaps powerful person. You seem to think that the endless contemplation of one's actions is an attractive trait that permits a person to consider himself better than other people and confers the right not so much to compassion as to respect and love."

"Well, isn't that so?" Karsavina asked naively.

She'd never talked with Sanin at such length, but she'd always heard that he was quite original; in his presence she felt the proximity of something new, interesting, and exciting.

Sanin started laughing.

"There was a time when man lived a narrow, animal life, never considering what he did or why he felt what he did. This was followed by an era of conscious life, and its first stage was the reevaluation of all feelings, needs, and desires. Yury Svarozhich stands precisely at this stage; like the last of the Mohicans, he represents this period of human development as it recedes into eternity. Like every final manifestation, he's absorbed all the essences of his age and they've poisoned him to the depths of his soul. He has no life as such; everything he does is subject to endless reconsideration: is it good or bad? He's developed this trait to the point of absurdity: joining the cause, he wonders whether it's beneath his dignity to stand in the ranks with others; abandoning the cause, he wonders whether it's humiliating to stand apart from the general movement. The fact is that there are many people like this; they constitute a majority. Yury Svarozhich is an exception only insofar as he's not as stupid as the rest and this struggle with himself has not assumed so ridiculous a form but at times even a genuinely tragic one. A man like Novikov merely grows fat on his hesitation and suffering like a hog locked in a pigsty, but Svarozhich really carries misfortune around in his heart."

Sanin suddenly stopped. His own loud voice and simple, ordinary words had dispelled the enchantment of night, and he regretted it. He fell silent and once again fixed his gaze on this young woman, on the dark brows on her pale face and her prominent bosom.

"I don't understand," she began timidly. "You talk about Yury Nikolaevich as if he were to blame for being himself rather than someone else. If a man isn't satisfied with life, then it means he's above life."

"A man can't be above life," Sanin replied. "He himself is merely a small part of it. He can be dissatisfied, but the reason lies within him. He simply can't or won't reap from the richness of life enough to satisfy his true needs. Some people spend their whole lives in prison, others are like birds that have been in cages for too long and are afraid to leave. Man's a harmonious combination of body and spirit, until that combination is destroyed. Ultimately, only the approach of death can do that, but we ourselves can also destroy it with our deformed worldview. We've stigmatized our physical desires as bestial, we've become ashamed of them, and we've cloaked them in humiliating forms and produced a one-sided existence. Those of us who are weak by nature haven't noticed it and drag through life in chains; but those who are weak only because they've been bound by a false view of life and themselves—they are martyrs: this repressed force tears itself free, the body begs for joy and subjects them to torments. All their lives they wander among dualities, grasping at any straw in the sphere of new moral ideals, but in the last analysis, they're afraid to live, miserable, afraid to feel."

"Yes, yes," Karsavina replied with unexpected force.

A host of new and unexpected thoughts arose within her.

She glanced about with shining eyes: the mighty, splendid beauty of the power embodied in the motionless river, the dark forest, and the depths of the night sky with its pensive moon flowed into her body and soul in great waves. She was gradually overcome by a strange feeling, one that was already familiar to her, and that she both liked and feared, a feeling of vague urge toward power, motion, and happiness.

"I keep dreaming of a better time," Sanin began after a pause, "when nothing will stand between man and his happiness, and when man can freely and fearlessly devote himself to all attainable forms of enjoyment."

"But what then? A return to barbarism?"

"No. The time when people lived like animals, merely to fill their bellies, was barbarously crude and miserable; and our own time, when the body's subordinated to the spirit and relegated to the background, is senselessly weak. But mankind has not lived in vain: it's evolving new conditions of life in which there'll be no place for either bestiality or asceticism."

"Tell me, what about love? Doesn't it impose obligations?" Karsavina asked unexpectedly.

"No. Love imposes severe obligations on people only through jealousy, and jealousy's born of slavery. Any form of slavery gives rise to evil. People must enjoy love without fear or prohibition, without limitation. Then the very forms of love will expand into an endless sequence of fortuitous and unexpected occurrences, a chain of chance events."

Back there I wasn't afraid of anything! the young woman thought proudly; then all of a sudden she saw Sanin as if for the first time.

He was sitting in the stern—massive, powerful, his eyes dark from the night and the moon, his broad shoulders as strong as iron. Karsavina stared at him with terrified curiosity. She suddenly realized that a whole world of unknown original thoughts and sensations lay before her; all of a sudden she felt like reaching out to it.

How attractive he is! The thought flashed surreptitiously through her mind. She began chuckling to herself in embarrassment, but a strange excitement overcame her body and manifested itself in nervous trembling.

He must have sensed this unexpected surge of female interest because his breathing grew stronger and faster.

The oars, caught now among the low branches of the narrow channel into which the boat had slowly turned, slipped weakly from her hands; and something seemed to sink within her as well.

"I can't row here. It's too hard," she explained, her words trailing off, her voice ringing softly and musically in the dark, narrow channel where the rippling of a stream was faintly audible.

Sanin stood up in the boat and moved toward her.

"Where are you going?" she asked with uncomprehending fear.

"Let me."

The young woman rose and tried to move toward the stern. The boat rocked vigorously and she instinctively grabbed hold of Sanin, her firm breasts pressing forcefully against him. At that moment, almost unaware, and not even believing in the possibility of such a thing, she prolonged the contact with an imperceptibly fleeting movement, as if that contact were entirely accidental.

At once he felt with his entire being the marvelous enchantment of a woman's closeness; and with her entire being she understood his feeling, she too felt all the power of his yearning, and was intoxicated by it even before she knew what was happening.

"Ah. . . ." The sound escaped Sanin's lips with astonishment and ecstasy; he embraced her so powerfully and passionately that she was forced back and, feeling herself unsupported, reached instinctively for her falling hat and her hair.

The boat rocked more violently and still invisible waves rushed toward the shore with a disquieting sound.

"What are you doing?" Karsavina cried weakly. "Let me go! For God's sake! What are you doing?" she said in a breathless whisper after a brief, uneasy silence, trying to extricate herself from his arms of steel. But Sanin, almost crushing her firm breasts, clasped her to him powerfully; she could scarcely breathe; all the barriers that had existed between them disappeared. There was darkness all around, the pungent smell of fresh water and grasses, a strange chill, heat, and silence. She suddenly experienced an inexplicable loss of will; she relaxed her arms and lay back, seeing and feeling nothing; with both burning pain and agonizing delight she surrendered to another's strength and will—those of a man.

## XXXIX

Not long afterward she began to recover, she recognized the patch of moonlight on the dark water, the fact that she was lying in the boat, Sanin's face with its strange eyes, the fact that he was embracing her as if she were his own, and that her bare knee was rubbing against one oar.

Then she began weeping softly and without restraint, not yet extricating herself from his arms, still submissive.

Her tears were filled with sorrow at the loss of something irretrievable, with fear, self-pity, and fragile fondness for him, emerging not from her mind or heart but from the very depths of her young body, exposed in its strength and beauty for the first time.

The boat moved quietly into a broader and slightly more illumined stretch of the river and rocked on the dark, mysterious water, its ripples running with their quiet, endless splashing.

Sanin lifted her in his arms and sat her down on his lap. She sat there dazed and helpless, like a little girl.

She heard as if in a dream that he was comforting and addressing her in a familiar way; his voice was full of tenderness, subdued strength, and gratitude.

I'll drown myself later, she thought vaguely, listening to his words and seeming to reply to a stranger who was about to demand an answer from her: What have you done and what will you do now?

"What shall I do now?" Karsavina asked unexpectedly and automatically.

"We'll see," replied Sanin.

She wanted to get off his lap but he held on to her, and she remained there compliantly. It was rather strange that she felt neither anger nor loathing for him.

Later, when Karsavina remembered that evening, everything seemed incomprehensible to her, as if in a dream. Everything around them was silent; it was dark and solemnly still, as if preserving a mystery. The light of the moon waning in the dark treetops was strangely immobile and transparent. The black shadows under the bank and in the depths of the forest watched them with fathomless eyes; everything was frozen in tense anticipation. Meanwhile, she didn't have the strength or will to recover, to remember that she loved someone else, to become the single young woman she had been, or to push the man's chest away. She didn't defend herself when he began kissing her once again; she welcomed this burning new delight almost unconsciously, with half-closed eyes receding ever deeper into a new, still strange, and enigmatically enticing world. At times she seemed not to see or hear or feel anything, but each of his movements, each force exerted on her submissive body she perceived with extraordinary piquancy, with mixed feelings of humiliation and eager curiosity.

Despair, descending around her heart like a chill, provoked her downcast and fearful thoughts.

It doesn't matter, nothing matters, she said to herself, but a secret physical curiosity seemed to want to find out what more this man could do to her—he who was so remote and yet so intimate, so aggressive and so powerful.

Then, when he moved away from her and, still sitting beside her, began to row, she leaned back and closed her eyes; trying not to go on living, she trembled at every movement of his firm, now familiar hands as they moved smoothly above her bosom.

With a soft crunching sound the boat reached the bank. Karsavina opened her eyes.

All around there was meadow, water, and white mist. The moon shone feebly and wanly, like a ghost expiring at daybreak. It was very light and clear. A fresh early-morning breeze was blowing.

"Shall I go with you?" Sanin asked softly.

"No, I'll go alone," she replied mechanically.

He lifted her in his arms and, delighting in his own powerful effort, he carried her from the boat, feeling both ardent love and grateful tenderness toward her. He clasped her firmly to him and then put her down on the ground. She swayed, unable to stand.

"What a beauty!" Sanin said with such emotion that it was as if his entire soul were striving for her in a torrent of tenderness, passion, and pity.

She smiled with unconscious pride.

Sanin took her by the arm and drew her to him. "Give me a kiss!"

It doesn't matter now. . . . Why is he so pitiful and intimate? Nevertheless, it's better not to think! These disconnected thoughts raced through her mind and she gave him a long, tender kiss on the lips.

"Well, good-bye," she whispered, getting lost in the sounds, not knowing what she was saying.

"Don't be angry with me, my dear," he said in a tone of soft entreaty.

Then, as she walked along the dam, swaying and tripping over the hem of her dress, Sanin stood for a long time watching her sadly, regretting the wasted suffering she'd have to experience, above which, he thought, she would be unable to rise.

Her figure melted away and vanished in the mist as she moved toward the dawn. When she was no longer visible, he jumped into the boat; the water began to churn merrily and noisily around the oars at his powerful, triumphant strokes. In the widest stretch of the river, amid the swirling white mist under the morning sky, he dropped the oars, stood up straight in the boat, and with all his might gave a loud, joyful cry.

The forest and mist had been waiting and echoed him with their own prolonged, jubilant cry, which slowly faded away.

## XL

As if stunned by a blow to the head, Karsavina dozed off immediately; after a short, sound sleep, she suddenly woke early the next morning, feeling ill and her body ice cold. It seemed that her despair hadn't had any respite: not for a single moment had she forgotten what had happened. She looked around keenly, surveying silently and attentively all the items in her room, trying to see what had changed since yesterday.

But everything in the room, including the icons in the corner, the windows, the floor, the furniture, and Dubova's blond head sound asleep in the other bed, looked back at her in the bright, calm morning light. Everything was as simple as ever; only her pale dress, crumpled and tossed on a chair, reminded her of something.

Through the flush of her recent sleep, a deathly pallor had begun to appear even more clearly on Karsavina's face; her dark brows were etched as distinctly as they'd been in the moonlight the previous night.

With the striking perception and lucidity of a sick brain, everything she'd experienced rose before her; clearest of all was how earlier that morning she'd made her way through the sleeping streets of the town. The sun, just appearing over the roofs and fences gray with dew, had shone unmercifully and dazzlingly as never before. Through closed shutters, as if through eyelids shut tight, the inimical windows of middle-class houses had seemed to follow her while lonely strangers turned to look back at her. She'd walked on in the morning sunlight, tripping over the hem of her long skirt, barely keeping hold of her green, plush bag. She'd made her way like an outlaw along by the fences, her steps uneven and hesitant.

If at that moment the entire human race came streaming out onto her path with gaping mouths and envious eyes, showering her with derision and laughter, lashing her with vulgar words, it wouldn't have mattered at all; she would've walked on, reeling from the blows, without either aim or purpose, with desolate anguish in her soul.

By the time she'd reached the meadow where the noisy strokes of his oars churning up the water had faded into the mist, Karsavina suddenly realized what a terrible burden had fallen onto her hunched woman's shoulders: despair overcame her heart, her mind, her life. She cried out, let her bag fall onto the wet sand, and clutched her head.

From that time on she would always feel under the influence of others; no longer would she have a will of her own.

She recalled the events of the previous night like some powerful intoxication. There was something extraordinary about it, deliriously gripping, more powerful than anything before; and now it was impossible to understand how all this had happened, how she could've been so oblivious to the loss of shame, reason, and the love of another man that had seemed to fill her entire life.

In her physical distress, like the feeling of sickness just before death, she slipped from under the blanket and, moving silently, began to get dressed, feeling that at Dubova's slightest movement her body was touched by the cold.

Then she sat down next to the window and fixed her strained, motionless gaze on the garden, where the trees bathed in morning light looked so yellow and green.

Her thoughts were burdensome and raced like black smoke carried on the wind. If someone could have opened her soul and read it like a book, he'd have been horrified.

Against the background of her unusually strong young life, in which every day each feeling and movement had been filled with passionate blood fired by the sun, monstrous images now swirled. The dark, immutable thought of suicide loomed large in her consciousness; impassioned anguish at having lost her pure, profound love for Yury gripped her heart; a dim wave of fear swallowed everything before the swarm of familiar and unfamiliar human faces in her mind.

At first she thought of going to see Yury, throwing herself at him, weeping, devoting her entire life to him, and then heading off somewhere once and for all. But the horror of seeing Yury overcame her and she wanted to die then and there, simply to cease living. Then the idea occurred to her that somehow she could still make everything right, that last night couldn't really have happened; but then, like a wild wail, the recollection of her nakedness rushed through her mind, the heaviness of the man's body, the momentary intense oblivion. Distraught and deafened by the overwhelming force of what had happened, she rested her bosom against the windowsill and sat there without either strength or thoughts.

Meanwhile Dubova woke up and heard her friend's movement and dazed cry.

"Ah, you're up already? That's quite unusual."

In the early morning, when Karsavina had returned, the sleepy Dubova had asked her, "Why are you so disheveled?"

Then she'd fallen asleep again. But now she sensed something; barefoot and wearing only her nightshirt, she came over to Karsavina.

"What's wrong? Are you all right?" she asked considerately and tenderly, like an older sister.

Karsavina withdrew, as if expecting a blow, but her rosy lips curled in an artificial smile; it seemed that someone else's voice replied much too cheerfully:

"Of course. I simply haven't slept."

Thus was her first lie spoken; it demolished without trace all recollection of the previously free, bold young woman she had been. That was one person, this was another, and this one was deceitful, cowardly, and defiled. As Dubova was washing and dressing, Karsavina glanced at her furtively; her friend looked so bright and pure, while she felt as dark as a lowly reptile. The feeling was so powerful that even the part of the room where Dubova was moving seemed lit by the sun, whereas her own corner drowned in damp, stuffy darkness. Karsavina recalled how she'd always considered herself above her aging, colorless girlfriend, given her own aura of youth, beauty, and innocence; now she wept in anguish—large tears, like drops of blood, tears of hopeless loss.

But all this took place inside her; on the outside Karsavina was calm, even rather cheerful. She put on a pretty blue dress and hat, picked up her parasol, and set off for school at her customary lively pace. She stayed there until dinner, and then came home.

On the way she met Lida Sanina.

Both of them—young, beautiful, graceful women—stood lit by the sun with smiles on their passionate lips, talking about insignificant matters. But Lida felt a morbid hatred for the happy, carefree young woman, while Karsavina envied the good fortune to be as lovely, lively, and free as Lida.

After dinner Karsavina picked up a book, sat down by the window, and once again began to look listlessly and intently at the light and warmth of the garden in the last days of summer.

The sharp pain had passed and in her soul everything had become indifferent, bruised exhaustion.

Well, what of it. I'll go wherever the road leads. I'll perish, she repeated to herself apathetically.

She caught sight of Sanin before he noticed her.

He was walking through the garden, tall and serene, glancing from side to side, reaching out to the branches of bushes as if greeting them. Settling back and pressing the book to her chest, Karsavina watched him savagely as he slowly made his way to her window.

"Hello," he said, offering his hand.

Before she'd managed to stand and recover from the turbulence of her chaotic feelings, he repeated with insistent affection: "I said hello."

There was something in his voice that deprived her of the chance to cry out, stand up, and walk away; instead, devoid of own will, she replied softly, "Hello."

Having answered, she felt that he was stronger than she was and that he would do with her as he wished.

Sanin leaned his elbows on the windowsill and said, "Come out into the garden for a while; we have to talk."

She stood up and, still in the grip of some strange power, didn't know what to do or where to go.

"I'll be over there," said Sanin.

She nodded in an agony of embarrassment over what she would say.

Sanin walked away at a slow, calm pace; Karsavina was afraid to look at him. For a few moments she stood there motionless, her arms folded tightly across her chest. Then she suddenly began fussing, even gathered up the skirt of her dress so it would be easier to walk in, and left the house.

Golden sunlight and yellow leaves filled the entire garden from end to end. From a distance Karsavina saw Sanin standing on the path. He was smiling at her and the young woman found it difficult and embarrassing to walk in his gaze: she felt as if her dress didn't cover her and he could see every movement of her naked body, which he now knew. Her feelings of helplessness and shame were so great that she grew afraid of the garden and the light. Hurrying, almost tripping over herself, she went up to him and stood so close that he couldn't see all of her at once, from head to toe.

Then he took her by the hand, led her to the thickest grove of tangled trees, and there, as he crouched on the stump of an old apple tree, virtually sat her on his lap.

From the side her downcast profile and round shoulders were visible, soft and weak next to his broad, strong chest, but it complemented hers in a nice, strange way. Unintentionally, feeling rapturous admiration for her beauty and seeming to kneel before her, he leaned over and softly kissed the flimsy, dry fabric through which her vigorous body felt so warm. Karsavina shuddered but didn't turn away. He overpowered her with his strength and audacity, and she him with her tenderness and beauty, and each was afraid of the other. Sanin wanted to say many tender, soothing words, but it seemed to him that at the first sound of his voice Karsavina would get up and walk away, so he kept silent. The young woman listened to the strained sound of his breathing.

What does he want? What will he do? she wondered, weak with fear and shame. Will he do it again? I'll tear myself away, I'll leave!

"Zinochka," Sanin said at last; the sound of his voice, awkwardly uttering this familiar form of her name for the first time, was both tender and strange.

She glanced up at his face for a moment; with ecstasy and fear she met his gleaming gaze, and she was frightened. She felt afraid, and at the same time felt instinctively that he was not all that terrible, and that now he was more afraid of her than she was of him. Something resembling sly feminine curiosity stirred in a corner of her soul; suddenly she felt easier and not ashamed to be sitting on his lap.

"I don't know," said Sanin, "perhaps I'm very guilty in your eyes and shouldn't have come. But I couldn't leave you like this. I so want you to understand me . . .and not to harbor any loathing or hatred for me. What was I supposed to do? There came a moment when I felt that something between us had disappeared and that if I let the moment pass, it would never be repeated in my life . . . that you would go by and I would never experience the delight and happiness I could have. You're so lovely, so young. . . ."

Karsavina was silent. Her translucent ear, half-hidden by her hair, turned pink and her eyelids began to flutter.

And just as gently, in vague, halting terms, Sanin told her of the enormous happiness she'd afforded him and that their night together would remain with him always, like a fairy tale. From his voice it was clear that he was suffering from the impossibility of conveying to her something that would ease her grief, cheer her so she could become as she was before and recover what she'd lost from her life.

"You're suffering, but yesterday was so good!" he said. "But this suffering is only because our life's arranged so atrociously; people themselves determine the price of their own happiness. But if we lived differently, this night would remain in both our memories as one of our most valuable, interesting, and splendid experiences, the sort that make life worth living."

"If only!" Karsavina replied mechanically, and all of a sudden, unexpectedly even for herself, she smiled slyly.

It was as if the sun had risen, the birds had started to sing and the grasses to rustle; it became so light and bright in her soul after this smile, which restored for a moment the former cheerful, bold young woman she had been. But it was merely a spark that soon vanished.

Suddenly she imagined her entire future in the form of dark, tattered, soiled shreds of rumor, ridicule, sorrow, and shame, reaching the point of disgrace. She saw all the familiar faces, and they were scornful and squeamish; monstrous images raced by; dark terror filled her soul and aroused her hatred.

"Go away, leave me alone!" she cried with a cruel expression, as if taking revenge on him for her own smile, blanching and gritting her teeth; then pushing herself away from his chest, she stood up.

A heavy feeling of impotence overcame Sanin. He felt that no words could console her for what had obviously caused her suffering, disgrace, and misery. She was justified in her rage and sorrow, and it wasn't in his power to remake her whole world instantaneously and remove from her woman's shoulders the horrible, stubborn burden that had fallen innocently upon her as a result of the joy and happiness afforded him by her youthful beauty. For a moment the idea occurred to him to offer her his name and assistance, but something restrained him. He felt it was too shallow and not what was needed.

All right, he thought. Let life take its course.

She stood not far away, her hands hanging down, her head drooping, crowned by her splendid hair; as she pondered something, a deep, unmaidenly furrow crossed her beautiful forehead.

"I know," he began, "that you love Yury Svarozhich. Perhaps you're suffering most of all because of that?"

"I don't love anyone!" she whispered in anguish, folding her arms painfully.

On her face, like physical pain, was sharply etched an awareness of her guilt before the person just mentioned and her impotent despair.

Meanwhile, in her soul an enormous and momentous question arose and trembled like a column of smoke in which was concentrated all her horror and the solution to what had transpired.

How can I say it? she thought without words. I love Yury and now I love him so much that it breaks my heart . . . to think that I won't be as innocent or as special for him as I was before. Everything's fading as if I were close to death. Meanwhile, something drew me to this man yesterday.

The thought of Sanin had no shape: it was a recollection of insane power, terrible enjoyment in which suffering was combined with a desire for even deeper intimacy and, at times, a wish to be tormented to death. Then there was the luminous and peaceful recollection of some melodious and inexpressibly intimate tenderness; this final memory revived her heart.

I myself am to blame! she said to herself. I'm a vile, depraved creature!

She wanted to weep, to atone, to inflict lashes on the same magnificent white body that had turned out to be stronger and more demanding than her mind, her love, her consciousness itself.

For a moment it seemed that she couldn't endure this terrible surge of feeling, that she'd lose consciousness and die. But it faded and passed, and there remained only hopeless, quiet sorrow.

Then Sanin said with particular poignant entreaty, "Don't think badly of me. You're still just as splendid and you'll provide another man with the same happiness you gave me. More, much more. And I wish you nothing but the very best and tenderest. I'll always remember you just as you were last night. Farewell. If you ever need me for anything, send for me. I would give my life for you if I could!"

Karsavina looked up at him quietly and began to feel sorry.

Perhaps it'll all pass! flashed through her mind, and for a moment everything didn't seem as painful and horrible to her. For an instant they looked each other in the eye, and at that moment something good emerged from the depths of their hearts and was joined together, as if they'd suddenly become related and familiar and had learned something no one else needed to know and that would remain in their souls as a warm, bright memory.

"Well, farewell!" she said in a low, girlish voice.

Joy and tenderness lit Sanin's face. She stretched out her hand to him but they ended by kissing each other simply and warmly, like brother and sister.

As Sanin left, Karsavina accompanied him to the gate and for a long time stood watching him pensively and sadly. Then she quietly went back into the garden and lay down on the grass, hands beneath her head.

The dry, still fragrant grass was rustling all around; closing her eyes, without thoughts or feelings, she lay completely still. Something was happening within her, and it seemed that it would happen all by itself: she would rise again and return to life as the cheerful, youthful, bold woman she once had been, a woman before whom life would reveal its happiest and most magnificent treasures.

The dark thought of Yury and whether she had to tell him her secret came into her mind, bringing new horror and shame, but she said to herself hurriedly, There's no need to think about that, no need at all. It'll pass.

And once more she lay still in anticipation.

## XLI

That day Yury woke late in an oppressive frame of mind, with a bad taste in his mouth and a slight nagging pain in his temples. At first he couldn't remember anything except shouting, clinking of glasses, pale fires, and the clear, transparent light of morning, so strange for his intoxicated, befuddled eyes. Then he recalled how Shafrov and Peter Ilich, stumbling and muttering hoarsely, had returned to their rooms to go to bed, while he and Ivanov, terribly pale from all the vodka but as steady as always, had stayed on the balcony for a long time, paying no attention to the sunny morning that was blue above and green below, to the meadow, or to the river sparkling like white gold beneath them.

They argued, and Ivanov demonstrated triumphantly to Yury that people like him were good for nothing; that they dared not take from life what belongs to them; and that the best thing would be for them to disappear without trace and to leave no offspring. He repeated Peter Ilich's words with inscrutably malicious delight: "Those I even hesitate to call people," and he laughed wildly as if he'd vanquished Yury. Meanwhile, for some reason Yury wasn't in the least offended and listened to him, objecting only when he was accused of a lack of experience, saying that on the contrary the lives of these people were especially subtle and complicated, but that it was true that it really was better for them to perish. Yury was unbearably gloomy; he felt like crying and atoning for his actions. He remembered with shame how he'd tried to excuse himself; he dwelled on the episode with Karsavina and was almost ready to share his encounter with that pure, sweet young woman with this smug, crude man. But Ivanov was so drunk that he seemed not to notice anything, and Yury now desperately wanted to believe that this was really the case.

Shouting for no reason at all, Ivanov made his way out into the courtyard and suddenly everyone disappeared. It became extremely deserted, and Yury was left completely alone. His vision was narrowed by a drunken haze; only the soiled tablecloth, the chewed ends of radishes, the glasses with cigarette butts and dregs of beer in them danced before his eyes. He sat there, his head bowed, rocking to and fro, and feeling abandoned by the whole world.

Then Ivanov returned, and with him came Sanin, who'd gone off somewhere. He was cheerful, boisterous, and completely sober, and looked at Yury in a strange way that seemed to be either excessively affectionate or rather derisive. Deeper in his recollections there was only an empty white spot; then Yury remembered the boat, the river, and a milky pink mist that he had never seen before. They were making their way across the cold, clear water, across the level sand lit by sunlight as if from below. He had a bad headache and was feeling nauseous.

The devil knows what sort of filth this is! he thought. All I need now is to become a drunkard.

And, squeamishly shaking off these memories as if they were dirt sticking to his feet, Yury began to think more deeply about what had happened in the woods.

At first he recalled the extraordinary, mysterious forest, the deep, still darkness under the trees, the strange moonlight, the woman's cool, white body, her closed eyes, her lazy, heavy scent, her burning desire, which reached the point of madness.

This recollection filled his body with a languorous, voluptuous trembling, but something appalling struck his temples and seized his heart; he recalled in much too great detail that distraught, monstrous scene when, without feeling any desire, he'd thrown her to the ground, and she, not wanting it, resisted and pulled away, and then he saw that he couldn't and wouldn't do it but climbed on top of her all the same.

He shuddered with shame and even became aware of the daylight. He felt like retreating into the darkness, burying himself in the earth so as not to confront his disgrace. But in a moment, no matter how difficult it was, he convinced himself that the most loathsome thing was not that he'd defiled and ruined a powerful surge of passion but that for just one minute he'd been close to intimacy with a young woman.

With a terrible, almost physical effort, as if wrestling with a man many times stronger than himself, he examined his own feelings and realized that he'd behaved just as he was supposed to.

It would've been vile if I'd taken advantage of that burst of passion!

But before him there arose a new, even more tormenting question: What's to be done now?

Amid this chaos of contradictory ideas and desires, one emerged crystal-clear: I must break with everything! I can't overpower her, amuse myself, and then abandon her. I'm not that sort of man. I feel other people's suffering too personally to cause it. Marriage?

Even the word sounded incredibly vulgar to him. He, Yury, with his extraordinary, altogether special powers of organization, always hesitating on the brink of great ideas and great suffering, couldn't conceive of such philistine happiness with a wife, children, and household. He even blushed, as if offended by the mere possibility of the fleeting idea of such a response.

So should I reject her and leave?

Like the greatest happiness irretrievably disappearing, like the loss of life itself, the distant image of the young woman flashed before him. As if repudiating her, he tore her from his heart and with her went his own bloody sinews, leaving ruptured, bleeding mortal wounds behind. Everything grew dark all around; his soul became heavy and empty; even his body seemed to grow weak.

But I do love her! he cried to himself in a final burst of excruciating incomprehension. How can it be that I ruined my own happiness? It's absurd, atrocious!

So what then? Marriage?

And once more ashamed at the possibility of even thinking about it, he sank into perplexed, painful anguish. He stopped noticing the sunlight itself, ceased being aware of his own life, and lost the will to see and hear. Trying not to think, he sat down at the table and began reading an imitation of Ecclesiastes he'd written several days before:

There is neither good nor evil in the world.

Some say: What's natural is good, and man is right in his desires.

But that's a lie, because everything is natural; nothing is born of darkness and emptiness; it all has the same origin.

Others say: What's good is from God, but that's a lie, because if there is a God, then everything is from him, even desecration.

Yet others say: What's good is doing good to others. But is there such a thing? What's good for one person is bad for another: freedom is good for the slave; slavery is good for the master; a rich man wants to keep his wealth; a poor man wants the rich man to perish; the outcast wants to submit; the one who cast him out doesn't; the unloved wants to be loved; the happy man wants everyone else to be rejected except for him; those living don't want to die; those being born want others to die and make room for them; man desires the death of beasts; beasts want the death of man. And thus it is and has been throughout all ages and will be until the end of time; no one has any right to what is good for him alone.

It's accepted among men that it's better to do good and to love than to commit evil and hate. But that's cryptic: for if there is retribution, then it's better for man to do good and sacrifice himself, and if there isn't, then it's better to claim his own share under the sun.

Here's another example of the lie among people: someone's destroying his own life for the sake of others. They tell him: Your spirit will outlive you because it'll be preserved in the deeds of others like an everlasting seed. But this is a lie, since they know that in the span of time the spirit of creation and the spirit of destruction are both equally vital, and it isn't known what will rise and what will fall.

Here's another: people think about how others will live after them and tell themselves that it's good and their children will reap the fruits of their labors. But we don't know what will come after us, and we can't conceive of the darkness for those who will follow in our footsteps. We can't love them or hate them, just as we can't love or hate those who came before us. The link between the epochs has been broken.

It's also said: We make all people equal before the source of joy and sorrow, and we reward everyone according to the same standard. But no man can perceive joy and sorrow or pain and pleasure greater than his own, and when people's share is unequal, they are unequal, and when the share is made equal, their hearts are not made equal for all eternity.

Thus says pride: both the strong and the weak!

But every man is both the sunrise and the sunset, the summit and the abyss, the atom and the universe.

They say: The human mind is great! But this is a lie, because man's vision is limited and he sees neither his own insanity nor his reason in the infinite universe, where reason and insanity flow like water.

What does man know?

Even Adam knew how to eat and drink and what to wear, but he protected his needs and his progeny; we know the same things and protect our progeny for the future. But Adam didn't know what to do so that he wouldn't die and wouldn't be afraid, and we don't know that either. Much knowledge has been created, but we haven't conceived the life and happiness to fill it.

From head to toe man's always had the aim of protecting his body from pain and death. And we can see: wasn't it with a simple stick that Cain struck down Abel, and wasn't it with the same stick that it was possible to destroy the first man standing on the highest step of knowledge? Wasn't it Methuselah who lived longer than anyone else, yet he still died; wasn't it Job who was more fortunate than anyone else, yet he was devoured by grief; and each and every man, having experienced in his life as much happiness and sorrow as his shoulders can bear, doesn't he die the same death as his forefathers did? Even now, when people crown their gods with knowledge, hold forth, and gloat!

Worms consume them all the same!

A cold chill ran up and down Yury's spine; a vision of white worms swarming in a thick layer over the entire earth from end to end upset him. The words he'd written struck him as unusually profound.

Isn't all this true? The idea hit him like a hammer, and a sense of pride at his authorship was combined with a sharp stab of grief.

He went over to the window and gazed aimlessly into the garden for a long time; the paths were already covered with a golden layer of yellow and red leaves; more dead leaves, swirling softly in the air, fell noiselessly to the ground. Deathly yellow hues lay everywhere and leaves were dying, as were millions of insects that lived only by light and warmth. Everything was perishing in the quiet, serene light of day.

Yury couldn't understand this serenity; such obvious death aroused painful, pointless animosity in his soul.

There . . . it all succumbs and shines, just as if it were given a special treat! he thought with deliberate harshness, wanting to come up with even harsher and more offensive words.

Many occurred to him, but they hung in the void and fell weakly upon his head. Such animosity overcame him to the very roots of his hair, so that he had to gasp for breath.

Beyond the window lay the golden garden; beyond the garden, the river reflected the greenish-gold autumnal sky; beyond the river were meadows decked in silvery gossamers; beyond the meadows was the river once more; in it the forest was turned upside down, as were its banks, oak trees, and quiet paths; and there, someone was walking.

 XLII

It was the drunken choir member Peter Ilich.

When autumn comes and the place where people have their summer cottages becomes deserted and quiet like a small cemetery of former revels, a special, exquisite beauty descends upon it: trees and bushes show through slender, delicate railings like lace, and hops adorn it with red garlands; little toylike cottages appear through the golden tracery of thinning branches; lonely red asters hang above deserted flower beds, pensively and coldly nodding their lovely little heads; balconies and green benches still preserve traces of their former cheerful, noisy life, and everything seems to have been replete with merriment, happiness, and particularly bewitching life. Sometimes, in a deserted avenue, a solitary, pensive female figure appears like a lonely bird abandoned by its migrating flock; she seems astonishingly beautiful, sad, and mysterious. Locked windows and doors assure stillness; the autumnal silence now seems to live its own enigmatic, elemental life here.

Peter Ilich is walking slowly along the deserted paths, his walking stick rustling in the yellow fallen leaves.

When it's crowded, noisy, and cheerful here, he never comes. Perhaps he instinctively feels his old age, infirmity, and unattractiveness; other people, with their bright faces and laughter, prevent him from hearing something that only he can discern.

He walks past the summer cottages, sits down on an abandoned bench, and for a long time, until the chilly autumn sky grows dark, he stares straight ahead, no doubt sensing the breath of eternity drifting invisibly above this place of other people's joy and amusement.

Then he goes down to the river, beneath the imposing green and yellow oak trees, to stare at the crystal-clear quiet water. He lies down on the dry, thin grass and remains there for hours, his head nestled on the earth, listening to its wordless talk, inhaling its grand, calm breath.

He frequents the wildest places—where the river approaches the hill and the hill tries to stifle it, but can't. The river laughs at the hill, rolling in blue and silver laughter, while the hill frowns and its leaves rustle. Sometimes huge oak trees hurl themselves into the water from the steep bank and drown their drooping, broken branches in the flowing, laughing depths.

The river frolics in her streams—blue from the sky and green from the earth—and it seems that someone is quickly scribbling incomprehensible, mysterious characters upon it. It writes and then erases them, again writes and then erases once more.

No one can ever read these characters, but apparently they touch Peter Ilich's soul because he watches them for hours at a time; they make him quiet and calm, like the flickering flame of the evening of human life.

The forest, river, fields, sky, and earth provide him with something that is missing in his drunken, squalid life, something that fills his soul to its deepest depths. The appearance of the old singer during his wanderings is solemnly pensive and imposing.

Returning and meeting one of his few acquaintances, he speaks, trying to convey with a weighty look something he can't communicate. For some reason he always concludes with the same phrase:

"Winter there . . . is superb! So serene . . . snowflakes dancing . . . bullfinches singing!"

His voice modulates to a high tenor and melts away into the air; one feels that this man, despite his infirmity, has the special ability to perceive a tiny fragment of life's beauty; when free from working for his crust of bread, free from vodka and illness, he satisfies his life so well and fully that his soul becomes joyful.

## XLIII

Autumn. It's already autumn. Then comes the winter and snow. Then spring, summer, and autumn again. Winter, spring, summer . . . what a bore! And what exactly will I be doing all that time? The same as I am now! Yury grimaced. At best, I'll become dull-witted and won't think about anything at all. And then—old age and death.

Once again an endless series of thoughts ran through his mind: life had passed him by; there was no such thing as a special existence; each life, even that of heroes, was filled with tedium, tiresome periods of preparation, dismal outcomes. He remembered that he'd always lived in anticipation of starting something new, considering what he was doing at any given moment only temporary; but that temporary pursuit stretched out like a caterpillar, revealing all sorts of new variations until it became apparent that the caterpillar's colorless tail would vanish in old age and death.

An exploit, a feat! Yury thought, wringing his hands in anguish. To blaze up and disappear, without fear or torment! That's the only kind of life.

Thousands of exploits, each more heroic than the last, appeared before him, but each of them looked him in the face with the skull of death. He closed his eyes and saw with utter clarity the pale Petersburg morning, wet brick walls, gallows outlined in a dim silhouette against the dark-gray sky. . . . Or else someone's fierce face, the muzzle of a revolver against his temple, a horror that seemed impossible to bear, yet one that must be borne, the force of a shot as it struck him in the face. . . . Or whips lashing his face and back and his naked buttocks. . . .

Is this what I must do? Isn't that what I must cope with? he asked himself and gave up, dejected.

Exploits paled, melted, and vanished; in their place appeared the mocking visage of his own powerlessness and the awareness that all these dreams of heroic feats were merely childish games.

What's the good of subjecting myself to abuse and death so that workers of the thirty-second century won't go without food or sex? To hell with them, all those workers and workless of the world!

Once again he felt a surge of impotent rage, agonizing and pointless. He was overcome by an insurmountable need to throw off something, to rouse himself. But invisible claws held him fast; a gradual feeling of ultimate exhaustion began to creep into his mind and heart, filling his active body with deadly apathy.

If only someone would kill me, he thought wearily. Unexpectedly, from behind, so that I don't even notice my own death. . . . Damn it, all sorts of nonsense invade the mind! And why does it have to be someone else and not me? Am I really such a nonentity that I lack the strength to take my own life, even when I'm fully aware that life brings only misery? After all, doesn't one have to die sooner or later? What's this all about . . . this petty reckoning!

But then mentally he crouched down on the ground and, covering his face, looked at himself from above with tormenting derision and contempt.

No, you're playing tricks, my good man, not on your life! You're an expert at thinking, but when it comes to acting . . . Not a chance!"

He felt a slight chill in his heart, bizarre and cowardly.

Should I try? Not seriously, but as a joke? Not really, but just so . . . Still, it'd be interesting! he said to himself, as if offering excuses.

It was very arduous and shameful for him to fetch the revolver from the table drawer; he was frightened by the absurd idea that this evening, on the boulevard, Dubova, Shafrov, Sanin, and most of all Karsavina wouldn't know and couldn't guess what sort of childish experiment he was performing on himself.

Stealthily slipping the gun into his pocket, he went out onto the porch leading to the garden. Dry yellow leaves also lay like corpses on the steps. He kicked them aside, listened to their faint rustling, and began whistling a slow, sad tune.

"What's that you're singing?" Lyalya asked in jest, coming from the garden into the house carrying a book and parasol. She was returning from a rendezvous with Ryazantsev at the river and was looking fresh and happy from their kisses. No one prevented them from seeing each other wherever and whenever they wanted, but in secret, in the solitude and silence of the deserted garden, there was something exciting that made their kisses ardent and aroused new desires in Lyalya.

"It sounds as if you're burying your youth," she added in passing.

"Nonsense," Yury replied angrily; from that moment he felt the onset of something stronger than he was.

Like an animal that senses that death is imminent, he began to fret and search for a suitable place. Not the courtyard: everything there irritated him. He went down to the river, where yellow leaves and gossamers floated; he tossed a dry stick into the water and watched for a long time as swift, shallow ripples spread in rings around it and the floating leaves shuddered. Then he went toward the house again, where the last red blossoms hung in lonely, sad mourning among the withered, yellowed flower beds. He stood over them and then returned to the middle of the garden.

There everything was already yellow and the branches appeared velvet black amid the tracery of golden leaves. There was only one green tree—an oak, imposingly preserving its lobed leaves. On the bench beneath this tree sat a large ginger tomcat, warming himself in the sun.

Yury began to stroke the cat's furry back gently and sadly, and felt tears welling up in his eyes.

Life's finished, it's all over, he repeated mechanically to himself; and although the words seemed meaningless, they pierced his heart like an arrow.

But that's nonsense! My whole life lies ahead of me. I'm only twenty-six! he cried mentally, suddenly freeing himself for a moment from the haze in which he was struggling, like a fly caught in a spider's web.

"Hey, that's not the point—whether I'm twenty-six or my whole life lies ahead!" he said dismissively. "What's the point?"

Unexpectedly the image of Karsavina arose before him, and the fact that after yesterday's sickeningly disgraceful scene it was impossible to see her and impossible not to see her. He imagined their meeting: shame overwhelmed his heart and mind, and it occurred to him that it was better to die than to go through that.

The cat arched his back and purred in delight, like a samovar singing a bubbling song. Yury looked at him attentively and began pacing back and forth.

Life's tedious . . . boring, sordid. . . . However, I don't know what's . . . But it's better to die rather than see her again!

Treading heavily, the coachman went by, carrying a bucket of water. There were dead yellow leaves even in the bucket. The maid came out onto the porch of the house, visible through the branches; she was saying something. For a long time Yury was unable to understand what it was. The bond between him and everything around him was beginning to tear and dissolve. With each moment he moved imperceptibly further and further away, withdrawing from the whole world into the dark depths of his own solitary spirit.

"Oh, yes, all right," he said, finally realizing that the maid was calling him to lunch.

Lunch? he asked himself in fear. Eat lunch? That means everything's just the same—to live again, to suffer, to decide how to behave with Karsavina, to be with my own thoughts, with everything? I'd better act quickly, or I'll have to go to lunch and I won't have time.

A strange haste seized him and a shudder ran through his body, spreading subtly into all his joints, his arms and legs, his chest. The maid, tucking her hands under her white apron, stood still on the porch, obviously trying to breathe in the autumn air of the garden.

Like a thief Yury hid behind the oak tree so he wouldn't be seen from the porch; peeping out at the maid to see if she could make him out, he very swiftly and unexpectedly shot himself in the chest.

Missed! The thought flashed joyously through his mind, together with a momentary, excruciating desire to live combined with a fear of death. But now he saw the top of the oak tree before him, the blue sky, and in between the ginger cat, who had jumped up from where he'd been sitting.

The maid rushed into the house with a cry, and it seemed to Yury that a crowd of people immediately gathered around him. Someone poured cold water on his head, and a yellow leaf stuck to his forehead, much to his annoyance. Agitated voices were shouting all around and someone cried and called:

"Yura, Yura! Why?"

It's Lyalya crying, he thought; at the same time, he opened his eyes and in savage, animal despair began struggling and shouting:

"A doctor! Send for him now!"

But with incredible horror he realized that everything was already over and that nothing would help. The leaves sticking to his forehead quickly became heavier and crushed his head. He stretched his neck out, trying to see something in spite of them, but they rapidly grew thicker in all directions and soon covered everything.

Then he was no longer aware of what was happening to him.

 XLIV

Those who knew him and those who didn't, those who loved him and those who despised him, and those who never thought about him, everyone felt sorry for Yury Svarozhich when he died.

No one could really understand why he had done it, but everyone thought they understood, and in the depths of their souls shared his thoughts. Suicide seemed magnificent: its beauty brought tears, flowers, and fine words.

There were no relatives at the funeral because Svarozhich's father had suffered a stroke and Lyalya wouldn't leave his side. Only Ryazantsev was present; he made all the arrangements for the funeral. The congregation became even more downcast at the isolation of the deceased, and his image grew even greater, sadder, and more imposing.

They brought him a multitude of lovely, odorless autumn flowers; among the combination of red, white, and green, Yury's dead face, lacking all trace of feelings he'd had or of things he'd done, seemed genuinely tranquil.

When they carried his coffin past the apartment where Dubova and Karsavina lived, they both came out and joined the mourners. Karsavina had a weak, beaten look, like that of a young woman being led out for a verbal reprimand and then an ignominious execution. Although she knew that Yury had no idea what had happened to her, nevertheless it seemed that there remained some link between his death and that event which would always remain secret. She had shouldered a great burden of unfathomable blame and felt herself the unhappiest and guiltiest person in all the world. She wept all night, mentally embracing and caressing the image of a man who'd departed forever; by morning she was filled with undying love for Svarozhich and contempt for Sanin.

Their chance intimacy now appeared to her as a horrendous nightmare, and on the following day even more horrendous. Everything that Sanin had said to her and everything in which she had believed instinctively seemed despicable, as if she'd fallen into an abyss from which she'd never escape. When Sanin came toward her, she stared at him with loathing and fear, and immediately turned away.

The fleeting sensation of her cold fingers in his hand, which he offered for a firm, friendly handshake, conveyed to Sanin everything she was feeling and thinking, and he himself now felt alienated from her forever. With a curl of his lip, he thought for a moment and moved toward Ivanov, who was lost in thought, lagging behind the rest, glumly tossing his straight, fair hair.

"Look how hard Peter Ilich is trying," Sanin said pensively.

Up ahead, beyond the swaying coffin lid, sad funereal voices rose, and Peter Ilich's low bass clearly and dolorously quivered and hung in the air.

"How astonishing," Ivanov began. "Such a weakling, and . . . now look what he's done!"

"I think, my friend," replied Sanin, "that three seconds before he shot himself he still didn't know if he'd do it. He died just as he lived."

"That's how it is. Still, he found a place for himself," Ivanov said incomprehensibly. Suddenly he tossed his fair hair and became cheerful, obviously realizing something that only he could understand and that could comfort only him.

It was deep autumn in the cemetery; its trees were sprinkled with red and gold rain. Only the grass showed green in places beneath its covering of dead leaves; on the paths the breeze swept them into thick piles and it seemed as if yellow streams were coursing throughout the graveyard.

The crosses showed white, the marble tombstones stood serenely black and gray, the railings shone golden; amid the silent graves someone's invisible but gloomy presence hovered, as if just now, before the arrival of these people disturbed the tranquillity of the place, someone sorrowful had been walking the paths, sitting on the graves and grieving without hope or tears.

The dark earth received Yury and swallowed him; people crowded round the grave for a while, glancing with inquisitive, awkward curiosity into the black darkness that was their own fate, chanting their plaintive dirges.

At the terrible moment when the coffin lid became no longer visible and eternal earth lay forever between the living and dead, Karsavina burst into loud sobs; her high voice rose wailing above the quiet cemetery and above all those who'd fallen silent in somber sorrow and pain.

She no longer cared whether people discovered her secret. Everyone had guessed it, but the horror of the death that had forever severed the bond between this weeping, lovely young woman who'd wanted to give him her whole life, her youth and beauty, and this deceased young man now buried in the earth was so evident to all that nobody dared offend the woman's bared soul with their dark thoughts. They merely hung their heads lower in instinctive respect and pity.

They led Karsavina away; her sobs, gradually subsiding into a soft, hopeless lament, fell silent somewhere in the distance. An oblong mound of earth grew above the grave, ominously recalling its concealed human body; and on it they quickly laid green fir branches in a symmetrical pattern.

Then Shafrov piped up. "Gentlemen, someone has to make a speech. Gentlemen, this won't do," he said hastily but at the same time plaintively, first to one, then to another.

"Ask Sanin," suggested Ivanov maliciously.

Shafrov looked at him in surprise but Ivanov's face was unperturbed and he obeyed.

"Sanin, Sanin . . . where's Sanin, gentlemen?" he said in haste, looking around nearsightedly. "Ah! Vladimir Petrovich, say a few words. This won't do!"

"Say something yourself," replied Sanin sullenly, still listening to Karsavina's fading voice. He thought he could still hear that high-pitched voice, resonant even in its sobs.

"If I could, of course I would speak. After all, he really was a re-mark-a-ble man! Well, please . . . a few words!"

Sanin looked him straight in the eye and said with annoyance, "What's there to say? Now there's one less fool in the world and that's that!"

His loud, shrill voice resounded with unexpected strength and clarity. At first everyone seemed to freeze; but while many had yet to understand what they'd heard, Dubova cried in a harsh tone, "That's vile!"

"Why?" Sanin asked, shrugging.

Dubova wanted to shout at him and shake her fist, but she was surrounded by several young women. They all stirred and began to move. Impotent but indignant voices broke out, agitated, flushed faces rushed by, and the crowd swiftly dispersed like a pile of dead leaves blown by the wind. Shafrov ran off somewhere then came back. Ryazantsev, standing in a separate group, was waving his arms excitedly.

Sanin looked carelessly into the furious face of someone with glasses, which for some reason had turned up right under his nose, but he remained silent, then glanced at Ivanov.

Ivanov looked uncertain. While turning Shafrov against Sanin, to some extent he'd foreseen an incident, but not what had actually happened. On the one hand, he was enjoying the coarseness of the whole affair; on the other, he felt rather unpleasant and awkward. He didn't know what to say and stared uncertainly beyond the crosses into the distant fields.

"What a bunch of fools," Sanin said with a genuine pang of regret.

Then Ivanov felt ashamed that he could have second thoughts about anything; feigning indifference, he set his walking stick behind him, leaned on it, and said, "To hell with them. Let's go."

"All right, let's."

They walked past Ryazantsev, who was glaring at them angrily, and the group beside him, and headed for the gate. But even from a distance Sanin noticed a group of young people with whom he was only slightly acquainted standing like a herd of sheep with their heads together. In the center stood Shafrov, fretfully waving his arms and speaking; he fell silent as Sanin approached. All their faces turned toward him and each wore a strange expression: a combination of generous indignation, timidity, and curiosity.

"They're plotting against you!" said Ivanov.

Sanin suddenly frowned, and even Ivanov was surprised to see his expression. Shafrov emerged from the group of students and young ladies with slightly anxious and enraptured little pink faces, and, his face as red as a beet and squinting nearsightedly, headed toward Sanin. Suddenly he stopped, as if ready to strike the first person who approached him.

Shafrov must have understood this because he stopped farther away than he needed to and turned pale. The students and young ladies, like a small herd following a goat, crowded behind him.

"What more do you want?" asked Sanin in a low voice.

"Nothing," replied Shafrov in confusion. "But on behalf of the entire group of friends, we wish to express our disapproval and . . ."

"Much do I care about your disapproval!" replied Sanin through clenched teeth with an unkind expression. "You asked me to say something about the departed Svarozhich and when I said what I thought, you express your indignation? All right! If you weren't such stupid, sentimental little boys, I'd explain that I'm right and Svarozhich really did live foolishly, tormented himself over trifles, and died an absurd death. But you . . . I'm simply fed up with all your obtuseness and stupidity. You can all go to hell! Go on! Quick—march!"

And Sanin walked straight ahead, parting the crowd as he passed through it.

"Don't push, please!" Shafrov protested in a thin, rather squeaky voice, his face bright red to the point of tears.

"This is outrageous!" someone started to say but didn't finish.

Sanin and Ivanov made their way to the street and walked in silence for a long time.

"Why do you frighten people like that?" Ivanov began. "You're a malicious fellow after all."

"If these freethinking young people had been pestering you so persistently all your life," Sanin answered in earnest, "you'd have scared them even more. But to hell with them!"

"Well, don't cry, my friend!" Ivanov replied half seriously, half in jest. "You know what? Let's go and buy some beer and drink to the memory of God's faithful servant Yury! What do you say?"

"Why not?" Sanin replied indifferently.

"By the time we get back, all the others will have gone," Ivanov said excitedly. "We'll sit down on his grave and have a drink. We'll honor the deceased and give ourselves some pleasure."

"Indeed."

When they returned to the cemetery, there was no one there. The crosses and gravestones stood as if in anticipation, motionless on the yellowing ground. Not a living thing was visible, and the only thing audible was a slippery black snake slithering across the path and rustling in the fallen leaves.

"Ugh . . . you disgusting creature!" said Ivanov with a shudder.

By Yury's fresh grave, which smelled of freshly dug cold earth, rotting fungus, and green fir trees, they dumped a pile of heavy beer bottles on the grass.

 XLV

"You know what?" said Sanin when after an hour or two they'd come out onto the dark, twilight street.

"What?"

"Come with me to the station. I'm leaving."

Ivanov stopped. "What for?"

"I'm bored here."

"Afraid of something?"

"What? I just want to go, that's all."

"Why?"

"Don't ask stupid questions, my friend. I want to leave and that's all there is to it. As long as one doesn't know people well, it seems they have something to offer. There were some interesting folk here. Karsavina seemed different, Semenov faded away, and Lida might have followed an unusual path. But now it's boring. I'm fed up with everyone. Isn't that enough for you? Do you understand, I've endured these people as long as I can. I can't take any more."

Ivanov looked at him for a long time.

"Well, let's go," he said. "Will you say good-bye to your family?"

"The devil take them. I'm sick of them most of all."

"Will you take your things?'

"I have only a few. You go into the garden; I'll go to my room and pass you my suitcase through the open window. Otherwise they'll see me and start asking questions. What on earth can I say to console them?"

"All right," Ivanov drawled. For a moment he seemed downcast but then dismissed it. "I'm very sorry about this, my friend. But what can I do?"

"Come with me."

"Where to?"

"It doesn't matter. We'll see."

"But I have no money."

"Neither do I," Sanin said with a laugh.

"No, go on your own. Classes start on the fifteenth. That's more secure."

Sanin looked him silently in the eye and Ivanov looked at him in the same way. Ivanov suddenly felt awkward and withdrew, as if he'd seen his own odious reflection in a mirror. Sanin turned away.

They walked across the courtyard. Sanin went into the house while Ivanov walked into the darkened garden, where he was greeted by the gloomy shadows of the autumn evening and the smell of quiet decay. He made his way across the lawn past bushes, rustling leaves, and snapping twigs toward Sanin's window. It was open and dark inside.

Sanin walked quietly through the hall and, hearing familiar voices, stopped, facing the balcony door.

"What do you want from me?" he heard Lida's voice from the balcony; Sanin was struck by its flat, tormented tone.

"I don't want anything," replied Novikov; apparently against his will, his voice sounded peevish and tiresome. "But it seems strange to me that you look as if you're making a sacrifice for me. While I . . ."

"Well, fine." Lida's voice broke off; the fragile sound of approaching tears unexpectedly resounded in the dim silence of the evening. "It's not me. You're making the sacrifice—you! I know! What more do you need from me?"

Novikov whimpered in perplexity and confusion, but it was clear he was embarrassed and trying to conceal it.

"Why can't you understand? I love you, so it's no sacrifice. But if you regard our intimacy as a sacrifice by one of us, what sort of life will we ever have together?"

Novikov's voice grew stronger and he sounded persuasive, even elated, as if he'd just discovered something important that would now convince Lida once and for all. "You must understand. We can live together only on one condition: namely, that there is no sacrifice made by either side. It has to be one or the other: either we love each other and our intimacy is sensible and natural, or we don't, and then . . ."

Lida suddenly burst into tears.

"What's wrong with you?" Novikov asked in astonishment and irritation. "I don't understand. I don't think I said anything offensive. Stop it! I was talking about both of us. The devil only knows what's going on here! Why are you crying? I can't say anything at all!"

"I don't know. I don't."

The muffled, pitiful female voice sounded unbearably sad in its miserable plaintiveness, powerless and speechless.

Sanin frowned and went into his room.

Well, that's probably the end of Lida, he thought. Perhaps she'd have been better off if she'd really gone and drowned herself. Maybe it'll turn out all right. Who knows?

At the window Ivanov heard Sanin fumbling hastily, shuffling papers and dropping something.

"Are you coming soon?" he asked impatiently.

He was bored and restless standing under the dark window in the dim autumn twilight before the dark, mysterious garden. The rustling reminded him of his dream.

"Right away," replied Sanin, so close to the window that he startled Ivanov. The darkness in the window flickered and a suitcase appeared, followed by Sanin's pale face. "Here, take this."

Sanin jumped lightly to the ground and picked up the suitcase.

"Let's go!"

They set off swiftly through the garden.

There was pale twilight with a faint, cold smell of chill earth. The trees were completely stripped of their leaves, so the garden looked totally deserted and vast. Beyond the river the sunset burned; the water sparkled, forgotten and abandoned at the end of the garden that was no longer of any use.

When they reached the station, the signal lights were lit along the endless dark tracks and the train's locomotive was puffing. People were running about, doors slamming, men shouting and cursing at one another in rude, foul voices, as if everyone were troubled and dejected, and wanting to conceal his feelings from others beneath deliberate malice. A crowd of dark, distraught peasants carrying bundles huddled together on the platform.

Sanin and Ivanov had a drink in the buffet.

"Well, bon voyage!" said Ivanov glumly.

"My way, my friend, is always solitary," said Sanin with a smile. "I ask nothing from life and expect nothing. The end is never happy: old age and death, that's all."

They went out onto the platform and found an empty place to stand.

"Well, good-bye!"

"Good-bye!"

And without either of them planning it, they embraced and kissed.

The train clanged, screeched, and started to move.

"Oh, brother! I've come to love you, I really have!" Ivanov cried out suddenly. "You're the only real man I've ever met!"

"You're the only one who's come to love me!" said Sanin with a laugh. He jumped onto the step of a passing car.

"Here we go," he cried merrily. "Farewell!"

"Farewell!"

The cars moved quickly past Ivanov as if they'd suddenly decided to run away somewhere. A red signal flashed in the darkness and for a long time remained there, as if not moving any farther away.

Ivanov stared after the train and grew gloomy and bored. He dragged himself mournfully through the town's streets and looked at the sparse ordered lights.

Shall I drown my sorrow? he asked himself, and the long, pale shadow of his lengthy, colorless life accompanied him to the tavern.

## XLVI

In the airless, crowded railway car the lanterns gasped for air and gaunt, shabby people stirred among wavering smoky shadows and pools of dull light.

Sanin was sitting beside three peasants. When he walked in they were talking about something; one of them, barely visible in the darkness, said, "So you say it's bad?"

"Couldn't be worser," replied the old, shaggy man sitting next to Sanin in a high, cracked voice. "They stood their ground; they won't take any risks for us. Say what you like, but when it comes to saving your own skin, whoever's stronger gets to suck blood."

"So what are you waiting for?" asked Sanin, who'd guessed at once the topic of this earnest and tedious conversation.

The old man turned to him and spread his arms wide. "What can we do?"

Sanin stood up and went to find another seat. He knew this kind of people who live like beasts, destroying neither themselves nor others, but dragging out their animal existence in the vague hope of some miracle they'd never live to see and in anticipation of which millions like them have already perished.

Night was dragging on. Everyone was asleep, except for a tradesman in a long jacket who sat facing Sanin and was maliciously cursing his wife; she sat there in timid silence and merely looked around with frightened eyes.

"You wait, just give me a chance and I'll show you, you bitch!" hissed the man like a repulsive beast.

Sanin was dozing when the woman, crying out in pain, woke him. The tradesman quickly dropped his hand but Sanin managed to see that he'd wrenched his wife's breast.

"What a beast you are!" Sanin said angrily.

The tradesman was frightened and fell silent, looking at Sanin dumbfounded with his tiny, mean eyes, as if grinning at him.

Sanin stared at him in disgust and went out onto the platform at the end of the carriage. As he passed through the car, he saw crowds of people piled up against each other. It was beginning to grow light and pale-blue sunlight was streaming in through the windows; as a result, their faces looked timid and deathlike, and sad shadows floated across them, lending them a defenseless look of suffering.

Out on the carriage platform Sanin took a deep breath of the fresh morning air.

Mankind's a sordid thing, he felt, rather than thought, and suddenly he felt a desire to leave all these people behind, to leave even for a short time this train with its stale air, smoke, and clatter.

Day was already breaking on the horizon. The last traces of night, pale and painful, were retreating without trace into the blue darkness beyond the steppe.

Without thinking for long, Sanin climbed down onto the steps of the carriage and, leaving his almost empty suitcase behind, jumped from the train to the ground.

The train went rushing by with a roar and a whistle, the earth slipped from under his feet, and Sanin fell on the damp sand of the embankment. The red light of the last car was already far away when he stood up, laughing at himself.

"That's better!" he said aloud, giving a free, ringing cry of pleasure.

It was spacious and open all around. Green grass stretched in all directions in an endless, smooth expanse and vanished into the distant morning mist.

Sanin breathed easily and gazed cheerfully at the endless expanse of earth, advancing with powerful, broad steps farther and farther toward the bright, joyous light of dawn. And when the steppe awoke, its distant fields blazing blue and green, when it spread itself beneath the immense vault of the sky, and when the sun rose sparkling and shining ahead of him, it seemed as if Sanin were striding forth to meet it.

# Afterword

## NICHOLAS LUKER

During the first decade of the twentieth century Russian realist prose enjoyed a vigorous revival, and by the outbreak of World War I it had become remarkably varied. Maxim Gorky, Leonid Andreyev, and Ivan Bunin, three of the writers prominent in those years, have long been familiar to Western readers, yet the author who caused the greatest literary sensation of that decade was until recently, virtually forgotten.

Artsybashev's life began and ended in obscurity. But during its short span, thanks to his novel *Sanin,* he achieved a reputation unequaled by any writer of his time. Whether readers agreed or disagreed with what his work advocated, all were impassioned by it, and the furor it provoked echoed throughout Russia and beyond its borders.

Mikhail Petrovich Artsybashev was born in October 1878 into a landowning gentry family in Ukraine. His maternal great-grandfather was the illustrious Polish statesman Tadeusz Kosciuszko (1746–1817). Years later Artsybashev boasted that there was Tatar, Russian, Georgian, Polish, and French blood in his veins. When he was three, his mother died of tuberculosis, a disease that would dog him all his adult life. In 1897, after expulsion from school and an attempt at suicide, he enrolled at the Kharkov School of Art, but he left it shortly before he was to take his final examinations. "I renounced my dream of becoming an artist," he explained later; ". . . this was very hard. . . ." But he had already begun to write and publish stories in provincial papers, and had drafted a novel, *Yury Svarozhich,* which would develop into *Sanin.*

At twenty Artsybashev married a young Kharkov woman. She bore him a son, but the couple soon separated. (The boy was to achieve the artist's career of which his father had dreamed. After settling in New York in 1919, he became the illustrator—notably for *Time* magazine—Boris Artzybasheff [1899–1965]). By 1905, even before *Sanin* appeared, Artsybashev's reputation as a prose writer was established. During 1907–8, already suffering from tuberculosis, he divided his time between St. Petersburg and Yalta. Moving to Moscow in 1912, he remained active in journalism, then during World War I turned to drama. Increasingly hostile to the Bolsheviks in his nonfiction work after 1917, he continued to live in Moscow, though he played little part in its literary life. In 1923 he left Russia for Warsaw, where he spent his last years as co-editor of the anti-Bolshevik newspaper *For Freedom!* Beset by financial problems and deteriorating health, he died in March 1927.

When Artsybashev's novel appeared, it was generally considered highly suggestive, and some scenes were thought to be unashamedly pornographic. Foreign publishers responded swiftly to public demand for titillating reading, and translations appeared in Germany (an edition of 100,000), France, Italy, Denmark, Bulgaria, Hungary, and Japan. In Russia the novel triggered such an avalanche of essays and reviews that its title became a household word.

It was the work's sensational aspects, not its literary or philosophical qualities, that attracted such attention. Though a minority defended it, "respectable" Russian society was hostile to it, an attitude epitomized by the critic Dmitry Mirsky's remark that Artsybashev had "contributed to the moral deterioration of Russian society, especially of provincial schoolgirls."[1] Sadly, most of his detractors had missed the point. "No one in Russia," Artsybashev complained, "took the trouble really to fathom the ideas of the novel. The eulogies and condemnations are equally one-sided."[2]

*Sanin* rests on its hero's unexpected arrival and departure at the beginning and end of the work. Returning to his southern provincial town after several years' absence, the self-assured Sanin comes home fully formed as a character before the work begins. Despite his youth, he possesses a maturity and wisdom that evidently derive from experience of a wider world. In the course of the story (it covers six months, from spring to autumn), he is the only character who does not change. Throughout the narrative he serves as a mouthpiece for the author's views, a didactic figure who considers it his duty actively to involve himself in the lives of his fellow men and women and to illustrate his weltanschauung in the process.

Sanin's physical self-assertiveness is vital to the work and has its origins in Artsybashev's earlier writing, notably his tale "The Death of Lande" (1904).

---

[1] D. S. Mirsky, *A History of Russian Literature*, trans. Francis J. Whitfield (London: Routledge, 1964), 402.
[2] Mikhail Artsybashev, *The Millionaire*, trans. Percy Pinkerton (London: Martin Secker, 1915), 9.

After striking Zarudin in self-defense, Sanin advises the submissive Solovei-chik that moral victory lies not in proffering the other cheek but in being right with one's conscience. Revealing that he once dreamed of a Christian life with its passive resistance to evil, Sanin explains that when he was struck by an attacker, he did not retaliate. Later, however, realizing the hypocrisy of his position, he ceased to take pride in his false moral victory and beat his enemy senseless.

That Sanin is a descendant of Nietzsche's *Übermensch* (the superman) was long assumed by the few critics who gave serious consideration to *Sanin* be-fore the 1980s. Curiously, Artsybashev himself declared that he had never "properly" read Nietzsche—a writer, he explained, "out of sympathy with me both in his ideas and the bombastic form of his works."[3] Moreover, as if emphasizing his rejection of Nietzsche, Artsybashev has Sanin discard *Thus Spake Zarathustra* (1883–92), spit in disgust, and fall asleep. While admit-ting that the events of 1905 "long distracted me from what I consider 'mine'—the preaching of anarchical individuality," Artsybashev revealed that he found Max Stirner "much nearer and more comprehensible."[4] Stirner (the pseudonym of Johann Kaspar Schmidt, 1806–56) was a German indi-vidualist anarchist philosopher and author of *The Ego and His Own* (1844), a work that attracted the attention of several Russian writers around 1900.

Stirner's work turns on the contrast between the ancient and modern worlds, and shows that modern men and women no longer know how to live in the natural world of the present. Stirner maintains that Christianity has de-prived his contemporaries of their ancestors' awareness of reality by directing their attention inward, to their own minds. He believes that since modern in-dividuals are preoccupied with the spiritual, they are ruled by abstract no-tions, such as morality and law, which derive chiefly from Christian ethics. But if individuals supplant Christianity with supreme love of their unique selves, then such notions become irrelevant. Denying any being higher than themselves, his self-conscious egoists see themselves as the gods of all that lives in a world where "God has had to give place . . . to Man."[5] This is the new raison d'être that Artsybashev offers a generation lost in the wilderness of self-doubt: egoistic concern with one's uniquely individual self.

The echoes of Stirner's thinking in Sanin's preceptive behavior are clear. A human being's role in life is purely passive, Sanin believes, and one's death is as necessary to the process of existence as one's life. But while alive, we must remain true to our essential selves. If Stirner maintains that life is filled with pleasure, Sanin advises us to take all that life offers. To enjoy life to the full, Sanin needs actively to satisfy his natural desires. A person who suppresses

---

[3] Ibid. The word "properly" in Artsybashev's remark may well be the most operative: it is well nigh impossible to deny some influence, at least, of Nietzsche in *Sanin*.

[4] Ibid., 8.

[5] Max Stirner, *The Ego and His Own*, trans. Steven T. Byington (New York: Boni & Liver-ight, 1918), 162.

those desires, he believes, destroys himself. So Sanin dreams of a happy time, he tells Karsavina, "when man will give himself freely to all the delights available to him."

Who, then, *is* Sanin? We cannot really know. We are told only that he has traveled Russia, suffered privation, and taken part in revolutionary activity. Moreover, notwithstanding his articulate utterances, he remains difficult to define as a character. He speaks for his creator, demonstrating his principles through his behavior. But if it is hard to believe in his existence *outside* the novel—he enters from and returns to limbo at its close—we are left in no doubt as to his physical reality within it: his prominent muscles, powerful shoulders, and mocking eyes are frequently mentioned. Moreover, his bodily presence is emphasized by his intensely physical response to the natural world, with which he feels organically joined, a response not only elemental but also erotic: he walks barefoot when he can, dances naked on the sunlit grass, and gives a cry of ecstasy after his union with Karsavina, a cry echoed by both forest and dawn. A second cry closes the work as, leaping from the train, he strides over the steppe toward the rising sun. Central to Artsybashev's portrayal is the primeval vigor of the earth and its life-giving sunlight. Indeed, Sanin's name apparently derives from the Latin *sanus* ("healthy"). With their focus on sensuality, pregnancy, and suicide, the few events of this novel all deal in a prescriptive manner with the equally elemental phenomena of procreation and death.

Paradoxically, it was the novel's excessively programmatic quality that most reduced its effect. The critic Kornei Chukovsky wrote that the work's argumentative tone not only detracted from its potential aesthetic success but also hindered its possible erotic appeal.[6] Not content merely to describe Sanin's uninhibited sexual behavior, Artsybashev called on his readers to behave likewise. In his attempt, therefore, to make a preceptive statement about the need for personal freedom and the gratification of desire, he perhaps protested too much.

What the novel loses in didactic monologues uttered by its hero it gains in evocative nature descriptions, whose pictorial quality reflects Artsybashev's experience as an art student. Those descriptions aside, his narrative devices are undistinguished, for they generally lack variety. Like its structure, the work's character definition is simple: its characters fall into socially defined groups such as army officers and members of the intelligentsia. Strategically placed among the latter are representatives of specific worldviews: Soloveichik, with his nonresistance to evil, is a follower of Tolstoy; Sanin owes not a little to Nietzsche; while Svarozhich, the hero's polar opposite, is an exiled revolutionary. In contrast to their male counterparts, the female characters serve merely to maintain the erotic tension that remains fundamental to the story.

[6] Cited in Laura Engelstein, *The Keys to Happiness: Sex and the Search for Modernity in Fin-de-Siècle Russia* (Ithaca: Cornell University Press, 1992), 386.

Seeking to explain the novel's popularity, the modern critic Neya Zorkaya argues that *Sanin* managed to fashion techniques of contemporary modernism into the accessible literary manner of "the boulevard"—the kind of writing designed for unsophisticated readers and devoted to pleasure and desire. Its characteristics are a "formulaic monotony" and the use of stereotypes and clichés.[7] Thus in *Sanin* the female characters are described in a virtually identical way, with recurrent adjectives and phrases. Artsybashev's programmatic stance was therefore at variance with his style, which reflected the gray uniformity imposed by the mass market on "popular" literature. Moreover, when portraying sexual activity itself, he could not escape the era's conventional assumptions: two seduction scenes in *Sanin* indicate that action has occurred, but nothing is described explicitly, and his message is conveyed in hackneyed terms.

Notwithstanding its widely perceived role in fulfilling Russian readers' supposed desire for erotic themes after 1905, is this overtly polemical novel quite what it seems? After all, both its exaltation of selfhood and its challenge to bourgeois respectability failed to convince more thoughtful readers. The work's message is ambiguous, and its assertion of the individual's right to pleasure is undercut by the hero's escape, like a latter-day noble savage, into untrammeled nature at the close. Is not his flight simply the result of boredom rather than of desire for further excitement? Moreover, despite its sexual suggestiveness, the novel curiously imposes its own scale of sexual values: while exalting the purity of natural desire, it condemns male sexual conquest for domination's sake.

For all Artsybashev's supposed reflection of the social preoccupations of his time, the portrayal of Sanin has for today's reader profoundly disturbing implications. Most significant are the incestuous overtones detected in Sanin's relationship with his sister Lida, an attraction that is mutual. In the first chapter, gazing lustfully at her, he embraces her, saying how beautiful she has become; at his touch she feels a frisson. Later, in an episode tense with sensuality, Sanin's desire for her is more explicit as he stands beside her, his breath hot on her cheek. His urgent closeness arouses her revulsion yet also her prurient curiosity. Though Sanin and Lida commit no incestuous act, Artsybashev implies that, like any man and woman, brother and sister should enjoy sex without censure.

Finally, if Artsybashev's literary technique is open to question, let us examine Sanin's behavior. Lacking a specific occupation, he may be seen as a manipulator whose movements from place to place are unpredictable, if not unnerving. By watching others and eavesdropping on them, he influences their lives as he sees fit. Artsybashev's hero may thus be viewed as a mysterious, sinister figure who has his real being outside the enclosed world of his town, enters it in pursuit of sexual pleasure, upsets its equilibrium, and de-

---

[7] Cited ibid.

stroys lives there. Moreover, his selfish hedonism allows him to contemplate the ultimate sin of incest. We may even conclude that the name Sanin suggests Satanin (from the Russian satana), and thus Satan himself. So can this questionable devil figure really be the new "hero of our time," as so many commentators regarded him? Is he "the natural and necessary product of our epoch," as Vladimir Kranikhfeld put it, "one of the boldly individualistic 'strong'"?[8] Or is he simply a descendant of Stirner's "king of the world," a defiantly egoistic man-god who acknowledges no authority save his own will?

Sanin's rarity as a type is underscored by his sudden departure at the novel's close. By the end of his brief stay in the town he has become bored. Though people around him appeared interesting initially, they have failed to measure up to his expectations. How marked has his effect been on this provincial community whose anonymity implies that it represents not only all Russia but also the world at large? He has indirectly caused the suicides of Zarudin and Soloveichik; by seducing Karsavina, he has tacitly passed sentence on Svarozhich; while he has discovered that both Lida and Karsavina possess the capacity to be true to themselves, he has realized they will shortly succumb to conventional social expectations; and, finally, he has found that even his disciple Ivanov lacks the strength to join him as he leaves. In social terms the novel's finale is decidedly pessimistic. Despite Sanin's wish to propagandize the ways of true being, he has had only a temporary effect on the townspeople. Convinced that he is infinitely above them, he considers his fellow human beings contemptible, for none possesses the courage to join him in the quest for an exclusive place in the sun.

However one views its hero, Artsybashev's novel cannot be passed over as merely a "curious and regrettable episode in the history of Russian literature," as Mirsky put it.[9] There was infinitely more to its appearance than the national scandal it triggered. Most commentators, failing to perceive its author's message because they focused on the work's sensationalism, were wide of the mark. Instead, serving as "an apology for individualism," its author explained, it aims to present in Sanin an emerging type who is still rare but whose "spirit is to be found in every frank, bold, and strong representative of the new Russia."[10] Bearing that significant message, Artsybashev's thought-provoking novel made a uniquely important contribution to the debate about both sexual consciousness and public morality in Russian society after the crisis year of 1905.

---

[8] Cited ibid., 383.
[9] Mirsky, *History of Russian Literature*, 403.
[10] Artsybashev, *Millionaire*, 9.

# Selected Bibliography

## Artsybashev's *Sanin*

Boele, Otto. "The Pornographic *Roman à Thèse:* Mikhail Artsybashev's *Sanin.*" In *Eros and Pornography in Russian Culture,* ed. Marcus Levitt and Andrei Toporkov, 300–337. Moscow: Ladomir, 1999.

Luker, Nicholas. "Artsybashev's *Sanin:* A Reappraisal." *Renaissance and Modern Studies* 24 (1980): 58–78.

———. "Mikhail Artsybashev." In *An Anthology of Russian Neo-Realism: The "Znanie" School of Maxim Gorky,* ed. and trans. Nicholas Luker, 213–31. Ann Arbor: Ardis, 1982.

———. "Mikhail Petrovich Artsybashev, 1878–1927." In *Reference Guide to Russian Literature,* ed. Neil Cornwell, 118–20. London: Fitzroy Dearborn, 1998.

## Popular Culture and Pulp Fiction

Brooks, Jeffrey. *When Russia Learned to Read: Literacy and Popular Literature, 1861–1917.* Princeton: Princeton University Press, 1985.

Clowes, Edith. "Literary Reception as Vulgarization: Nietzsche's Idea of the Superman in Neo-Realist Fiction." In *Nietzsche in Russia,* ed. Bernice Rosenthal, 315–29. Princeton: Princeton University Press, 1986.

Gracheva, Alla. "Early Twentieth-Century Best-Sellers and the Aesthetics of 'Mass' Consciousness." In *Twentieth-Century Russian Literature,* ed. Karen Ryan and Barry Scherr, 15–23. New York: St. Martin's Press, 1999.

Kelly, Catriona, and David Shepherd, eds. *Constructing Russian Culture in the Age of Revolution: 1881–1940,* 107–194. New York: Oxford University Press, 1998.

## Sexual Issues and Eroticism in Turn-of-the-Century Russia

Berdyaev, Nikolai, et al. *Landmarks: A Collection of Essays on the Russian Intelligentsia (1909)*. Ed. Boris Shragin and Albert Todd. Trans. Marian Schwartz. New York: Karz Howard, 1977.

Engelstein, Laura. *The Keys to Happiness: Sex and the Search for Modernity in Fin-de-Siècle Russia*, 215–53, 359–420. Ithaca: Cornell University Press, 1992.

Naiman, Eric. *Sex in Public: The Incarnation of Early Soviet Ideology*, 27–78. Princeton: Princeton University Press, 1997.


## Radicalism and the Russian Intelligentsia

Morrissey, Susan K. *Heralds of Revolution: Russian Students and the Mythologies of Radicalism*, 127–54. New York: Oxford University Press, 1998.

Stites, Richard. *The Women's Liberation Movement in Russia: Feminism, Nihilism, and Bolshevism, 1860–1930*, 178–90. Princeton: Princeton University Press, 1978.


## Other Bestsellers in Turn-of-the-Century Russia

Nagrodskaya, Evdokiya. *The Wrath of Dionysus: A Novel*. Trans. and ed. Louise McReynolds. Bloomington: Indiana University Press, 1997.

Verbitskaya, Anastasya. *Keys to Happiness*. Trans. and ed. Beth Holmgren and Helena Goscilo. Bloomington: Indiana University Press, 1999.